Amorica's Wager
Twelve Dancing Princesses Book Two

Christine Young

Published by Rogue Phoenix Press, LLP
Copyright © 2018

ISBN: 978-1-62420-647-4

Credits

Cover Artist: Designs by Ms G
Edited by Christie L. Kraemer

Chapter One

Coast of England 1816

"It's a bloody cursed day." Damian Andrews swept the child into his arms and waded through the pounding surf to the beach. He braced himself against the out-going current then sloshed through the crashing waves. Salt spray clung to the wind, stinging his nostrils.

Damian turned. Beneath his ribs, his heart pounded a cadence hard and fast. "Merde." He swore again as he watched the captain shout orders to his crew. The French brandy that was supposed to have arrived this night would have to wait.

Standing in the longboat, the captain of the ship that brought the brandy as well as the political refugees from the Germanies held a torch aloft—the only light in the vast darkness. "Hurry, laddie. We have human cargo tonight and the tide is changing."

A little girl whimpered.

Damian pulled her into his arms, bent on protecting her at all cost.

"It's all right. You will all be together soon." The smuggling of French brandy was a cover for the cause that meant so much to him. Religious and political refugees—at times it seemed they came in droves. All were seeking a better life. A life of freedom. "Your mother is coming as well as your baby brother. You will be safe."

Damian looked to the captain. "The father?" he queried.

"He didn't come with his family. He said he had one more thing to do. You must hurry."

The child leaned into Damian, her little face nuzzling his shoulder, her silent sobs gut-wrenching. He pulled her closer, cursing at the elements as well as mankind and wishing he could find a way to shield the tiny child from harm. He knew the feat to be impossible. The little girl touched a place in his heart and for a moment filled that broken space with light. Yes, the mother would be with her children, but why had the father stayed where his life was in peril? He had learned long ago one could come to regret rash actions. And he'd also learned one could lose all chance at love in one instant.

Lord, but he'd lost his concentration and in losing that, he could well lose his edge.

No secrets— no lies. The thought haunted him.

His life was a lie, but he would change nothing until his penance was paid. A constant drizzle soaked him to the skin. The wind sent goose bumps rising on his arms. He reached shore and handed the girl over to Aric Lakeland, a trusted friend and accomplice in this night's work, then turned and walked back to the longboat. Her baby brother as well as her mother waited.

He had never meant to get involved. It was the greatest of ironies that he was here now. He'd been a man who loved his family and his home.

He'd been content but that seemed years ago—a life time.

It felt like centuries.

The captain spoke, his voice hushed. "Hurry, now, Master Damian.

It's the watch. They are due to ride by here any time now. The patrols have doubled these last few weeks. I fear it's not as safe as it used to be." The captain handed over the baby wrapped in blankets. Damian stared at the child. The babe couldn't be a year old. The child didn't make a sound, not even a whimper.

This was injustice, a travesty. He looked at the mother. "Can you make it on your own?" He prayed the fragile lady standing before him had more courage than she appeared to have. She nodded and with the captain's help, she stepped into the ocean, struggling for balance. Yet her shoulders were squared and her spine stiff.

As soon as the captain placed the babe in Damian's arms and the three of them were headed for land, he gave orders. Two sailors rowed out to sea, moving toward the black ship that rose and fell on the distant waves.

On a cliff above, the dark silhouette of a third man, Ryder McClaren, could be seen for a brief moment. He waved his arms then disappeared into the shadows once more.

"Hurry," Damian bade the mother, his hand resting on the small of her back, urging her forward.

Damian ran with the mother and babe, joining Aric in a rapid dash to the cave. Inside they groped their way through the darkness. He smelled the moldy dampness and wished for light. Settling in the eerie blackness behind several ledges, they held still. For long seconds, Damian didn't breathe. He listened for the sound of pounding hooves and the thundering of the patrols as they rode past. All he heard was his heart hammering against his ribs and his pulse beating in his ears.

A flash of light in the front of the cave warned them someone entered.

Aric rose. Damian stopped him, his hand on his friend's shoulder. He shook his head then nodded toward the mother. Aric pulled her close and motioned for silence.

Two men entered, a pine-pitch torch held aloft. Light skittered across the walls and glimmered where minerals imbedded in the rocks caught its beacon.

The men walked farther into the cave. A crash outside made one of the men whirl. The torch fell to the floor, the light extinguished. Blackness invaded once again.

"Bloody eyes," one of the men cursed. "It's haunted. Me grandma told tales of this place. It's not called the Devil's Cave for no reason. And the lights we saw glimmering in the distance was ghosts, I say. No one should be in this cursed place at night."

"Someone is here," the other said. "I know I saw a boat on the horizon. It's smugglers, I say. Have you forgotten the bounty? Why, if we find just one of them scurvy mates, the reward will keep us in wine and whores for months."

Damian swore silently and pulled the little girl closer once again touching her lips with his finger in a motion to make sure she knew she should not make a sound. He'd heard of the bounty. The money on their heads had increased. Now the risk was tenfold. Damian decided he would have to find another place to bring the contraband into England.

"My neck is pricklin'. It's haunted, I say. I got chills sweepin' up my spine. What you saw was a ghost ship. I'm getting outa here. Nothin's goin' to keep me in this cave. Nothin'."

"Curse you, there is no such thing as ghosts and goblins. 'Tis your imagination runnin' wild with you." The man paused "But I know someone's in here," he persisted. "My informant is always right," he snarled under his breath. "Bloody hell, I'll shoot you in the back if you run on me now."

"Yer crazy, I don't see anyone," the other man growled in answer.

"Ye don't want the bounty on their heads? There's smugglin' goin on here. It's more than brandy they smuggle. Thousand pounds for each man captured. Dead or alive," One Eye said. "The woman they're bringin' tonight is a witch they say."

An eerie, moaning wail filled the emptiness inside the cavern. And then another. Damian felt cold sweep down his spine, even though he knew it was Ryder sending the ghostly warning through a natural vent in the cave.

"I'm gettin' outa here." The man whirled, sand rustling beneath his feet as he raced from the cave.

"Bloody eyes, I'll give you nothing."

One Eye's labored breathing sent chills down Damian's spine. He held the babe close to his chest, praying the child would not cry. He had hoped to get through this without a fight.

Aric kept the little girl still.

"Lookee there. Someone's on the cliff above," a shout came from outside the cave.

Damian swore silently, mentally counting three men in the patrol.

Ryder would put his life in danger for them. He would play the decoy. The baby whimpered but all attention was directed toward Ryder. The men raced from the cave. In the stillness of the night, Damian rubbed the babe's back and rocked. His legs cramped. Still they waited in silence.

They would wait until Ryder returned—if Ryder returned.

Hours seemed to pass. He could hear the mother's quiet, terror-filled sobs. The little girl had long ago climbed from Aric's arms and gone to her mother. Finally, the cry of a hawk pierced the silence. Damian rose then helped the mother to her feet, handing the babe to her.

"Stay behind me," Damian ordered. In stealth, he moved through the cave to the entrance.

Ryder stood on the narrow path that wound to the top of the cliff.

Damian met him, hand extended in greeting. The night's chill deepened; the wind blew rain until drops pelted the mossy hillside.

"Our enemies are closing in on us," Ryder said, tightening the cinch on the saddle. "Can you ride, lass?" he asked.

She nodded.

"Then we must make haste. It's a long way to travel until we reach the first safe house."

Aric fashioned a makeshift sling around his body then set the baby inside. Ryder pulled the little girl up to sit behind him on his horse. "Hang on to me. Wrap your arms around me and don't let go," Ryder told her.

"Where are we going?" the little girl asked and strained to reach around the big man.

"To America," Ryder said softly. "To a place where all of you will live safely."

"Do you promise?" she asked, her eyes wide, tears smudging her dirty cheeks.

"Aye, I give you my word," Aric said.

Damian heard him whispering to the little girl as they moved away from him. He wished he could go with Ryder. The city life left him bored and restless. He would give most anything to have a family and a home— a wife who loved him. He'd done that once, and he'd lost all he held dear.

Now he paid penance for his mistakes. For what he'd wrought upon his house.

A sense of urgency filled him. They didn't have time to waste.

Aric Lakeland mounted his horse, the baby nestled in front of him.

"You don't have to do this. Times are growing more dangerous. The patrols come closer each time. I would hate to see harm come to you."

"I will be fine. I have nothing to live for, so I have no reason to be cautious. I learn more in a day than either of you in a month. It's better this way. You'll see. And while I'm in London, I can come and go as I please. No one notices or cares what I do," Damian said.

"There are plenty who care. I worry that you take too many chances."

"You are like an old woman, worrying all the time. Have you nothing better to do with your time?" Damian laughed. "I'll be fine."

"Still, we cannot chance running into a British patrol."

"We cannot stop. The cargo is too precious, the cause too important," Damian said. "But I understand why you may not want to continue. You must make your own choices."

"Is all this more important than your life?" he asked. "The time may well come when you have to decide that your own life is worth more. You might find happiness—a woman."

"I would not burden a lady with the secrets I carry or the danger that surrounds me," Damian spoke from deep inside, the constant pain residing there still too real to ignore.

Aric's eyebrows drew together. "When will you learn to forgive yourself? This penance you make yourself pay daily will get you killed.

No matter what you want to believe there are many who have your best interest at heart."

Damian grinned at his friend. "Go with speed and may God be with you," he said quietly. "I'll send you word of another mission as soon as I know."

Aric leaned forward, his forearm resting on the saddle. "I have more names." He turned and reached into his saddlebag. Then he handed a parchment over to Damian. "I know I don't need to tell you to guard this with your life."

Damian unrolled the paper. A list of names wishing asylum and safe passage to America appeared. "When?"

"As soon as possible."

Damian grinned. "You should heed your own advice. You are as reckless as I. More so. You do not need to do this." He paused a moment, "I will meet with my informant and add any new names."

Aric shook his head, a grin spreading across his ruggedly handsome features. "We both know it's the right thing to do." Damian laughed and swatted Aric's horse on the rear. "Ride hard and fast my friend and take care. I will look for your next message." Damian watched Aric ride over the hills until he could see him no longer. Then he turned and walked down the treacherous path to the cave.

He strode, quick-paced, along the beach for several miles until he reached the natural shelter where he'd left his horse. The black stallion whinnied when he saw him.

Damian mounted and rode through the night and into the next day. He stopped at an inn for a few hours sleep, a bath, and a hot meal. Then he rode once more. It wasn't until the sun began to set that he touched the outskirts of London.

He rode through the city until he reached his townhouse and dismounted at his stables, handing the reins over to the boy.

"Lord Andrews," a freckled faced young boy called out. "We were getting worried, we were. Did you see any highwaymen?"

"No," he said and ruffled the boy's hair. "Your imagination is running away with you."

He turned and strode to his home. The night before he'd been chilled to the very marrow of his bones. His thoughts had been bleak, and he'd wondered several times while they hid in the cave if they would survive.

Yet here he was. Much to his chagrin, it seemed an angel of light looked after his worthless soul.

He inhaled deeply, wondering why he had been permitted to live while his tiny daughter and his beautiful wife had been chosen to die. He'd done all in his power to save them. God had forsaken him.

It had been his fault, too. He'd urged them to go to the lake with him.

His wife had said no, that it was too cold that day. If he'd just listened to her, they would all be alive today and perhaps he would not be risking his hide to save the lives of those he did not know.

He'd understood their cause, and he'd been caught up in their stories.

All they wanted was a place they could live their lives in peace. No, he would not cease. He had nothing else to live for.

He grimaced when he began to tie the enormous neckcloth. The starched muslin made the garment exceedingly uncomfortable. Anguish filled him. Everyone he'd ever cared for had died because of him.

Cheerful and far too flamboyant clothes, gaudy—for his taste—came from his dresser. Swearing under his breath at this debacle and wondering why he'd chosen to send Feroz, his valet on a mission, he donned one of his most extravagant waistcoats, a skintight garment with lace and brass buttons and tight-fitting breeches that fit his legs as if painted on them.

He grimaced when he put the wig on his head. He hated the bloody neckcloth just as he despised the lavish wig that decorated his head as well as the tight-fitting clothes

He much preferred more casual and plain clothes. He looked much as he wanted: a foolish English dandy. Displeased but accepting his appearance, he took meticulous care. He wondered if his pants wouldn't split while he made his way to the Dowager Duchess's home where he'd been invited to attend a coming out for the Lady's new charges.

Damian looked into a mirror one last time before muttering to himself. "It's off to the soiree and the jester I will be." He tucked the new list of names into a pocket to give to Ryder later this evening.

~ * ~

"Damian." Lord Dickens, who was deep in his cups, waived his hand in greeting. "Where've you been keeping yourself? We've missed you," Dicky said. Dicky's friend, Lord Rathen rocked precariously on his heels, his wig slightly askew, his neckcloth had long ago become limp, dangling precariously.

Under his breath, Damian swore then purposely stumbled into the wall. He crossed his eyes and looked at the ceiling, wishing he'd had some time alone before encountering these men. "Let me see—" he said, his words slurred. "Kathryn," he said, unable to think of another name. The Lady Kathryn's I believe." Later, he would apologize to the lady. His back to the wall, he slid to the floor, wishing the two men would vanish. He was exhausted and wanted this night to end.

The pair laughed. Dickens pushed Lord Rathen. "Watch where you're goin, Richy." Wine sloshed from their crystal glasses pooling in a blood red pattern on the floor. "She's your new mistress?" Legs sprawled, his head resting against the cold stone behind him, Damian nodded while he whisked away an imaginary piece of dust. His lies piled higher.

"You need more wine, friend," Dickens said.

"You have any?" Damian slurred. Dickens held out his glass. Damian drank deeply.

Dicky leaned against the wall. "Friends? Got plenty," he said. "Wine, it's easy to refill the glass, just have to find my way to the parlor."

"What was that?" Rathen asked. All three men turned.

Instantly alert and on guard, Damian looked in the direction of the sound. A tiny giggle escaped the curtains. Damian rose and stumbled toward the hidden alcove, pausing a moment. With the tip of his finger, he pushed the heavy velvet drapery aside. The walls of every townhouse seemed to hold spies.

"Who do we have here?" Damian asked. "A gaggle of girls? Pretty girls," he chuckled. Despite his inbred caution, his gaze was drawn to one dark-haired lady. For a moment, their eyes met and held. Charmed by her beauty, he nearly forgot who he pretended to be or what risks were involved if his true purpose in the city was discovered.

"New to London? Or just reclusive?" Dickens asked.

~ * ~

"New," Amorica Hepburn said, looking to her cousins for help and holding tight to a letter that slipped beneath the curtains just before the men discovered them. Amorica was the second oldest of all the cousins. She and Ravyn Graham were English while Christel was Scottish, of the McLellan Clan.

The Duchess, their Aunt Charlotte, would storm the halls looking for them. They were supposed to be upstairs, dancing. This was not a situation that would give them a good name or ease them into English society. They had just arrived in town and wanted to look around. And they were far too used to having the run of their castle and estates at home.

They managed to escape the dance floor and thought it was great fun, but now they had to find a way to get back without being noticed. The man who had opened the curtain appeared, like so many of the English, wearing a ridiculous costume.

Amorica wasn't sure why, but her heart did a giant flip-flop and her breath caught in her throat. She could tell little about him. His eyes seemed to shimmer. He was laughing at her. Or was he?

"We really must be going," Ravyn said, rising from the bench. Two of the young men stepped in front of her, blocking her path. Eyes wide, she gasped and sat back down.

"Not so fast," one said smoothly, rubbing his chin as if deep in thought. "No, a boon first." His own gaze focused unswervingly on Ravyn.

"Your names," the second one said. "You must give us your names, and we will let you pass. Moreover, we will give you ours so you can remember us on the morrow. I am Lord Dicky Dickens, this is Lord Richy Rathen and this," he sneered, "is Lord Damian Andrews." He reached out to pick up Christel's hand.

"No," Christel said, pushing against the wall behind her.

"I say," Damian said. "It's not proper to delay them. Truly, at this hour they should be upstairs dancing the night away." Dicky whirled awkwardly, nearly losing his balance as he addressed his friend. "You have had your pleasures tonight. Do not try to dissuade us in ours. We will have their names, and then we will escort them back to the dance floor."

Amorica hesitated then decided the only way out of this was to give these rascals what they wanted. But she didn't need an escort, and she couldn't figure out how to politely forego the company.

"My name is Lady Amorica, this is Lady Christel and Lady Ravyn." Amorica pointed to each girl as she gave their names. "Now you must let us pass."

Her bravado seemed to be amusing to Dickens and Rathen. When Dickens stepped forward to stop them, Damian waved a lace handkerchief haphazardly, his footing precarious. He appeared just tipsy enough to give the other men pause. Once again, he waved his hands, slicing through the air clumsily. "You must let them go," he said. "It would not be gentlemanly to keep them longer. The hour grows late. The Duchess will be—"

"There you all are."

"Livid," Damian finished.

The Duchess swept around the corner, her skirts held high, her plump cheeks rosy with exertion. "I've been looking most everywhere for the three of you. Shame on you. You girls must learn the proper rules. Etiquette—it's important. I will not put up with your antics. You must be perfect ladies, or I will send you back to your indulgent fathers."

Amorica had never been happier to see The Duchess than she was now. Yet she managed a wide smile for Damian. When he bowed, nearly falling over his feet in the process, she could not help feeling there was something not quite right about the man.

"I will call on you tomorrow," Lord Rathen said, pointedly gazing at Ravyn with lovesick eyes, sending what seemed to be a silent challenge to the others.

Amorica wasn't sure, but she thought she saw Damian Andrews frown. For a moment, his brows drew together, then he smoothed his features and Amorica wasn't sure if she'd imagined the look. She hoped Lord Andrews would call on her tomorrow. He was perfect for her purposes here. Her father would never agree to a marriage to a man of his caliber—an obvious wastrel. Perhaps with his help, she could postpone the inevitable marriage her father so diligently sought for her.

Glancing over her shoulder, she smiled at Damian and gave him a small wave then what she hoped was a flirtatious wink. He stood gape-mouthed, his hands dangling uselessly at his side while his friends slapped him on the back and called out ribald names.

"You got another one wrapped around your little finger, old fellow.

How do you do it?" Rathen asked. "Tell me and I would wind Ravyn around mine—finger." He held up one hand, staring at the appendage as if he wasn't sure what he'd just said.

Amorica heard the comment as they dutifully followed The Duchess back to the dance floor and the incessant stream of English lords. Amorica felt a lightheartedness she hadn't known for a long time. She smiled to herself as she looked forward to the next day.

"Girls you need to heed my rules. You don't want your names besmirched before you have even one suitor. Now behave yourselves. I know your fathers gave you the run of your estates but this is London and you can't behave that way. The guests are leaving. You must say good night, then it is off to bed with you."

~ * ~

"Goodnight, Duchess," Ravyn said sweetly a few hours later as she brushed a light kiss on the old lady's cheek.

"Goodnight, sweet dreams," Amorica said. "And don't fret over us.

We will not give you any more headaches. I promise."

"Really." Christel stepped forward and gave The Duchess a quick hug.

"I will make sure Ravyn and Amorica do nothing they would regret. They will behave themselves. I promise."

"I will hold all of you to your word. You are a dear," The Duchess told Christel. "But I doubt you can keep your cousins from finding trouble. It seems to follow them. Now to bed with you. You must look your best tomorrow. Hopefully a few of the Lords you met tonight will call on you." When the door closed, they all collapsed on their beds, giggling like little girls. Amorica laughed so hard her sides hurt.

"You cannot use Damian Andrews to keep yourself from the altar," Christel told her cousin. "It would not be fair, and it might backfire."

"I have an idea," Ravyn said a bit sheepishly. "We can make a wager."

Let us see who can dissuade our new suitors first." Christel gasped. "You cannot mean to use those men."

"They are plotting to use us. Did you not see their minds churning?" Ravyn asked. "I'm sure the three will have some dastardly plan concocted by the morn'."

"I saw they were despicable, and they already pursue us. I will have no qualms about getting rid of them."

"What about Damian? He seemed rather—nice. I do not want to dissuade him. At least not yet." Amorica fidgeted with her dress, her eyes on the floor, barely able to contain the laughter bubbling up inside. She could think of no one else she would rather spend time with, even though he was not a man her father would approve. She didn't plan on marrying him; neither did she plan on winning the bet with her cousins.

Christel threw up her hands. "Do what you want, but I will have no part of this plan."

Ravyn smiled sweetly. "So, when Lord Dickens courts you, you will pretend to fall in love with him?"

"No," Christel said. "I will do nothing to confuse the issue. I will not let him think I care for him in any way."

Amorica could not help but shake her head at Ravyn's smug smile.

Christel had fallen into place. "Then you will do your best to discourage him," Amorica said softly. "You can do naught else."

"Very well, but it is Damian I am worried over. He could not help gazing at you, Amorica. His eyes were wide as plates. It seemed he was smitten upon first sight," Christel said.

"As I was not," Amorica laughed. "He is the most self-absorbed dandy I have ever set eyes upon, but he was nice." She paused. "Well, he was nicer than the other two. Father would never approve of him. That makes him safe company."

"Then I would wager that you will lose this bet, Amorica. It will be doubly hard if the both of you are smitten," Ravyn said.

"I am not smitten. Without those flamboyant and tight-fitting clothes, he might be easy to look upon, but what else does he have to recommend him? If he were to be husband material, father would have to approve, and I doubt if he would allow me to marry a man who spends most of his time tying a cravat and gambling away his inheritance."

"So, we are all in this together?" Ravyn asked, extending her hand.

Facing each other, they placed their hands together. "Yes, we are in this together. We will see who can lose their dandy first. Even though we know Amorica will lose."

"There is something else," Amorica said, her voice a bit hesitant yet filled with curiosity. "I found this. I think it belongs to one of them." Her fingers tightened around the letter she'd found in the hallway. She smoothed it out. "It's a list of names. I wonder what it means." Christel stared in horror at the parchment. "You must return it."

"Do you know whose it was?" Ravyn asked. "If you give it to the wrong man, you might stir up a nest of hornets." Armorica gazed at the list of names. She recognized none of them, and it might not be more than a list of people to attend a ball or something.

And yet—she bit down on her lower lip in fierce concentration. "We cannot keep this." Christel rose and walked to the window. Moonlight streamed in through the glass.

"We cannot give it away." Ravyn joined Christel at the window, her hand resting on Christel's shoulder. "I know you believe in doing right, but we don't know what that is."

"Perhaps the owner of the list will come looking for it." Amorica sat down on her bed, still staring at the names, memorizing them. A little frission of excitement surged through her. Despite the bet, she wanted to see Damian again.

Something about him intrigued her.

So much did not ring true.

Moreover, before she left London, she meant to appease her avid curiosity. Even if he came looking for the list, she wasn't sure she would give it up easily. No, it had fallen into her hands for a reason, and she vowed she'd discover that reason.

Chapter Two

Damian's heart skipped when he realized the list of names had vanished. The list in the wrong hands could mean disaster. He was a link in the underground chain. The men he helped relocate were courageous men who had spoken their mind during a time when countries were trying to rebuild after the Napoleon wars. Knowing they could no longer live in their own countries, they would relocate in the United States, hoping to build new lives. To cover his unease and nervousness, he grinned, trying for a lopsided smile.

"What is this?" Dicky asked, bent over at the waist and peering at the floor. He nearly lost his balance, grabbing hold of Richy's shirt to steady himself.

Damian shifted position and stared at the floor where Dicky was bowed over diligently watching a tiny insect crawl along the stone.

"It's a bug," Damian said, sarcasm touching his voice, loathing the situation at hand. All Damian could think of was the list of names and the danger to the people whose names were written upon it if he didn't find it soon. He raked his mind for clues. He remembered quickly stuffing the paper in a pocket when Dicky rounded the corner.

"A bug," Richy said with disgust and then a crazed kind of curiosity.

He sidled over for a closer look, kneeling. Then stooping on all fours, he prodded the bug to make it move.

Dicky sat back on his haunches. "I bet," Dicky began, pinching his nose before pushing off the floor clumsily.

"What?" Richy asked, still staring at the tiny bug. "I'll bet, too."

He sat on the floor, his legs sprawled in front of him, looking around as if he tried to remember what he was about to say. "Damian, old boy, are you with us?"

Damian nodded, his mind focused, his body tense, yet he slumped, pretending to be just as drunk as the other two. His gaze fastened on the alcove intently, praying that what he sought would be found there. All he wanted was for the dandy duo to leave and let him search.

"Aye," he said slowly. "I'm with you."

"What is it you want to bet, Dicky? Can't think of anything—"

"The ladies," Dicky said slyly, a bit of whimsy in his tone. "The ladies. If I wasn't mistaken, one of them took a fancy to Damian. That sweet little brunette. And I have a fancy for the fairest damsel, Christel." A wave of nausea swept through Damian. This did not bode well.

Despite his sodden state, Dicky had not missed his strange infatuation with Amorica.

"And what about the ladies? Shouldn't they have a say in this?" Damian asked, even knowing that once Dicky had a thought, for good or bad, no one could dissuade him.

"I'll bet both of you," Dicky paused once more, pointing at Richy and then Damian, "that I can win the hand of the fair Christel before either of you can win your lady fair." He rubbed his stomach then scratched under his arm. "Damian, it's obvious you are smitten with the fair Amorica, and Richy, you will try to win Ravyn's hand. The first one to get the lady into bed and to the altar wins."

Damian's already stretched too-thin nerves skittered then catapulted.

He didn't want to involve Amorica in his life. Yet, to keep his true purpose in London unknown, he would have to go along with these two— at least pretend. In addition, he would have to concentrate his efforts in that direction—courting Amorica.

Ah, but Dicky had the right of it. He had felt an immediate surge of heat sweep through him, and a fine sheen of sweat broke out on his body the moment he'd seen the Lady Amorica. Even thinking of her made him short of breath.

He knew the dangers. He also remembered the promises to himself.

He would never risk her life. He would bet and play the game, but he would put up a wall between the sweet Amorica and himself, one that could not be broken even if he won the bet. Yet if she ended up in his bed—well that, he mused, could never happen.

"Very well," Damian said. "I believe I'm half-way to having her heart, and I smell a quick victory."

"You should not be so confident. Perhaps you underestimate my prowess with the ladies." Dicky swaggered down the long hallway, Richy close behind. "Perhaps we should raise the stakes. The first one to get a promise of marriage. Yes, that will be the gist of it. I for one am willing to settle for a wife with money. I can always keep a mistress or two on the side. When all is said and done, marriage might not be such high stakes."

"You are too drunk to remember what you bet come morning. You do not even recall that the winner must end up at the altar," Damian said.

Dicky gasped.

Damian followed them, casting a wary eye over his shoulder at the little alcove where he thought the list of names had fallen.

"And you are sober, Damian?" Dicky retorted.

"More than either of you," Damian sidestepped. "I will not wake with a pounding head and a sick stomach." True enough. He'd had only one mug of ale and little wine.

"You lie," Richy said. "You have matched us drink for drink."

"And why," Damian stumbled then groped for the ornately papered wall, "would you want to tie yourselves to a lady fair?" Dicky staggered into the wall before finally reaching the entrance to the townhouse. He opened the door and stumbled. "My father has decided I should join the ranks of the socially correct. If I am to inherit, or even receive one more pound of spending money, I must marry and beget an heir before the year has passed. Otherwise, he has said he will cut me off without a farthing. What about you?"

Damian grunted, once again looking over his shoulder. "Ah, but you forget. This was your idea. And yet, Amorica is quite beautiful. It will not be difficult to woo her and bed her."

"Ravyn is finer," Richy cut in, a bit of drool sliding down his chin. He wiped it away. "I, on the other hand, must wed a wealthy heiress. I have no funds. My father was a wastrel as well. Together we have left the family without resources. It seems not only my sister must wed for money, I must also find a fat purse to bed down with. I would not be averse to having Ravyn under my thumb."

Repulsed by the depravity here, Damian looked away. Light from candles upon the walls lit the hallway with an eerie glow that did little to dispel the gloom settling around Damian's heart.

His carelessness had put countless lives in danger and his own disguise in jeopardy. The list was not meant to be seen by anyone except him. He was becoming increasingly more terrified that one of the ladies had found the parchment. He swore beneath his breath while trying to banter with Dicky.

"These ladies may not be easy conquests. They are in the capable hands of The Duchess. I'm sure she will keep a close eye on them," Damian said then immediately regretted his words.

"And what would you know of inner strength?" Richy questioned, laughing and slapping Damian between his shoulder blades. "The ladies I have seen you with are—well, they have little of what you have just described."

"Nothing," Damian muttered, wishing for a quick and immediate respite from this conversation and the situation he'd stumbled into.

The men laughed then fell into a strange silence. The hour had grown late, and Damian needed to return to the alcove to look for the list. If it wasn't in the alcove, then what?

He would have to go to the ladies.

He would have to find a way to search their rooms. His heart thudded against his chest.

"We will meet in the morning and determine the rules to this game," Dicky said.

"Rules?" Richy called out. "Are there to be rules? Don't know if

I want to play then. Don't like rules." He roughed his hands through his hair. His eyes were dark with smudges beneath them then he muttered once more, "No, I don't much like rules."

They had reached the front of the townhouse. Richy waited for his carriage. "Are you coming?" he asked Damian as he stepped inside, Dicky on his heels.

"Not yet, I saw someone I need to speak with," he lied.

"Then, to the morning and the rules."

Damian watched them leave then whirled quickly, shaking off all signs of his drunken stupor and strode purposely down the hallway to the alcove where he'd first seen Amorica.

Pushing the curtains aside, he knelt an hands and knees and searched.

He ran the palms of his hands over the wooden surface, his fingers slipping into every groove. He pressed his nose to the floor and peered beneath the seat then he threw each pillow onto the floor.

Nothing.

His body strung taut, he felt a fever within, heating him. Disgusted with himself, he swore softly and sat back on his legs, inhaling the soft scent of the girls that still lingered in the air.

Roses.

She had the list.

He had no doubts, because he'd seen her fingers pressed tightly together as if she hid something. Bloody hell, but the danger she courted.

No, the danger he'd sent her way. He was a fool. The hair on the back of his neck stood on end.

"Wolfy. Wolfy, stop!"

Suddenly, Damian was bowled over from behind, a furry slobbering animal on top of him. Wolfy?

Rolling over, he encountered Wolfy. Two huge front paws on his chest, he wanted to laugh even while he didn't know if the dog was friendly or mean as sin.

"Wolfy, behave yourself."

He'd bloody well recognize that voice anywhere. Amorica.

Wolfy slowly backed off Damian's chest. "What are you doing here?" Damian asked, his voice a little too harsh, his eyes riveted on the animal hovering above him. Yet a sudden fear for her coursed through him. "The soiree is over. You should be tucked safely into your bed. What on earth are you doing?"

"I couldn't sleep. Wolfy was restless. Besides, he needed to go for a walk," she said, her mouth pursing into a pretty little pout. He wouldn't mind softening those lips with a kiss.

"Wolfy doesn't look vicious. In fact—" Damian paused.

"I don't need you to tell me what to do," Amorica said, even while she seemed to be taking in his prone position. "What are you doing here?" She sat down. "Shouldn't you be on your way home?"

"Looking for something," he hesitated, knowing that if Amorica had indeed found the list, she might guess who lost it.

Her lips thinned and the truth was clear in her eyes. Amorica had found the list of names and was far too curious for her own good. In fact, if he had to guess, she'd used Wolfy's need for a walk in hopes she would learn more, mayhap discover the owner of the list.

"Are you?" She spoke softly, pulling Wolfy's leash until the dog sat on his haunches, his long tongue lolling from his mouth.

"I am. You wouldn't happen to know anything?" he queried, watching her eyes, believing she would give herself away.

She shook her head; yet, she lowered her lashes, hiding her eyes from him, perhaps even pretending innocence. Moreover, if he guessed right, she was not experienced in subterfuge or lies. He wanted to see her eyes.

If he remembered right, they were green, a deep, sea green. She was slender, almost fragile, and yet as he'd thought before, even with her slight form, she had steel for a spine, strength of conviction and an overindulgent father—if he didn't miss his guess. She was spoiled and willful. She should have been taught long ago that a woman did not wander alone at night.

"Now why don't I believe you?" He lifted one eyebrow, waiting for an answer.

Her lashes rose slowly, and this time she did look at him directly.

"Because you have never learned to trust?" She cocked her head sideways, a tiny smile gracing her delicate features.

"Perhaps," he said, watching her fidgeting fingers before his gaze rested on the deep rise and fall of her bodice as she tried to hide her agitation. She reached out for the dog, distracting his attentions. Once again, he gazed at her long slender fingers. His pulse jumped.

"Really, you should not insinuate such things," she told him.

Damian found himself touched by her innocence and intrigued by her curiosity. Yet he warned himself that she knew far too much. He did not want her in this position, a place where he might have to silence her. His gut churned, and he wasn't at all sure of the source of discomfort. In a few moments' time, she had touched a part of him he'd no longer thought existed. In that same amount of time, she'd jeopardized all he worked for over the years.

"That you lie?" he asked, meaning to challenge her. The sooner the truth was revealed, the sooner he could deal with her.

She inhaled sharply. "No, sir, I do not lie."

"You do, though. Even your haughty indignation cannot cover the fact that you have not told all you know. Nevertheless, I will pursue this no more. What I lost was inconsequential, meaningless." Once again her lips thinned and her brows furrowed together as if she concentrated fiercely. Instantly, he knew she didn't believe him.

"I see," she said.

"But I don't believe you understand the consequences," he told her, his voice changing its timbre. He sat down on the seat beside Amorica.

"Perhaps."

"What is it you want?" he asked, his hand resting on her knee. He felt her tremble beneath his touch, and he also felt her warmth.

"To take my dog for a walk," she said quickly and without seeming reservation.

"Ah, and so why do you linger here? Do you trust me? You shouldn't." He spoke smoothly, his confidence rising. "I am a rogue, a man with no feelings or scruples. I take what I want."

A dangerous man.

She pushed his hand from her leg, her fingers cold and soft. "I have noticed. Yet strangely enough you no longer seemed to have over-imbibed."

Beneath his breath, he swore once more. He had been so overcome with her presence, he'd lost his focus. And by losing that edge, he'd placed his friends, Aric and Ryder, in grave danger as well as the people listed on the parchment.

Haphazardly, he clung to his mission. Yet she tantalized him. Even after berating himself, he wished he could learn more about her. And wondered if he seduced her, just how soft she would feel? He was struck once more by the thought. What was it he so suddenly coveted? Was it Amorica in his arms or the list of names he'd sworn to keep secret?

"I will walk you and—Wolfy—back to your chambers."

"The Duchess will not be pleased. You should go." Good God, but he would have to find a way out of this mess he'd created through his carelessness.

~ * ~

Amorica woke to the chirping of birds outside her window and golden beams of light slanting through intricate stained glass panes.

Wolfy groaned and rolled on top of her. She wound her fingers in his soft fur. He was her sunshine. He made her heart smile with happiness.

Suddenly, thoughts of Damian were in the forefront, too. He was not for her, she reminded herself. He was all her father abhorred in a man.

However, he was not dangerous nor did he present a challenge.

"Wolfy, you great beast, get off me," she said, pushing at the big animal who was still really a puppy. Wolfy's head popped up. He whirled then growled softly. A slight tremor in the draperies that had been pulled back and tied at the edge of the window caught her attention.

"Who's there?" She rose. Hesitantly and with Wolfy beside her, she approached the shifting curtains and the partially open window.

She paused, hands touching the edges of the fabric. Then she spoke to the dog. "Wolfy, I shut the window last night." Her heart fluttered.

"Who's there?" she asked again but no one answered.

The breeze brought in the scent of fall roses. She placed her hands on the sill and leaned out, staring into the courtyard below.

Damian stood below her window, his gaze directed her way. He waved and pointed, making funny little gestures she didn't understand.

She looked around, unable to keep from smiling at Damian's antics.

Wolfy's paws rested on the windowsill.

"What is it?" she called out, leaning precariously from the window, Wolfy barking constantly.

Damian pointed and grinned then he turned and did a skip with a little twirl before facing her again. He bowed low then brought his hands to his mouth cupping them so the sound would travel farther.

"Look on the floor by your door."

"What?" she yelled at him.

"By—your—door." He called out again, kneeling, his hand clasped at his chest.

She laughed, waving at him. "Oh." Then she spun from the window and hurried to the door. On the floor between the Persian rug and the heavy oak door, she saw an envelope. He must have paid a servant to stuff it under the door. She picked it up and turned it over. It was sealed with scarlet wax. She remembered the heavy signet ring on Damian's finger.

She traced the design in the wax with her fingertip, memorizing the intricate crest. This was far from proper. He should have addressed the invitation to The Duchess.

She ran back to the window, but he'd disappeared. When she'd seen him in the gardens, she was sure he'd been in her room and had somehow climbed up then down one of the trellises by her window. But that would have been impossible. Thorn-filled white rose bushes covered the trellises.

Amorica turned from the window, leaning against the wall. She slowly opened the envelope and pulled out the parchment within.

For a long moment, she didn't unfold the note, afraid to read what was inside. Her stomach fluttered and churned. She caught her lower lip beneath her top teeth. Curiosity overpowered any concerns she might have had.

My Dearest Amorica,

Meet me in the gardens by the duck pond this afternoon. With great anticipation I await your sweetness.

Your Ardent Admirer,

Lord Damian Andrews

Amorica refolded the parchment and sat for the longest time staring out the window. Common sense told her not to reply to Damian's request.

Her heart told her she had no choice. She was supposed to dissuade her suitor. Yet she did not want to do so.

Giggles floated from the other private rooms connected to hers.

Ravyn and Christel emerged, grinning and chatting, their girlish behavior endearing to her.

At twenty-one, she was the matron in the group.

Their welfare was her responsibility.

"See what we have?" Ravyn held out her own request to meet Lord Rathen in the gardens this afternoon. "It's an invitation." Christel didn't give Amorica a chance to reply.

"What do you make of this?" Christel asked, sitting down, nibbling on the cheese and drinking the chocolate sent by their chaperone to appease their hunger until breakfast.

"So," Ravyn began, "How will you dissuade Damian and what did you do last night? I heard you leave the room after we all retired."

"I won't say," Amorica told her cousins. "But I did take Wolfy with me, and Damian was a perfect gentleman. He made sure to tell me what grave dangers lurked at night." Amorica paused. "Damian is safe. I am not sure—"

"Oh, how sweet," Ravyn said then she leaned toward her cousin and placed her hand on top of Amorica's. "But do you think it was wise? We don't know if the men are safe. You've made assumptions."

"No, it was not wise, but it was necessary. We will tell them no. We cannot go to the gardens. I don't trust either Dicky or Richy," Amorica said. "Neither do I, but I suspect they are as harmless as your Damian.

And—I believe—there is something they want from us." She paused, her brows coming together in a flat line. "I don't like being used," Ravyn said.

My Damian? Amorica thought.

No, he was not harmless. An underlying danger surrounded him. The heat that had swept through her when he placed his hand on her knee was vivid in her mind, as well as the way just the sight of him left her breathless and her heart pounding.

Wolfy sat beside her and nudged her hand, wanting to be petted. She smiled and bent low, framing Wolfy's head with her hands she spoke to him. "You are so sweet," she told the puppy. "And you have never before liked a man, have you? You don't growl at Damian. Why is that? Do you like Lord Andrews?"

Probably because he wasn't a threat. At least not like most men were.

He was a dandy, she reminded herself. Most likely Wolfy knows that.

Mayhap Wolfy senses he is risk-free.

Christel rose and walked to the desk where she kept her parchment and pens. "I will send a message that we will not meet them in the gardens. We must dissuade them of any ideas."

"This is exciting. We have a chance now to put our plans in action.

Do you all think they will give up easily?" Ravyn asked.

Amorica wanted to be alone with Damian, she suddenly realized. She wanted to discover the truth about him and why he confused her so. She wanted him to touch her again and perhaps—she placed one finger on her lips—wondering what his lips would feel like. Beneath her trembling fingers, Wolfy nuzzled into her hands.

Ravyn lay back, her hand across her heart. "It will be far too easy to fool these men. They have little to no backbone. Spineless. Simpering." In her very quiet way, Christel spoke. "We should have a picnic. The Duchess can oversee, and if she learns about the invitations, she will make us go. She is charged with finding us husbands. I suspect Lord Dickens is looking for a wealthy wife. I would dissuade him, and if I do have to marry, I would hope for a real love not a man who has to take a wife because he is a wastrel."

"A picnic is a grand idea. I heartily agree with you, Christel. I would not wish to marry a man who—is not a man," Ravyn said. She lay back on the couch. Wolfy jumped up beside her. Then, sitting up and gazing at Christel, Ravyn said, "I've never heard you be more romantic."

Christel finished the last message and sealed it. "I am far from a hopeless romantic. It's just that I don't know what I want any more. Once I thought I wanted to give my life to God. But now—"

"Don't tell me you've fallen for Lord Dickens?" Amorica gasped, scrunching her features together and clearly dismayed by Christel's statement.

Christel shook her head. "I have fallen for no one. It's just that I've looked at life differently since Father sentenced me to London. Perhaps I do have obligations to my family I've never realized. Mayhap I've been selfish."

"Sentenced?" Ravyn laughed. "Many would love to have such a sentence. All this is not life threatening. And I'm sure we will find the city life fun and exciting."

"Traveling to London did seem like a punishment when father first told me. The worst of it was that I had no choice. He gave me no say in what was to become of me," Amorica said, watching the gardens below, hoping for another sight of Damian. What was it about him that attracted her to him? She couldn't figure it out.

He was nothing like any man she'd dreamed of falling in love with.

"What are you thinking?" Christel handed the message to Amorica.

"I am thinking of Damian," Amorica said truthfully. And his huge brown eyes. They were sad eyes, she realized suddenly—very sad.

What was it that had him drinking and carousing his life away? A woman, Amorica decided. Someone had broken his heart.

Mayhap she could heal his heart or perhaps ease the pain. Yet she didn't believe she could turn him into a real man, a man who would stand up for her, a man who would fight for her. A man her father would approve. No, he most likely knew naught of anything save tying a cravat.

Heal his heart? That was far more than she meant to do. She was supposed to push him away. Common sense told her she should do just that. Yet Damian might be as he appeared. He could be a dangerous man, and if he was, she was stumbling into uncharted territory. So why did everything she knew and sensed about Damian Andrews contradict itself?

If he was indeed a dangerous man, perhaps he wasn't spineless. She inhaled sharply, surprised at the circuitous route her thoughts had traveled.

Behind her she heard Christel and Ravyn receiving very specific instructions about the picnic. The Duchess insisted they meet the Lords and would make sure all was perfect. The wine, the cheeses, and breads they should take. The chaperone. Or would The Duchess chaperone? It seemed Aunt Charlotte had received a proper invitation from the lords.

"We will find out what those men are about. It's not a good idea to meet with them without knowing all we can."

"Yes, and I'm sure the servants will be willing to talk. They will most likely tell us more than one tall tale," Amorica said.

She sat down at her dressing table. All her belongings were there but they weren't where she placed them. She touched the white linen, traced the embossed pattern of roses, leaves, and vines. Her brows furrowed in concentration while she pulled the drawer open.

Goose bumps rose on her flesh. The parchment holding the list of names had vanished. She whirled, upsetting the belongings on top of the table. They fell with a clatter to the floor.

"Whatever is wrong?" Ravyn asked.

"He was here," she said softly, her words caught in her parched throat.

"Who?" Christel asked. "No one could get in here without disturbing us—without Wolfy setting up an unholy racket."

"Damian," she breathed, her heart stomping on her ribs. "Wolfy likes him."

"True, Wolfy would have sounded an alarm. There is not a man alive that beast likes."

"I'm telling you he was here." Amorica closed her eyes and watched the dark and light patterns flash across the back of her eyelids. She saw the names on the list. The ones she'd taken great care to memorize. No, it could not be true.

"Wolfy," she turned her attention to her puppy. "Did you let that man inside? Did you allow him to come into our rooms?" Wolfy whined softly and hung his head as if he knew he'd failed his mistress.

"It's impossible. The door was bolted from the inside. Unless one of us walked in our sleep, he could not have gotten in and then out and thrown the bolt across it again."

"Then did one of you take the list? It's not here, and I remember when I tucked it safely inside as well the very spot I placed it." They both shook their heads.

"Look again," Christel bade Amorica. "Perhaps it fell into a crack or beneath something else."

Once again, Amorica searched for the list of names. Whether they were here mattered little to Amorica save the knowledge that Damian was able to get inside this room and out with no one being the wiser. She closed her eyes, another shiver of unease slithering down her spine.

"Perhaps you are right, Amorica," Ravyn approached her cousin.

"Mayhap Damian Andrews is not what he seems. Is it up to us to give him away? We do not know who he is or what he stands for."

"We do not know it was Damian who stole the list. We cannot presume something so ludicrous. Damian does not possess the skills of a thief," Amorica insisted, yet she was not so sure.

"And are you willing to bet your life on that fact?" Ravyn asked.

"No. We cannot go anywhere with them. We must tell them no!"

Chapter Three

"No lies, no deceit, only truth between us," Damian gazed at the shimmering lake, his mind reeling.

He knew what he wished for was not possible. Everything between them was false.

He sat on a rock near the duck pond, waiting for Amorica. He tossed a small pebble into the water and watched the ripples spread across the surface growing ever wider just as the lies between them grew. Sunlight filtered through the leaves on the trees, playing chase with the ducks and swans.

He tossed another pebble. His thoughts were a mixture of yearnings long buried which now warred with loyalty to his commitments. Donning the facade of a court dandy had once intrigued him. Now he abhorred each moment.

Amorica—she made him feel again—completed him. She filled an emptiness within his heart. He didn't understand why, but she did. He could not close his eyes but he would see her. His dreams were filled with images of her.

Yet her presence in his life jeopardized everything he worked for, all he believed. He wondered how much she knew and if he could trust her.

She had found the list. Moreover, his excursion into her chamber had told him nothing about her intentions or if she had shown the cousins the list of names.

No, he could not take any chances. The gamble was too big and concerned too many people. The lives of his friends were at stake as well as their families. For a while, this mission had made him forget his past.

Now, all he could think about was Amorica, and learning to care again.

He tossed another pebble. This ludicrous bet he'd wagered with Dicky and Richy might well be the best thing that happened to him. He would not offer marriage even though the thought of bedding her made his heart race and his mind whirl. She was a lady born. He could not bed her without the sanctity of marriage vows. But he could spend time with her.

To preserve the ruse he'd created, he needed to go along with the bet.

He rubbed the back of his neck, wishing he could ease the building tension. The midnight raids an ever-increasing peril to all who participated.

The conquest of Amorica would not be easy. She appeared to be intelligent and stubborn—not easily duped. No, he would not be able to win her compliance with sweet words and subtle seduction. Even though she was innocent in nature, she was smart and would see through any ploy he might conceive. He might never be able to hold her in his arms.

He could think of little else.

She had rejected his advance the night before even though he'd seen her eyes widen and darken. He'd watched a soft rose color paint her cheeks which told him she was not adverse to his touch.

She would follow all the rules. She would not end up in anyone's bed before marriage vows were said. And so he could not win this bet, but still he didn't want Lord Dickens or Rathyn to win either. He could not picture the fair Christel with Dicky or Ravyn with Richy. The cousins were too proud and too intelligent to be duped by the wager.

The sun chased a cloud and hid behind its fluffy softness. Shadows covered the pond and the grassy knoll beyond. A swan swam nearby and regally gave him a wary eye, casting Damian's thoughts into another direction.

Ryder was due in London tomorrow with directions for the next mission. In addition, he hoped Aric had found another cove, one that would not be discovered by the patrols or spies, searching for the men who he brought to freedom.

Damian smiled inwardly, his heart warming with more thoughts of the sweet delectable Amorica.

He had come here early, hoping to see Amorica alone, although he doubted she would arrive without her chaperone or her cousins.

Ah, but a man could dream. He had plans. One of those plans was to find out what Amorica knew or guessed about the list of names. She could not possibly know who these people were. If she did, she would not want to place any man, woman, or child in the path of death. That is what she would do if she inadvertently revealed anything. He could not give himself away. He could not warn her of the danger. First, he would have to know her political views.

Ah, but women were not supposed to have political leanings. Yet he knew firsthand many did.

The sun slipped from behind the clouds. Damian loosened his shirt, the heat of the day warming him. He suddenly longed for his home and the small lake nearby. He wanted to swim naked and make love to Amorica in the water. He imagined the sweet feel of her flesh against his, the water a thin but erotic barrier between them—the tender, light touch of her fingertips. He closed his eyes and let his face tilt to the sun. Warmth descended and penetrated. Heat built within. He marveled at the new feelings and how right they felt even while he fought to keep them at bay.

While Amorica touched him like no other, she was untouchable.

Then he scoffed at himself and his daydreams. He didn't deserve a woman such as Amorica. He didn't have time to waste his life in fantasy and useless daydreams that could easily turn into nightmares.

He clenched his fists together and stared over the water. Nothing would deter him from his purpose, not even a pair of beguiling green eyes and a smile that would melt ice.

"Lost in thoughts, Damian?" Dicky stepped up to the boulder, laughing. Richy behind him. "No doubt you are thinking of the fair Amorica."

Damian swore softly, knowing once again he'd let thoughts of

Amorica intrude when he should have been alert. No human, let alone a woman, had ever affected him this way. He leapt from the rock and walked a few paces.

Back and forth he paced, brooding within himself. Then he stopped.

"How long have you been standing there?" Damian asked, studying his fingernails.

"Only a minute." Richy replied defensively. "We thought you were brooding, perhaps making plans on how best to win the lady's hand and the bet."

Girlish laughter flitted on the sunny breeze. All three men turned.

Amorica led the way, then Ravyn, Christel, and their chaperone trudged behind them. Amorica skipped up to them.

"It's such a beautiful day. Have you been waiting long?" she asked, smoothing her skirts and her hair, her smile piercing Damian's heart as if he'd been struck once again by an arrow.

Wolfy bounded behind Amorica, instantly spotting the ducks. The hound chased several, jumping into the water with a resounding splash.

"Wolfy, no," Amorica called out, setting the basket she carried on the ground and racing to the spot where Wolfy jumped into the pond. "You will get everyone wet. Whatever am I to do with you?" Loud quacking and fluttering of wings reverberated as the birds took to the water and the air in terror.

"Wolfy," she said softly, then shook her head. "I cannot get him to obey. He does just as he wants no matter how stern I am."

"I see," Damian said, laughing, rocking back on his heels as he watched the commotion in the duck pond. "You are too softhearted, too kind. If you are unsure of how to train him, I could lend a hand." He touched a lacy handkerchief to his lips.

"I—" she began then cut herself short.

Wolfy bounded from the water, barking, darting from one bird to another. The dog suddenly stopped and shook water over everyone, wagging his tail happily in the process. Amorica ducked behind Damian, hiding from the onslaught.

"What is this?" Dicky wailed, water dripping from his nose. "Get rid of that beast. He is nothing but trouble, I say."

"I'm so sorry," Christel said, brushing water from his clothes, trying to hide the laughter that all but bubbled out with her words.

"He is like that." Ravyn shrugged her shoulders. "He is only a puppy.

What would you expect? We have two more just like him at home." She tossed her head.

"Well," Richy said, annoyed. "Does the dog have to stay?"

"He goes wherever I go." Amorica walked to the dog, standing in front of him in a protective manner and looking as if she wanted to wrap her arms around him. But he was too wet even for her.

"Of course he does," Damian said. "Now what do you have in the basket? Food, I hope. I am famished." Ah, he was a starving man.

Nevertheless, Damian was wise enough to know it was only Amorica who would appease his hunger.

"The Duchess stocked it with food from the kitchen. We'll have to see." Amorica opened the basket. Peering inside, she rummaged the contents.

Damian grabbed one of the quilts the girls held then took Amorica's hand and led her away from the others. "I see a grassy knoll—over there—and I'd like to spend some time alone with you." He watched her blush prettily. The rose color that settled upon her cheeks was more endearing than ever.

"But—" she began.

He stopped her, one finger on her lips, silencing her. Ulterior motives uppermost in his mind. Her lips were soft and warm. "I won't take no for an answer. And if The Duchess finds out the truth, I will tell her I absconded with you."

"Now just a minute." the girl's elderly chaperone stepped forward, her bosom heaving. "Take your hands off her."

He did not comply. "You can see us from here," he promised, leading Amorica away, unwilling to hear more protests from the chaperone. His behavior was supposed to be reprehensible. He meant to take full advantage. To Damian, it suddenly seemed the sun shone brighter and the air smelled fresher. Good feelings pooled in his gut.

"You don't mind, do you?" he asked Amorica but he didn't slow his pace. "I want to get to know you." He winked.

"I don't mind," she said, her lashes lowered, fluttered a moment before she looked at him. Her voice was soft, and the sweet scent of roses floated whimsically around him.

Wolfy followed, chasing bees and butterflies then returning to his mistress for a head rub. Damian cast the dog a wary glance. "He's not much of a guard dog, is he?"

She watched him, her eyes shining with laughter. "No, he seems to like you. However, I wouldn't wager on the other two. He's never liked men. You are the only one he doesn't growl at."

"I'm pleased," he told her, grinning at Amorica then the dog. He spread the quilt on the ground then set Amorica's basket down.

The wolfhound lay down at one edge, resting his head on his paws, his eyes wide open.

"Are you hungry?" he asked, thinking about feeding her tiny morsels and following with soft daytime kisses that would lead to long, lingering, seductive kisses. Knowing he didn't dare do either.

"Not really. My stomach is fluttering and—" she hesitated, her upper teeth resting on her lower lip. His shoulders tightened. His body hummed with long repressed need. Good, God, but he'd had women. He'd not been celibate over the years. But this was so very different, so special. He wanted to hold onto this moment and make these feelings last forever. He wanted to understand everything about her.

He placed her hand in his, touching the softness, reveling in the warmth, tracing each finger to its tip, exploring all he dared. She shivered, her eyes wide with sensual innocence and wonder, but she didn't pull her hand from his. He meant to move slowly, but good intentions were easier thought than accomplished. He wanted to make love to her.

Fantasies— ah but for the wonder of them.

They were so very dear to the heart and yet unreal.

"Should you do that?" she asked, wonder thrumming in her voice.

"Yes," he told her and placed a kiss in the heart of her palm. He inhaled a long deep breath before letting her go. He rummaged through the basket and brought out cheese and bread; a leather skin of wine.

Fascinated by every little move she made, he watched her place each small morsel on her lips, butterflies churning in his stomach. His imagination wild, he pictured her in his arms.

The sun shielded by clouds cast a shadow across the hill. She shivered, drawing a shawl close around her shoulders. She looked at him with anticipation in her eyes.

"Would you like to go for a walk?" he asked, looking across the pond to the others, wishing he was alone with her—completely alone.

"My cousins appear to be going home. I—" she began but he cut her off. "It's early still."

"I'm not sure this is a good idea. The Duchess will not approve.

Aunty Maddie might try and follow." Her lashes fluttered flirtatiously. "I fear she cannot exert herself so. She gets tired easily. My father, the laird, would never forgive me if I let anything happen to his sister."

"Hush," he said, once again placing a finger on her lips. "We won't go far. I promise—a short walk." He watched her hesitate then look away.

He wanted her beside him.

She looked up, her eyes sparkling. She looked to Maddie then back to him. "Very well," she told him as if she were resigned and rose, shaking out her skirts. "Where will we go?"

"Around the pond. See the gazebo? We will go there, rest a moment before we return. Then I will walk you back to your house."

"You are a rogue," she said, smiling then blushing. "But I will hold you to your promise. And you will behave yourself."

"Perhaps," he said. Behaving himself was the last thought on his mind, yet Damian knew he would have to do just that. He scooped the quilt and basket up from the ground, throwing it over his arm. Then he placed her hand in his.

"What is it you do? You know, when you are not with Dicky and

Richy." She looked at him as if she trusted him with her life.

"Nothing." His gut tightened, suddenly reminded of the list of names.

"Do you have a home and a family somewhere?"

"I do as little as possible," he said, wishing that at least for the moment they would not delve into his past—a past better left forgotten.

"I do not believe you."

His back ached, his mind wandering, instinctively roaming the land, searching out possible danger.

"You should. I live south of London. My family is wealthy, and I have no need to work. I gamble and wager money that has been given to me with no strings attached. I am a father's worst nightmare."

"Everyone must do something," she told him. "Who oversees your crops and the servants?"

He nodded, his neck muscles tensing, sensing the disapproval in her voice. "My oldest brother does a fine job."

"So," she said, tilting her head slightly as if she meant to judge his reaction. "That leaves you free to play."

"That leaves me free," he agreed, knowing he must continue the ruse he'd started. Yet it was a role he must follow to its bitter end.

As they walked the banter was easy, but he didn't dare ask what was uppermost on his mind. Because of him, many people were in danger. His mind wrapped around the names on the parchment. There had not been so many that she could not have memorized them. Yet without knowing who they were, why would she bother?

A gust of wind caught them broadside. The sky was mottled with dark clouds as well as bright blue patches. Yet he hadn't noticed. Rain showers threatened. Yet the sun warmed the ground in uneven patches. The weather had changed while he spoke about his past and tried to remember why he should stay far away from this lady.

"Do you think it will rain?" She looked upward. A fine mist floated around them, a drop of rain catching the tip of her nose. Amorica laughed.

"I suppose it will. Although the sky is blue in the other direction."

"Quick," he said, "run to the gazebo." But he didn't give her the chance.

Laughing, he swept her into his arms and ran, reveling in the feel of her body against his. She felt fragile in his arms, her weight feather-light.

She laughed too.

"Put me down," she said between her laughter. "You cannot carry me so far."

"I am no fool. I would not give up a chance to hold you." I would steal a kiss if you would allow me.

"But I must weigh as much as a whale."

"You have no idea. I can barely stagger across the ground." With a small tight fist, she hit him on the shoulder. "Do not tease so."

"My apologies. Look, we are here."

Damian two-stepped the stairs into the small shelter. The skies opened in a torrent of rain. He set her down on a wooden seat, although he searched his mind for a reason to keep her close.

Amorica wrapped her arms around her, goose bumps rising on her flesh. "It's cold," she said.

"Here. The shower will pass in a moment." Damian wrapped the quilt around her shoulders. A steady staccato of drops hit the roof. Wind whipped around the pillars.

"You must be cold, too," she said, her lips quivering slightly as she spoke.

"Is that an invitation?"

"I don't understand."

"Ah, but I wondered. Perhaps I should only hope." He stared at the quilt. Her eyes wide, she opened her arms to him. "You want to share." He sat next to her and pulled her close. Huddled inside the quilt, they stayed in the gazebo and watched the rain.

~ * ~

Amorica's heart thundered with nervous energy. "I—I'm cold."

She rubbed the goose bumps on her arms as Damian pulled her closer. Her insides fluttered helplessly, her breath seemed to catch each time she inhaled. She could not stop the tense trembling of her body.

She should be pushing him away. She had such confusing thoughts about this Englishman—this man who knew nothing of a hard day's work.

Power and strength emanated from Damian even while she felt the gentleness of the embrace. "Not for long, I pray. I will do all that I can to ease your shivering," he whispered next to her face, barely touching her cheek with his lips.

The gesture was not a kiss, but Amorica felt heat rise within and her breath once again catch in her throat. Her entire body tightened, shook with a strange pleasure.

The sound of her pulse beat within her ears. She didn't understand the unstoppable trembling encompassing her.

She wanted to know more about this man. She wanted to understand why he wasted his days and drank away his nights. Even while she knew he would never make her happy.

Lord, but her father would loathe him.

Instead, she watched the rain and the ducks in the pond in front of them. While she watched, she felt his embrace and could not stop the heat or the racing of her pulse. She closed her eyes for a moment and listened to Damian's heart and his strong, even breaths. She felt things she'd never imagined. She felt sheltered and protected within his embrace. She felt as if she was meant to stay there forever. Yet the tension would not abate.

The heat rose.

She had questions about Damian's character as well as his business.

Her fears settled like so much steel in her mind and stole pleasure from her soul. The names on the list were a constant reminder that he was not what he appeared—a court dandy—a rogue. A secretive air wove around everything he said and all he did. She prayed he was a man of honor, a man to whom she could trust her life. But the secrets surrounding him seemed to increase ten-fold upon each meeting. She was terribly afraid he would hurt her or someone she loved. She wanted him to be honest with her, yet she knew she had no right to demand honesty. They meant little to each other, and she had vowed to try to dissuade him from courting her. It was a vow that would be terribly hard to keep.

Because he was safe, he represented a means to an end and somewhere deep inside, he intrigued her. Despite all she had been taught about men and all she had been brought up to believe she should seek in a husband, she liked his arms around her and the closeness she felt this moment.

Her heart controlled her mind. For all apparent purposes, he was a rogue and a wastrel. She reminded herself once more that she was supposed to dissuade him.

It seemed she was fatally attracted to him. Her mind reeled circuitously. Or was she attracted to the man she thought he could become?

Wolfy bounded into the small shelter, his tongue lolling, his fur soaked. He shook from head to tail, splattering droplets of water everywhere.

"Ah," Damian said, "I would that Wolfy did not like me so. Perhaps I could stay dry."

She laughed and pulled the quilt tighter, hoping the trembling would cease. She pressed away from Damian's chest, all the while knowing she should not be here.

"I would think you would prefer a wee bit of water over bite marks," she told him, turning toward him and gazing into his dark brown eyes—eyes that seemed to Amorica to be fathomless and filled with deep sadness. How on earth could eyes that seemed so sincere belong to a man who cared nothing about anything save himself?

"Perhaps I would." he touched her nose with a fingertip, his eyes now a deeper, darker brown. She wanted to reach inside him—to know what he thought.

She looked away, afraid of the strange sensations pooling within. A simmering heat swept throughout. She wanted to see inside, to understand who he was and why—at times—he seemed to be two different people.

"I miss my home," she said sadly, wondering why she would reveal such a thing to a man who was an enigma—a man she wasn't at all sure she could trust. She wanted to talk about the people she loved. She needed to recall their images and the way they spoke and thought.

"And where is that?" he asked, his powerful forearms settling beneath her breasts, pulling her close even while she'd thought she should distance herself from him. The sheltering security she felt surrounded her in a tension-filled aura, even while his touch unnerved her. It was a strange feeling to be filled with excitement and anticipation.

"On the eastern coast. My father, our fathers, want to see us married.

They sent us here without consulting us despite our protests when we discovered their intentions."

"Is it common for a father to consult a daughter about such things?" he asked, a lightness in his voice, the note of humor clear.

"Of course it is, at least in my family and my cousin's families. I have three sisters and eight cousins," she found herself saying. "Last year my uncle took matters into his own hands and sent out a handbill offering his oldest daughter's hand in marriage to the first man who could discover her secret." She paused a moment, remembering those awful days and the turmoil her uncle had caused.

"Did the ploy work?" Damian's laughter reverberated around the small gazebo.

Still within his arms, she turned swiftly. "It's not funny. Hunter Gray followed Allura night and day until he finally found our island sanctuary.

Now none of us can go there alone—unchaperoned. We must be accompanied by his men."

"Are you a disobedient daughter?" he queried, his arms tightening around her, her heart hammering and her hands shaking. She could not escape his embrace, nor did she want to. "And will you be a disobedient wife to some unlucky lord?"

"My cousin was not disobedient. Her father promised she could marry for love and then he went back on his word," she quickly shot back yet she found her voice softening. "You have a great deal of nerve asking that question." It was not Damian's fault what happened. He had only inquired.

Damian smiled at Amorica, her breath catching in her throat. "I did not ask about your cousin, yet I am glad you told me."

"True." She thought about his question. "I am not disobedient and so this sentence in London is unbearable. I do have a mind of my own and do like to be independent. In this world it seems to be impractical as well as difficult for a woman to speak her mind."

He cleared his throat, his voice so low and soft she leaned into him so she could hear. "Am I unbearable?"

She sat up too quickly. His arms brushed across her breasts.

"Damian," she said, startled by the sudden intensity of the sensations the slight touch caused.

He smiled as if he knew what had just happened and was pleased, but he didn't say anything.

"No, you are not unbearable." She lowered her lashes and looked away from Damian. She didn't want him to see into her eyes—read whatever emotions pooled there. He already knew far too much about her.

"I would like to see this sanctuary of yours," he said, settling her back into his arms, pulling her so very close. His chin rested lightly upon the top of her head, unsettling her, unraveling her nerves one tiny strand at a time. She could barely speak. Her voice faltered. "The island is beautiful and secluded. A bubbling spring is near the hut we built and each of us brought a special stone to place on the island. It is just off the Southeastern Scottish coastline. Christel is Scottish as is Allura."

"No one goes there? I would think such a beautiful spot would be a popular place."

She shook her head, caught up in the memories of her special place.

"Allura, my oldest cousin, called the island a sanctuary, and it was until her father sent that hated handbill throughout the land and Hunter Gray arrived to turn our lives upside down. When she married, all that changed.

Hunter, her husband, is building her a small summer home there. Of course we are free to visit if we take a man with us but—"

"But," he interrupted, his voice whispering against her ear. "Would you allow me to take you there some time?"

"You would want to see it? I would show you the island." They didn't speak for a while. She watched the mist and knew this time with Damian would end. Wolfy's eyes were closed, and it seemed the puppy slept, possibly dreaming of the havoc he could create when he woke.

"Aunty Maddie is sure to be displeased when you return me to the townhouse," she finally said. "We should never have gone off alone."

"I will take full responsibility. We can leave anytime you wish." They didn't speak for a long moment. She wanted him to be someone he wasn't. She would tell him they were not suitable.

Damian broke the silence. "Tell me their names." Amorica stiffened at the sound of his voice, unsure suddenly of what he wanted from her. It seemed to her that he was probing for something—perhaps more information about herself. She turned to face him once more, his arms relaxing around her and allowing her the leeway to turn.

"My sisters?" she began.

"Yes," he laughed, "From oldest to youngest. Your cousins too." She paused in mid-thought. "Why?"

"For a challenge," he told her, one eyebrow lifting.

"Do I have an allotted amount of time?" she inquired.

"Five meager seconds."

She inhaled a long deep breath, paused thoughtfully for a moment then, "Allura, myself, Ravyn, Christel, Storm, Faith, Ella, Eveleen, Larena, Tavia and Tira the twins, and last but the most flamboyant, Aidan."

He chuckled softly. "I did not believe you could perform such a feat.

Of course I have no way of knowing if you said them in the right order. I am amazed—all daughters. Your fathers and uncles must have been beside themselves."

"That is not very flattering," she told him indignantly.

"Do you recite and memorize things easily?" Damian asked, his probing gaze unsettling Amorica.

She nodded. "It's a gift I have. I can remember most anything just from looking at it." She glanced down, suddenly realizing what she'd just revealed. If he was—as she suspected—the owner of the list of names, he would know she had memorized them. How had she let herself forget?

He rambled off a long list of countries. "Can you recite them back?" She nodded, her eyes wide, feeling the coldness emanating from him.

He was no longer the carefree dandy she had been exchanging words with.

He was distant, his eyes shadowed and cold—hard. He appeared to be a very dangerous man.

He watched her. Waiting.

Instead, she rose and shook out the wrinkles in her skirt. "It's time we returned. The mist has cleared and while the sunshine is distant, I believe we will stay dry."

"Your reputation will be ruined," he told her, leaning back, his arms crossed in front of him. His gaze traveled the length of her.

"I did nothing wrong. My reputation is what I make of it, nothing more."

"But no one will see it that way. People are quick to believe the worst.

They will delight in spreading the gossip. Your cousin's will be involved as well as The Duchess."

She swayed. Suddenly, she felt dizzy and lightheaded. The ground seemed to whirl while her stomach churned. She had thought of no one but herself.

"Sit," he told her. "I will think of something. Perhaps we can find a way."

She sat down. Her mind filled with Damian's words. She did not want to cause The Duchess problems. The Duchess had been good to them, and she knew the same people who condemned her would gossip about the stately woman.

"I will return alone. You can follow later," she told him, thinking her decision to be obvious. "We should not see each other again." She watched his eyes darken.

His voice hardened. "Everyone knows we came here together. Neither Lord Dickens or Lord Rathen understand the meaning of discreet. They thrive on conflict and gossip. The story will spread through the ton faster than you could ever believe."

"Bah, it doesn't matter to me," she said, erratically waving her hands in the air. I don't wish to marry, and I would relish the chance to return to my home. This is nothing I cannot live through. Yet I would not be the catalyst to hurt The Duchess or my cousins."

"Nor would I be the reason for your fall from grace and a possible scandal. We will do this my way."

He placed her hand in his, his thumb rubbing gentle circles on her wrist. Circles that sent tremors racing up her spine. She shuddered and closed her eyes, bracing herself against the onslaught of sensations.

"Ah, just as I suspected. Your chaperone has returned for her young charge. Your return will be completely acceptable."

"That is not Aunty Maddie. She is most likely asleep in her room. I'm sure the day was taxing for her."

"Then it must be one of your cousins, come to make sure your reputation remains intact. I'm sure they will not wish to stay in London by themselves."

"Christel." Amorica waved at her cousin then she turned to Damian.

"We are lucky I suppose."

"I suppose," he said. "I cannot tell you, though, how disappointed I am to hear that you wish to remain unwed and that you do not want to see me again. Wouldn't your father be displeased by this revelation?" he asked, a strange expression on his handsome features.

"I came to collect my cousin," Christel said. "Maddie is waiting at the townhouse."

Minutes later, the three stood by the back door. The scent of white roses filled the air. "I will see you on the morrow," Damian told Amorica before politely kissing the back of her hand.

"That won't be possible." She escaped inside and wondered just what sort of lecture Maddie was about to give Damian.

"Young man, I know what you are about and I want to help," Maddie began.

Chapter Four

Damian stepped back, shocked by the intrusive thrust of Maddie's words and the implications they inspired if she had seen the list of names.

With his hand on his hip, he looked away. Then he turned to Maddie, smoothing his frock coat and picking at imaginary flecks of dirt. "I don't understand. I'm not about anything." With a huge yawn, he looked away.

"I am what you see." He held his arms out for the insightful lady to inspect him, praying all the while she would not be able to see inside his heart—praying she would not see behind the powdered wig and the ostentatious bow in his hair.

Maddie approached him, finger stabbing his chest, her expression too determined to give him peace of mind.

"Do not lie to me, young man. I've seen you sneaking about in the dead of the night, and I've listened to what you and your young friends have to say to each other."

"Maddie," he said, this time his hands raised defensively into the air.

"Maddie, Maddie."

"Don't you Maddie me. I'm not talking about you shamelessly cavorting with Lord Dickens and Rathen. I'm talking about that man you call Ryder and the other one, Aric. Those fellows are different— dangerous. They are more like you. And the three of you are about something. I saw the three of you sneaking around at Vauxhall a week ago. You were acting strange. I wouldn't have thought twice about it, but now you're here. I won't let you embroil my young charges in your mischief. I will have the truth."

Damian stepped back, his heart in his throat. "You mistake me for someone else." He spoke softly. "I suggest you watch them more closely.

"No, I don't," she said.

The girls have far too much time on their hands. They do as they please. I would put an end to that." Damian pulled out a lace handkerchief and delicately touched the corners of his mouth. "Now, if you will be so good as to excuse me. And—" he said pointedly, "—you should see to your impressionable young charges."

"This is no longer your choice. You had best tell me your secret." she told him, bringing her hands to her ample hips, her eyes narrowing to stare accusingly upon him.

"I am exactly what you see," Damian said. "An admitted wastrel. You are a shrewd woman and it seems a determined one, yet you are wrong in this matter."

"Nay, I am not. If you want to see Amorica again—" she began.

He cut her off with a wave of the hand. "Do not think to blackmail me." He grew agitated with Maddie. "It will not go well for you if you try.

I have ways to make your life miserable." He could not stop the low growl in the back of his throat.

"Bah, beneath all that posturing and preening, you are a different man—dangerous, perhaps even threatening. Yet you are not cruel. You would never hurt me or make my life miserable as you say." With all the patience Damian could draw forth, he lightly touched her elbow and led Maddie to a dark corner. "Very well, you can help by keeping a closer eye on your young charges. I would never forgive myself if anything happened to them, especially Amorica."

"I will do more." Maddie's voice held a combative tone.

"There is nothing more to do."

"This does no good to your cause. I will keep my eyes and ears open, and if I hear anything I will make sure to get a message to you." She whispered, her voice rising with the agitation, her fear apparent in her features.

"You will not give up on this nonsense?" he asked clearly puzzled.

All his dandified airs could not shake her. "You must see to Amorica and her cousins. There is no cause."

"I can do both."

He stepped back still stunned by Maddie. She was not what she seemed, and Damian knew he would have to take great care—more care than he had in the past. He had been living in a dream world. He had become too cocky and far too sure of himself. He had relegated all at court as inconsequential, perhaps boring and with nothing more on their minds than drinking and womanizing. Yet this woman had seen through his ploy.

She was right. Others would discover his ruse.

"Forget this nonsense," he told Maddie before taking his leave. He didn't wait for her to answer, but he did pray she would heed his advice.

Outside, a light mist coated the gardens, and the daylight grew dim.

Aric was due to meet him soon with news of the latest stowaways. Ryder would be in London at the end of the week, and they would all meet at Hyde Park.

A few hours later, Damian strode down a cobbled path, through an archway adorned with purple flowers and into a section of his garden where large shrubs and trees gave him the privacy he wanted.

Aric stood by a large oak tree. As Damian approached, Aric slowly turned, his expression unreadable.

"You are late," he said. "It's not like you. Is there something wrong?" Aric held his hand out in greeting, his gaze focused on Damian's. And Damian was sure he read his mind.

"Nothing is wrong. There are just a few complications." Damian pulled the powdered wig from his head.

"A woman?" Aric inquired, his voice a whisper, low yet curious.

Damian nodded. "A chaperone of a young lady I find myself courting seems to know more than she should." Damian related the conversation to Aric. "Then—what do you plan?"

Damian shrugged, wondering the same thing. They needed a new place to land, a safe place. Yet he did not want to involve Amorica's family in this subterfuge. If Ryder found another cove or a safe bay, he would not mention the island.

"I will wait and watch."

As if they knew each other's mind, they turned and walked to Damian's home.

Inside, Damian poured them both a glass of wine. Damian usually enjoyed the camaraderie with his long time friend. Tonight he had too much on his mind, too much to tell Aric.

"I will protect her with my life." Damian spoke in a slow measured voice while he slipped out of the ornate jacket he wore.

Aric leaned forward, his forearms resting on his thighs. "Who?" he asked, his brows drawn tightly together.

"Her name is Amorica."

"A lady who has come to London with nothing on her mind save finding a Lord to marry?" Aric's voice held a wealth of condemnation for her type. Until Damian met Amorica he'd felt the same.

"She is not like that." Damian drank long and deep, letting the wine settle warmly in his stomach just as thoughts of Amorica were sharp in his mind. He spoke as if he wished to convince himself that Aric spoke false.

She was not as she seemed. At times, he caught a side of her he didn't believe she wanted him to see. "She viewed the journey to London as punishment. Yet she batted her eyelashes shamelessly and seemed to play a game."

"You cannot expect me to believe that," Aric said laughing. He rose and sauntered around the room, stopping only to stare out the window.

"Women want only three things, marriage, a title and wealth."

"You are right. I cannot expect you to believe that this jaded heart of mine might well be thawing and that a woman might prefer her home to life at court. But it is the truth."

"Perhaps you have been misled," Aric said, turning to face Damian once more. "It would not be the first time sweet words and a beautiful face deceived a man."

"And whose heart is more jaded? Yours or mine?" Damian laughed.

"I have not claimed to have fallen in love—only that I will protect her to the best of my ability. I fear her curiosity and intelligence may well place her in a position she cannot escape."

"There is more here than you are telling."

Damian nodded. "She has seen the list."

"What?" Aric whirled on Damian, his face pinched tightly in anger.

"You cannot have been so careless. People's lives are at stake."

"It's the double life I have to live. I was pretending to stumble around in a drunken stupor, and the parchment fluttered to the floor and into an alcove. Before I could retrieve it, Lord Dickens and Rathen appeared then I discovered the girls inside the alcove. As it turns out, when I returned to the alcove the list had vanished."

Aric could do little but shake his head.

"I stole into her chambers that night and retrieved it, but I am sure she knows all the names. She has quite a remarkable memory."

"You must leave. None of this is worth risking your life. There are others who are willing to carry on the work we started. The close call the other night is proof our enemies may well discover us and if they do, we will not be able to defend ourselves."

"Wait until we hear from Ryder. I have a safe haven in mind if Ryder does not find one on his own. We will at least do as we have promised and escort to safety those of the brotherhood seeking political asylum from reactionary Austria."

Aric set the chalice he'd been drinking from on a table. "I must go.

I'll return in a week with Ryder. You must keep all eyes open and do not let your mind wander. Use her, ease yourself with her, but do not let this woman you covet steal your life or your heart. All could be lost if you let down your guard."

~ * ~

"I don't understand." Amorica sat on the window seat, her chin in her hands, saddened by the absence of Damian's attentions.

"I dinna ken why he has not called on you or sent a message either," Christel said showing her Scottish heritage. Christel was the second daughter of a Scottish laird. "I thought that he cared for you. I thought that perhaps he might even be falling in love with you."

"Neither do I," Ravyn added. "As for love, I doubt his attentions have been sincere. I've received countless, meaningless notes from Richy, and I've had afternoon tea with him twice. No matter what I do, he continues to send invitations."

"What have you tried?" Christel asked. "Where your ploy did not work for you, it might for me."

"I've played this relationship as if I'm a dimwit," Amorica said. "At the time I did not think he noticed my stupidity. Now I believe I have won the wager."

"I tried the same ploy," Christel sighed. "But it hasn't worked for me.

What else?"

"I brought Wolfy who growled at him for the entire time we were together," Ravyn said.

"I tried that too," Christel said with a huge sigh. And I thought it would be Amorica who would have trouble getting rid of her suitor."

"He hasn't called on me once," Amorica joined the conversation with a wistfulness to her voice she didn't understand. Wasn't this what she wanted? To escape marriage and return home? Until she'd met Damian Andrews, that had been her fantasy. Had she done something wrong that day when they'd picnicked at the pond? Perhaps she had been too bold, too sure of herself. Perhaps her ploys had worked too well.

She remembered the way his arms felt around her, his scent, the touch of his hands. All too well, she could not forget the sensations he evoked when he ran his hands along her arms.

"Enough of this pouting," Maddie entered the room in a bustling hurry. "There is to be a ball, a costume ball. You each have to decide what to wear. We must make sure your costumes are demure."

"A costume ball," they echoed in seeming unison. "What fun."

"Who do you suppose Dicky and Richy will go as?" Christel asked.

"I'm afraid to venture a guess."

"What would be in character?" Ravyn asked.

"They don't have to dress up. They already parade as court jesters," Christel giggled.

"Well," Maddie interjected her opinion, "Each of you will go as a fair maiden. I will not see you do anything scandalous. I ken the way your minds work, and I will have none of it."

"Perhaps I will go as a nun," Christel paused, looking up from her stitching.

"You will not. While I agree Dicky is not the man for you, someone will come along. I ken the man of your dreams is in your near future." Maddie, Christel's aunt and Scottish to the core, rearranged the bath sheets, folding and refolding each one as if she needed something to keep her hands busy.

"What about mine?" Ravyn asked, a pretty pout on her lips. "I would have you see into my future as well. Do you carry a crystal ball with you?"

"You will find your man without encouragement from this old lady."

"Oh, I don't know." Ravyn walked to the window and leaning her elbows on the sill gazed into the night. "There are no real men here. I think they must all be out there somewhere trying to right all the wrong in this world. I would like to meet one—a man who could set everything right—and give some brave man my heart. If he were a knight fighting in a tournament, I would blow him a kiss and he would bow before me, before he joined the lists."

"You are an incurable romantic, Ravyn. There are few decent men these days. And where you find one would not be in high society in London or at a debutante ball."

"Like Hunter, Allura's husband. God could send me one just like him.

He is gentle and kind, and he would put his life before Allura's."

"True indeed, he is noble and all that knighthood is supposed to be about. But none of the Lords we have met are like that."

"Damian Andrews—" Maddie began but she cut herself off, her hand across her mouth stifling a tiny gasp.

"Damian what?" Amorica insisted. "What were you going to say, Maddie? Out with it."

"I will say nothing. But mark my words, time will tell, and I think you will be pleased."

Amorica shook her head at Maddie who had now turned her back to the girls while she hummed and refolded sheets that were already perfect.

"We shall all go to the ball, each as a different goddess."

"Don't you think that is presumptive?" Christel asked, yet she was smiling and her eyes seemed to sparkle with laughter and the promise of something.

The smooth skin between Ravyn's eyebrows creased together. "No, it's a costume ball isn't it? We are not proclaiming ourselves goddesses.

We are just dressing up for fun."

"I will go as Diana, the Huntress," Ravyn said. "Who will you be?" She looked from one sister to the other.

"I will go as Athena, and Christel can go as Demeter," Amorica said thoughtfully.

"We will have to put our heads together and design something spectacular," Ravyn said.

"Is it Lord Rathen you wish to impress?" Both Amorica and Christel laughed. Amorica watched her cousin who seemed to be smiling wistfully even while she shook her head.

"I saw someone the other day," she spoke softly. "I caught his eyes but he disappeared into the gardens," she paused. "While his actions seemed harmless, they also seemed—secretive, perhaps even furtive. I do not think he was pleased that he was seen."

"What did he look like?" Amorica asked between stitches. She had her own fantasies but this seemed much too much like the scene she'd come upon the other day when she was riding in the park. Two men spoke with Damian, both dressed in dark clothes. All three whispered then another piece of parchment was handed to Damian.

"He was dark and brooding after he saw me. His first reaction was to smile but then his features hardened. There was a third man also," Ravyn said. "I saw him," Christel said looking up with a curious light in her eyes.

"The sight of him stole my breath, my heart pounded so hard I nearly thought it would jump through my skin."

"You saw him? The third man?" Amorica asked.

"Where were you?" The demand from Ravyn was unexpected.

Christel paused and looked out the window. Her cheeks were pale yet her shoulders were squared and her chin high when she looked back at them.

"I was in the garden, reading and trying to think of a nice way to tell Dicky that I truly do not welcome his attentions. He is crass and vulgar, and I do not want to see him but despite all I do, he continues to pester me.

I even said no to him. I told him I did not return his affections but every time I turn a corner or think that I am alone, he shows up."

"I did not know you were distressed," Amorica said and walked to Christel's side, resting her hands on her cousin's shoulders. "We must put an end to this. In such a short time, I feel we have done all a disservice by our wager."

"How can you say that?" Ravyn asked.

"We have not deceived them. We have been honest and straightforward. They all know how we feel, don't they?" Amorica asked, but she knew the truth. In her heart and in not so subtle ways, she had encouraged Damian. She knew it was Damian who had rejected her.

"Well, none of this matters. Our costumes must be perfect," Ravyn said. "I mean to discover who conspires with Damian Andrews in the dark of the night."

"You must take precautions," Christel told her cousin. "I fear for your safety."

"Come let us forget this intrigue. I cannot imagine Damian as a dangerous man or that he conspires with anyone. He cares of nothing save spending his father's fortune and acting the fool."

"His friends are the same," Ravyn agreed.

"What will we wear?" Amorica asked.

"You have only three days to put something together," Maddie told them. "The ball will be held to celebrate the new seasons." With that said, Maddie left the room.

For a moment, Ravyn stepped from the common room the three girls shared. She reemerged wearing a sheer sky blue gown that lovingly caressed her body.

She carried two other gowns. One was a soft meadow green and the other was snow white. "We will wear these," she said, a mischievous smile forming on her lips.

"Where did you get them?" Amorica asked.

"I heard of the ball two days ago, and I had them made."

"You can see right through them," Christel protested.

"True, but we will decorate them in such a manner that our gowns will leave those staring at us able to see nothing more than their imagination." Ravyn turned so the girls could see the gown.

Amorica rose, circling her cousin. "We will fashion a bow and arrow for the goddess Diana. The quiver will hang from the shoulder and a soft scarf will cover her breasts."

"And for the goddess Demeter, we will fashion autumn leaves and perhaps a few flowers to signify the changing of the seasons." Ravyn twirled.

"Well, if you wear those dresses, you will never rid yourselves of the men you seek to elude," Christel said. "And what will Athena wear with the gown that hides nothing."

"Circlets of gold and perhaps gold and silver scarves sewn carefully to disguise and hide but also to invite a man of my choosing to look but not touch."

"You are shameful." Christel said.

"Here," Ravyn handed a gown to each of the girls. "Try them on." Ravyn's unabashed smile touched Amorica in a way she could have never imagined.

"It's scandalous. You know that," Amorica said.

Amorica hesitated for a second only then disappeared with the gown into her chambers. Christel did the same, and Amorica could only imagine she did so with reluctance.

A few moments later, she reappeared along with Christel into the main room. Her heart stopped beating for a moment when she saw Ravyn and Christel. The gowns hid nothing. They showed off every curve the girls possessed. Amorica felt a strange connection and power while she wore the gown, knowing she could decorate the garment to entice yet not reveal.

"Amorica, we will have to go shopping, but I'm not sure where.

Athena will need a helmet to make her costume complete. I will need a bow and arrow. I changed my mind, Christel, you will need be Hestia the goddess of the hearth. I will finish with the scarves."

"I dinna think—" Christel began but was quickly shooed away by Ravyn. "We must take care."

"What if someone was to recognize us?"

"They cannot," Christel's voice rose in agitation.

"Of course they won't," Ravyn reassured her cousin as she continued to artfully drape scarves around Amorica while Christel watched with an expression of horrified fascination.

"It's wicked," Amorica murmured, yet she knew she would wear the costume.

"We will disappear before the masks are taken off. Make sure we stay close to each other," Ravyn said.

"Stay close to the nearest door."

"Something will happen. It always does when we do something like this—something so scandalous. We cannot think to make it through an entire evening unscathed," Christel fidgeted with the newly draped scarf.

"You are breathtaking," Amorica said of her cousin. "I would give anything to see the look on Lord Dickens' face if he were to realize your identity."

"I would not like to think of such things." Christel lowered her lashes.

"I suppose you do not. Since you mean to become a nun, I don't suppose you would want to entice any man, even Dickens."

"I do not."

"What of the man we saw with Damian Andrews. You could not keep your eyes from him," Ravyn teased.

"Let me in."

From outside the door, Maddie's voice rose several decibels, the pounding incessant.

"You cannot go inside. This is not proper go back downstairs. Be off with you, Lord Dickens, Lord Rathen, No." Maddie's voice rose.

Maddie stepped inside and closed the door behind her with a resounding bang. Inside, she leaned against the door, panting, her cheeks rosy. Then she saw the girls. Her eyes grew wide. She inhaled sharply.

"Ye cannae mean to wear that!"

~ * ~

"There are Austrian spies about and pirates." Lord Henry Rathen, second Earl of Devonshire spoke to Damian while he sipped smuggled brandy. Richy had been summoned home to give an accounting of his deeds to his father. Along with Dicky, Damian had kept Richy company.

"So you say." Damian stared out the window of the Earl's summer home, watching the roads leading to the entrance.

"Come now. You cannot tell me you have not heard the stories floating about."

"I've heard—things," Damian meant to sound vague. Yet everything the man said disturbed him.

"They have found the pirate's caves. They are smuggling rebels,

Germans, Russians, and anyone who dares defy their government. I cannot tell you how disgusted I am. They are bringing rebellion to English soil."

"You don't like liberal thought," Damian spoke to the older man.

Lord Dickens waved his hands in the air. "That is beside the point. I cannot abide dissidents either. No Englishmen want to see governments brought down by commoners."

Damian yawned, pretending boredom. "What can all this possibly have to do with me?"

"You and Dicky should take more of an interest in your government.

Life is not just about drinking and whoring. You should become—involved."

"Ah, but I do believe those are the more pleasant pursuits of life. I do not wish to become involved."

"Bah, have some backbone young man. I daresay my son will never change. I've had hopes that some of his friends might perform the miracle I cannot."

"Do not look to me," Damian said, sitting down on a chair and closing his eyes. "I have no wish to reform anyone."

"The pirates have changed their meeting place. In two days they will smuggle another family onto English soil. I know where they plan to go."

Damian was sweating from the inside out. There was a traitor in their midst.

Chapter Five

"It's a godsend, I say," Aric Lakeland told Damian. "I am heartily glad the girl's chaperone showed her hand. We must know who is loyal. Who we can trust."

"There is no proof," Damian cautioned. "I would know more before I condemn the old woman. She seemed sincere."

"She must have had a bone to pick with someone. We do not know her history or why she would care about the politics of the time."

"Perhaps it is not what we think. Perhaps she means to implicate the girls in her scheme and discredit them," Aric tossed out.

A shudder ran down Damian's spine. He had thought along those lines more than once. The girls would have to be protected.

How would he protect Amorica from himself? He had stayed away from her, tried to put her from his mind. But now he was about to return to high society. He would have to attend balls, be seen riding in the park and at Whites.

They would meet.

He would have to see her. If he did not appear smitten, Dicky and Richy would question his motives.

His choices were limited.

A costume ball...

The Duchess would guard her charges. Did she have their best interest at heart? He prayed she did.

If Maddie was loyal to the girls, could she be trusted to keep his secrets too? She offered her loyalty, pretended to understand his cause.

Maddie had inferred she might have a new asylum for the political refugees. A safe haven.

Damian's heart sped. Different scenarios to this raced through his mind.

"Do not trust her and do not let down your guard. We cannot know her mind," Aric cautioned.

"I will heed your warning."

"You must do more than that. You must watch your back," Aric said.

"Would that she had some out-of-the-way place to offer."

"Ryder has spoken of Christel's family. The Scottish clan is well known. It seems there are islands nearby. Her ancestral home is on the coast. It sounds perfect," Aric said, yet his eyes had narrowed.

"You do not trust Maddie."

"I trust no one save you and Ryder. Do not trust the girls," Aric cautioned.

Damian nodded. He would not trust easily and yet something about Amorica stirred him. Deep in his heart, he wanted to trust her. He wished he could set aside his fears and doubts.

"She knows too much," Aric reminded him.

"Maddie?"

"Amorica. She has seen the names of the refugees." Silence clung in the small room. Aric was right. She had seen the list of names. Now she had the power of life or death over everyone on the list. And all who had possessed it.

"What will you do?" Aric asked.

Damian had no answers to his friend's questions. "I do not know." Damian turned to leave but Aric stopped him.

"If Amorica is involved—then you must silence her."

~ * ~

"This costume is scandalous," Ravyn said, stepping back and studying her handiwork.

"You promise the mask will hide my identity?" Amorica asked.

She lovingly touched the fabric.

"I promise. No one at the ball will guess. We are safe behind our masks. For once we can act and do as we please."

"Something will go wrong," Christel said. "Father will hear."

"And they will banish the lot of us to a tiny village in the Highlands."

"That would make you happy."

"And both of you miserable." Christel set aside the brush she'd been using to comb her hair. "If I did anything to make either of you unhappy—" "I apologize," Ravyn said coming to her cousin. "Our fathers will hear nothing. In the morning, we will look back on this night with fondness.

Our small moment of daring will be remembered and cherished forever. It will become an event we can tell our grandchildren about. Trust me." Amorica watched her cousins with fondness. And while Ravyn meant well, Amorica had the same feeling of foreboding Christel had.

Her stomach churned with butterflies, her heart raced, and all Amorica could think of was seeing Damian. He would attend the ball. He had to. Christel had told her Damian would attend. Dicky had told her.

"Have you heard news of the smugglers?" Christel asked, changing the subject.

"What are they smuggling?" Ravyn walked toward her cousin. "And where have you heard this?"

"Dicky told me. They are smuggling people. Dissidents from other European countries. People who would be prosecuted for crimes they have not committed. All they have done is speak their mind." Amorica stiffened. She'd heard the rumors as well. "They say an aristocrat is involved. I pray they catch them soon." She spoke with deep bitterness, memories welling from the past.

"Well, we can rest assured it isn't any of our suitors."

"Thank God for that. Father would arrest the man himself," Amorica said, remembering the night her mother died.

The night smugglers landed in a cove near her home.

The night her mother had gone for a walk in the moonlight.

"What would you do?" Christel asked.

Without batting an eyelash, Amorica said, "I would have him drawn and quartered."

The men had struck down Amorica's mother as if she were nothing.

The men had been desperate. They had been running for their very lives.

But it had not given them the right to kill another.

Amorica tucked a wayward strand of hair behind her ear. Her mask covered her face, some of it hand painted by Ravyn, who had an artistic bent. Suddenly this night did not seem quite so jovial.

She adjusted the scarf at her shoulder. She knew that even if the knot came undone, she would be fully covered. The gown beneath the scarves covered her from her neck to her toes. She turned to study herself in the mirror.

"Shall we?" Ravyn asked.

Amorica drew in a long deep breath then nodded. She made her decision where Damian Andrews was concerned.

Thank God he was too much the dandy to be one of the smugglers.

~ * ~

"I cannot stay away a moment longer," Damian said as he watched the cousins walk into the ballroom. They were naïve, he mused, if they sought to hide their identity behind the tiny masks they wore.

"It is not wise to go to Amorica. Do not dance with her," Aric cautioned Damian.

"Where Amorica is concerned, I am not a wise man." Damian stepped forward into the light. He waited for a moment before approaching the girls. His heart stopped for an instant. His breath rushed out. Bloody hell, he whispered to himself, his gaze riveted on Amorica and her scandalous attire. A gown that left him awe-struck. While it revealed every curve, it also concealed. It was, just like the woman, an anomaly, fascinating.

"She cannot mean to parade herself in such a costume," Damian said.

Aric stood behind Damian. "Breathtaking," he said. "I would like a better view."

Damian growled low in his throat. "Not if you value your life, friend." The word friend was said with an edge Damian had never felt before.

"It is not the fair Amorica I care to see." Aric spoke quietly, an edge to his own voice.

"Then who?"

"Ravyn," Aric replied. "She has caught my eye each time I have seen her. She is—" he paused for several long seconds. "She tantalizes my senses. Makes my breath catch in my throat."

"Caution, friend. By the look of it, every man in the house is—tantalized. And, if you recall, you are no more free to court a lady than I am."

"I do not mean to court the lady."

"She is a lady," Damian reminded his friend, his emotions spiraling.

He did not mean to imply that Aric would treat her without regard and yet this conversation headed in that very direction.

"A dance would not hurt," Aric moved from the dark corner and stepped toward the girls. Damian held back, letting his gaze travel the length of Amorica then back to her eyes.

The artfully draped scarves covered every part of her and danced whimsically around her.

Yet with every move she made they teased and taunted and said look but don't touch.

Even for this court, the gowns were scandalous. Why had The Duchess let them get away with something that would be the talk of London for the coming weeks?

Richy reached Ravyn before Aric did and claimed the first dance.

There was little Damian could do to protect Ravyn. She would have to fend for herself. He decided he would manipulate Amorica's time.

He would let no one close to her. As soon he could, he would whisk her away from the ball where every court dandy could not speculate as to the soft virgin flesh beneath her gown.

Ah, and Dicky appeared at Christel's side. She flushed a deep shade of crimson, even while her back stiffened. Dicky would not be the first man to win the bet and neither would he. Yet he prayed Richy would not succeed with Ravyn. If Aric intervened, Richy would never be able to mince his way to Ravyn's bed then down the aisle to the altar.

The music changed tempo. Damian smoothed the non-existent creases from his jacket. He stepped forward, wishing he did not have to pretend to be something he wasn't.

"Amorica," he bowed low.

~ * ~

She laughed softly, hiding behind a lace fan. "You are not supposed to know my name," she said. "You are such a rogue." She turned away from him, realizing the mask concealed nothing. She had seen him in the corner. His eyes dark, his countenance brooding, and she had wondered if he'd seen through her disguise. Instead of fear now that she'd been recognized a tingle of excitement swept through her.

"I would know you anywhere." Damian bent low to whisper in her ear. "Nothing you do to yourself could conceal your true identity." His breath whispered like a warm spring breeze across her cheek. Her body tightened, her pulse racing. He left her feeling weak-kneed.

"You speak too intimately," she said, turning from him and fanning her heated cheeks.

"I would know you more intimately," he returned, his hand upon hers.

He led her to the dance floor, his thumb rubbing circles on her wrist, his gaze never leaving hers.

She did not understand the sudden emotions enveloping her heart. He had left her alone for more days than she wanted to count. She had thought he'd lost interest. Too late, she remembered her ploy. She must act ridiculously naive. The ploy was difficult since it seemed she had an opinion about everything. She had never worn her heart on her sleeve, and she never shied from a conflict. Yet this moment she had butterflies in her stomach, and she had the uneasy feeling she should turn and run from Damian Andrews.

His touch was always upon her, his fingers lightly brushing her skin.

They stopped and stepped away from the dancers. Yet they went nowhere.

He stood beside her, his fingertip trailing across the top of her hand, exploring her palm and her wrist. His gaze never left hers. She moistened her lips and his eyes grew darker. She turned her head, watching the others in the room flit whimsically about, and wishing she could think of something witty to say. He toyed with a strand of hair then let his fingers brush across her cheek.

Christel danced by with Dicky, her brows creased together as if she were in deep thought. Then Ravyn danced by in Richy's arms, her smile wide and infectious. Richy appeared to have lost his heart to her.

Before this night ended, Amorica would understand Damian's intentions. She needed to know just what his motives were. Why would he stay away for so many days then not let her from his sight? She meant to find out.

"You must dance—get the lady something to drink," Dicky said, his words slurred, his eyes dazed.

~ * ~

Damian wobbled on his heels. Yet a moment ago he seemed fully aware of his hands and legs. He leaned against a pillar and closed his eyes.

Richy stumbled into a spot in front of Ravyn, nearly toppling her.

"I say," Dicky began, "It's time to start a party of our own."

"We could go to my home," Richy said, his head lolling to one side.

"Or mine," Dicky volunteered.

"The duchess will hunt us down," Christel said softly. She gazed down the hallway leading from the ballroom as if she wished The Duchess would appear magically. Amorica's heart went out to her younger cousin.

"I would like to go," Ravyn said.

"No." Amorica nearly jumped from her skin. "You cannot mean such a thing."

Ravyn's eyes twinkled with mischief. "Why?" she asked.

"You know why."

"May I?" Damian bowed low over Amorica's hand.

"A dance?" she queried, her breath catching.

"Of course," he said, his manners impeccable.

With her hands in his, Damian twirled Amorica in a tight circle before passing her to the man next in line. His throat constricted. From a distance Ryder nodded. The gesture was subtle but recognizable. Aric stood in a dark shadow, his features drawn tight. They all knew what had to be accomplished this night.

Slowly Ryder walked toward him, assuming his place in the dance line. Damian stepped away from the dancers, waiting for Amorica to move past him. When she did, he reached out to her, gently pulling her from the line, then with her hand within his, he led her away from the gaiety and into darkened corridors.

"What are you doing?" She sounded breathless, her voice a soft sweetness that would tempt the most determined man. "Where do you take me?" Her steps were quick and light.

"I am taking you—" he paused. He wasn't sure what he intended, just that he had needed to get her away from the staring eyes and the lascivious grins of his friends and enemies. The sight of her in the flimsy scarves she'd draped over her sent surges of heat raging within. Enveloped in jealousy, his needs driving him, he strode faster.

"Damian, slow down." She stumbled into him, her small fingers gripping his shirt.

Beneath his breath, he swore then he swept her into his arms. Her breasts pushed against his chest, her hair fluttered lightly against his face, tickling his skin. She pressed her head against him, and he was sure he felt the tender slide of her lips against his neck. The sensation vanished.

You must silence her.

He could not. Yet their lives were at stake and for better or worse interwoven. She knew far too much.

Yet without further knowledge, she knew nothing.

He felt her gaze upon him. Felt the inferno once more. He had not determined his course. He had acted with no thought. Yet what he did now, he would not change.

He kicked open the door. Outside the air was heavy with moisture. No wind blew. Fog hung on the ground and wound itself through the trees.

She shivered.

"Damian—"

"Hush, you will be warm in a few minutes. There is something I want you to see." He could hear the river ahead of him. He moved faster. He strode toward a building that housed rare and beautiful flowers. He had brought some of them to the grounds himself. Just as he brought Amorica to the gardens.

She pressed herself closer. "I do not believe I will ever be warm again."

"You remind me of white roses," he told her.

Inwardly, he smiled. He liked the tone she spoke to him with. He longed for a woman who had the will to stand and fight. A woman who would challenge him. Perhaps she was not as she seemed.

Yet that misplaced determination might lead her into trouble.

The Duke's glassed in gardens were kept warm by an elaborate set of furnaces supplied with coal. Inside the glass conservatory the scent of roses touched his heart. He breathed in deeply once more wondering about Amorica, about things best left alone. He wanted to understand her. He knew he didn't have the right to probe into her thoughts. Another wife and family were not meant for him.

He strode with her to a balcony, looking over the river then he set her on the railing. "Hold on to me," he told her. His voice rasped. He cleared his throat.

Her fingers tightened around his neck, the soft pads brushing his flesh, evoking carnal thoughts. He had a mission here. He had to manipulate her until every waking thought of her was about him. She would dream of him at night. She would yearn for him during the day.

Yet he was repulsed at that image.

You must silence her.

So she would never betray him.

He would bend her to his will. She would cry out at night for him, for his touch and she would forever give her loyalty to him and to his cause.

For him, she would stand beside him, loyal and true of heart.

And silent. There was no other way.

Yet he closed his eyes and let his imagination roam where it shouldn't. "What would happen if I tugged on this tiny scrap of fabric?" He stared at the knot tied provocatively atop her shoulder. His heart sped.

It was not his intention to seduce, yet it seemed he lost all common sense where Amorica was concerned.

She looked at him, moistening her lips, tilting her head sideways as if she was trying to figure out the answer to his question.

"I don't understand," she told him. Her eyes widened then darkened.

Desire rimmed the beautiful hue.

"But I think you do." He kissed the line of her jaw, soft teasing kisses.

He nibbled softly, caressing and licking the tender flesh. Her chin rose, giving him further access. She moaned softly.

Her fingers tightened around him once more. He pushed her slightly backward, watching the water below, knowing she would pull herself closer, press her body against his. He growled low in his throat, wishing she were his alone, understanding she would never be. He was not worthy of her, could not give her the security and love she deserved. Yet her softness so close to him made reasoning impossible. His body hardened with need. Fire swept within.

His lips trailed kisses down her neck, resting on the tiny knot that held her gown. He could loosen the ties—discover her hidden secrets.

The fabric would slip lovingly down her body. She would be open to his eyes. Her secrets revealed to him. The thought left him gasping for breath—his body raging with need.

He had forsaken his home and his family. He had torn asunder all ties with his kin when he'd devoted himself to the cause.

He had made a solemn vow to himself.

Now he held this lady's life in the palms of his hands. And the vow he'd made might soon be broken.

"Damian—"

The soft sound of her voice penetrated his thoughts, left him needy with desire. She had no idea what she did to him.

"What are you doing?" she asked, her fingers tugging gently on his hair. Yet the sensation she evoked was a caress. She needed him—wanted him. I am seducing you until you will do my bidding. He didn't dare tell her his thoughts. "I am curious."

"Curious?" she queried, her cheek resting against his head.

"Oh, yes. I would know why you would wear this costume?"

"Because—" she began but then inhaled swiftly, her body responding to his caress and then his teeth closed on the tie. He tugged and experimented, sensing the slight loosening of the fabric.

"You should not tempt me so." He wished he could dare pull on the ties. The fabric would break free from its restraint and slide down her body. He closed his eyes, imagining her unveiling. Inch by sheer inch the material would uncover her alabaster flesh. Then it would cling to her breasts, hugging her nipples as if taunting him even more. It seemed to Damian that the scarves conspired against him.

"I do not mean to," she said.

In front of him, she was covered still. Yet the back of his hand grazed forbidden territory. He heard her indrawn breath and when he lifted his gaze from the beauty of her, to her eyes, he saw them widen in understanding. Still she had no choice but to cling to him. The water raged behind her. Her fingers tightened around his neck.

"What do you do?" she asked.

He heard no sound of protest. Her voice sounded soft and sultry

70

to his hungry ears. If she gave him a reason, no, he could not. Still, she said nothing and her voice was more curious than anything.

"I mean to see all of you." Touch all of you. Bury myself inside you.

"It's not right," she breathed softly against his cheek.

"Then tell me no."

She looked at him as he watched her, waiting for her to give him reason to stop. Her words haunted him. He had no right. She was not his and never would be. He did not deserve her, did not deserve to know her sweetness. He touched her lips with a finger.

Bind her, silence her.

He would have to find another way to keep her safe. Yet so much was at risk here. He lowered his lips to hers and ran his tongue along the seam, praying she would open to him. He buried his fingers in her hair, loosening the tendrils until they fell in disarray around her shoulders. This moment was his. This time in eternity would forge a place in his mind forever.

She moved closer to him, pressed herself against his length. Her lips parted, and she met him with her own innocent explorations.

He pulled back. His hands framed her face. Her lips were kiss-swollen, tempting, alluring. His gut tightened. He'd never felt so damn helpless in his life. She embedded herself in his heart. He could not withdraw so easily from the silken web she wove around him.

He ran his fingers through her hair. The soft scent of roses permeated the air, mixing with the other flowers in the greenhouse. As if she were lost in thought, her lashes lowered to her cheeks, resting there for a moment before she looked at him again.

He imagined her on his bed, her hair spread across his sheets, her limbs wrapped around him, white rose petals scattered around her. His thoughts might indeed condemn him to a fiery grave. He could not stop himself. He did not want to stop. He needed her as he needed air to breathe. He kissed her again. With no hesitation, she accepted him. He was afraid his heart as well as his very soul belonged to Amorica.

"Damian! I say, Damian. Where are you?"

Damian swore softly then quickly lifted Amorica from the railing, setting her behind him. "Hush, sweetheart," he said.

He watched her push her hair back then touch the knot at her shoulder as if she checked it. She should have never worn the outlandish costume, he thought.

"Damian!"

He could not avoid them. Even as he searched for a way to escape Richy and Dicky, the footsteps closed on them.

"There you are."

"I say. You've had more luck than we have."

"Aye, this dark brooding man yanked Christel from my arms just as I approached a private nook. I thought for sure I'd have her in my arms and my bed for the night."

Behind him, he felt Amorica's trembling touch. He felt his own anger grow, wishing there would have been some way to avoid the wager.

He sensed she was about to step from behind him. He moved so she could not show herself to these men who were rapidly becoming his enemies. He did not want anyone to see Amorica now—in her state of dishabille.

He grabbed Dicky by the arm and led him away.

"Hey!" Dicky said but offered no resistance. Richy slanted a lingering look toward Amorica but followed, a wry smile on his face.

"What is it? Let go." Dicky's words slurred.

Damian heard the rustle of leaves and the soft slide of fabric. He breathed in deeply, wishing this evening had not ended this way. Yet there was no changing this. He watched Amorica leave the greenhouse and run across the grass.

She disappeared in the darkness.

It was for the best, he told himself. Yet his heart did not want to believe.

Chapter Six

"You cannot mean to go with Damian—without a chaperone?" Ravyn spoke as she paced the confines of Amorica's room.

"It has been two weeks since I saw him." Amorica protested while she leaned on the windowsill, peering down at the gardens below, then farther, imagining the glass conservatory where she was sure she had lost her heart to the rogue.

"And that is a better reason not to go. You cannot mean to fall right into his plans whenever he crooks a little finger. Your reputation will be ruined," Christel said.

"I do not care a fig for my reputation. He is the perfect gentleman, too perfect at times. He would never—" she stopped, remembering the greenhouse—his kisses—the way he touched her and the way her heart had raced.

Ravyn stood, feet apart, hands on hips. "All the more reason to stay away from him. And what of the wager? You will not win if you give into him so easily. What would your father say?"

"He would not be pleased. No respecting lady would ride off for an afternoon picnic with a man—alone."

"It is morning." Ravyn reminded Amorica. "And if I read your mind correctly, it is for the entire day, this outing of yours."

"What is the difference? A day or half a day?"

"Probably nothing. It is just—I fear for your heart."

"The sun is shining, the sky is blue, and I don't believe there is a cloud in the sky. I will have a fine ride and a nice picnic, and I will be home before dark."

"You cannot be sure he does not have some nefarious motive in mind."

"And I was afraid to say anything of this to Christel. I knew she would object but I didn't think you would. Damian is neither dangerous or nefarious."

"Well." Ravyn blew a strand of loose hair from her face. "I didn't think you would lose all common sense where that man came into play."

"What are you thinking?"

"I am thinking I might never see him again. I am thinking I deserve to have a ride on a fine day. I am thinking he is up to something, and I mean to find out what it is."

"Then all the more reason to let it go." Ravyn tried to convince Amorica to stay home.

"And his other friends? Who are they?"

"Besides dark and brooding? Frightening?"

"They are all that, but they are also gentlemen."

"What on earth would make you say that?" Ravyn stepped closer to her cousin.

Outside on the lawn Damian stood and waved toward them.

"He beckons you, and you run right into his arms. You should learn to distance yourself from him, make him work to have you."

"If I seem too eager, he will turn tail and run the other way. Isn't that what he does each time I see him? I have found the perfect way to win our wager that I do not want to win."

"Do not be too sure of yourself?"

"Where Damian is concerned, I am not sure of anything." Amorica muttered, wondering if she answered her cousin's previous question or addressed her doubts. Amorica had watched Christel and she had watched the dark man known as Ryder. He appeared sinister yet he was Damian's friend. Perhaps Ravyn should know. And perhaps she should not. Amorica had seen the way Aric Lakeland stared at Ravyn. Amorica whirled on her cousin. "I must go."

"Damian has called."

"Yes, and I think you should keep a closer eye on yourself as well as Christel. Ryder watches her and Aric cannot keep his gaze from following you."

"Well." Ravyn chose to ignore Amorica's warnings. "Don't forget your cloak."

"Very well, if it makes you feel better." Amorica grabbed her cloak from the peg, kissed her cousin on the cheek. "I will return before dark. I have Damian's promise."

"And that makes me feel better? Take care, Amorica. You have little experience in affairs of the heart."

"You worry too much." But Amorica shivered, goose bumps prickling her arms. The truth of her own emotions settled into the pit of her stomach and would not let go. What did she know about Damian Andrews? Not enough, as her father would say. Not nearly enough.

Yet the sun shone, and her heart was light. She raced down the servant steps and to the door leading to the stables. As she reached for the door, it swept open seemingly of its own accord. Before she could step inside, she found herself lifted into the air and twirled around and around, the grass and the shrubs blending into a fuzzy blur.

"Damian!" she laughed. "Set me down."

"Never, you are as light as a feather. And I enjoy having you in my arms."

"I am dizzy." She breathed softly, taking in the hard planes of Damian's chest and tightening her hands around his arms.

He set her on the ground. "Are you ready?" he asked, his voice low as if he wished for no one to hear.

She smiled at him, pleased with his words, touching his jaw with a finger, feeling the light beard stubble there.

"I am," she said, then set off toward the stable. She stopped suddenly.

The horses were saddled and waiting. "You were very sure of me."

"No, I was not. I saw you in the window and then your cousin and I feared you would change your mind."

"She said your motives might be dark."

He grinned. "Indeed."

"Indeed? Is that all you can say?"

"I would not deny wanting you. But I would never harm you nor would I spirit you away from your friends for dark purposes."

She cocked her head and touched the nose of the horse he had saddled for her. "I prefer to ride astride. Are you shocked?"

His smile grew. "Nothing about you shocks me. I can have the saddle changed if you wish."

"No, just help me up."

He gave her a boost. In a few minutes he'd mounted his horse. They rode away from the stables and toward the vibrant countryside.

They rode in silence for several minutes. "Where are we going?" Amorica asked.

"I know of a sweet spot near a lake. It is beautiful and the scent of the forest behind fills the air. I would go there if that is all right with you." She blinked, a sudden surge of moisture from her eyes. He was kind.

The guilt at what she planned to do to Damian swamped her. Yet she should know what he was about, she told herself. She did this to protect herself, her virtue, her reputation. No, she did not. For she was never in fear for her virtue or her reputation.

She did this because she wanted to discover his secrets. And for the short time she had known him, he had a multitude of them.

"I'll race you to the edge of the trees," she cried out, nudging her horse forward before he could reply.

She heard his throaty laughter behind her and for a moment, she thought he might give her the win. But then she heard the pounding of his hooves behind her. She laughed when he pulled up next to her.

"You cheat," he said, staring at her as if he were measuring her. For a few moments, they galloped side by side. "Do you want me to give you the win?" he queried, the pounding of the hooves and the thundering of her heart nearly drowning out his words.

"Of course not," she urged her horse faster. But her efforts were to no avail. He passed her then, and she saw only his back. A few seconds later, he had stopped at the edge of the trees. She stopped beside him, laughing and pushing her hair from her eyes. The horses sidestepped.

"Where have you been the last few days?" she asked, noting the sudden stiffening of his shoulders and the tick at his jaw. Secrets. He had too many.

"Hunting," he told her.

She supposed his inane excuse might be true. "Hunting what?" she asked.

"What would you like?" The joy went out of his smile.

"I don't know," she said, "the truth."

"The truth would only hurt you." He dismounted and helped her down. He pointed toward the south. "The lake is over that rise."

"Truth should not hurt," she said, no longer quite as breathless but much more disillusioned.

"The meadow and the lake." A gust of wind caught Amorica's scarf.

The ends whipped behind her. He had changed the topic, and Amorica guessed the subject of his whereabouts would not be broached again.

He dismounted then helped her from her horse. "They are winded." He led the horses over the hill and when they crested the rise, Amorica drew in her breath. Sunlight rode the ripples on the lake that had been stirred by the slight breeze.

Damian spread the blanket. He bowed low and offered her a seat before he set the basket of food beside her. "What is it you brought to eat?" "Are you hungry?" he asked.

"Famished." Amorica wished with all her heart Damian would find a way to trust her with his secrets. Hunting, yes, and she was fishing for information. He was far too tight-lipped.

"I have cheese and bread and roasted deer and I don't know what other delicacies the cook packed." He pulled out a wine skin and offered her a drink.

She held it up and let the sweet wine drip slowly into her mouth. She felt a rush of pleasure and decided she would not question him further—at least not until later. She watched him eat then leaned back on her elbows and lifted her face to the sun. Warmth radiated through her and it seemed she felt the heat of his gaze upon her.

She opened her eyes and stared at him. "What are you thinking?" He laughed and drank wine. "That you are the most refreshing woman I have ever met."

She sat up, cocking her head sideways. "What does that mean?"

"Are you always so full of questions?" He bit into a piece of cheese and tore off a hunk of bread. While he chewed, he watched her and then he drank more wine, holding it out to her when he was finished.

"I wasn't going to ask any more." She drew her cloak more tightly around her.

"Are you cold?"

"The wind seems to have picked up, and the sun is sliding behind those clouds."

Damian swore softly, his gaze now on the horizon. Dark clouds grew and the wind whistled through the trees. "Come on," he said, springing to his feet and holding his hand to her.

She started to question him but bit back the words, knowing he had some plan.

He rose and walked to his horse. Opening his saddlebags, he withdrew a bright, colorful object and began assembling it.

Curiosity drew her to him. She looked around him, straining to see what he did even while he attempted to keep her from seeing.

"Go back and sit down. It's a surprise."

"Do not dismiss me so easily. I want to see." She pushed against the hard muscled planes of his back, understanding his strength and if he wished, he could forcefully keep her from her mission. Yet it seemed he only turned away.

"There!" He held the object aloft.

She clapped her hands together. "A kite!" she cried out. "Are you going to fly it?"

He smiled at her and slipped the ribbon from her hair. Her heart leapt.

"Of course."

"My ribbon."

"The kite must have a tail."

"Then I offer it as a favor for my knight in shining armor."

"As any damsel would."

The string was attached as well as the tail. He began to run, slowly letting the kite fly higher and higher. The wind cooperated. The kite soared into the sky. Breathless, he walked to her and held out the wooden stick where the other end of the string was wound.

They sat on a rock and watched the kite dance and sway high in the air. "I've always wanted to fly," he said.

"To fly? It is not possible."

"True, but that fact does not change what my heart feels."

"You are a dreamer," she said matter of factly, wishing for the same ability.

"No," he said softly. "I am not."

"I found a list of names." She ventured into uncharted territory. She watched his jaw tighten. He watched the kite.

"Really?"

"Someone stole it."

He turned to her, his eyes darkening, a muscle in his neck twitching.

"How?"

She breathed easier. He spoke with such calm his reaction must have been from concern through her. "I don't know. I found it the night I met you. The next morning it was not in my dresser."

"Your rooms were locked?"

"I thought so."

"Then you must have misplaced the list.

"I did not. I remember where I hid it, and it is no longer there."

"Your cousins?"

"They are innocent," she said, feeling very much relieved. "What do you know of the smugglers?"

He played out the line on the kite. She didn't think he meant to answer and then, "You should not listen to gossip."

"I haven't. It is my cousin, Ravyn. She says they are in London, in every drawing room and at every ball."

"What do you think of smugglers?" he laughed and let out a bit more line then handed the kite over to her. "Here."

"I loathe them."

"Really," he said, but there was no laughter in his eyes. "Why?" Wind shrieked through the trees on the edge of the forest. Fat drops of rain sluiced from the sky.

"I—" she began.

"Let the kite go."

"No," she said. "I could not."

"Let it go," he repeated, taking the wood from her hand.

"No," she sputtered.

"It is not worth your health to hang on to something so inconsequential."

"Damian," she began, yet the rain pelted her and she knew they must find shelter.

"Hurry."

"Hurry where? There is nowhere to go."

Damian grabbed the reins of his horse as well as hers. He offered her a hand up, but the storm frightened her horse. The animal reared up, pawing the air.

"There is shelter about a half league from here." He steadied her horse, yet she could not mount. He led both horses toward the line of trees.

"More secrets?" she asked, and then, "I would have them drawn and quartered." She did not think he heard her because he made no answer.

~ * ~

Damian felt the ice crystallize around his heart.

Drawn and quartered.

Her words echoed in his mind. As they rode, he watched her pull her cape tightly around her shoulders. Then he turned his attention to the trail and what he would do with Amorica.

Silence her.

No, he would never harm her. But he had the welfare of so many resting on what he did.

She despised him.

Tonight?

He would decide how to keep her from harm's way while making sure she never spoke of the list. He would take no chances.

Inside the forest, the rain did not beat so harshly, nor did the wind batter the terrified horses. Yet he felt drenched from the inside out.

Soaked through all the layers of their clothing, Damian and Amorica reached a small cottage deep in the forest. This morning he'd had no intention of bringing her here, yet he'd taken great delight in showing her the meadow and the land surrounding the cottage.

"Go on, get warm," he said, while he unlocked the door. "I'll see to the horses."

"What is this place?" Amorica stepped through the door and paused, turning to look over her shoulder at Damian. Her eyes were wide—questioning. His heart skipped.

He watched her, debating with himself, then deciding not to answer her until he returned. He did not like lying to her, yet he could tell her only partial truths.

"More secrets," he heard her say as he turned and left her in the room.

Yes, he thought, far too many secrets.

A few minutes later, he stepped inside the cottage. A fire burned in the hearth. "Resourceful as well as beautiful," he said with a whisper, tension centering in the back of his neck.

"I'm as much Scottish as English," she replied, a soft lilt to her voice.

"I see. Are you trying to tell me that—"

"I can take care of myself." She smiled, yet she'd wrapped her arms around her waist, and he watched her shiver.

In most situations, she could probably take care of herself. "But you are still cold?"

She nodded, an impish smile on her face. "The rain sent chills through to my bones."

He dropped his saddlebag on the floor and shucked off his cloak. The cloth fell to the floor in a sodden puddle. He had not planned on a downpour, but he always rode prepared.

"I've never seen it rain so hard. You've got to get out of your wet clothing." While he tried for a light-hearted air, he wondered how she would react.

"I've nothing to put on." She shrugged, watching him with her haunting green eyes.

He handed her shirt and trousers he pulled from his bags. "You can go over there, draw the curtain, and change."

"What will you do? You are just as wet as I am. You will take a chill then who will get me home? I've no idea where we are." He was sure she knew exactly where they were. Leastwise, he didn't think she'd have trouble finding her way back to the London townhouse.

"My clothing will not take as long to dry as yours." When she vanished behind the curtain, he drew his shirt over his head and draped it across a chair to dry. "Bring your gown and other things out here. We will dry them by the fire."

"Um, the trousers won't stay up," she said, stepping through the curtain opening and holding on to the waistband with one hand while trying to hold her wet hair from her back with the other.

He inhaled a swift, sharp breath. What he'd given her to wear concealed nothing.

"You've taken your shirt off." Her voice wavered slightly then thinned as if in disapproval.

"I did not want to catch a fever."

"I see," she murmured. Then she looked at him. "I'm not going to wear the trousers. They are useless, and you can wear them instead of the wet ones."

"Ever practical?" he asked a slow grin growing from the pit of his stomach.

She thinned her lips. "I try to be," she said, before disappearing behind the curtain once more. When she reappeared, Damian could not speak or move. Beneath his voluminous shirt, her legs were long and her feet were tiny. She held the trousers out to him, and when she moved, he could see her nipples press against his shirt. Quickly, he took the clothes, pushed the curtain shut and slipped out of the wet pants and into the dry ones. He didn't feel any more in control of the situation than when she'd told him she'd see him drawn and quartered.

He inhaled several deep, cleansing, mind-clearing breaths and entered the room. She sat by the fire, finger combing her long damp hair.

"Let me," he said, sitting down beside her, taking up the task of combing her hair, hoping desperately the simple chore would keep his mind from the sensual fantasies that warred with the reality of their situation. He must make sure she never realized the raw tension ripping through him.

The very essence of Amorica filled his head and soul.

She turned to him, smiling, then gazed toward the fire once again. For a moment, he watched the flames dance in the grate. Her hair smelled of roses. His gut tightened. He swore softly beneath his breath, suddenly realizing this would be the longest night of his life.

Amorica leaned into him. His hands slid through the softness of her hair. She sighed, and he was sure she had no idea what she did and how her slightest gesture affected him. Her eyes closed. Dark lashes swept across alabaster flesh. The storm had not been planned, and yet the isolation, the night alone, all served the sinister purpose he was destined to fulfill. Silence her. Bind her so thoroughly to him she could never leave. After tonight, no matter what he did or did not do, she was his. She would be ostracized by those with influence—and shamed.

His heart wrenched into two pieces.

Her cheek touched upon his chest. Her hand rested on his abdomen.

He sucked air.

She pushed away from him, her eyes open now and shining with trust.

Her innocence and courage always unmanned him.

"You have so many secrets," she said. "And I have the feeling you distrust me."

Faith was so very elusive.

Now, he trusted her to betray him.

"I trust few people." He pulled her close, letting her rest against him and reveling in the feel of her so close, yet so very distant. He could not have her, he reminded himself.

Because he did not want to hurt her.

Bloody hell, he had already hurt her irreparably. She would have to go home.

Unless he wed her.

He could not. He could never put her in danger or condemn her to a life of misery with a man she loathed. Damaging her reputation was nothing compared to her life—which would be in jeopardy everyday if they wed.

Her fingertips lightly traced his collarbone. His body shuddered at the sensation. She followed her fingertips with her lips, kissing him lightly.

She set a blaze within him, her every touch mercuric. She seduced him with every gesture, every look. Her hands ran across his chest, touching him everywhere.

"Amorica," his voice rasped. He could barely breathe, could not think. "This is not wise."

She stopped, her fingertip resting on his chest and gazed at him wide eyed. Then she touched him—with her lips—her tongue.

With one finger, he touched her beneath her chin, lifting her face gently. He needed to see into her eyes. Then he framed her face with his hands. For the longest time, he watched her.

"Do you have any idea how beautiful you are?" How very treacherous you would be if you knew the truth of my mission. All the names on the list would be in jeopardy.

She started to shake her head, but his lips met hers, melded sweetly with her warmth. He traced the seam of her lips, and she opened for him.

Her nails bit into his skin. She made a low sound in the back of her throat.

Her urgency amazed him.

"Did you know you appear the braw handsome highlander?" she asked in return, pushing away from him then moistening her lips, her eyes wide, the centers dark with passion.

He kissed her again and pushed her back on the fur in front of the fire.

Embers crackled then he heard nothing but the roar of his blood pounding in his veins.

He rolled so she lay atop him, straddling his hips. "You should tell me to stop."

She settled her hair behind her. "I don't want you to stop," she sighed, her smile lighting his heart.

"It does not matter. Tell me to act the gentleman and walk away."

"I like you the way you are." She bent low, her breasts softly pushing against his chest, her lips seeking his own.

He groaned, knowing he was damned.

Lord, but he could not stop himself and she made no effort to tell him no. He kissed her again, running his hands down her legs. They were long and soft. He turned her again, his leg resting between her thighs, his hands smoothing her cascading hair from her face. One fingertip traced her bottom lip. His mind fantasized in directions it should not wander.

He had to stop.

With willpower born of determination he'd never known before, Damian set her gently aside then left her. Running his fingers through his hair, he walked to the small window in the front of the cottage. Rain still sluiced from the sky. He realized he'd forgotten to leave the signal lantern in the window. He swore again.

Quickly, he moved the lantern then lit it. He placed it in the window, telling all who might seek shelter here that it was occupied. No one would enter here now unless the need was dire.

She sat up. Her legs tucked neatly beneath her hips, her lips swollen slightly from his kisses.

"Go to bed," he said in a voice harsher than he'd wanted.

She looked at him as if he'd spoken in a foreign language. Then she shook her head.

"Amorica, you must be exhausted. Go to bed." He spoke more softly now. Distance from her seemed to give him the power to forget how much he wanted her.

Power to remember her feelings.

She pushed her hair behind her back and sat up a bit straighter. Her nipples pushed against his shirt.

"What about you?" Her eyes were wide.

He was a man well and truly damned.

"I will sleep by the fire."

"There is no need for that. The bed is large enough for two." Good God, was she so very naive or did she mean to tempt and seduce him?

"No bed is large enough for the two of us," he told her.

Her brows drew together as if the words he'd just spoken were taking root in her head. "You're wrong, it is plenty big."

"Is this an invitation?"

"For what?"

"You have no idea?"

"I do." She rose and walked to him. Her hands extended and he wondered what she was going to do. She was like no maiden he'd ever encountered.

She placed her hands on his shoulders and rose up, kissing him lightly.

He groaned deep in his throat. He placed his hands on her back and pulled her close. Once again they kissed. He wondered why he was playing the fool. She wanted him in her bed. Why on earth should he deny himself the pleasure? He slipped his hands beneath the shirt she wore, touching her tender untried skin, reveling in the softness he found there.

Drawn and quartered.

He could not stop. He kissed her hard and sweet and urgent. She responded to his kiss, pushing herself against him, winding her fingers through his hair. She made soft sounds in the back of her throat. Sounds that drew him to her, that made pushing her away impossible.

I cannot do this.

He ended the kiss. "Go to bed," he said, once again. "I will join you later."

She smiled. "I knew you would come to your senses."

"You are wrong. This is wrong." He made a sweeping gesture.

He watched her walk to the small room. She didn't draw the curtain.

He studied her while she pulled back the covers and tucked herself into the bed. He turned and closed his eyes. Then in silent desperation, he rested his hands against the window sill, his forehead touching the pane of glass.

She would have no idea what this cost him.

"Damian. Damian, are you there?" The voice on the other side of the door startled him.

He reached for his pistol.

Chapter Seven

"Stay inside," Damian told Amorica. His hand was outstretched. "Don't leave."

Her wide eyes filled with concern, yet he didn't see fear. He stepped into the curtained bedroom and pulled a quilt from the bed. She turned her back to him and let him wrap it around her shoulders.

"Who is it?" Amorica asked. "I could—"

"Ryder." Damian spoke, abruptly cutting off any further questions.

He strode to the corner where he stowed his saddlebags. His pistol was loaded.

"Ryder? I thought." She paused, her forehead creased.

"Can you use this?" He handed her the gun. Putting a loaded gun in the hands of a woman who vowed to have him drawn and quartered might not be prudent. Yet he saw no other choice.

"Yes," she nodded, "Damian."

"Keep this close," he cautioned. "Don't leave the cottage." The strange light in her eyes unnerved Damian.

"Very well," she told him as if she were used to dark secrets and dangerous nights.

Ryder would not show himself at the cottage unless something had gone horribly awry. Fear crept beneath Damian's skin. He stepped outside but not before looking over his shoulder at Amorica. Her face was pale, her eyes large, curious, and yet he felt sure she could handle most anything.

She sat on the bed, candle light behind her casting a yellow-gold halo around her. He wanted to keep this image of her in his mind. He prayed she didn't have more courage than common sense.

"Are you sure?" he asked, trying to reassure himself she did not need his protection.

"Go on," she said, her voice soft. "Whatever it is, I'm sure you need to give it your full attention."

"Most likely it is nothing," he said, brushing off Ryder's sudden appearance.

"Most likely," she agreed, setting the pistol on the bed beside her, yet her fingers did not leave the handle. Nor did the rigid line of her spine or the stiffness of her shoulders lessen.

"I will be back as soon as I find out why he is here." She nodded, a small smile forming on her lips. "Damian," she said.

"What?"

"Go. I will be fine."

He didn't want to leave her. He didn't want to chance her discovering what he did. But he did want to discover what had led her to loathe smugglers.

And he wondered if he could convince her he was not a scurvy nave.

Most likely he could not.

"You need not worry about me." She rose and walked to him, touching his arm lightly with her hand. "I am no fragile lady." To Damian, she appeared far too delicate. The slightest breeze might blow her away. He was so very afraid this was a hurricane of monstrous proportions that was about to find release here tonight.

"In that you are wrong," he spoke from deep within. The need to protect and shelter her rose to overwhelming levels. He strode to her and touched her lips with a fingertip. "Remember—do not leave the cottage. I will be back for you as soon as possible."

"This cannot be so dangerous," she said. "I would know what you are about."

"The less you understand the safer you will be."

"Damian." Her fingers gripped his arm. Her nails bit into his flesh.

"You're frightening me."

"I do not mean to scare you. Promise me you will take heed. You will do as I've bid you."

"An order then?" she queried, tilting her head in question.

"If you wish to think of my words in that light, an order it is." She rose, her hands trembling. For a moment Damian thought the shaking of her body was anger and not fear. The tight set of her lips, the widening of her eyes, and the indignation he read there were all telltale signs of what?

"Take heed," he said softly. "This could mean life or death. Do not do anything foolish."

Outside the night was dark, rain sluiced through the sky and wind set up an eerie wail. Damian headed for the barn. He heard horse hooves and their soft nickering answer to Ryder.

Damian pushed open the door. One torch gave some light to the space while casting lengthy shadows across the stalls.

Ryder lay atop several bales of hay, propped up with one elbow.

"Did I interrupt something?" Ryder asked, rising in one lithe movement. His dark eyes and brooding countenance gave nothing away.

Damian waved a hand in the air. "What has happened to bring you to this out-of-the-way spot in the middle of the night?" Ryder's expression turned solemn. He rose to his feet. "An accident."

"Aric?" Damian jumped to conclusions, his heart pounding.

"No. The next shipment crossing the English Channel had trouble. The ship went down."

"Anyone we know?"

"Our last rescue," Ryder said. "The father was aboard. He decided to leave sooner than he had planned."

"Dead?"

"Probably."

"Then we wait."

"'It is getting too dangerous. What does the girl know?" Ryder asked.

Damian had not been eager for this question. "Nothing."

"She will understand what you are about soon enough. London is ripe with gossip. Richy's father is handing out a reward for anyone with information. Also, an operative from the Austrian court has arrived. He is seeking information and looking for the men responsible for smuggling the wanted men from his country. We cannot trust The Duchess. Can we trust the girls?"

Ryder's question was pointed and harsh, full of implications Damian did not want to think about, let alone talk about with Ryder. He had just learned her intentions. He wasn't ready to share the danger with Ryder.

"I wish I had better news," Ryder paused. "She is not loyal to you?"

"No." Admitting his fear was not easy. He had hoped the girls could be allies.

"A shame."

"Worse than that, she wants to see me drawn and quartered." Damian paused, wishing he could see the raw humor in all this. "You too if the words she spoke this afternoon are true."

"Me? What have I done?"

"It is not as you think. I have not seduced her, although she has given me every provocation. Perhaps the circumstances would be better if I had." He sat down on a bale of hay intensely involved with his conversation with Ryder and the knowledge of Amorica's feelings.

"What then?"

"She loathes smugglers," Damian said. "Not just me. All."

"You must get rid of her. She is too much a threat," Ryder said.

"God knows I've thought about it, but I don't know how. I cannot harm her." Damian turned on his friend, anger simmering within as well as self-disgust. "And I don't believe you are advocating that. I have no wish to leave London. The information that comes our way is worth the risk."

"Ah, but now we have more than our own lives to consider," Ryder reminded Damian. "Your lady will be in harm's way every moment of every day even though she despises all that you do. Guilty because she has been seen with you more than she should. She will be condemned without a trial."

The blood in Damian's veins chilled to ice. "What do you suggest?"

"Take her to your ancestral home," Ryder said. He rose and adjusted the stirrups on his saddle. "By doing so, you will keep her safe from herself and from those who would act out against her because of your dealings."

"I had thought of that but dismissed it. I don't wish to soil her reputation further."

"After today's outing do you even believe she could make up a story that would redeem her in the eyes of those who would judge her?"

"What are they saying?"

"I will tell those who ask that you eloped. You were so smitten with her charms you could not spend another night without her in your bed." Ryder shrugged his shoulders and grinned—the smile a rare event.

"Her father would come for her if I sent for him. She would be safe in her own home," Damian said, tossing out every solution.

"And he would make sure the two of you wed," Ryder told Damian.

"I will never wed," Damian said with little conviction.

"I know something of Amorica's father. If you refused, he would shoot you. Perhaps even see you drawn and quartered."

"Which is worse? Drawn and quartered or shot?" he asked, a wry grin on his face.

"Drawn and quartered."

A soft yet determined female voice behind Damian startled him then a cold sweat broke out on his skin.

"Hold your hands high, both of you. Stand up, then turn slowly around." Amorica's voice was utterly feminine, but Damian didn't doubt the wealth of determination he heard.

"What did you hear?" he asked. Hands held high, he looked at Ryder who was leaning against the horse's stall, his arms crossed in front of him.

"Enough—too much," she said.

"I don't suppose you'd like to hear an explanation?" Damian asked.

"I believe you said enough to hang yourself. But you will not have to concern yourself with me or my reputation. I will leave of my own accord." Tears streamed down her face.

"I cannot let you do that," Damian said. "You cannot think to overpower two men with one pistol. I cannot let you leave with the knowledge you gained here this night."

He watched the tiny lump in her throat, saw the trembling of her arms as she struggled with the weight of the pistol. Yet she held her ground, arms outstretched, the weapon pointed at his heart.

"I can shoot you." Her voice was frighteningly calm—devoid of emotion.

Ryder stepped forward. "Take your best shot. One of us will be left standing when you're done."

"I don't like the way that sounds," Damian said. He turned his attention back to Amorica. "Easy, put the gun down. We can talk about whatever troubles you." His arms began to lower, his hands outstretched, reaching for the pistol as he spoke.

"Talk won't change how I feel. You are a horrible, treacherous man. It is your kind that would shoot a helpless woman as easily as you would squash an ant."

Damian moved closer.

Amorica stepped back, her hands shaking. He watched her eyes and heard Ryder's deep snarl.

"Tell me what happened. What woman?" Damian asked, moving closer once again. The wind wailed around the eaves. Rain pounded on the rooftop.

"Do you want help?" Ryder asked.

"No," Damian said, disliking the tone he heard in Ryder's voice. "If I were you, I would watch my own back. It is not just me she wants to shoot."

"Ah, but your advice falls on deaf ears at the moment." An owl flew from one rafter to another, wings flapping loudly.

Amorica did not look away. Damian studied her eyes, her shaking arms and faltering backward steps.

"Put the gun down, Amorica." He tried again.

She shook her head and stepped away from him once more. "Don't come any closer."

"Or you'll shoot?" he queried.

"Don't doubt it."

He moved forward more quickly. Her back was now against the door.

"Shoot. Or give me the gun."

"Damian—"

Gale force wind shook the door.

Amorica stumbled. The sound of the gun echoed in the tiny space.

"Amorica!"

Chapter Eight

"Damian!"

"I'm here," his voice sounded too controlled, too stiff.

"You're bleeding." Amorica dropped the pistol, her hand to her heart.

The gun landed with a thud in the hay on the barn floor.

"Damn right."

"You're angry?" Her body shook. Fear rose to the back of her throat.

She choked on words that couldn't be said—words of pleading.

"Shouldn't you be asking if I'm hurt?" he queried in a low deadly voice.

"Are you—are you all right?" Amorica asked.

"What does it look like? I'm breathing."

"And bleeding," Amorica added.

"Bleeding like a stuck pig."

"I'm not sorry." Her chin rose a notch. "You're a smuggler." She watched him pluck the gun from the hay.

"That I am, and I should treat you in the manner you expect." He rubbed his chin, looking to Ryder who had not moved from his nonchalant pose. "Go to the cottage," he told her.

"If I don't?" With every breath she challenged all that he was; all that they would be.

"Wherever you go, Amorica, I will follow. Do not deceive yourself. You are not a free woman nor from this moment will you ever be."

"You cannot think to kidnap me."

"Kidnapping would be far too easy. Hold you hostage for a ransom. No, I would not do that. Take heed."

For a moment she considered running. How far would she get without a horse? For another moment she thought of her home and her family. She felt a sudden emptiness. She suddenly understood that Damian Andrews was a hard, cold, dangerous man. He did not spend his days gambling his fortune away.

He'd duped them all.

She would never underestimate the man. She would defeat him.

Because he would not expect her to be strong, too hold firm against him.

She nodded, wrapped the quilt around her shoulders and quietly walked back to the cottage. Damian and Ryder would talk then he'd return. She couldn't escape unless she had a horse. They'd ridden too far.

Somehow she'd find a way to flee whatever he planned for her. She would never concede to his demands.

Once inside she sat down by the fire. A strange stillness surrounded her. A deep foreboding settled in the pit of her stomach. The door opened then closed. She knew he stood inside the room watching her. She felt the hair on the back of her neck prickle, felt goose bumps rise on her arms.

She wanted him to say something—anything.

Long, deep breaths didn't ease her unraveling nerves. Memories of the man she had thought he was gave her pause. "You are no gentleman." She heard his footsteps. Knew he was securing his weapons.

Then he knelt beside her, his fingertip lightly touched her chin, encouraging her to look at him.

"Why?" he asked. "What happened to you?"

She stiffened. She didn't need to explain her feelings to him, didn't owe him an explanation. He was a smuggler, a criminal, a man who was sought by the Crown for illegal activities.

"Go away," she told him.

"I can't do that," he said softly. "Like it or not, you have put yourself in a position where you have few choices. I did not want this to happen."

"What are you going to do?"

He dropped his hand, rising and turning his back to her as if challenging her. He ran his hands through his hair then faced her.

"I don't know what I'm going to do," he told her. "You threaten all I hold dear. All I care for. Ryder has made a suggestion."

"Don't listen to him," she told Damian.

"Why is that?" He was so close she could feel his breath whisper across her cheek.

She turned her back to him, her fingers clasped tightly in her lap. She chose not to answer. She heard him let out his breath, heard him walking again.

The bed creaked. She turned. He had stretched out on the bed, his hands clasped behind his head, his eyes closed as if he meant to sleep.

"Aren't you afraid I'll shoot you in your sleep?" He didn't open his eyes. "No."

"You didn't want to sleep there a few minutes ago," she said.

Damian didn't answer. Amorica wrapped the quilt around her shoulders and tried to find comfort on the rug in front of the fire.

Her hips dug into the floorboards. She turned over then sat up, resigned to discomfort even while she eyed the bed and the man sleeping there.

His breaths had deepened. He turned over, pulling the blankets to cover him. She walked to the bed and knelt beside it, wondering if she dared. She was exhausted. And she didn't know what fate awaited her.

She wanted nothing more than to close her eyes and find herself in her rooms with her cousins. She closed her eyes. When she opened them again the candle had melted down, the flame striving to stay alive. Damian had rolled to the other side of the bed, leaving plenty of room for her if she wished to share a bed with him.

With her quilt rolled around her like a bag, she lay down beside Damian and fell into an exhausted, restless sleep.

"No!" Her cry echoed in her head. She struggled, but strong arms held her down. "No." She cried out again and again but she could not fight free.

To no avail, Amorica kicked and scratched at the man holding her. "It's all right," she heard the man whisper.

But it wasn't. Nothing was alright and it never would be again. Blood splattered the ground around her. Her mother lay still, her face pale, her eyes closed.

"No," she said, but her voice sounded thin and child-like.

"Hush, it's just a dream." Damian's words whispered across her cheek. He held her and rocked her as if she were a babe.

Amorica swiped at the tears running down her cheeks to slide down her neck and soak into his shirt. "No," she whispered.

"Tell me," he said. "Sometimes it helps."

"No." She could never tell him—a smuggler. She could never confide in him the heartache she felt, the recurring nightmares she suffered since that horrific morning. She had stumbled on her mother. Amorica had gone outside to play, and she'd found her mother in a pool of her own blood.

Her sisters had been too young to understand. But she'd carried the weight of that day with her for what seemed an eternity.

Damian held her until she stopped sobbing. He didn't ask her again to tell him about the dream. He didn't speak at all. She found his silence as well as the dark foreboding expression he wore now unnerving.

He rose and walked to the fire. Someone had kept it burning during the night.

"Are you hungry?" he asked, his voice devoid of emotion. She felt as if he spoke to a servant—a stranger.

"Yes," she said.

"There is bread and cheese here—compliments of Ryder. No one is going to wait on you."

She rubbed her forehead. Gone was the gentleman, the man she'd thought he was.

What had she believed?

Well, she could easily tell her cousins she'd lost the wager if she ever saw them again. This man despised her as much as she loathed him.

She walked to the table and tore off a hunk of bread. She looked at him then the knife. He shrugged and handed her the weapon. Yet she could hear his unspoken words. Don't even think of it.

She cut a piece of cheese and set the knife on the table. It lay between them. Its cutting edge and the meaning of all that had gone on the night before, knifed into her.

"What now?" she asked, expecting him to take her back to London as soon as the rain stopped.

"We ride," he said.

She nodded, but there was something in his expression that made her question. "Where?"

"North—then south," he said and walked from the room before she had a chance to question him further.

What?

If she wasn't mistaken, London lay to the West. But then she'd felt turned around ever since they entered the forest where the cottage sat.

He poked his head back in the door. "Your clothes are dry. Get dressed. We are leaving as soon as the horses are readied."

"But it is still raining." Her protest ricocheted off the closed door.

She didn't doubt for a moment he meant she would go as she was if she didn't concede to his orders and dress.

"Stupid girl," she mumbled to herself. "You are acting the child." She wanted nothing more than to be completely clothed when he came for her.

She slipped on her shoes.

"Ready?" he asked, holding the door open. She saw the horses and the pouring rain. Damian held out a great raincoat.

"Compliments of Ryder?" she asked sweetly, thinking he'd probably just as soon see her drenched from head to toe.

He nodded, holding the door, waiting.

She walked through and Ryder helped her onto her horse. She pulled the coat close to her, wishing for sunshine, yet knowing it would be some time before gentle warming rays would heat the earth.

A few hours later Damian broke the silence.

"We will wed in Gretna Green."

~ * ~

"Surely you jest. I will not wed you," she said, her voice ripe with anger.

"I suppose it was too much to ask. Very well, then you understand you will be presumed to be my mistress. Nothing I could do or say will change what people think."

"My father will kill you." She pushed her horse so they were riding side by side. Yet she did not look at him.

"Your father as well as your cousins will think you dead in the fire." He nodded his head, wishing there was another way, knowing she would give in to marriage. For Amorica, marriage to him was a high price to pay.

Through the forest and the rain, flames leapt into the sky.

"The cottage?" she asked.

"No, it is a small hovel nearby. Aric and Ryder will weave a tale no one will dispute."

"I despise you," she said.

Yes, he knew the truth.

~ * ~

"You can change your mind." Damian avoided eye contact with Amorica. They did not ride to Gretna Green. It was too far. His gaze traveled over the countryside, resting for a moment on the small village church where he meant to wed. Its white spire reflected sunlight, and he wished for a bright future for Amorica.

He heard her clear her throat, thought he also heard a silence filled with regret. Despite the sunshine, gray clouds dotted the sky and the scent of rain hung on the air. "About the marriage."

"Never," she said.

Her voice wavered. Somewhere deep inside, Damian knew she would regret every moment he spent with her. His heart ached for her. To be tied to a man she reviled through all eternity was a fate he would not wish on anyone.

The hill where he stopped was high above the village. While they rode, she'd said nothing. He wondered when she would voice an opinion—spew her frustration and anger.

Now he knew she would keep her emotions within. She pushed a windblown strand of hair from her face. A face paled by sadness.

"Never," he repeated her words. "You would do well to reconsider my proposal."

He turned to her and watched her straighten, saw the tilt of her chin.

Her fingers wove through the reins, gripping them more tightly. Her horse nickered softly.

"What would you do?" she asked.

He cleared his throat. "If we wed?"

"I would not sleep with you." She turned her face away from him. A silent protest to what she was about to agree to do.

She would never make this easy. He knew the answer to her question, but he chose not to tell her he did not mean to force her to the marriage bed. He wasn't sure why, nor did he understand his motives.

"I have a home near the coast. I would take you there." And leave you to your own devices.

That thought bothered him more than he wanted to admit. He didn't want her to suffer in any way and yet together they had charted her future.

The threat she posed was far too dangerous. He could not trust her.

Without trust, she could not have freedom.

"What would I do?" Her voice dropped a level. He heard the tears in her voice. When she turned back to him, he could see no moisture in her eyes. "Act the dutiful wife."

He watched her. Even if she loved him, and their circumstances were ideal, she might never be dutiful. And, he would not want her submissive.

He liked the fire he saw in her eyes when she was angry. He loved the challenge she posed when she disagreed.

"And how is that? I've had no one to teach me." Her voice was as rigid and as unbending as her back.

"You will have free run of the estate."

"Your prisoner there?"

She guessed more than he was willing to admit at the moment.

"Never," he told her. His lie did not sit well with him. "A wife is not a captive."

A soft wind swept across the land, freeing the scent of falling autumn leaves. Birch leaves fluttered gently against each other. She had brought herself to this. If she'd just obeyed him. If she'd stayed inside. Instead, her curiosity brought her to an untenable place.

She laughed then, but her eyes held no warmth. The tears he'd not seen earlier formed in her eyes.

"What rights will I have?"

He breathed in deeply. "Have you changed your mind? Will you accept my hand in marriage? My hearth for your home?"

"Will you answer me honestly?" she asked yet she seemed resigned.

Her destiny lay in his hands now.

"I cannot. You know more than you should. But understand this. I will treat you with the respect due your station."

"You will ride away and leave me."

He braced himself. "I have no other choice."

"Then you will not consummate the marriage."

"I would not force you," he told her. His heart constricted—squeezed the air from his lungs. He would not take that which she would not give willingly.

She nodded toward the church, body tense.

He nudged his horse forward, hoping she had not changed her mind and would follow. She was stubbornly courageous.

The trail wound down the cliff. The journey seemed forever, the village miles away. Warming rays of the sun felt too hot. Moisture beaded on the back of his neck while his heart raced.

He didn't like this ending.

The marriage would be no beginning.

Misery and regret would haunt their lives.

He heard her horse behind him, and breathed a silent prayer of thanks.

He wasn't sure what he would do if she refused, but this first step gave him time to think of arguments if she were to say no.

The small church was at the far end of the village. The white spire reflected the sun. He had never thought to wed again. Yet this was no marriage. It was a means to an end that should have never come about. He wrestled with his thoughts, wondering how he might have saved her from this fate.

She would have discovered the truth soon enough. Because he could not let her go. Because something drove him to seek her out, even when seeing her was foolhardy.

No, this had been inevitable.

A marriage to a woman who despised all he was, all he believed. His heart froze at the prospect.

At least she wouldn't expect anything from him. She spoke of her hatred. The last thought lingered in his mind. His pledge to his cause meant he would never find forgiveness. She would despise him the rest of their lives.

But then why would he care? He had wanted this no more than she had. He didn't love her. He'd known a true love once before.

This was a marriage of necessity.

Her hand clutched the reins. He dismounted then helped her down.

Her body was stiff, distant. He felt the chill emanate to the marrow of his bones.

His mind went over what he must do. He could not begin to imagine what she would do when she discovered he would leave her. Rejoice, he thought. Yet she would have no friends, no family, not even Wolfy to keep her company. The elderly man and his wife who kept his home would prove little company for her. He could not risk her safety, could not give her freedom to leave. He prayed she would stay of her own accord.

Her eyes had once shimmered with laughter. They had been chameleon, the color changing with the subtle variations of light. Now they were cold. He knew how she felt. Cold and emotionless—empty inside. He had made it clear he was not interested in her in any way save silencing her voice.

She stumbled toward the steps. She had the look of a cornered animal.

He'd told her he wouldn't force her. She shouldn't look so frightened. Not the woman who had blindly held a gun to him. Or was this a ploy so he would let down his guard? She couldn't leave him. She didn't understand what her knowledge in the wrong hands could mean for his friends—for him. Ah, but she wanted to see him drawn and quartered.

"Christel," she whispered, her voice holding a desperate edge. "Give me your faith. Help me through this journey."

Christel was not here to help her. No one would rescue her. Perhaps time would. When this was done, he would grant her leave to go home. He would let her go.

The wedding was as cold and bleak and heartless as he'd known it was going to be. Only one person besides the priest stood in attendance.

He guessed the man was the grounds keeper. He didn't know nor did he care. How was he ever going to get through the ceremony knowing his bride loathed him? He had never felt so empty—so alone.

The priest stared at them with furrowed brows as if to ask if they truly wanted this, yet he asked no pointed questions. He stood before them, his hands clasped around the bible and waited.

Silence filled the room until it echoed with its emptiness.

"What is done here today cannot be easily undone," the priest said in solemn grandfatherly tones.

Annulment? Nay. Even if she left him, she would always be his wife.

She would never seek to leave him. Her father would never allow such a thing. Damian had never met the man, yet he guessed the truth.

Fool. He had thought he could play both ends against the middle. He had thought he could wager and come out unscathed.

Wife. He had learned in the weeks she'd been in London that he would inherit her estate. She was the oldest and all the siblings were female. The father looked to secure his land before he died.

He did not want her estate. He wanted nothing save to give her that which he was unable to give. Her happiness.

He understood he would be frowned upon by her father. He did not appear to be the type of man a father would want for his oldest daughter, any daughter. For the sake of appearances, he was a wastrel of the worst sort. A second son, one who had found wealth by gambling and not a hard day's work. Yet he had earned all he owned. He had been given nothing by his own father, a man who had disowned him when he refused the military commission offered.

He had to admit though, much of his wealth had come from illegal smuggling of brandy. But that had been a ruse to cover the other purpose.

Smuggling political and religious refugees to America.

She deserved better than him. She should have a huge wedding with all the gaiety and friends of the family. Here they were alone with one elderly gentleman to witness their marriage—a marriage that was doomed from the start. No love existed between them. They shared only fear and hatred.

Damian swallowed the lump in his throat. He had no intention of backing down now. He could offer her more as his wife than he could if she were labeled his mistress.

She would be one or the other.

The rock in the pit of his stomach grew. He loathed himself and what took place this day.

The priest nodded. He was ready to begin the ceremony.

For another brief moment Damian had second thoughts. He quickly pushed them away. She stiffened. He held out his arm to escort her to the altar. She did not accept his gesture of goodwill. Instead she pulled away, refusing to make eye contact or to touch him. He was her enemy now, her jailor. He would give her no freedom in the days to come. She should say no to the vows and no to the man. Yet the alternatives were not acceptable either.

"Take it, Amorica," he said.

"I will not."

"Have you not learned you will suffer if you do not do my bidding?" he asked in a low tone. "This wedding is inconsequential. Nothing to what you will be asked as my wife."

~ * ~

The threat went straight to her heart. Biting on her lower lip, wishing there was another way she slowly took his arm, and allowed him to escort her down the aisle and to the rest of her life. Inside, the church smelled musty and unkempt. She rubbed her arm in a futile attempt to ward off the chill encompassing her.

She felt as if she walked in a fog. They reached the altar and stood in front of the priest. He smiled kindly at her. She needed to look away, wishing this wasn't a lie. She was about to take vows before God. Vows she loathed. Her lips trembled and her heart felt as if icy hands squeezed from within.

Her breath rasped. She had no choice; yet she wanted to turn and run out the door. She wanted to grab her horse and ride and ride until she was home. But her father would send her back to London. He would insist she find a husband. He would not give her shelter, because he'd made his wishes clear. He had made them more than clear. Do not return unless you are wed.

She tried to believe it was someone else inside her gown, but she could not disassociate herself from her body. The man walking beside her would be her husband, with all the rights associated with that state, regardless of his promise.

They stopped and he turned her to face him. Her gaze met his. His dark eyes were void of emotion. He wore buckskin breeches; his shirt was made of the finest white linen. His dark hair was tied back with a leather thong. He no longer appeared the simpering dandy she'd once thought him to be. In a protective fog, she listened to the words that would change her life. She heard her toneless whispers in reply to the questions. She made her own answers in her mind.

No, she did not take this man.

No, she would not love him until death do us part.

No, she would never obey him.

But the words she spoke aloud were the opposite, while she desperately tried to keep the moisture in her eyes from spilling down her cheeks. She would never let him see her cry. When the priest declared them husband and wife, her heart died.

Amorica knew what came next, yet she hoped it could be avoided. He cared no more for her than she did for him. He did not seal the marriage with a kiss. She was right about how he felt. He thanked the priest and paid him, then he turned on one heel and walked from the altar with his new wife.

She watched him leave, wondering what he expected of her now. In less than a second, he stood in the doorway, silhouetted by the filtered light. His face cast in shadows, yet she felt sure she knew his mind.

Woodenly she walked to him then followed him from the church.

His silence foreboded nothing good. The scent of late fall filled the air. A lazy breeze swept through the trees, shaking colored leaves to the ground.

She was a married woman now.

Amorica had always imagined her wedding day would be a day of joy, a time for song, dance, and sharing of love. How ironic that today was so very different. She wrapped her cloak around her and tried to take solace in the sunset.

What would the night bring?

What would happen to her now?

He had promised her, but he'd also pointed out she'd done this to herself. Whatever happened she had no one to blame—save her own curiosity.

The skies darkened. Clouds cloaked the sky and kept the moon from casting light upon the land.

Still they rode. Exhaustion filled her body and mind. She closed her eyes, wishing he would stop, dreading what might come. He'd told her he would not force her. But she was his now, and he had every right to take her to his bed.

Willing or not.

I do.

No! Her heart cried out.

~ * ~

In the dimly lit room, the scent of strong coffee as well as male sweat permeated the space. Richy sat beside Dicky, their heads drawn close in private conversation.

"We can do it. I know we can," Richy whispered into the dark recesses before he swallowed the dark rich brew that sat in front of him.

"I don't like the idea. If the rumors are true, these scoundrels are dangerous. Do you think they would think twice before shooting either of us?" Dicky's voice wavered, sweat beaded on his forehead. He tapped his nails on the wooden table.

"I have no choice. My creditors are knocking on my door every day.

Father says he won't help. I have to have the reward."

"But the smugglers?"

"It is not my choice." Richy said. "I will give you half if you find the courage."

"Propose." Dicky paused. "Propose to Ravyn. There is a fortune to be had if you marry well. She is an heiress, a rich one."

"I haven't been able to see her. Since Amorica disappeared, she has remained in seclusion. The Duchess has taken to her bed."

"I saw her with that scoundrel, Aric Lakeland. You come from much better lineage."

"No," Richy moaned, his head in his hands. "The man is dangerous."

She cannot think to find solace in his company." Richy reached into his pocket. A few seconds later he held a rumpled note. He leaned closer to Dicky. "The next boat will arrive on the morrow.

I will split the reward," he promised once more.

Coffee steamed in front of them.

Dicky didn't answer. His lashes lowered, and for a moment, Richy thought he would agree.

Richy did mean to give him a chance to change his mind. He continued, "I'll wager the smugglers won't put up a fight. They always run. We will either capture them or not. If we succeed, you can offer for Christel."

"I don't know." Dicky hesitated a moment too long and Richy knew he'd persuaded him. "I—"

"I've hired a few men. They don't know it's the smuggler with the reward we are after. They think I just want to intercept the shipment of brandy. We will share what we capture."

"You are sure there is no danger?" Dicky asked.

"I am sure." Richy prayed he was right. Suddenly this night seemed filled with good tidings. He looked upward to the rooms and let his gaze roam the coffee house. He looked for a bawdy woman, needing a good time now that his future was secured.

"To the reward." Dicky said, saluting in the air with his drink.

"To the reward," Richy echoed.

~ * ~

Jab. Jab. Ravyn's needle punctured the fabric in her lap.

"Where is she? How dare she run off and leave us all to worry." The piece she worked exploded across the room. She jumped up, her heart pounding. Fear for her cousin overwhelmed her.

"She will come home," Christel said, her gaze riveted on Ravyn.

"I've not your faith." Ravyn whirled on her cousin, all her pent-up emotions bursting. The scent of rain hung on the musty air. "The duchess has taken to her bed."

"No one sends invitations save Richy and Dicky. The Duchess cannot abide them."

Ravyn ran her hands across the smooth wood of the windowsill. "As if you care. I do not want to be with them either. At least they would provide a way to leave this tiny room. I feel as if I'm in a prison."

"You are not a loner, Ravyn. You need people to keep you happy. I am content to watch the birds fly. If I could do something to ease your pain, I would."

"You are a saint, Christel." Ravyn inhaled deeply, pushing back the moisture in her eyes. "And I should not complain so much. I saw Aric Lakeland two days past. I fear he knows more than he will tell."

"You think he knows where she is? Perhaps Ryder does too."

"They would never tell."

"I miss Amorica. I am so afraid for her, but there is nothing we can do to help. We must be patient and wait for word."

"I don't believe Damian would harm her. I thought he was half smitten with her."

"He is not what he seems, Ravyn. He is dangerous and—" Christel broke off.

"He has something dark he hides. I would know what. I would know what he has done with Amorica. He is not to be trusted."

"As I would. Do you think Aric and Ryder might be involved as well? We have both seen them together, whispering with Damian and plotting some dastardly deeds."

"If I had to venture a guess, I would agree. But to condemn a man without knowledge is not right."

"Then we must discover the truth," Ravyn said, whirling to face Christel.

Chapter Nine

"This is to be my home?"

Numb inside, Damian watched Amorica gaze dejectedly at his sprawling home sitting high above the ocean on a rocky ledge. Salt-filled spray saturated the air. Wind swept from the ocean, misting the land.

"My home is no prison," he told her. Yet in some ways it was.

"So you say." Her cold voice ripped his heart in two.

He thought he heard tears in her voice. Yet her back was stiff, her jaw thrust forward. Her beautiful hair cascaded down her back, her green eyes flashing.

"Your home," he said, wishing in truth that together they could make it a home, that somehow they could have a life together. He had wanted her, yearned for all he could not have. Now he could reach out and take what he wanted. But he'd made promises, vows he meant to keep.

"I made my choices. I will live with them. A marriage of convenience is not unusual." Her voice shook when she spoke.

Still he heard determination in her voice. And he feared for her. "You will like it here." Even to his ears, his words sounded like an order. She would loath the lack of freedom. Yet he could not offer that which her soul desired. He could not give her love, nor could he give her permission to roam the land.

She turned to him. It was the first eye contact they had made since the day of the wedding. "I will try."

His heart lightened. Yet he dare not read too much into this. "I believed you would."

He saw the smile begin to form at the corners of her mouth. "You never had doubts?"

"I did." he admitted reluctantly. The doubts were about us, not my home. I will not be here and so you can make what you will of your life."

"You are leaving? I will be alone here? No friends? No family?" The lightness he'd felt earlier vanished. A chill swept within. This would never work. She would find a way to leave, and in doing so, all he had worked for would be in jeopardy. His gut churned. He'd never thought— he'd never thought she'd be so determined, so absolute in her decisions.

Perhaps more.

He nudged his horse forward, knowing she would follow him. He'd sent word of their arrival, and all should be ready for them. A home that might never be a home to her waited for them.

The sun abandoned the earth. Hidden behind heavy clouds, the meager light cast a dismal gloom upon the land. Never before had he regretted his actions. Binding this woman to him for any amount of time had been reprehensible. She did not want anything to do with him or his life. She despised him.

Drawn and quartered.

The words echoed in his mind. Her sentiments would haunt him the rest of his life. And theirs.

Amorica was spirit, free and wild, and he had bound her to him. Her courage was immeasurable.

His home grew closer.

His future awaited him.

He dismounted and helped Amorica from her horse, giving the reins over to a groom.

"There you are, Master Damian. And your bride," Erline, Damian's aging housekeeper met them inside. "As you instructed I have been to the village and bought, clothes and other items for her convenience."

"Yes, my wife, her name is Amorica. Our rooms are prepared?" He dreaded the unspoken thoughts. The glances he knew Erline would cast her husband. Yet, he reminded himself it was not their concern how he and his new bride spent their nights.

They dare not ask why they did not share a bed. Nor would they gossip. He would make sure all he employed understood what was at stake here. "I'm tired. I'd like to—"

"Of course." Erline said. Her kindly smile was sure to melt Amorica's heart. Erline took Amorica's arm and led her further into the house.

Damian had given instructions to put Amorica in the suite next to his.

He heard their talking fade as he watched Erline lead Amorica away.

Blair, Erline's husband, stepped forward. Blair watched over the farmlands as well as the stables. Damian relied on these two. Both Blair and Erline had seen him through happier times. Now they would wonder.

They would wonder why he and Amorica had wed. He would never make excuses, but he would not tell them the truth either.

He would have to speak to Amorica.

"Sholeh?" He watched the woman walk into the room. How could he have forgotten Sholeh?

"Master."

"How have you been?" Damian asked, admiring the tiny woman. She had been with him for several years now and had been one of the first he rescued. She had been a friend when he needed one, and a lover after his wife died.

"It is not my health I worry over," Sholeh said, glancing to the stairway and the direction Amorica had gone. "It is yours."

"You need not worry. I haven't taken leave of my senses." For the first time, Damian wondered at the wisdom of bringing Amorica here.

Sholeh had always been loyal to him, but he saw the fire in her eyes when she spoke and sensed the underlying anger.

"That is not what I meant," Sholeh said. "Who is she?"

"My wife." Damian felt torn in half.

"I did not expect to see you with a wife, but if I did, it would not be to see the two of you in separate rooms. You are a man of fire and great passion. You must have a real wife." She lowered her lashes and demurely folded her hands in front, beneath her breasts. Her long black hair shimmered where the light from an upstairs window caught the lengths.

Damian raked his hands through his hair then accepted the drink Blair offered. He turned to Sholeh. "I want you to watch her like a hawk. Do not under any circumstances allow her to leave here alone." Immediately, he knew the mistake of his words. He cleared his throat. "Forget that. I will have Feroz watch her."

Sholeh frowned. "She sounds more like a captive than a wife." The scent of jasmine hung in the air, wafting toward him. Sholeh always smelled of Jasmine. He was not so sure this plan of his would not backfire.

"She is neither," Damian blurted. He had not meant to divulge such a thing. The humiliation to Amorica was undeserved. She had done nothing wrong. Her curiosity had gotten the best of her and jeopardized countless lives. "I do not understand." Sholeh cocked her head sideways, seeming to study Damian, all the while searching for some obscure clue to his thoughts.

"I do not expect you to. It is best you know as little as possible."

"I will not be her jailor," Sholeh said, her voice strained with the tension she must surely feel.

"Be kind to her," Damian said. Two women—Perhaps he had made a huge mistake.

But this had been her domain—her home. He'd given her free reign.

Now he changed the rules. He'd brought a wife home.

Sholeh lowered her lashes. Damian wished he could see inside her mind. Then she looked at him. "I will do what I must. I will treat her as your wife—with respect due her position."

Damian heard a slight edge to her voice he'd never heard before.

"I will hold you to that, Sholeh." Damian turned then, and it seemed as if his household had all assembled during his conversation with Sholeh.

He nodded to his servants then walked into the parlor and poured himself a strong drink, swallowing the contents in one gulp then he poured another. Sholeh followed and seemed to busy herself with little things, straightening the curtains, rearranging the flowers she must have cut earlier in the day.

"Will you behave yourself?" Damian asked.

She nodded, but a slight noise from above caught her attention. Her gaze strained to see around the corner and to the landing above. The scent of roses blindsided him.

Amorica.

There would be hell to pay. For some strange reason, he relished what might come. He smiled and leaned against the wall, waiting for what would surely be an explosion.

He turned and saw Amorica. She had pulled back her hair and Erline had wound the length around her head, dressing it with pearls. She wore a pale white gown that Erline had brought her, one that clung to her and flared out from her tiny waist then seemed to float like magic around her feet. She appeared regal. Thoughts of royalty came to mind. She walked down the steps, her head held high, all-knowing eyes.

"Damian," she said.

He read nothing in her voice, no inflections to give her emotions away.

Yet her gaze was riveted on Sholeh. Her chin jutted up, her shoulders squared.

Would she be pleased another woman occupied his home?

Or jealous?

Perhaps she would be angry.

Amorica stopped in front of them. "She is beautiful? Who is she? And what is her role here? Servant? Mistress?" Damian watched as Amorica lowered her eyes then looked back to him. It seemed as if she took that moment to compose her thoughts and her emotions.

"She works for me."

"I run the house," Sholeh spoke.

"I thought Erline did. My mistake. However, I will run the house now."

Damian's gut churned. He had brought a kitten into a viper's den.

Or had he brought a lion? If he had wanted peace, he would not find it here beneath this strange facade of civility. Another woman would not rule Amorica, and he had the strange sense a husband would not rule her either.

How long had it been since he had thought of peace?

He had known tranquility before his wife died. His life since had been a living hell. He wanted a wife and children. He yearned for what he'd once had. Yet Amorica might never give him that.

"Perhaps you should go to your room," Damian spoke pointedly to Sholeh. His fingers clenched in tight fists, apprehension concerning this meeting taking its toll. He had proceeded with blinders on and now he had a horrible sense of foreboding.

Sholeh lowered her lashes then nodded. "Whatever you wish, Damian," she spoke softly, but then she turned toward Amorica.

Damian wondered if fire had flashed from her eyes, and if Sholeh would treat Amorica with the respect she claimed.

She would, but begrudgingly.

"You need not protect me. I am capable of taking charge of your home." Amorica paused then. "If you will allow it." He felt as if she slapped him. "Of course," he said, realizing she was more competent and confident than he had thought.

What did he know about his new bride?

Not nearly enough.

What he did know pleased him, he thought suddenly.

Amorica turned to a smiling Erline. "Will you show me around?" she asked. "Tell me everything."

"Of course, m'lady," Erline said grinning.

Sholeh said nothing more. Nor did she move.

Amorica and Erline walked through the parlor and into the kitchen.

He heard the soft sounds of their voices and felt strangely forlorn when the scent of white roses dissipated from the room.

"Sir." Blair seemed to appear from nowhere. "A missive for you. From Master Ryder." He handed the parchment to Damian then stepped back to wait for orders.

Damian stared at the parchment, knowing it was a summons. They had made plans for tomorrow night. Two refugees were to arrive on the morrow then leave in two days for Virginia. He walked to the terrace overlooking the ocean—breathed in deeply. He closed his eyes, imagining all that could have been before shoving the thoughts to the back of his mind.

Sholeh stood beside him, her hand on his back. She knew everything about him and the demons that chased him. Many times he'd woken in her arms, trembling and sweating with the horrific memories.

"Another mission?" Sholeh asked. "Now that you have a wife, do you think you should risk all?"

Of course not. "My wife has nothing to do with this. Risk or not, I have made vows to myself that I must keep. People depend on me—on us—Ryder and Aric."

"Vows to the dead," Sholeh reminded him. "If she loved you, she would want you to move on with your life."

Yes, vows to the dead yet they were no less valid, no less binding. He did wish to move on with his life. He owned land in Maryland as well as Virginia. He had once hoped to move there, work the land, live in harmony and watch his family grow. He had laid those plans to rest with his first wife.

A gull swooped in front of them. A spray of water from crashing waves sent salt spray into the air. Whitecaps danced on angry waves.

Damian's heart leapt with excitement. "I will find a new home for you," he told the woman who stood by his side, the woman who had eased his pain for too many years.

"That is not necessary," Sholeh said.

He thought he heard tears in her voice, unshed moisture in her eyes.

"A mistress and a wife under the same roof?" he queried, studying the woman who had been his friend and paramour. "I do not think so."

"Send the infidel away," Sholeh said with a shake of her head that sent her hair swirling around her shoulders.

He laughed. "Send my wife away and let my mistress stay?"

"You do not love her," Sholeh insisted, stepping around Damian. She ran her finger up his chest until her hands wound around his neck, pressing her body against his, enticing him, seducing him. Yet he felt no response, no rush of desire.

"What makes you think that?" he reached for her hands, intending to gently ply them away and make sure she understood he would not break his vows to God or to himself.

"The way you look at her."

"How is that?" he queried, knowing what she said would be true.

"With anger in your eyes. You do not want her here. You do not share beds. You do not love her as a husband should."

"It is none of your concern, Sholeh. When I return, I will see to your future. Until then, take care. I do not want to hear any reports from Erline or Blair that you have been less than kind to Amorica. Remember, she is my wife."

"Excuse me," Amorica said from behind the pair. Her hands folded in front of her she waited patiently. Yet she held her head high. She was no innocent maiden, his wife.

Damian stiffened then quickly dislodged Sholeh's hands from his neck. He set her aside. But she moved closer, testing his will as well as his determination. Perhaps she tested Amorica too.

"I will be leaving in the morning," Damian told her, his voice stiff.

"You will have the house to yourself. It is yours to do with as you please." Amorica looked pointedly at Sholeh then back to Damian. "I can redecorate?"

"Sholeh will leave as soon as I find her a new home—a place where she will be safe. Until then, I'm afraid you will have to allow her the freedom of my home that she is used to having."

"I will abide by your wishes." Devoid of emotion, Amorica's words knifed through him.

Helplessness overcame his common sense, and he felt the need to go to her, to take her into his arms and reassure her that all would be well—that she had nothing to fear from Sholeh.

Nothing would ever be right again.

Amorica did not say anything else. She turned and left. A part of Damian's heart bled. He had never intended to hurt her. Yet Sholeh's presence here could not hurt Amorica unless she cared at least a little for him. Nay, Sholeh's presence would serve to undermine Amorica's authority. Pride. Amorica's wounded pride. There was a price to pay for everything. So why did he send the one woman who cared for him to another home?

Sholeh touched his arm. She looked at him with sorrow-filled eyes.

"You do not love her," she implored.

"Do not presume to know how I feel," he spoke harshly.

~ * ~

"He doesn't love you."

"I am his wife." It did not matter if Damian loved her or not. She had married him and Sholeh would treat her with respect.

"You don't love him either," Sholeh said

The two women stood in the doorway and watched Damian ride from their lives. Amorica knew she would have to find a way to deal with this woman. Damian's mistress. Was she Damian's mistress? He had not said as much. But what else would she be? Sholeh was almost right though.

She did not want to love Damian. So why did so many emotions surge through her when she looked at this woman? Anger, jealousy, hurt. She shouldn't feel anything. She should be pleased he would not come to her bed. She should be relieved he would keep his word to her.

She was not.

The woman knew where Damian had gone and why. Yet Damian had chosen not to divulge to her his mission.

Smuggling.

Chills crept up her spine. Sudden, unexplained fear swept through her.

She hated all he stood for—despised what he did.

She had wanted to see him drawn and quartered.

Damian was her husband now. She owed him her loyalty.

Until death do us part.

She did not want to argue with this woman. Damian had told Sholeh that Amorica was mistress of this home.

"Sholeh," Amorica began, "this is a big home. Until Damian returns, we will avoid each other's company. Stay in the east wing. I will have your meals sent to you."

Sholeh lowered her lashes and nodded her consent.

Amorica's stomach churned. Sholeh complied too easily. The small twitch of the woman's mouth, the slight clenching of her fists, all sent signals to Amorica that Sholeh would not give up Damian without a fight.

Did Amorica want Sholeh to give up Damian?

No! Her mind screamed. But her heart echoed the opposite.

"I'm going for a ride." She turned to Blair. "Send word to the stables to have a fresh horse saddled."

"But you have just arrived," Erline said. "You must rest." Amorica paced the wood floor. She could not rest. She would not know a minute's peace until she settled her mind—until she understood what she felt for Damian Andrews—smuggler—thief—criminal.

A man with a dark black soul.

She strode out the door and to the stables. "M'lady," a large black man stepped from the shadows. He stood more than a head taller than she did. His shoulders were broad, his arms huge. "I will accompany you."

"My jailer?" she queried.

He showed no sign of emotions. "Feroz is my name," he told her.

"Feroz, I wish to be alone. I will ride by myself."

"I cannot allow that," he spoke with the same accent as Sholeh.

"I do not understand." Yet she did, and she felt anger rise within.

"I have been told to watch over you and to protect you." Feroz was soft-spoken for such a big man. Amorica accepted his help onto her horse then nudged the mare forward, not waiting for Feroz to mount and follow. She rode a path to the sea, the wind blowing her hair.

The sound of hoof beats followed her.

High on a rocky cliff, she stopped and watched the surf pound the ledge. Farther out the sea appeared calm, the waves moving rhythmically.

A spray caught her attention, then the back of a whale, then another.

She watched the two whales move across the ocean. Watched as they undulated, cruising along the coastline.

Feroz waited behind her, somehow sensing her desperate need for solitude. He said nothing but she felt his presence. Her heart was heavy with loneliness. When she closed her eyes, she saw her home, saw the gentle surf lap the beach, remembered the island sanctuary the cousins had created. She remembered the first time she saw Damian. Simpering popinjay.

She had never been so wrong.

Her cousins would laugh at her, and they would wonder how she could have been taken in by his posturing. Would wonder why she had not seen the underlying man, the coldness in his eyes, and the danger emanating from every pore.

She did not want to leave the rocky perch she'd found. By staying here, she felt a small measure of freedom. When she returned, the walls would close in on her, just as they had when she'd seen Damian's mistress. When she had realized by marrying Damian she'd lost her identity.

The sky darkened. The sun rested on the horizon, and the wind gusted.

"We should return," Feroz said. "The rocky path back will not be safe in the darkness."

Men such as her husband roamed the hills during the night. Men who did not care if they hurt the innocent. Men who believed anything justified reaching their goals.

She nodded acceptance. She was hungry. Her stomach growled. She had not eaten since early this morning. And she was bone weary. A night of peaceful sleep might help calm her nervous apprehension.

~ * ~

"The tide is rising," Ryder McLaren whispered.

"The ship. See." Aric Lakeland pointed toward a black silhouette, rising and falling with the waves.

"The dory will come ashore anytime now. All is quiet." Damian leapt from the rock he had been standing on, searching the countryside for any sign of patrols.

A gull shrieked, the cry hovering on the windless night. On the sea, lantern light bobbed.

Damian's heart raced with excitement and anticipation. He did not want the patrols to come anywhere near this place, yet he would relish a good fight. His emotions had churned and rolled in his gut since he left.

Now he needed his wits and his concentration. He could not jeopardize this mission with wayward thoughts of the nightmare brewing at home.

"Ready lads," Ryder said. The dory rolled closer. Two men sat in the front, a third rowed and one man held a small torch. A slim golden line of light stretched across the ocean. Waves lapped gently on the beach.

Quickly, Ryder and Aric strode to the boat. Damian resumed his perch, searching the landscape. In the distance, he saw horses.

"We've company," he turned and spoke to the crew who were now helping the two men from the boat.

"Hurry lads," Ryder said.

"Run." Aric spoke with a quiet calm to the men before helping Ryder shove the dory back into the water.

Through the darkened night, the men raced to their horses. Damian's heart sped. By the time he had jumped from the rock and followed his friends, the riders had closed the distance to the sea.

"Can we out race them?" one of the refugees asked.

"We must head into the hills. See that line of trees? Once we reach the forest we will find a safe hideaway."

"There they are!" Damian heard the cry. He pulled on the reins, tempted to fight.

"We will fight another day." Aric stopped too. "These men are at risk.

Do not let your turmoil at home endanger others." Damian swallowed the anxiety, swallowed the simmering fury and turned once again, sending his horse in pursuit of his friends. He pushed his horse to a gallop. He would ride into the mouth of hell if he could find the way. The forest closed in around them. The sounds of their horses' hooves pounding the earthen floor silenced the night sounds. Off the road, they dodged through thick brush, racing across tiny glades, headed for the caves on the other side of the hills. Once there they would be impossible to find. Hunkered down deep inside one of the many caves, no one would spend the time to find them. All they need do was wait out the patrols who would soon grow weary and tired then would decide to find their way home.

"There it is, just ahead," he heard Ryder call out.

Damian saw a dark shadow. Small in the distance, yet he knew the depression well. It hid the passage into a small cave, which wound in a circuitous manner to another larger cave, which in turn opened into a valley—a valley where no one lived. To Damian's knowledge few entered because it was damn hard to find.

For a moment the exhilaration of his race to safety had given a time of respite from the helplessness he felt where Amorica was concerned. Now that they were safe, his thoughts went back to the dark-haired virgin he had wed—the temptress who had captured something indefinable within him.

She had embedded herself into his soul, and he would move heaven and earth to dislodge her presence there. Sholeh had been safe. A woman who made no demands upon his heart or his soul. But he knew now he'd been wrong about Sholeh. She had wedged into his life when he wasn't aware. He didn't love her, but he'd become used to her. She had always been there for him. He'd used her, taken advantage of her loyalty to him.

He would have to find a home for her or someone to wed her.

The five men dismounted and walked their horses deep into a cave.

"How long must we stay?" the one man who spoke English, a language professor asked.

"Ryder will check on the patrols in the morning. If there are none about, we can leave then. If not, we wait until it is safe. We have enough food and water for a week," Aric said.

"Good God, a week? I thought we would be headed to Virginia by then. I've family there who need my protection." Damian cleared his throat. "We will do all we can to speed this up.

But you knew the danger when you agreed to accept our help. We will not allow anything to happen to any of you.

Chapter Ten

"It's not so. Say it is not true!" Amorica sat up, startled awake from a sound sleep, her hair disheveled and damp. She pushed hair from her eyes while she tried to see through the dark room. She had walked across her grave—and Damian's. She had heard shots ring out in the night, had seen the horse stumble and fall, a rider tumbling from the mount. Her heart sped. She placed a hand on her chest as if she could ease the pain. Her fist tightened around the sheet. It was not the first time she'd had this nightmare. No, the dream had been the same every night since Damian left. Her life had tumbled and churned, her soul turning to stone each time she encountered Damian's mistress.

She swung her legs from the bed and walked to the balcony adjacent her room. It overlooked the ocean and in the short time she had lived here, she'd spent most of it on this balcony staring dazedly out to sea.

As if he would rise from the foaming ocean and find his way home—He had abandoned her—had left her with a seemingly mild and meek woman, who beneath the tender façade was a hellcat. Amorica never knew what waited around each corner. Yet every incident was easily explained away; the spiders in the chimney, the worms in the ashes, the maggots in the rotting meat. Amorica knew it was a craftily conceived plan to chase her away.

She placed her hands on the railing, leaning out, reaching for the emptiness while embracing the elements. "Damian, where are you? Come home." She wasn't sure where the words came from unless it was from the deepest part of her. "I miss you. I would that you were safe and the graves are not ours or soon to be."

Had she gone insane?

No. She wished for Damian because she was lonely—because no one else would find her here. Neither Ravyn nor Christel would think to look for her here even if they knew she had married Damian Andrews. She did not think anyone in London knew of this home in this desolate place.

"Why couldn't you be the man I thought you were?" She closed her eyes and turned away from the ocean. When she opened them, shadows danced on the walls in front of her. "A simpering English popinjay. A man who was safe. Who I could say goodbye to."

"A man your father would despise?" Damian stepped forward.

"What?" Amorica whirled, her hand to her mouth. "What did you hear?" She gasped for air. Her heart sped erratically.

He did not move. He stood as still as death and stones and watched her. He could have been a dark ghost in the foreboding night. "More than you would have wanted me to hear."

"Everything?"

She watched him nod.

"Watch out!" Damian lunged toward her, pulling her into his arms.

She felt herself falling, tumbling to the ground and Damian rolling to land on the floor of the balcony. Above her, a vine twisted and turned. "Bloody hell, get inside. Now!" He thrust her toward the door even before he had wrenched her to her feet.

She cried out, stumbling in an attempt to gain her footing. She watched him clasp what appeared to be a vine and throw it from the balcony. She sat on the floor in her room, trembling, shaking. He leaned over the balcony, his head bowed as in prayer. Then he turned and strode inside.

She tried to push off the floor but she found herself pulled upward in one swift move and in the sheltering security of his arms. She pressed her cheek against his chest and let her fingers wind into the white linen of his shirt. His hands ran the length of her back then down to her waist. Her breathing slowed, her heart calmed and yet she did not move away. She savored the sensations, finding comfort in the tenderness he offered.

After a while, she pushed away and looked into his eyes. Amorica remembered fathomless eyes, eyes filled with sorrow and what seemed like a deep-seated longing. "It wasn't a vine, was it?"

He inhaled sharply, his eyebrows narrowing. "No."

"What was it?"

"It was harmless—meant to frighten not kill."

"Damian, don't hedge. I want to know what Sholeh planted on my doorstep."

"A snake. It was a harmless one. It doesn't bite and carries no venom." Damian shrugged, "Sholeh has always liked snakes. She keeps them as pets."

She realized he denied nothing. He knew what his mistress was capable of. Her hands on his chest she moved further away. "I'm not afraid of snakes."

He chuckled softly. "I did not think you were. I am."

"But—"

"Hush," he pulled her closer. She allowed it, knowing he would not come to her again but wishing her life had taken a different turn—wishing on that long ago night she had not been so very curious.

He scooped her into his arms and carried her to her bed, settling upon it with her in his lap.

"Stay with me," she said into the crispness of his shirt. "I don't want you to leave."

Damian ran his fingers through her hair, sifting through each strand.

"Why did you cry out in your sleep?"

She stiffened and yet the warmth from his hands calmed her. She need not answer. She could tell him something far different and yet she wanted to tell him of the dream. Yet there were more pressing things on her mind.

"Where were you?"

"Very nicely done," he chuckled, tracing the contour of her chin with one fingertip.

She liked his laughter. She had always enjoyed the sound. "What?" she asked innocently, knowing what he spoke of.

He brought a strand of her hair to his cheek, to test its texture or its scent? "I wanted to make sure you were all right before I retired for the night."

"You've been gone near a week," she said reproachfully.

"Were you worried?" he queried, touching her lips.

"Yes," she admitted, not wanting to argue with him or change the magical spell that seemed to bind them together.

"I'm glad to hear that."

"You found me on the balcony and listened to me," she said. She felt the calm begin to dissipate—felt it change to anger.

"What did you expect?"

"I did not expect you." She sat up, too quickly, surprising him and knocking over a glass of water on the bed stand beside her. "How did you get on the balcony?"

He cleared his throat, but she did not give him time to answer.

"My door was locked from the inside. And it is a hundred foot drop to the rocks below."

"A very good question," he said, running his fingertip across her eyebrow. "You should not frown so. It will give you wrinkles before your time."

"And you would care." She suddenly realized he had gone to great lengths to find his way to her balcony. Heart-stopping lengths. She recalled the incident in the townhouse and the missing list of names. She had shrugged that off. That door had been locked from the inside too.

"'You did not go through the door." She accused.

He shrugged. "My room is next to yours. It is an easy leap from one balcony to the other."

She could do nothing more than shake her head. "You could not wait until the morning to check on me?"

"No." He kissed the tip of her nose, her cheek then he closed her eyes with kisses. Within his arms, she shivered and trembled, and she thought how could this man do such strangely delightful things to her?

"Are you cold?"

"No, but I cannot stop shaking. I do not understand what makes my body tremble."

He feathered light kisses along her neck and across her collarbone.

"Do you know?" she asked.

He stopped and smiled at her. "Tell me to stop." She shook her head. "I do not know why but I like to be in your arms. "I feel protected and sheltered."

"And would you have felt that way if you still thought of me as a simpering English popinjay?"

"You were safe."

"You were using me."

"No more than you used me. I don't know how or why but I sensed the three of you were using us. But I trusted you, and I wanted to find out what made you the man you were."

"You never planned to marry me."

"I never planned to marry anyone I did not love. My father promised me, and I meant to hold him to it."

"But he got anxious. You did not find someone to love, and he grew older. He did not want to leave his estate, his lands, all he had worked for up to chance."

"How did you know?" Amorica asked, wondering if he knew all her thoughts, if he could read her mind.

He shrugged. "It's the way of the English aristocracy."

"I do not like their ways." Amorica relaxed, closing her eyes and wondering if she could fall asleep in his arms and not be plagued by nightmares. For the moment, she just wanted to forget who he was and the horrific things he'd done.

"You never told me what woke you." He stroked her back, easing the tension that had built in her muscles.

"It's silly."

"Nothing is ever silly. Telling makes it seem less real. I don't want you to be afraid in my home."

That was far too honest of him. It was his home, despite the fact they were husband and wife. "My dream," she paused, pushing a tendril of hair from her face. "I was walking on grave stones—yours and mine. I heard shots, and you cried out." She wanted to forget he was a smuggler—to forget she loathed the very ground he walked upon. Yet right now, at this moment, she could not.

She trembled, and she could not stop herself. His arms tightened around her but the shaking would not cease. He rocked with her.

"It's just a dream, and as you can see we are both very much alive." She had nothing left to say to him. It seemed all had been drained from her. She closed her eyes and drifted into daydreams of a life far different from this one.

He lifted her chin with a finger, touched her bottom lip with his thumb. She opened her eyes and looked into the darkness of his gaze. She felt the heat from his body, the tension rising between them. Slowly, his lips closed over hers. She tasted mint on his breath and felt the trembling of his body next to hers. His hands framed her face. He feathered kisses on her lips, soft kisses, ones that tantalized and teased every sense she possessed. His tongue traveled across her lips, urging them to part. She opened for him. He deepened the kiss.

He is a smuggler, she reminded herself. Yet she needed him—desired him. Amorica responded; imitated all that he did. His hands explored and caressed her, touched parts of her she had never believed a man would touch.

Damian knew he should stop. He had promised her he would not force her. Yet the caress of her hands, the trembling they caused within, and the inferno sweeping through her did not speak of force.

She wore only her nightdress. The fabric was elegant, sheer. The straps were wispy and the gown was ribbed with lace. The fabric clung to her breasts, molding them, shaping each lush curve. The garment was soft, elusive, sensual, clinging to her waist then flaring free—and sheer—to the floor. The gown did little to shield the rouge-colored crests of her nipples, nor did it do anything other than add mystery to the ebony-dark triangle at the juncture of her thighs. It emphasized her slender beauty in the glow of the moonlight. For a moment, he could only gaze upon her.

It was impossible not to want her, and when she pressed against him, he could feel the hardening crests, the opulent fullness. Amorica was a temptress, a goddess of sensuality. She pulled forth all his baser needs, beckoned to him when he should put up barriers to resist her charms. He didn't know what he was after.

"Damian?" she questioned him, and all they did. Unwittingly they seduced each other. He wanted her with a need he had never felt before.

Not even for his first wife.

"Tell me to stop. If we continue, there will be no turning back," he whispered, close to her cheek.

Within his arms, he felt her stiffen. She would tell him no. She would stop this fiasco before it could end in something they could not erase.

"I've been so lonely, so very afraid."

His gut churned. He would not change who he was or what he did.

She had accepted him and his life with the wedding.

"I don't know what to tell you," he said.

His hands rested beneath her breasts. He wanted to cup their fullness.

He wanted to bury himself in her heat and somehow ease her loneliness—and his.

There was no magic, no miracles.

"You don't have to tell me anything. I understand my choices."

"Do you," he said, knowing she could not possibly know or understand the dangers surrounding her.

She nodded. He wanted to trust her, to share more deeply.

You may kiss the bride.

The words echoed mockingly in his mind, then faded away. She should struggle, protest. He had promised her, yet she'd married him.

Despite everything, she'd made vows before God.

But that wasn't why he had touched her. And it wasn't why he couldn't seem to leave her. He had come here only to make sure Sholeh had not terrorized her. But he stayed because—Her lips were full and beautiful. The taste of them was sweet. More than that, the passion that filled her trembled within her, within her body and her soul, waiting to be ignited by the right man. That didn't seem to matter. Maybe it was the passion of his desperation. Perhaps it was anger. He had never intended to wed another.

That didn't matter either. He wanted to kiss her, wanted to taste that sweetness that was so unique to her. His fingers curled into her hair, holding her close. His tongue touched her lips, smoothed across her teeth as she gave into his explorations. He discovered the fullness of her mouth.

The taste was amazing. It seemed the tiny cries of returned passion swept through him as an aphrodisiac might.

Maybe it was more than her lips that spurred him. The first time he had seen her, he had been surprised by her beauty—perhaps even captivated by it. He could remember staring at her and forgetting where he was and why he pretended to be a bumbling fool.

What a strange beginning they had had.

Once again, he found himself surprised, fascinated, and intrigued.

Beneath the sheer fabric of her ribbed and laced nightdress he could feel the sensual curve and shape of her body. Full breasts crushed against his chest. Despite them, he felt the wild pounding of her heart. Her legs were long and shapely, nearly entwined with his. He felt the flatness of her stomach, and the rise of femininity, for he had crushed her against him.

The taste, the scent, the feel of her, all were suddenly blinding.

The sensations were so arousing he could think no more. Her hair was silk to his touch. Her body was fire. He could forget his pain. He could forget the past. Forget love, and the dreams that had been cast to ashes. No matter that it was a passion born of all the wrong emotions, Amorica seethed with it. She was raw and exciting. The sparks that shimmered from her and around her evoked a shattering burst of desire within him. It made him long to drink of her lips; to savor the sweet taste of her mouth, to delve further and further within it. As the seconds passed, it seemed she responded with curious explorations of her own initiative. Perhaps her body yielded to his. Perhaps her lips surrendered, parted of their own accord.

Let her go, he warned himself.

This was his mistake. He should have never come so far—kissed her so—taken her into his arms.

Anger with himself clouded his judgment. Anger with Amorica for allowing him to be seduced surged to the forefront of his mind. She never ceased to surprise and amaze him.

She was pure rebellion—and beauty. She fought all that society dictated she should be, yet she succumbed to the unwritten morals. Her eyes were wide and seductive, innocent yet curious too.

Her hair spilled about her like a black cloud, her lips were red and moist from his kiss. Her coloring, even in moonlight, was glorious. He tugged on the laces holding her gown together and the fabric fell free. Her naked breasts and flesh were radiant and beautiful. Heat cascaded from her in great waves. It seemed to touch him. To sweep into his body, constrict his muscles, and quicken his pulse. The heat entered into his hips and his loins, and he was stunned by the savage and volatile way in which he wanted her.

He clenched his teeth hard together. He should walk away from her.

Bloody hell, he could not walk away from her!

Tomorrow he would leave again.

His finger caressed her hardened nipple. She inhaled a swift, deep breath yet she did not pull away. He lowered his lips to hers, touching her, exploring the soft sweetness that was Amorica.

Her senses seemed to take hold. "Stop," she said, her word a barely discernible whisper.

"Amorica?" he questioned.

He pushed away, while he berated himself for his foolishness. She caught her lower lip beneath her teeth, her breasts rising and falling with her exertion, her eyes alive with passion and bewilderment.

"I'm sorry," she said. He could hear the humiliation in her voice. He had never thought to cause her shame.

Nor had he thought to confuse the issue. In every sense, this was a marriage of convenience.

"Don't be," he said.

He felt her tremble more fiercely. He pushed away from her, furious with himself. He rose. He saw her eyes widen with amazement. She sat up, quickly pulling on the ties of her gown.

He bowed to her, mocking himself as well as their sham of a marriage. "Pleasant dreams."

"You're leaving," she said quickly.

"You want me to stay?" he queried softly, leaning close to her, feeling the warmth of her once more.

"I—" she began but it seemed she did not know what to say next. She paused, moistening her lips. He could see her pride battling with her absolute relief that he seemed to have second thoughts.

"You need to remember what you want from me, Amorica. Bloody hell, I think I need a drink." He turned and started for the door.

To his amazement, a pillow hit him. "How dare you. How dare you seduce me and—" she began.

He did not give her time to finish. "And walk away? I will come back to your bed if you ask."

"You did this to humiliate me, to strip me of my modesty, to show me you could have me if you wanted. I am not at your disposal, Damian Andrews. I do not love you."

He walked back to her quickly, catching hold of her even as she protested, pulling her back up into his arms. "Amorica, I can't strip you of anything. You have agreed to be my wife. No one would think twice if I stayed here this night with you. Indeed, tongues are already wagging about our sleeping quarters."

"And your mistress has done nothing to dispel the gossip."

"She has no reason. You have taken that which she once thought of as hers. I never wanted to humiliate you. You walked into a room where I forbade you to go and set all this in motion. God alive! I have tormented myself. But there is more to all this. You married me. You made your choices, and for the time you must honor that commitment. But for the moment, good night!"

He set her down. She sank back to the bed, her eyes huge pools of despair and perhaps anger. He had not meant to fight with her.

When he left her this time, she didn't say anything. Her eyes seemed to shoot daggers at him. Even as he walked away he could feel them slicing into his back.

Just who had taken whom tonight, he wondered. Almost taken, he amended. For Amorica might well lie awake questioning all that had transpired and how close she had come to giving herself to him. But he was suffering the tortures of the damned.

As he closed the door, he thought he heard her whisper.

"I will never be your wife."

Chapter Eleven

"Don't say a word." Damian came down the stairway with tense, heavy footfalls, trying to ignore Ryder, Aric, and Sholeh who seemed to be staring at him. He didn't want to think about what almost happened with Amorica. The memory of his wife, naked and growing more angry with him by the second, seemed branded in his mind, and Amorica was too much for him to think about now. He still felt the sparks that had seemed to leap from her, like pitch-drenched kindling in a blazing campfire, Amorica in all her glory. He remembered all that magnificent black hair streaming down her back, every curve and nuance of her perfect young body.

Her eyes, those green fire-ice-eyes, blazed as she watched him.

Indeed, he'd had a small taste of her—and she was sweet.

Then why did he feel as if an inferno swept through him now, the one suffering the pain of the damned? Who was the fool now? A simpering English dandy? Perhaps there was more truth to that than he wanted to believe. How the bloody hell could he want her so? When there was nothing but hostility between them after this travesty of a marriage. How could he have allowed himself to come to this end?

He reached his study and burst irritably into it, lighting the candle and sinking into the chair behind the desk. He poured himself a decanter of smuggled French brandy from the side table then leaned back in the chair, swallowing it down, wincing at the fire that seared his throat. He didn't dare close his eyes, and he didn't dare open them. Either way he saw her.

Amorica. Naked. Maybe emotions didn't mean anything after so many years, and so long a time since passion meant something. Maybe the wanting was enough. Amorica was perfect. Tall, slim, a little bit too thin, but nothing could have taken away from the natural dips and curves of her body. Her naked flesh was a beautiful ivory shade, and it had the sweetest scent and the most inviting appeal.

He exhaled a long groan. He should have left her the hell alone. He didn't understand the forces or the demons that drove him this night. He knew only that she had been in his thoughts and his dreams since he left her here a week ago.

He didn't know what she thought. He didn't know if she'd adapted to her captivity. Because that was what he'd arrogantly imposed upon her.

She had felt so compliant in his arms, so ready to explore her demons.

Marriage. He had thought she would refuse, but she had agreed.

Perhaps too easily, but he hadn't taken time to question. It had been no more than a quick excursion into the small village chapel, an afternoon's escapade, easily done, easily forgotten.

Did she care? Did she give a damn about the danger? Or did she only have designs upon marriage to a wealthy Lord?

Not that he resented having done something to secure her future. She was a wealthy heiress in her own right. He understood she played him for a fool. Yet he had wagered that she would wed him. She wasn't in his bed though.

Damian lifted his brandy glass high. "To you Aric and you Ryder." The first time his friends had come here, they'd sat in this room drinking brandy.

"To the prosperity of our endeavors," Aric said.

"Aye," He and Ryder saluted.

They had begun that night. A ship struggled off shore, caught in the tide and the rocks. As it floundered in raging elements and an angry sea, the threesome rescued the people aboard.

And so the tale began. The patrols grew closer now. It seemed there was a spy in their midst. Damian wondered if it wasn't time to pass the torch on to someone else, to find something else to do with his life.

For now, though, they had two more people coming from Calais seeking refuge. He could not stop yet. As for Amorica, he could only pray that her curiosity would not land her in the wrong place at the wrong time.

When she'd shot him that night, he'd wanted to throttle her.

Bloody hell. Men knew how to forgive, and they knew when to surrender. Amorica would never stop fighting her demons even though they belonged in the past not in her future.

Nor, he thought soberly, would she ever realize she wasn't the only one to give up something held dear. For a moment, the pain returned to him, though he thought he had learned to suppress it a long, long time ago.

It returned harsh, brutal, tearing into his heart.

He gritted his teeth. Meara Kildare had died because she was different. He could still remember that day and the helplessness. Meara was a healer. Still no amount of money or power could stop those who feared her and her ability to cure the sick and injured.

Meara. He hadn't known her for a year when he married her. He had first met her in the forests. He'd been hunting, and she'd been gathering herbs. Meara had been beautiful—blonde, blue-eyed, delicate, and lovely.

She had been so very proud, but so sweet and soft-spoken. Three little children had clung to her skirts, and all were threadbare and thin looking.

Later he had come to discover they were siblings. Both parents had died, and she'd been left the task of taking care of them.

He didn't know when he'd fallen in love with her. He'd always been popular with the ladies. He'd even been growing serious about the daughter of a squire who lived nearby, but something had been lacking and he'd backed away.

Once he realized just how deeply he cared for Meara, he learned what had been missing. Love. She was, indeed, unique. She was sweet, dignified, and strong, too, he realized. She pretended to bow to him in all things then she went her own way.

She had been dead a long time now.

As the second son, he had few obligations and had always known he would have to make his own fortune. He'd done just that.

On that awful day, he'd left her and their child for just a moment. When he returned, a roving band of thieves had attacked. He fought them all. And he managed to kill three of them before they ran off.

It was too late. She'd been shot through the heart only moments before he returned from picking wildflowers for her. Bloody hell, she'd died because he'd left to pick flowers.

He brought her and their child back to his home and once they were buried, he left.

Meara was dead; he began a new life away from everything that would remind him of her. He found Aric and Ryder and together their smuggling efforts seemed to grow. With each new band of refugees, more asked for help.

Then he decided to go to London. No one would expect a simpering fop to be the dangerous smuggler that had a reward on his head that was growing as fast as the lists of refugees. He had come to know Richy and Dicky, and the wager had been inescapable. Amorica had infatuated him from the first moment he saw her—his green-eyed siren upstairs—the one who had married him, condemning him, hating him.

"To you, Amorica!" He swallowed down another two-fingers of brandy. He wondered if she sat at his desk while he was away, sipping smuggled brandy—or swigging it down—just as he was now. It was a fine study, with the massive desk and rows of books. His ledgers and all his books were kept there.

For a moment, a heartbeat of pity slipped its way into his heart. She had thought her excursion to London a punishment. Yet she had managed well, until she ran into him. She had every right to be angry with him.

Pity. Because she was going to have to stay here alone for a long time. Because one more group of refugees would reach Britain, and he would send them on to Virginia. Because he had to return to London.

He smiled suddenly. When he returned from London, he should take her to the States. She was a fighter. She had magnificent courage.

She would do well there.

She was beautiful, desirable and it had always been his dream.

He set his glass down, sobering. The States were really no place for royalty. Some of the men did bring their wives, but those wives loved their husbands.

The states were wild, primitive, dangerous, savage. Then again, Amorica was all those things too.

Somewhere in the house, a clock struck. He counted the chimes.

Twelve, it was midnight.

He'd not had a wedding night.

His first marriage was so different. Despite his strained marriage to Amorica, he'd imagined laughter and caring, and making love deep into the night. He'd imagined sleeping with midnight black streams of hair tangled all over his naked flesh. He'd imagined her smile and her welcome, touching her stomach in hopes there would soon be a child.

But he'd lived this before, and he could never hope to possess another such love. He wanted to be anywhere—anywhere but sitting alone in his home, unable to go to his wife and make love to her.

It probably wasn't what Amorica imagined either, he reminded himself. Maybe it was worse for her.

He stood up suddenly. He wasn't going to sleep alone. One didn't marry an ebony-haired enchantress and sleep in the guest room in his own home.

He took one more swig of brandy. He sighed aloud, lifting his glass again to the air. "To all the poor wretches!" he said. He threw the glass, and it smashed against the fireplace. He left the room behind him, and started upstairs.

His damned ancestors looked at him, and they condemned him. Yet they mocked him too. Mocked him for the promise he made to Amorica.

"Bloody hell, she's my wife! Not a word out of any of you." The word wife sounded too damn strange in connection with Amorica.

He walked past the portraits and to her room. The door was closed.

He entered the room and shut the door behind him.

Moonlight streamed in on the canopied bed. He walked to it and looked down at her.

She had fallen asleep. Another woman might have cried herself to sleep, but he doubted Amorica had done so. She lay on her side and he wanted to reach out and touch the curve of her back. It was plainly visible in the moon glow. Black hair spilled all around her, her fingers curled below her chin. Her lashes swept her cheeks. He reached out and touched her face, wondering if he didn't feel just a bit of dampness there, just a hint of tears.

"This isn't what either of us wanted. But it will ease the gossip while I'm away."

He sat at the foot of the bed and pulled off his boots. She must have been exhausted—she didn't stir. He watched her face all the while that he stripped out of his buckskins, folding his clothing neatly, piece by piece, and setting them upon her dressing table. He crawled in beside her, not touching her. He stared at the ceiling then swore silently at himself once more.

He knew damned well he'd never break his promise. He was on fire again, from head to toe. He had tried to pull the covers over his body, and now the damned sheet was rising, just as if there were a ghost down in the center of the bed. It was impossible to lie beside her and not want her.

Remember Meara! he told himself fiercely. Remember what it should have been. Remember Amorica's words. Remember the way she says "smuggler" as if it were the filthiest word in the English language.

The ploy didn't work. He was as hard as a poker, and with the sheet, flying up he felt like a flagstaff.

Well, he wasn't getting up. They were married, and whether there was anything between them or not, he was suddenly determined they were going to sleep like a married couple tonight. And he was equally determined that they stay married. At least it would dispel the gossip, he told himself again.

She was his enemy as no man had ever been, but she was also soft and supple. Her flesh was silk and he could just feel the whisper of it against his own. He turned slightly and her hair teased his nose, smelling like roses, feeling like a swatch of velvet. He turned his back on her, making sure their flesh didn't touch. He slammed his fist against his pillow.

He started to count sheep.

It was damned funny.

It was torture.

Bloody hell, but he was glad he would not be doing this every night.

~ * ~

He usually woke early, and from the slightest sound. All those of years from running from patrols, he'd become alert to the slightest danger.

Those instincts had done something to his ability to sleep deeply. But that night he slept as if he were dead.

Oddly enough, he had beautiful dreams. He was in a forest. He had always loved his home. In the distance, he saw the white cliffs fall to the churning sea below. Ocean spray drenched the rocks above. He was coming home. He was running because he could see her, Meara. Delicate, feminine, her hair a cloud of sunshine around her, she ran down the trail toward him, her arms outstretched. He ran harder. He felt his heartbeat against his ribs. He felt the muscles cramping in his legs. The smuggling was over. It was time to stop. She was reaching out to him.

The vision faded. In the dream, he knew she had died.

Vaguely from the deep, deep recesses of that dream, he heard a noise, and he realized the noise came from the real world of consciousness.

"Damian," it was a rough masculine voice. He opened his eyes, fighting the last vestiges of sleep.

Someone was directly beyond the door. With his present feelings he couldn't help but have recriminations that he was about to be found in Amorica's bed.

Why did Aric pound on the door?

Damian looked at the clock. It was well past ten. He'd overslept.

He was startled at just how quickly he found himself aroused at the sight of her. She had turned from him as if she could ignore his presence.

Her back was beautiful and sleek against the bedding that was falling from it. Her hair was pure ebony against the snow-white coloring of the sheets.

It fell in wave after wild wave down her back, and despite himself, he found himself making comparisons. Meara had been so delicate, ethereal, blond, pale and soft. Amorica was as slender, perhaps more so, but even slender she was richly curved, and she was not in the least ethereal. She was passion, fire, and sensuality.

He wanted her.

He undressed her.

"Amorica...?"

She had been asleep when he came to her. Until this moment, she had not known she slept with him. She turned and looked at him with absolute horror in her beautiful green eyes.

"What in God's name are you doing there?" She pointed at him, at the bed. Anger simmered within her and sparked the fire in her eyes.

"You've got to get up. You've got to get out of here."

He leaned back against the bedstead, studying her, shaking his head slowly. He crossed his arms stubbornly over his chest. "I intend to do just that, but in my own good time."

"You can't be found here. What will people think?"

"What do you care?"

She flashed him a furious glare. "You're a horrible person, Damian Andrews. No less than I'd expect—"

"From a smuggler. Yes, I know."

She flashed him another furious look then pushed up from the bed determined to find clothes even if he wasn't going to do so.

He reached out quickly, sweeping an arm around her, and drawing her back down.

"Damian, let me go—"

"Cover up, my love. Aric, Ryder and Sholeh, if I have missed my guess, are about to burst through that door."

And he was right. He'd barely brought the covers up over the two of them when the door did burst open.

A loud gasp escaped Sholeh.

Aric and Ryder stood in the doorway. Both men sported huge grins. But they weren't alone.

Erline and Blair were behind them.

Shocked, they didn't move.

"You are late, Damian," Damian heard Ryder say just as the door closed behind them.

"I will be right there," Damian called out.

Amorica turned to him, green eyes blazing. "I don't like the sound of that. What are you late for?"

He cleared his throat.

"No! You are leaving again and—" She sat up straight staring at Damian. "Why on earth would they be here? Aric, Ryder? And does Sholeh make a habit of looking for you in the mornings."

"Only when I'm not where I'm supposed to be, but rest easy, my love. This will make it easier for you to take command of the household. You can thank me later."

She leapt up, too distracted at first to realize she was swirling around the room in all her naked glory as she searched for her clothing. The tangled fall of her hair was wild and sensual. The contrast between the rich color of her hair and the ivory of her flesh was exotic and tempting. He realized she had two small dimples at the base of her spine, one over either buttock.

She wretched open her dresser. "We'll have to try to explain this to them. It wasn't as it seemed to be," she murmured, not even glancing his way. Damian rose more slowly. He walked over to stand just behind her back. She found the chemise she been searching for. "I know there is something we can say."

He took hold of both her shoulders and stared into her eyes. "Didn't you hear me? It will be in your best interest not to say anything.

Not to try and explain away what they just saw."

She shook her head. "You climbed into my bed without my permission."

"I don't need your permission. Everything I have done, I have done for your well-being. Remember, you are my wife." Her breath quickened. He was gazing into her eyes, but he could see the rise and fall of her breasts. Bloody hell. A part of his anatomy began to rise along in response.

Amorica's gaze slipped from his. A gasping sound escaped her, and she tried to elude his hold, her chin rising, her eyes narrowing. "You cannot believe this is what is best for me."

He had never thought her to be so stubborn. He heard the grating of his teeth, the comment made him furious. He pulled her against him.

"Amorica, I'm not your father. I will not cave in to all your whims. While I'd like your stay here to be at least pleasant, I do know what is best for you. Can't you understand the seriousness of what we've done and repercussions," he said. "You knew you would either be perceived as my wife or my whore. I've given you every consideration, and you made your choice."

She had grown very pale. She no longer resisted his hold upon her.

Her lashes so long, rich and black, fell over her eyes. "Will you let me go, please? I apologize. I understand what I've agreed to do, and I understand how they must look upon this marriage. Perhaps what you have done has helped."

Instantly, he released her. "Ah, I think I like you better when you are not caving into my every wish."

She turned her back on him and slipped into her chemise. He strode across the room and picked up his neatly folded clothing, dressing quickly. He could hear the splash of wash water from the pitcher to the bowl. With his back to her, he waited for her to finish dressing.

"You can go down without me," she told him.

Leaving her right now was best. He could walk down the stairs and ride away from his home. He should do just that and yet if he did she would, he knew, be tempted to follow.

"We will face my friends together. Shall we go, Lady Andrews?" He offered her his arm. Amorica accepted it with a regal air. They walked from the room together.

This would not be easy. He would do nothing to make it so. Amorica walked down the long stairway, feeling the warmth of his body next to hers, painfully aware of him beside her, remembering.

She suddenly felt a rush of blood to her cheeks. She remembered waking beside him. It had been almost like a dream.

She had wanted Damian to hold her, and she was a married woman.

The fact had not sunk into her head until this moment. They were married, and she wanted him to make love to her.

"What are they going to say to us?"

"They aren't going to say a word. All will seem normal to them."

"Sholeh will say something to me later. I can promise you that."

Damian nodded. "Most likely. I'm sure you will think of something appropriate to say in return."

He sounded exceptionally curt this morning. Nothing like the man she'd met in England and more like the one she'd married over a week ago and just slept with. She didn't think he had anything to be curt about. He acted as if he were impatient with her now, and as if he truly regretted all that he had gotten himself into.

His motives seemed pure. He hadn't forced her. He had crept into her bed without her knowledge, but what he said did make incredible sense.

Sholeh might back down a bit if she believed they had slept together.

He was a tall man and she felt the disadvantage of looking up to him.

His hair was still slightly askew falling rakishly over his forehead. Her heart took a hard thud. He was a handsome man but a very hard and dangerous one. He leaned against the banister and casually studied her.

"I will be back before the sun rises."

She couldn't help feeling there was something else going on here. She suspected he was about to leave on another smuggling mission. She wanted to protest, and she wanted to stop him.

Chapter Twelve

"Stop." Amorica pulled on the reins of her galloping horse. "For God's sake, stop!" she leaned over her horse and whispered to him.

"Please, please, please."

Wind whistled around her yet the dry sand grass did not bend with the wind. The night was still. Patches of fog danced on the ground.

When she pulled her horse to a stop, the world was quiet—deathly quiet.

She watched dark shadows of clouds cross the moon, and she listened.

But she didn't listen for normal nocturnal sound. She waited to hear Damian's voice—and his friends. For the longest time all she heard was the gentle lapping of waves on the beach.

Then she heard what she'd come here for.

"Damian."

She urged her horse forward, racing to meet the sounds. She meant to stop him. She would not allow him to continue with this.

"No," she cried out. Gun shots then the sound of metal hitting metal echoed through the night. Curses and an anguished cry crashed the very air around her.

"There is another one," this cry shattered through the battle noises slicing it into two pieces. Silence followed.

Shadowed forms turned toward her—pistols held in ready position.

One lone rider whirled his horse, tugging on the reins to halt its progress. The sudden change of speed making the horse's hooves rise high in the sky. She felt the searing gaze of his eyes upon her.

Damian.

"Get her," a patrolman cried. "She's one of them." She was not. She had nothing to do with smugglers. She had come here to stop this madness.

You are married to one, she reminded herself. You came to stop him, to interfere in his business this night. The patrols would not think her one of them. She had naught to do with any of this. But she was here, and she would be found guilty by association.

"Run." Damian's voice chilled the night air around her.

"Bloody hell, run." He cried out again. Terrified, her hands froze to her reins. She could not move. She could not think.

"Run," the desperate cry rose again on the night air. Thunder pounded behind her.

She watched as two of the men broke away from Damian. The patrol split. Some chased Ryder and Aric—the ship out to sea forgotten. She watched the small torch bob in the water before it changed directions, seeming to return to the ship.

Her horse sidestepped. Her heart in her throat she raced from the grisly scene she'd come upon. The powerful horse moved beneath her, the ground passed in a blur and she heard hooves behind her—ever closer—always closer. She leaned farther over the saddle. Her heart raced, her breaths coming in shallow pants. She felt his presence beside her before she could see him. Damian.

"Head to the trees," he yelled.

She nodded, expecting recriminations, expecting his anger. They reached the trees. He sped in front. The trail he headed down was narrow.

Dense foliage slapped at them.

She grit her teeth, wishing he would stop, knowing he could not until they were safe. She would have been safe with the patrols. She need not put herself through such a horrific ordeal. Still she did not have the courage to stop. For in the end, she would have to face Damian. She would have to answer to him.

They twisted and turned through the dense forest. She was sure they wound around on the same trail. Once he bade her stop and wait for him.

She waited and waited. She suddenly became quite afraid for he did not return, and it seemed he might not. A fine trembling swept through her.

She had no idea where she was or in which direction she should go. She was sure he had been so angry he'd left her to find her way on her own.

Without warning, a shadowed figure appeared in front of her. She started to cry out in fear.

He held his hand up. "Amorica, it's me."

She trembled harder. "Where are we? I was so afraid."

"We are safe. It's all you need to know."

All I need to know? She wanted to learn where he'd taken her. She needed to know how to return. "What has happened?"

"Hush now. It's not the time or the place. Follow me." Amorica swallowed hard. She felt as if she was going to pass out. No, she never passed out. She never even pretended to do such things. She clamped her hand to her mouth. A sudden panic seized her.

His shadowed form faded into the forest trees. Then he was gone. Damian.

He would not leave her here to die. If he wanted her dead, he would have to do it himself. She urged her horse forward. Terrified, she didn't want to lose him.

She rushed forward. Around the next bend she saw him. He had noticed she did not follow and stopped to wait. But would he have returned?

Most likely not, or perhaps he would have. Perhaps he wanted her around so he could torment her at night. Until last night, he'd left her alone, she reminded herself wishing there was some way she could cast blame upon his shoulders.

He turned his horse from the trail. She followed and once again, she wondered if he wasn't leading her to her doom.

After the longest time, he stopped. The night was black, the tiny space letting in no moonlight. She could barely see her hand in front of her face.

"We'll stay here." His words were curt and abrupt. She felt the cutting barb of his anger knife through her.

Yet after he dismounted, he helped her from her horse. He set a blanket upon the ground spreading it out.

"You can rest for the moment." He told her.

He turned on one boot heel and without glancing over his shoulder, he walked back the way they had just come.

She did not feel like resting for she was trembling from head to toe.

She was cold and hungry, and what she'd done was not prudent or safe.

Nothing made sense to her. She could have died. He could have died. She would die if he didn't return.

She wrapped the blanket around her shoulder and leaned against a tree. She didn't know when she closed her eyes.

She felt the touch of Damian's fingertip. "Ah, my love," he whispered. "You have a great deal of explaining." Against her will, she opened her eyes. "Damian?" she asked terrified.

Her hands shook and the corners of the blanket she clung to fell to the ground.

"What were you doing on the beach?"

He didn't sound angry. No, he sounded determined.

"I want the truth, Amorica. How did you get away from Feroz?"

"He was sleeping." She could barely speak. Her body shook, and she wanted nothing more than to have Damian hold her and chase away the terror she created. "The truth, Amorica."

She bit down on her lip. "I gave him something to drink." She didn't dare tell Damian she drugged him, but she knew he would guess. She swallowed hard, wishing she could erase her mistakes.

"I see." He rose. He'd been sitting on his haunches staring at her. She couldn't see his eyes but she knew they simmered with anger. He clenched his fists then unclenched them. He was trying, she thought, to keep his fury in check. He might have every right to be furious.

She had shot him then she'd married him. She'd put his friends and his mission in grave danger. Yet she loathed what he did.

"It was not Feroz's fault," she whispered, knowing she did not want Damian to blame Feroz. She had acted rashly and without thought.

He had been standing with his back to her, the dark outline of his form barely discernible.

"It was his duty."

"Please, do not punish him on my account."

"What lies between my servant and myself is not your business, wife." He said the last word pointedly and with great determination.

"Do you have any idea what you have accomplished this night?" he queried his voice growing surprisingly soft yet deadly.

"You're angry," Amorica said.

"You have no idea. All I tried to accomplish by bringing you to my estate and marrying you has been erased. If you were recognized by the patrol, you have put us all in mortal danger. You will lead them to our doorstep."

"You have always been in mortal danger."

"No one has known my name," Damian said.

"There is no reason anyone would know who I am."

"While I am willing to risk my own life, I'm unwilling to risk yours.

I've always been well aware my identity might be compromised some night."

She gasped. "You say that just to intimidate." Yet the words he spoke did terrify her. She breathed in deeply, hoping the air would ease her fears.

He crouched beside her once again. "I have never meant to intimidate you or frighten you. I have only wanted to keep my friends alive—and now you."

"Just because you lost a shipment of brandy—"

He waved his hand, his features contorting. "It was not a shipment of brandy I am concerned about. Do you know what we smuggle?" She was shaking her head.

"Smuggle?"

"The truth, only the truth." It seemed he had trouble speaking. He was angry—furiously so.

Indignation clouded rational judgment. "I do not lie. I have no idea what you speak of."

"And I cannot risk further mistakes. I thought I had found a way to silence you. And yet you follow me, putting all at risk." His finger touched her lips, his breath feathered across her cheeks. "I would bind you to me in another way. Get you with child. Perhaps that would put an end to your curiosity."

Once again, she shook her head. "You promised not to—"

"Force you," he finished for her. "I would never force you, but if you were willing."

She watched as he traced a feather light caress down her arm to her fingertips.

"Never," she said. Yet she lied to herself. At this moment, she wanted nothing more than to have Damian hold her. She wanted his warmth close to her, and she remembered the times so long ago she'd been so very attracted to him.

"Surrender to me, Amorica. Surrender to me tonight. Prove to me you can be trusted."

"Tonight?" She felt as if her eyes widened while her pulse thundered in her ears.

"I mean to find a way to keep you alive. We are safe here. The glade is well hidden and far from any routes the watch might take."

"Damian," her voice trembled. "I am so afraid. Hold me."

"You know what you are asking?" he queried softly. "In this, I will not allow you to play games. If this is what you want, when we ride from this forest, Amorica you will be my wife in every way." She nodded. "I do not know what I want save for you to hold me." If she did not surrender to him, she would surely die of the terror this night held for her.

She realized suddenly she could see his eyes. A ray of moonlight filtered through the foliage. Just enough light so she could see his face, his features, and his grim, chilling expression.

He ran his fingers around the beautiful embroidery and lace at the high collar of her gown. "You are sure," he asked her, his voice flat.

Suddenly she was no longer sure of anything, save she was about to let her husband, a smuggler, make love to her. She felt as if he held the winning hand, and the choice she was about to make would forever change her life.

"Bastard," she told him in a soft whisper, unsure if she meant the word but knowing she had to protest. Even in wanting him with such a strange desperation, she felt the need to fight him.

He nodded. "A smuggling bastard. One you are going to remember if I'm hauled off to jail?" he questioned.

"You said I was in just as much danger." Panic suddenly overwhelmed her. Her body trembled harder. She shook with a ferocity she had never felt before.

"Feroz would see you to your father's home before I allowed any Englishman to touch you."

"You would protect me?"

He nodded. He would always see to her welfare first. He could almost feel her relief.

She began to speak again, ignoring him, pushing him to simmering, heated emotions.

She wasn't getting out of the night ahead of them. He was not that easily distracted. "Amorica, decide now." Lord, but he wanted her. "If you want this, take the gown off."

"But—"

"Amorica, come here." He opened his arms to her, thinking she would come to him. Thinking she would surrender herself, give to him what he'd wanted so desperately from the first moment he'd seen her.

He'd been a lovesick fool.

Next thing he knew she was hissing that he was a smuggling son of a bitch, a snake, and scalawag, but she sat up and nearly ripped her gown herself wrenching it over her head.

"Amorica!" What was happening here? He had not thought she

would give herself to him and curse him at the same time.

She swore at him just as quietly as she could manage.

Furiously, she threw the gown as well as the rest of her clothing on the moss-covered ground beside the blanket, then she sat naked beside him, seething and trembling. Her eyes rose to meet his. They were liquid, green, and shimmering. She threw herself back on the ground, an artful sacrifice to him.

"Go ahead then. Do it. Just do whatever men do and be over with it." Hard put not to laugh aloud, he stretched out beside her, resting on one elbow, wondering how to proceed. This was not how he had imagined making love to his wife. Yet he had never thought it would be candlelit.

He rose and quickly disrobed, folding each piece of clothing and setting it nearby. It was not too cold out yet he wondered if he should provide another blanket. Naked, he walked to his horse and drew a blanket from one of his saddlebags. They had always ridden prepared. There was food in the bags too, enough to last a couple of days.

Blanket in hand, he lay on his side beside her. Strangely enough she hadn't moved. Her eyes were closed tight. He ran his hand down the length of her body. How had she been created so damned perfectly?

Muted moonlight fell over the rise of her breasts, and added mystery and shadow to the clefts at her hips and the dip between her breasts. At first, he just touched her, running his fingertips lightly over her flesh.

"Amorica, I would hold you. It doesn't have to be this way." She shook her head, her eyes still closed tightly. She looked as if she was going to her execution. He wished he could turn away, but she had aroused him to a burning need. Unless she told him no, they would make love this night.

His hand resting upon her, he felt her inhale sharply. He paused, running his palm over one nipple. Her breasts were perfect, firm, rounded, the peaks large, and deeply rouge in color.

"Amorica, tell me no," he prompted her. Tempted by her glorious beauty, he leaned over her, running his tongue slowly around the aureole, then encompassing the whole of her nipple. She shifted beneath him. He felt the slam of her heart, the quickening of her body. He cupped her other breast with his hand then rose, meeting her eyes before lowering his head to take her lips.

He knew she didn't mean to respond to him. She didn't exactly fight him, but neither did she simply allow her lips to part for him. He threaded his fingers into her hair, and with a growing passion, he gently invaded her mouth, bathing her teeth with his tongue then plunging deeply into her mouth. He could still feel her heartbeat. And he could feel the trembling that still riddled through her.

There was so much passion in her, if he could only reach it—touch it.

But she was afraid and he didn't know if she were afraid of him or of the night. Bloody hell, but he didn't want her to fear him or his touch.

Her mouth was sweet. The taste and feel of it seeped into his system, adding to the hunger that had begun for her, creating a harsher throb of desire within him. Perhaps she did not aid him, but she did not resist him either. He lifted his lips from hers. Her eyes were open now and on his. Her breathing came quickly and shallowly. Was she afraid? Was Amorica Hepburn Andrews, afraid?

He didn't even know if she'd kissed a man other than him or if she'd ever been in love. She was old enough for both. But then her father would have protected her. Just how experienced was she? How much was innocence? And how much was fear?

"You've never done this before?" he queried.

"Oh, you brute!" she cried out, struggling then to free herself from him. He laughed softly, pleased, and not at all sure why. He caught hold of her chin and kissed her again, deeply hungrily, giving her no chance to protest. The heat surged swiftly to his loins now. He tasted her lips and tasted them again. He rose above her.

"I will try to be very gentle," he told her.

She didn't answer him. Her eyes were closed. She was on the blanket, her beautiful face pale against the ink-dark cloud of her hair. He kept his eyes on her as he lowered himself against her. He caressed her breasts once again, feeling the pulse within her, feeling the heat. He lowered himself still, burying his face against the dip of her belly. Then lower. He brushed his fingers over the triangle between her thighs, stroked her lower and lower. Her thighs parted for him.

He stared up at her. Still, she kept her eyes closed. There was so much inside her, he thought. He had felt the quickening in her when he touched her breast. He felt the rampant trembling anew.

But she wasn't going to give to him. She did not mean to meet him halfway. No matter what, she was determined in some way to deny him.

She would not tell him no, but she would fight this in her own way—because he was a smuggler and she just couldn't surrender her innermost passions to a man she loathed.

Still, he didn't want to hurt her. He slid his thumb through the thick ebony of her pubic hair then into the damp softness of her sex. He felt again the trembling. Slowly, gently, he stroked her. He lowered his mouth to the tender, intimate regions of her flesh and began to tease her thus, moistening her at least, if he could not arouse her.

But he did arouse her, he was certain. Scarce had he touched her before she jerked and surged. Her fingers tore into his hair. Whispered words flew from her lips but he ignored them all, delving deeper and deeper within her, bathing her, savoring her. She began to shake. Hunger gnawed raw and painfully within him, a surge of heat came like a rush of anguish.

He rose over her at last, and at last, those magnificent green eyes were upon his. He said nothing more but seized her mouth once again, taking her lips just as he took her body. He tried to take care, tried to go very slowly. She hadn't lied. Her body protested the invasion of his; she cried out briefly at the pain, catching her lower lip between her teeth to keep from letting out any other sound. He forced himself to stop completely, gritting his teeth against the will of his body as he awaited the acceptance of hers. Then he began to move within her slowly—filling her with the length of his shaft, feeling the hug of her body around him. Sweet God, it was good to be within her, sheathed by her—even if she bit her lip—even if she damned him for all eternity.

She had been made for him, he thought. Despite everything that lay between them, she gave to him, her body beautifully encompassing his. He thrust slowly at first, very slowly, bracing his arms at his sides, watching her face. But her eyes remained closed, her head to the side— her teeth upon her lower lip. Yet as he moved, she began to move with him, instinctively, naturally. The subtle undulation of her hips against his body, inflamed him. He closed his eyes, clenching down hard on his jaw, fighting for control. He maintained it as long as he could. Then his rhythm came faster, his drive stronger. He slipped his hands beneath her buttocks, molding her to him, and he gave free rein to the voracity of his hunger, taking her then with a volatile and fierce passion. Again and again, he drove into her. Perspiration broke out in a fine sheen on his skin. He stiffened and thrust once more, hard and deep. His climax burst fiercely upon him, spilling his seed within her. And that same moment, she cried out, her nails biting deeply into his shoulders His weight was upon her, and his sex remained within her. He had given her pleasure, yet she struggled beneath him desperate, it seemed to distance herself from him. Somewhat ashamed, he quickly lifted his weight from her, rolling to her side. Instantly she turned her back on him, like some creature deeply wounded. A rush of frustration and impatience came to him. Bloody hell, she was his wife. She had put herself in jeopardy. She had risked countless lives. And he had told her she could say no. He would have stopped. He would somehow make her understand she had no options left. She could play the role of a dutiful wife—even if she thought him to be a simpering popinjay or a notorious criminal. It seemed, he realized suddenly that she preferred the simpering dandy. She must learn what was at stake and act accordingly.

He set a hand on the shoulder she had set so defensively against him.

"Amorica, I'm sorry if I hurt you. It's fairly natural. I understand, for a woman to cry the first time—"

"I am not crying," she whispered.

But he thought she was. He wanted to comfort her. He ran his hands down her beautiful, sleek back.

"Amorica—"

Her back stiffened like a poker. "You've had what you wanted. Now leave me alone."

As if he'd been burned, he withdrew his touch. He laced his fingers behind his head and stared at the sky above them. Dawn was almost upon them. He wanted to comfort her. He had felt the response of her body. She was beautiful, passionate, sensual, and he could feel it all. Feel it in her hunger for life, in her will, in her spirit.

Even in her hatred. Hate me then, he thought. But you will always respond to me, Amorica, you will. He let her lie there, fuming, stiff, and keeping her distance. Then he reached for her again.

He saw her eyes. They were shimmering green, cold, ice and fire. Rebellious, furious, she stared at him.

"It's over," she cried.

"It's just begun," he corrected. This time he swept her into his arms.

From the very first touch of his lips to hers, she filled him with a force and passion that brooked no resistance. He kissed her until her lips were wet and swollen, then tasted her earlobes and her throat.

He suckled her breasts, one then the other, taunting them with a slow rubbing motion with his thumbs then suckling them again until she cried out. His hands, his lips were everywhere. Her fingers flew about, exploring hungrily or something else, he was not sure, but he moved on.

He rolled her onto her stomach, teasing the line of her spine with the caress of his fingers and tongue, nipping her buttocks then rolling her over once again, parting her thighs, and having his way. When he took her again, he was so fiercely hungry himself he could scarcely believe it. He should be sated with her. He wanted more of her. He knew her from head to toe. He had touched her, tasted every part of her. Whether she wanted him or not, she writhed, and trembled, and created an ever-greater fire.

And it burned. Burned so that he was nearly mindless himself, and then amazed at the force of the climax that seized him again. She shuddered as he filled her. But no sound escaped her. No surrender even came in a whisper from her lips.

He fell to his side. Once again, she turned her back to him. Frustrated, he stared at the sky once more.

"Amorica—why?" he demanded.

She didn't answer. The silence echoed between the trees in the moss-covered glade. The sun rose higher and burned brighter.

He touched her again, stroking her back whether she wanted his touch or not this time.

He clenched his teeth. "Amorica, you're my wife. Why won't you give in to your own hunger and passion?"

He rose up on an elbow. "Tell me, Amorica. I want to understand. You're flesh and blood, and you're very much a woman. You're doing your best to deny me in every way save telling me to stop."

"I didn't deny you anything," she said.

"You did, and you know it."

She was silent again then burst out. "I don't owe you anything. You take what you want. There is nothing else that should be yours. You're a—" She broke off.

He caught hold of her shoulder and rolled her around once again. He met her eyes, those green eyes that were brilliant with tears that she would die before she shed.

"I'm a what, Amorica," he demanded harshly.

She shook her head.

"Answer me. No? All right. I'll answer for you. I'm a smuggler. Well, my dear Mrs. Andrews, you're one too. Your presence on the beach tonight made it abundantly clear that my wife could be involved in the same nefarious schemes. You might well be subject to the same punishment."

She stared at him. But then her lashes fell over her eyes. "I would take my chances with the patrols." She whispered vehemently.

"Bloody hell, Amorica," he said quietly. "Fine, have it your way. Like it or not, you will go to Newgate and hang with us if we are caught." Her eyes rose to his. "I would turn you in before I hung beside you." He traced a path across her neck. "I don't know, Amorica. You will think differently when you see the handbills seeking out the woman with the ebony hair, placed beside those seeking me. I wonder what bounty they will put on your head. Would you surrender to me or the hangman's noose?"

"I will surrender to no one."

Chapter Thirteen

Amorica sat cross-legged on a cliff overlooking the ocean. Wind whipped her hair and heat from the sun beat down upon her. She cast a pebble onto the rocks below, listening to its tiny thuds.

She rose easily from her sitting position and walked along the edge of the cliff, wishing for the real peace of being alone. Feroz stood guard behind her, watching her like a hawk. It seemed he knew where she was every minute of every day. Except when she retired for the night and a few moments of privacy, he never let her from his sight.

He rode behind her when she went to the small village nearby. He sat in silent vigil when she rode to the cliffs. He watched her watching the ocean. Both Erline and Blair reported to him.

Amorica had just ridden from the village but stopped here before going to Damian's home. She bought yards of fabric for new draperies, which might never be sewn. She wandered along the path and found a seat on a boulder. She braced her hands behind her and leaned back, her head facing the sun, and closed her eyes.

She never wanted to remember the night her mother died. But she did remember. It had been bitterly cold and the rain had been falling in sheets.

Her mother had been gone too long and so Amorica had wandered outside to find her. Her father had been hunting. Blood covered her mother. Her beautiful face had been so pale, so very ethereal. Amorica could not believe she was dead. She sat for what seemed like hours, holding her, rocking her, crying and wishing fervently she would open her eyes. She did not.

Her father found her the next morning, frozen to the bone, still holding her mother. She did not cry again until the funeral then it seemed she could not stop. No one, not even her littlest cousin, Aidan, with all her antics could ease the heartache.

She would never forgive the men who killed her mother or their kind.

Damian Andrews was a smuggler—she would never surrender to him.

He was no good, and she owed him nothing. But he owed her, her mother's life.

She clenched her teeth suddenly. Angry feelings soared. With all his words to her ringing true, she wanted to scream her fury at the world.

Feroz had told her about the wanted poster in the village by his home.

Feroz had said the people who lived there were loyal to Damian. Her picture now hung next to his but Feroz didn't know if they would harbor the same loyalty to her. But then Feroz told her the pictures didn't hold any resemblance to either of them. They had called her the phantom's mistress. Chills ripped through her. If she were caught, they would take her to Newgate, perhaps deport her. She had not asked for any of this. A smuggler of French brandy should not have such a high price on his head.

What was Damian Andrews really doing?

Amorica stood up, stretching, her hands against the small of her back.

The lower part by her spine had been giving her trouble lately. It was because of her efforts to refurnish and decorate Damian's home. She and Erline had spent countless hours scrubbing the kitchen and the halls as well as the rooms. Then they had measured every window, every piece of furniture.

When he returned what was she going to do? If he returned, she reminded herself. He might well intend to keep her forever—alone—isolated. He'd sent a messenger with letters from her cousins. They knew she had married Damian and were eager for news. He was still in

London—not so very far away. Occasionally, he wrote a few words to her.

She pressed her hand to her forehead, frowning then shaking her head against a moment's dizziness that seized her. It was the sun, or the fact that she had not been sleeping or eating well.

The day was unseasonably warm. It was Damian's fault, she was certain. She knew she was being perverse.

He'd been gone a little over five weeks now, and she wished fervently that she didn't think about him. At first, she'd been delighted to wake up and discover he was gone. On the first morning, she had been exhausted and sore from head to toe, and she had wanted nothing more than time in which to convince herself she had healed her wounds. Instead, she'd had to ride back to the estate on trails no humans ever traveled. He'd left for London as soon as he'd seen her inside and called out to Erline to fetch a bath for her.

Days had passed. When she thought about him, and that night between them, she had alternated between moments of deepest humiliation and fascination.

Thinking of it now, she nearly groaned aloud, raising her knees to her chest and hugging her arms around them.

Thoughts of Damian preoccupied her too much now, when she was awake and when she was asleep. There was no denying the strength of the man, the size of him, and the sleekness of his power. She tried to close her eyes and her mind from such thoughts, but they came to her repeatedly, unbidden. She could see his dark brown eyes, warning her that his will was law, the rakishly tousled auburn hair, the naked length of him, exploring her, touching her.

Then a flush of heat would rise in her, and her cheeks bloomed crimson. She swallowed down the thoughts. Thank God, he was gone. She didn't have to withstand the challenges he tossed at her.

Or feel the horrific tug to surrender, the desire to reach out, to touch something sweet and magical and elusive. She wanted to keep her feelings to herself.

She leaned back again, opening her eyes to watch the sky around her.

It was crystal clear today, a robin's egg blue. The air was crisp but everything the sun touched it heated. It was such a beautiful day. But the rain would follow soon. It always did, and she would have naught but gray mist to look upon.

She sighed, watching a gull swoop and dip with air currents. Damian would be caught. She heard him say the patrols grew closer each time.

What then?

She bit her lower lip. She had wanted to see her cousins, and she missed her puppy. Would she ever be trusted enough to leave here, or could Damian be persuaded to let her have company?

She'd half expected her father to show up at Damian's doorstep. But then her father did not know where she was. Damian had guarded all his secrets well.

She rose, having forgotten the feeling of dizziness, and walked back to the edge of the cliff. She bent down to pick up another pebble, wondering if she could toss it far enough to hit the water. After she threw it the dizziness seized her once again. She hurriedly stepped back from the cliff's edge. A sudden surge within her stomach startled her. She leaned a hand against a rock and paused for a moment. She'd felt queasy a few mornings ago, but she had swallowed hard and the feeling had passed.

She'd ignored the sensation then, and she would ignore it again.

She waited. The feeling didn't pass. To her astonishment, it worsened.

There was a small pool of rainwater down the path a ways. She walked quickly down the path. Bending over, she splashed cool water on her cheeks and let it slide down her face. She put the back of her hand to her forehead. It didn't help. She clutched her stomach and found herself being sick into the midst of rocks. She straightened; dismayed, wondering what sort of strange disease she might have caught. She splashed more water on her face then cupped some of the water in her hand and washed out her mouth. Maybe she was going to be all right.

She ripped her petticoat and soaked it in the water. Then she leaned against a rock and held the rag to her forehead. As she did so, she felt a curious feeling of unease slip over her, as if someone watched her. She pulled the cloth from her face and stared down the trail in the direction of her horse.

Damian.

As usual, he seemed to be in excellent condition. From his gold-buckled shoes to his scarlet frock coat, he was perfectly attired. When he dismounted from the horse and walked toward her, she noted that he hadn't lost a whit of his sleek, muscled tone or his suppleness. He was clean-shaven and his features seemed exceptionally striking.

She didn't want him to see her when she wasn't at her best. Now she was in old worn clothing. Her hair was damp and her cheeks were flushed.

She had just been wretchedly sick. The closer he came, the more fiercely her heart began to pound.

"Would you like help?" he offered easily. "Which one is it? Are you going to faint or fall?"

She stiffened, not wanting him to see any sign of weakness. "Of course I'm not going to faint or fall. I'm perfectly fine." But she wasn't.

The queasiness rose unbidden.

"Would you admit to me if you were sick?" He paused, hands on hips, his head tilted at an angle as he watched her. Why did he appear in those clothes when she'd thought he'd given up on them? Of course, he'd just spent five weeks in London.

She stared at his face, and despite herself, she felt a slow rush of heat rising to her cheeks. He was back and unwanted emotions seemed to race through her.

She turned quickly, using a huge boulder beside her as a brace. "How long have you been there?" she whispered, trying desperately not to be sick in front of him.

"Long enough."

"How did you find me?"

"I've been to the stable."

She nodded, needing something to do, and feeling so ridiculously flushed, she dipped her ripped piece of petticoat into the water again, pressing it against her forehead. "I'm sorry, I must be catching something. Perhaps you should go back to London. You wouldn't want to catch what I have."

She was surprised at the crooked smile that slid easily onto his lips as he slapped his riding gloves against his leg.

"You think you are ill?" he queried her, an amused glint in his brown eyes. He chuckled softly, looking well pleased with himself.

She threw up her hands. "Well, Lord Andrews, I'm ever so glad my misfortune amuses you."

"I'm sorry to disappoint you, but no misfortune of yours would amuse me. I just don't think you are ill."

"Then—"

"Amorica, my sweet innocent," he said with exasperation, making her sound anything but sweet or innocent. "Hasn't it occurred to you that you might be expecting a child?"

~ * ~

Perhaps she had flushed red before. Now he saw every drop of blood drain from her face. No, it never had occurred to her.

He was sure she'd been queasy before this. If she had given the least attention to the time that had elapsed, she might have noticed.

"Have you missed your monthly?" he demanded frankly, watching her intently.

The blood came surging back to her face. She stood in front of him, speechless. She looked as if she wanted to run from him.

"Bloody hell, Amorica." He reached out to her, wishing only to comfort her, knowing she would never accept the soothing gesture.

She found words. "You shouldn't know about such things," she blurted out.

His good humor returned. He felt keenly amused once again. "Do forgive me. We both grew up with responsibilities to our families. Be it true that I am a second son and will be left with nothing and you are sole heir of your family's fortune. It's rather difficult for a man to have reached my age with a total lack of knowledge about the opposite sex."

She flushed deeper. "I don't think you are lacking anything," she charged him, looking miserable. It seemed she was going to be sick again.

He was sure she did not want to show weakness. Not with him here, right on top of her, asking such personal questions. "Could you please just go away?"

"Amorica, I want to know—"

"Don't, please," she whispered miserably, holding her hands in front of her and backing away. "Maybe you know such things. Perhaps you shouldn't talk about them." She placed the cloth on her forehead again and turned away from him.

He didn't go away. "Amorica, turn around and look at me." She shook her head. Bloody hell, Amorica, she never told him the truth unless he pried it from her. Her reticence needed to stop here and now. He put his hands on her shoulders and turned her around. The glint of amusement vanished from his eyes. He could not help himself. He was at her side, sweeping her up into his arms, holding her close and wishing he could protect her from everything, including herself.

"Put me down. I'm not going to fall," she protested weakly. If he were lucky, she would not be sick again.

He walked her down the path toward the ocean cliffs, sitting her upon a rock where he could brace his back against a tree. He used his right hand to gently press the cooling rag over her forehead and cheeks. She closed her eyes, most certainly unaccustomed to this gentleness from him.

It felt curiously soothing to him. He hoped this helped ease the tension and strain he saw in her features. She appeared worn out, fragile.

He wanted to protect her now, shield her from anything that might go awry. It seemed especially nice not to feel the need to fight with her or defend what he did. It was just too difficult to defend something he could not explain.

If he was right, she was going to have his child. From that one amazing night when he had determined that it was going to be a real marriage, that in order to protect her from her own folly she would be his wife. Well, maybe he hadn't been entirely right. Perhaps he had shaped events to ease the incredible need he had for her. Maybe he wanted her to understand the consequences of what she'd done the night she'd interfered with the mission.

Her lashes suddenly flew open. His eyes were looking at her, dark, brown, intense. "You're wrong. It was only one night." He felt a cold chilling distance between them.

"Amorica, it certainly can happen from one night."

Her shoulders shook and she looked frightened—no, terrified. Was she ready for the responsibility? Of course she was, he told himself. She had nothing else to think about or do. Perhaps it was truly for the best. He could only hope she would not put herself at risk again—or the baby.

He watched her. "Oh, you'd like that, wouldn't you?" She seemed to lose control. "You'd get to feel wonderfully puffed up and arrogant and proud of your male prowess!"

He sighed, his teeth grating, so very tired of the animosity between them yet not having the vaguest clue how to change it. "Amorica, I wouldn't feel a thing save grateful and exuberant. If you haven't done enough with the animals at your keep to know about breeding, you would know that it can happen anytime. If it's the right night for you to conceive, then it's the right night, and it would have bloody little to do with any magnificent prowess on my part." He paused for a moment, raking his hands through his hair. "I've found suddenly that I'm thrilled by the idea of being a father."

Her lashes fell quickly, covering her eyes, hiding whatever she might be thinking or feeling from him.

He was going to have a baby. His heart leapt.

She opened her eyes again and met his. He didn't know if she was pleased or displeased or still rejecting the idea. He saw her swallow, suddenly trembling and looking as if she needed to escape. "I'm sorry," she murmured quickly. "I'm all right now."

She was pushing away and so he helped steady her. "Really," she said. "It may just be nothing, you know. The heat—"

"It's not hot today. In fact it is decidedly chilly," he said blandly. "I know what you're thinking, Amorica. You couldn't be having my child. You barely know me. I'm the enemy, a smuggler." She had touched a part of him he thought long forgotten. She had made him feel again — feel whole. In a strange way, she completed him.

She lifted her chin, "You don't know what I'm thinking."

He bowed slightly. "My apologies." She would never back down or admit to anything she did not want to admit to. Not until she had no choice. Well, he had lots of time.

"You've done this before? You act as if you know something about women—" She broke off, some startling intuition coming to her. "You've had a baby. You've fathered a child."

"I've no living children," he stated coldly, retreating into his own shell. "But—"

"I've no living children. Drop it, Amorica." He felt the hair on the back of his neck rise. The dark shadow that filled his heart at the mention of his child seemed to wrap around him.

It appeared she decided to do what he asked. "So, what are you doing here? What brought you back?"

"What do I want? Why, I want my wife. And I want her to show me how loyal she is. Remember my love, your neck is on the line now, just as mine is. You are..." he paused, "the phantom's mistress. They hang mistresses too." He regretted the statement as soon as he said the words.

Yet she had to remember how serious the accusations against her were.

All the blood seemed to drain from her face. He thought for a moment she might faint. She started to reach out to him for support then seemed to realize what she did. She would not touch her enemy, even if he fathered her child.

As if she meant to run from him and all he'd revealed, she started down the path toward her horse. He watched her running until she spooked her mare, and it raced off toward his home and the stables.

His gut churned. He wanted her blind loyalty as well as her affections.

He didn't know how to reach through to her though. It seemed whatever he did came out all wrong. He wanted a child but he wanted Amorica to want the child too.

He came up behind her, swinging her around, his arms about her in support. "Come on, we'll take my horse. It is only a short way. We'll ride together."

"I can't—"

"We'll see."

"I'll ride with Feroz."

"He returned home the minute I arrived."

She stumbled. He lifted her again, walking her down the path to where his very well-trained horse still stood. Her arms slipped around his neck. "I didn't mean to overhear a private conversation. I didn't mean to get in the way. I just wanted to know, to understand why Ryder was there."

"You are too curious, Amorica."

She nodded. He saw tears in her eyes. And it seemed she tried valiantly to hold them back.

"I am so afraid. I went into the village—"

She didn't need to say anything more. She'd seen the posters.

"Amorica, I won't let any harm come to you. I've been thinking of sailing to the States. I own land in Virginia and Maryland as well."

"I can't go to the States," she said tonelessly.

"We'll see."

She looked up, hearing the pounding of hooves. Down the hill and toward the valley, she could see four men.

"Amorica."

She turned. Damian put a finger to his lips warning her to silence. She obeyed his silent command.

"This is your first test," he said as the men came closer. "They are patrols, and I'm sure they have just come to ask a few questions."

"About smugglers?"

"Remember, my love, you are one now too."

She stiffened, holding still in his arms. He did not set her down but pulled her closer, wrapping his arm around her.

"Is that why you showed up here in those ridiculous clothes?" She queried him.

He nuzzled the column of her throat. "Play the dutiful wife, and they will leave all the sooner."

She ran her fingers through his hair, yet she did nothing to dispel what he was trying to accomplish here. "Always," she murmured, lowering her lashes.

He kissed her then, a long lingering kiss, not a daytime kiss, but one meant to seduce. He heard a soft moan of what he hoped was pleasure.

"My Lord," the voice intruded, his thoughts nearly a jumbled mess.

Bloody hell, but he wanted her, needed her. He could not quench the fire she ignited within him. It was just a kiss.

Slowly, he ended the kiss. He turned. The man was short and square, his mustache thick and curly, his chin soft.

He cleared his throat and set Amorica on her feet, keeping an arm around her trembling shoulders.

"Quickly now, what is it you want here?" He swiped an imaginary piece of lint from his frock coat. "Can't you see I'm busy? I've just returned from London, and I've yet to greet my wife properly," Damian said.

The man cleared his throat. "If you don't mind—"

"Of course I mind. Didn't I just tell you I have unfinished business here." Damian waved his free hand in the air. "I suppose you want to know if I've seen illegal activities going on in these parts. Of course not. Do I look like a man who would be traipsing about in the dead of night looking for scoundrels and scallywags?"

"No, no I suppose not."

"Then be on your way and allow me my pleasures. I've been weeks away from my wife."

"My Lord, I have instructions to interview everyone."

"You've interviewed me, now be off with you."

The man cleared his throat again. His horse sidestepped, clearly intimidated by the tone of Damian's voice.

"Your wife has answered no questions. I merely—"

"Does she—" Damian cut the man off and in turn was cut off by Amorica.

"Please excuse my husband. He does tend to be impatient and rude. I have seen no one. I was at home, alone. Now I want to be with my husband—doing things. He's been gone so long." Amorica fluttered her lashes at the man and pressed her breasts against Damian's chest. She was flirting with both of them.

His body responded instantly.

Amorica was very nearly purring her love for him. He found he was quite intrigued by her ability to play the coquette. She ran her fingers down his chest then up again, lingering at each button, provocatively toying with them.

Little minx, he would make her pay.

"Do you have any more questions?" she asked softly. "My husband and I were engaged in—a," she moistened her lips. "Activities. If you understand."

Damian decided two could play at this game. He kissed her ear, nibbled on it a moment and felt her jerk in response. He kissed her cheek and then lower to feather kisses down her throat. His fingers traced the line of her bodice, inching lower with each pass.

He heard her unnatural breath, heard the tiny gasp of air she inhaled.

The man cleared his throat then tipped his cap to her and spun his horse around. Damian watched them ride away.

"They will be back," he said. "And their questions will be more difficult to answer."

Chapter Fourteen

Later that day, Damian stood at the window of his study, watching Amorica play ball with her dog. Her cousins Christel and Ravyn sat on a patchwork quilt nearby. Laughter floated through the window. She had been genuinely pleased when Wolfy bounded through the front door to meet her. She had screamed with unabashed joy when both cousins followed more sedately.

This place was no one's heritage. It held no history or memories for him. He wanted to build a life in a land far away from here.

He wanted Amorica to dream his dream.

She hadn't asked him to bring her cousins to see her. He had wanted to see her smile, and so he'd made sure the cousins brought her dog too.

She hadn't asked him for anything save to leave her alone. When they arrived, he'd made it a point of telling her he had something to do. And so he'd disappeared down the hall. Maybe he needed time himself. It wasn't as if he meant to bundle up all their possessions and sail to the states on the first ship to leave port. She had some time. He had to work out arrangements. He had to return to London right away, and from there, make sure everyone believed the Phantom was dead as well as the woman who had been seen with him. He would have to arrange for Amorica's father to see her one last time.

Amorica would join him in London. Feroz would make sure her journey there was safe and uneventful. She could see The Duchess before they left on one of his merchant ships. One of his vessels was due into London from the East Indies soon, carrying tea and spices. He still had to find a home for Sholeh.

She wasn't saying good-bye to her cousins for good today, but he supposed it felt like it. There was certainly no turning back for her.

A soft sound of laughter rose up from below. It was faint, for Amorica was at a distance, but it evoked all kinds of nostalgia and wonder within him. How had they been before they'd all left for London to find husbands? Each one of the girls seemed to harbor their own demons. Each one would have to find their own means to vanquish them.

Amorica would be giving up so very much. She must have been the uncontested mistress at her father's home since her mother's death. She was the oldest of four sisters. She must have been sheer elegance and beauty in those days, allowing the spill of laughter to fill the halls, to lighten the days. She laughed so seldom now.

He closed his eyes. For a moment, he could almost imagine he was with them on the lawn. What were they saying, three cousins below him?

His eyes were sharp, and he could see her face, even as she turned to Christel. She was smiling. Her head was tilted back. Her hair, free and lustrous as the blue-black wing of a bird, flowed in rich waves and curls down her back, catching the sunlight. She laughed at something Christel said then threw the ball for her dog.

Ravyn rose from the quilt and walked to Amorica. She gave her a fierce hug then stepped back. For a moment, the three were posed there, arm in arm, in a continuing triangle. All three were so beautiful, two with black hair the other fair, golden and shimmering with the catch of light—and entwined by love—and that sometimes stubborn nature that seemed to be as much a part of the other two as it was with Amorica.

He sighed, catching hold of the rise of his temper. He didn't begrudge her, her cousins love, or loyalty between them. It was something precious to her, something he hoped they would have forever. Things were terribly different in his family. They held little love between them and less loyalty.

His eyes narrowed as he watched Amorica. She was so alive, so exuberant, so vivacious. Her spirit was as deep and bewitching as her vibrant coloring. Her passions ran so very deep.

But not for him.

How would it feel if she were ever to set her eyes upon him like that?

So sparkling, so brilliantly green, so tender? And that smile...

Never in a thousand years would she smile at him that way. Heaven help him, he decided dryly, if she did. He might melt into a puddle at her feet. He needed a strong guard against Amorica Hepburn—Andrews knew.

Her will was as strong as steel. If she ever felt that she really had any power over him, she would do her best to break him. She'd be free from him, taking what she wanted on her way.

He leaned back against the wall, closing his eyes for a moment.

Maybe he judged her too harshly. Maybe he spent too many hours mourning a gentle blond woman who had never even thought to disagree with him. No, Meara had been blessed with her own type of strength. She hadn't needed to spend countless hours fighting him. But he was married to Amorica now, and unless he missed his guess, he was expecting another child. They were going to make it work.

Every time he saw Amorica, he found himself doing things he had never planned to do. He had never intended to marry her. He had never meant to order her to go to the States. He had actually come back to say good-bye and perhaps discuss the possibility of her joining him. But once he had seen her, the order had just slipped out. Once he had issued it, he realized he had meant it.

He was a married man. He didn't intend to live without his wife. She might protest the trip, but she would go with him. In all the long nights he had been away from her, he had dreamed about her, and he had yearned for her. A slight sound from outside attracted his attention and he resumed his vigil at the window once again. The girls were leaving her. She watched them go, smiling. But when they had come up the knoll leading to the house, when she felt herself sheltered by the foliage between them, she turned back. He saw her shoulders hunching over.

He knew she cried. She slipped slowly to her knees. Her shoulders shook. She did not cry; she sobbed, in great, gulping waves. He clenched his jaw, torn by a wave of sympathy. He would not change his mind. She would go with him, because she was his wife.

"Actually, I don't think it's all just because of you," he heard a soft voice beside him. It surprised him. He had not heard footsteps.

He turned. Christel stood in the doorway. Amorica's cousin was beautiful too. He wondered what affect Dicky's amorous suit had upon her. She was a woman who would love deeply if she found the right person.

"Thanks for the words of confidence." He reproached her mildly.

Christel was seldom fooled. She seemed to be able to see inside one's soul. She could bring out the best in a person.

He crossed his arms over his chest, leaning against the wall. "What brought on such a comment? What does she say about me?"

"Never a word. Even when I ask her outright. She stares me straight in the eye and reminds me that some things are private and sacred. And that I, of all people, should understand."

"Does she now?" he murmured. He shouldn't have been surprised.

Amorica would never give herself away, not to Christel, not to anyone.

Yet she might give him away. He remembered the inquisition by the patrol. She'd remained steadfast and loyal, even flirting with him in front of the man to complete the ruse.

"You forget, I know her well, Damian." She flashed him a quick smile, came inside, and stared out the window with him. "I know what she's thinking."

"You do?"

He saw Christel nod slowly. "She's thinking of everyone she might never see again when she leaves. Not just her father or the mother she lost.

She's thinking about the people she's spent her entire life caring about."

"Christel, my God, I've lost people I love too. And she's my wife. She will go where I go."

"I know, but you control everything she does now. She doesn't have a choice. You have to try and remember that. She's not used to following anyone's orders."

Amorica had risen. As he watched, she strode toward the cliffs once more then she veered to the right, heading for a small clearing overlooking the ocean and disappeared into a cover of trees.

"Where in bloody hell is she heading now?" he demanded, then realized his language, and remembered that once upon a time he would have never thought to have been so crude in front of any lady. He closed his eyes, "Sorry, Christel—"

"It's quite all right, I've most certainly heard those words before," Christel said, then asked, "Why are you so angry with her?"

"I'm not angry," he denied, but Christel was right. Fine, Amorica was indeed stubborn. She wouldn't cry in front of him.

But she was sobbing behind his back and he wanted to shake her. He wasn't forcing her into a life as a scullery maid. No, just into a life with him.

"Where has she gone?" Christel asked.

Damian sighed. "A small clearing that overlooks the sea. You can see a corner through the trees right there. See..."

"She won't stay long. Since her mother died, she likes to go off by herself."

"I think I'll go find her," he murmured. He turned from the window, long legs carrying him quickly from the room. He was down the stairway before Christel seemed to have found the energy to come after him. "Damian!" she called his name, but he pretended not to hear her. By the time he had left the porch behind him and passed by the extensive maze of rosebushes, he heard Christel reach the porch herself. But she stopped there.

Ravyn came beside her.

"Let them be," she warned her. "They need time alone. Remember, he has been away, in London."

"He's angry, Ravyn."

"They'll solve it. They have to have some privacy to talk out their problems and their fears. Amorica has to have the chance to tell him how she feels."

"It won't change anything. She cannot stand the sight of him."

"Then so be it. But they are married. Give Damian a chance to prove himself to her. He can't do that with our interference."

"Christel, don't be ridiculous."

The voices faded behind him. He came to where Amorica had stood.

He'd come here before. The view was always spectacular. The ocean had always fascinated him. Sailing was in his blood. He loved the feel of a ship, and the way it would ride the swells and dips of the sea.

He stared at the sea. The waves crashed upon the cliffs. He hoped Amorica would weather the trip across the Atlantic well. He really didn't know. The apprehension ate at him. He followed the path Amorica had taken. Through the foliage, he could see the sun glisten off the grass.

He walked around the front. The trees made a natural canopy and he strode through it. There was a fire pit, circled with large rocks.

With a smile, he remembered the clearing in the early fall. He imagined how it would feel, a blaze snapping warmly, winds blowing the leaves from the trees. He'd spent so little time here.

Amorica hadn't heard him. She was sitting, leaning against a large rock and gazing at the ocean view. The sea crashed and churned dark today, but enchanting. Its color, its turbulence, warned that harsher weather was fast approaching.

Some sound or instinct alerted her to his presence. She turned, somewhat alarmed.

Most women, he thought, didn't look good when they cried. Their eyes usually got puffy and their face became a blotchy red—not Amorica.

Her cheeks were damp and flushed and her eyes remained crystal with the wetness of her tears. As she stared at him, she brushed her hands over her cheeks, and the wet glimmer of tears became that of defiance. He'd never seen eyes more vividly, beautifully green. He'd been so sorry, so touched by the pain she had been feeling.

Seeing the lightening-quick change in her, he felt his resolve stiffen.

Her pride was greater than any emotion within her heart.

"What are you doing here?" she whispered.

He lifted his hands. "I could ask you the same question." She turned back around, staring at the ocean. "I want to be left alone, nothing more."

"I cannot do that," he spoke softly.

He remained behind her in silence. His presence must have disturbed her, though, for she was quickly up, swinging around to meet him as if she feared to have him at her back.

"You could if you wished it."

"Perhaps," he said.

She stared at him, and he must have betrayed some surprise at her movement. She flushed slightly and strode closer to the fire pit. Her feet moved silently over the grass. Amorica looked over her shoulder. She caught his gaze then turned away quickly.

"I think I know why you're doing this, Damian." She was suddenly very prim, her hands folded before her, her eyes steady on his.

He took up a military "at ease" stance, legs slightly apart, his hands together at his back. "Oh?" he said politely. "And what am I doing?"

"Making me leave my home and my country. You have given the order and I must do your bidding."

"You're my wife."

She waved a hand in the air, unable to continue meeting his eyes.

"There must be another reason." He was dead silent, and she continued in a sudden rush. "I don't know what it is, but I saw you, Richy and Dicky talking, heads together as if you had some great secret and then all three of you looked at me and my cousins. You all smiled—"

"Because I smiled?" He interrupted her at last, struggling to keep a cap on his rising temper, "I am a man condemned because I smiled?" She didn't flinch. Her eyes narrowed and she stared him down in her very regal manner. "I didn't think you'd agree with me. I—" She broke off because he was striding across the clearing to her. He caught hold of her waist, lifting her, swirling her around.

"Let's get this straight right now, Amorica. Nothing Richy or Dicky could do or say would have any bearing on what I expected of my wife. I want to live with my wife and if I choose to do so in America then, my love, you will go with me."

"But—"

"No, no, no, hear me out. My turn, my way. This is between us, Amorica."

"I see," she said coolly, staring downward where he touched her with a scornful command. "All your animosity is strictly toward me." He released her. He'd hurt her if he didn't. "I have been patient, too patient."

Her lashes fluttered. She started to turn away. He brought her against him. "This is why you're coming with me," he said softly. He did what he'd been itching to do since he'd first seen her. He raked his fingers through the soft wealth of her hair, and kissed her. Touched those lips that were so warm and passionate that denying what was between them was ridiculous. Hunger and dreams bubbled to the surface. He kissed her hard, determinedly. Tasted the sweetness of her mouth, the mold of her lips, the very indefinable femininity about her that was so very elusive and so very beautiful and seductive.

Perhaps he took her by surprise. Perhaps he had been so determined to touch her that he left her no room to protest. A single sound escaped her.

Her arms rose between them, falling against his chest once then no more. His arms encircled her while his lips molded to hers. He sank down to the ground with her.

They were upon the grass.

He'd never meant to do this. To disappear for such a length of time then return and take his reluctant bride in a sunlit clearing. But he continually discovered himself doing things he didn't intend in the least with her.

Her lips were parted to his. Perhaps she was not so willing a participant in the kiss, but she did not deny it. She made no effort to twist from him. He kissed her and kissed her, and her breath came too quickly and her heart hammered. When he brought her down, her arms laced around his neck. To keep her from falling, of course. But still, there was no protest.

She was upon the ground, her hair spread across it, ebony blue. He leaned over her, aware of her eyes again and the sweeping richness of her black lashes. He stretched out beside her, cupping her breast beneath the fabric of her gown. Her lashes fell, her cheeks found color. He covered her mouth with his once again, his hand tugging upon her skirt and petticoat. Bloody hell, they wore so much clothing. His palms moved over the naked flesh of her belly. He massaged it and slipped his fingers between her legs.

He heard the rumble of sound from deep within her throat. Touching her, feeling the silky hair of her triangle, the tender, damp flesh of her sex, added fuel to a fire that had tormented him all the time that he had spent away from her. He had sworn that seeing her would be hell. It was indeed his own hell, for he burned in it, wanting her. Now the flames were rising to a peak. He wedged his weight between her thighs, fumbling quickly with his buckskins. Some sense of sanity within him cautioned hem that she was still new at this game, and not exactly an avid player—no matter the torment of his own desire. He touched her again, seeking erotic zones to tease, to arouse. To his surprise, he was rewarded with a startled gasp.

He rotated his touch, moving more deeply inside her. Another sound escaped her as she felt the first thrust of his sex, just at the very vulnerable portals of her own. He could feel the charge and the friction, the heat of his desire and hers. Her fingers bit into his shoulders. She buried her face against his neck. He lifted her hips and thrust deeply and cleanly within her, feeling her arms tighten about him as he did so. No sound escaped her. Slow! He warned himself. He tried. But his dreams blended with reality. The sweetness of her scent pervaded his blood. The hunger he had lived with since he had left her gnawed with a burning ache for fulfillment. The flesh of her buttocks and thighs was like satin beneath his touch, and being within her, clothed and sheathed by the hot liquid heat of her body, touched off depths of desire he had scarcely known existed.

As reluctant a bride as Amorica might be, she was wild and passionate and exciting. Whether she meant to give to him or not, she did.

Perhaps she merely rode the storm. As the intensity of his need rose in a sweet and merciless spiral, he locked her into his embrace and rhythm. He enticed her hips into a liquid smooth undulation. He swept her into his tempest until it burst upon him, wonderful and volatile. He drifted downward, amazed at the sensations she created at just how damned good it was to have her. Nothing had ever seemed quite so fierce or quite so sweet before.

Imagine! He mocked himself, if she were just not so reluctant.

She was quiet, breathing hard, her eyes downcast, still defying him.

She tried, which was futile with him still half atop her, to straighten her knees and bring down her skirts.

He bit his lip, rolling from her. He'd done well, he taunted himself.

Let me see, he'd invaded her privacy then taken her fully clothed on the very spot where she sought some measure of peace and solitude. Now she was trying to cover a slim, shapely leg and to his annoyance, he was discovering that he could be aroused again.

Meara would have looked at herself and giggled. And she would have whispered in his ear. "Well, that was fun, but really, Damian, shouldn't we shed our clothing next time?"

But, no! This was Amorica, with her flaming green eyes and midnight hair. And the sweet passion that simmered beneath everything, driving him to distraction. Making him want her more than he had ever wanted Meara.

He rose, adjusting his trousers. He walked to the edge of the clearing and looked out over the ocean before gazing back to her.

"I'm sorry," he told her quietly.

She didn't answer him. She was sitting up, her black hair a fall over her face hiding her eyes. She was still trying to straighten out her attire.

Her shoulders were squared. "It's really to be expected—" she began, in that regal voice that set his nerves on edge. And he heard what she didn't say. For a smuggler.

He was back beside her in a number of seconds. He didn't touch her, but he hunkered down before her. "All right, Amorica, I'm not sorry. I'm not in the least damned sorry. You're my wife. This is what married people do!"

"Actually, most married people are completely polite and respectful of one another," she said smoothly, tossing back that mountain of hair.

"They don't just couple like—"

"Bloody hell, Amorica. You cannot be so naive. You don't have the vaguest idea about married people."

She was gracefully on her feet in seconds. "So why bother to apologize?"

He stood, hands on his hips, facing her. "I won't do so ever again, Amorica, I promise." He smiled, remembering her secret torrent of tears over the fact that she was to come with him. He hadn't the least control over the twinge that came to him when he reached for her, pulling her close once again. "Never. And so much—truly decadent, by your standards—lies before us. There is the dirt on the floor of a log cabin.

There are streams galore out there, abandoned Indian dwellings, and wonderful, savage places to couple just like a pair of wild animals. And with my willing, imaginative bride, I just can't wait." She jerked her hand free. Her chin was high, her eyes blazing. "If you're trying to shock or frighten me, Damian, you can go to blue blazes.

I'll survive anything you can put in front of me. I'm strong and resilient and I won't let you scare me."

"Yes, you are a survivor. No one fights so damned well, Amorica." She threw back her full mane of ebony hair, her eyes sizzling, her hands on her hips, all of her trembling. Actually, he'd never seen her quite so vital, so passionate, so wild.

So beautiful, sensual, and appealing.

"You sorry excuse for humanity!" she lashed out. "You can just stop it, or I'll—"

"You'll what?" he taunted. "Call the patrols? Hang me from my boot heels? Remember, if anyone figures out who you are, you will be accused along with me."

"You've done this to me." A cry of fury brought her flying against him. He had goaded her on, and still, he hadn't quite been ready for her.

She nearly knocked him flat. He caught his balance just in time. He trapped her fingers just seconds before she could bring her nails raking across his face. Husky laughter spilled from him then, even though he gave himself an inward warning. She was someone to reckon with.

"Amorica—"

"Let go of me." She kicked him hard, right in the shin. It hurt like hell.

"Amorica." He jerked her around so her back was flat against his chest and her arms were tightly locked over her breasts.

She tried to bite him. He wrenched harder still trying not to hurt her. She went dead still, rigid as steel.

"Don't raise a hand against me. And no more kicking. Or biting. It would do well for you to recall the facts in this. You did this to yourself. Your curiosity seems to get the better of you all too frequently."

She remained still. And trembling. She tossed back her head. "Or what?" she whispered vehemently in turn.

He lowered his mouth against her ear. "Or I'll make love to you, I promise."

He knew, from the feel of her, that she longed to tell him, he didn't begin to know what sorry was—not yet. She'd see to it that he did.

But she was quiet for a long while. Then words seemed to explode from her. "I'll best you yet, you simpering English smuggler."

"Ah, yes." He pushed her from him. When she was spun around quickly to face him again, he swept her a low bow. "You're perfect. You've done nothing wrong, have you? Well, my love, if it wasn't for the handbills that want you for smuggling that are posted all over the south of England, I would not be forced to take refuge across the sea."

"You exaggerate—"

"Exaggerate? I've no choice, do I? I've wed a common thief. A smuggler it seems. You are what I am."

"That's despicable. Leave it to a—"

"Simpering smuggler. Yes. Well, I do apologize for disturbing your peace. Your cousins will accompany you into London. We don't need to start our journey until sometime tomorrow. I'm interested in some of the books in my library, so if you find yourself pining for me, you'll know where to find me. You can have hours and hours to yourself to go cry over lost memories. Enjoy yourself."

With another exaggerated and courtly bow—certainly as well executed as any member of the English aristocracy—he left her.

But as he walked toward the house, his shoulders squared, a tempest of anguish seethed within him.

He was sorry. Sometimes it seemed all he could do was bait Amorica.

When he wanted so desperately to heal the breech between them, he didn't want to be crude with her. Or cruel. He kept finding himself wanting to put his arms around her. Soothe her. Shelter her from all harm. And yes, do whatever she bade him to do.

She would just as soon be soothed by a snake, he was certain.

He stood still, suddenly wincing. Bloody hell! Her pride, and her courage, and her beauty, and all the fire that spilled from her soul. Even before the strange day of their wedding, he had been touched by that fire.

But he'd been able to keep his distance then, avoiding the fact that most of his hostility stemmed from desire.

Even now, he wanted to go back. Take her into his arms. Tell her that things would work out. But no, because then she'd want her own way again.

He had to take care. He couldn't let her know just how much he understood all she felt. Couldn't let her know how he dreamed of her, wanted her. He stiffened and gave himself a mental shake. Fool. He accused himself. He would not weaken. And he wouldn't fall in love with her.

Chapter Fifteen

"It's untamed country. A vast land where there are untold freedoms and countless opportunities." Amorica heard Damian saying when she walked into the house at last. She didn't know where her cousins were, but she heard the murmur of male voices coming from the parlor. She moved toward the doorway, hesitating as she listened to the men speak. "It can be dangerous sailing. The English navy is looking for deserters. And the American Privateers are really pirates praying on the English merchant ships. Then as one moves farther west some of the Indians are civilized, others are not."

"If one stays in the cities all is fairly civilized," Feroz added.

"You do not have to accompany us. You know you can stay here as long as you want." Damian rubbed his hand on his chin while he studied his long-time friend.

"And who will keep you from trouble?" Feroz asked.

Amorica heard Damian chuckle. She looked silently through the doorway. Three men stood in the center of the room with a map spread out on the table before them.

"Around the major cities the Indians are all fairly civilized," Damian was pointing out.

"Some more so than some of the Englishmen we've encountered recently," Feroz agreed, grinning.

"If you're referring to some of my London acquaintances, remember they've served their purpose nicely," Damian said.

"I'd never imply anything," Feroz responded easily enough. Amorica leaned back against the wall, biting her lower lip. Feroz didn't seem to have a problem with traveling all the way to the states. She breathed in deeply, trying to calm her rattled nerves. Maybe it was easier for him. He was a man. He didn't have nearly the number of things to worry over as she did.

Damian spoke. Because of his words, Amorica imagined he pointed at the map again.

"Once you go over the Appalachians you're in the hunting grounds, and you can come across just about anyone there. I read that the plains beyond the mountains are filled with bison and deer and the grass grows higher than a man's thighs."

"You plan on traveling beyond the mountains?" Feroz asked.

Damian shrugged his shoulders. "I don't know what I'll do. Amorica and the baby have changed everything."

"You are sure about all of this? Will the ladies be safe?" Amorica smiled then she remembered the other lady Feroz spoke of was undoubtedly Sholeh. Feroz was so blunt. He was a servant who seemed to transcend the usual respect due his boss.

"Wives have always followed their husbands," Blair said, who until this moment had not spoken.

"Will there be a ship's surgeon? One that has some training other than mending the sails?" Feroz asked. A clink of glasses followed. Someone was pouring smuggled brandy. Amorica held her breath. She should not be listening to this.

"I will make sure I find a man willing to travel to the States, someone willing to start a new life there. The western settlement where we are going could most likely use a doctor."

Well, no one was going to be worried about her medical welfare, Amorica decided.

"It's still dangerous country," Feroz mused. "You know that, Damian—you were just reading to us from Colonel Lyman's letter to you." She heard a rustle of paper then Feroz's deep voice as he began to read.

"Two women were picking berries behind their cabin when a couple of Indian braves kidnapped them. Search parties were sent out, but no one could find them for weeks. A trapper finally found the women. They had been taken into the tribe as slaves." The paper floated down. "Allah!" Feroz exploded.

Amorica swallowed hard, leaning against the wall. She felt as if she were going to pass out. No, she never passed out. She never even pretended to do such things, But the pictures Feroz's reading had evoked in her mind were dreadful. She clamped her hand to her mouth. A wild panic seized her.

"And those women did not want to return," Damian said. Amorica heard the clink of glass. Obviously, everyone had seen mental images of the two unfortunate women. "Captured and abused to the extent that their shame would not allow them to return to civilized society," Damian commented.

"You will tread softly and not venture west."

"No one can go unseen," Damian said. "But I mean to discover the truth about the country west of the Appalachians. I refuse to be ruled by gossip and fear. I will not lose my wife."

"This is good. I did not think you would. But does she understand the danger?" Feroz asked.

Damian sighed. "Listen, it isn't a perfect life. Yes, it is what I want with all my heart. There is nothing for me in England. I will make sure she understands the dangers and what she must do to protect herself." Amorica closed her eyes, bracing herself against the wall. There was silence for a moment. Then she heard Feroz speaking softly. "Well, maybe you've got a point. I would like to be as excited about this move as you are. But unless Sholeh wants to go—I don't know." he murmured.

"You know you do not have to come."

Feroz smiled slightly. "It will mean a new life for me too. I think the move will be fruitful. I have nothing to lose."

"Amorica is too courageous to fear Indians," Damian said.

No. Terrified! She wanted to cry out. But she didn't.

Maybe Damian sensed she was at the doorway listening. Maybe he even realized she might be listening and he was enjoying a moment of feeling a little bit smug.

Amorica swirled into the room, her skirts rustling around her as she entered, her chin high. She smiled, although it felt like her smile was chiseled in stone. Damian had seen her skirt, she realized, from his vantage point behind the map. He had known she was listening.

She headed straight to the brandy decanter, determined to ignore Damian if he should give her a look that insinuated she was being in the least improper.

So much for manners and mores, they were overrated anyway. She poured out two fingers of brandy then stared at Damian. He didn't appear shocked. He seemed amused.

So that was to be her fate in life—to amuse him at every turn. She pushed the brandy aside. Her stomach churned. She didn't want it anymore.

"Well, what do you think, Amorica?" Damian asked her.

It was her opportunity. Her golden opportunity to tell Damian to play explorer all on his own. She would stay in England, thank you.

Damian moved around the table, away from the map, fingering his brandy glass. He strode to Amorica and added a new shot to his glass, his eyes probing hers. Then he poured more brandy into her glass.

"They're really fascinating, you know. We whites, especially here in England, have a habit of grouping Indians together. They are very civilized in their own way, perhaps more so than we are. For example, they would never let their own starve to death while they had plenty." She didn't know Damian's ploy. If he meant to frighten her even more, it was working. She wouldn't show him she was afraid. She smiled, determined that he would not see her fear.

"Tell me about the Natives," she said pleasantly.

"Amorica, maybe you shouldn't—" Christel had just entered the room. What had Christel overheard? Amorica wondered.

"Oh, no. I'm just dying to hear anything Damian can tell me," Amorica said.

"I will forego for the moment." He lifted his glass and swallowed the contents in one gulp.

He had dismissed her quite handily. Yet, she did want to hear.

Maybe not at this moment though.

"Christel, it's quite all right," Amorica said quickly. "This is going to be my life. I should know everything. Perhaps the more I know, the safer I will be."

"You'll begin a new life frightened and miserable?" Christel asked.

"Perhaps you should stay home. Until the baby is born, until Damian is established at the very least."

Here it was again—her opportunity handed over to her on a silver platter.

"But Amorica is never frightened, are you, my love?" Damian challenged her.

She spun around. His eyes sizzled out a challenge of his own. Maybe he was goading her into doing his will. One or the other, it did not matter.

He wasn't going to win.

She smiled broadly at her cousin and Feroz. "My, my. How on earth could I ever be frightened of a sweet, little Indian?"

"They don't tend toward sweetness," Damian said suddenly. She spun around again. His fingers were now tense around his glass, and his eyes blazed into hers. "Perhaps you should stay in England." Even Damian was saying it now. All she had to do was speak.

But she didn't speak, and the moment was swiftly gone. He lifted his glass to her. "But Lady Amorica Andrews is going to America. I say that the Lakota and the Crow and any other tribe—all—had best take care. Right, my love?"

"Of course," she replied, and lifted her glass in kind. "After all, I shall have the great Damian Andrews at my side. No Indian brave would dare to steal his wife, I'm sure." Her shoulders shook with the images her words evoked. "Tell me. What is the difference between a smuggler, a pirate, or an Indian?"

"Pirates—Indians. Let's hope you don't encounter either," Ravyn swirled into the room. Her eyes darkened with concern. Amorica could sense Christel was about to jump in, and there was only so much Damian could do to keep peace with her cousins.

"I know I will be just fine." Amorica said, with a vocal enthusiasm she didn't feel, her eyes rising to Damian's. He seemed to want her to back out now, to cause some rift between them.

He sighed suddenly, reaching out for her. She remembered the last time he had touched her, and an inferno of simmering heat rushed through her. He merely slipped an arm through hers and led her back to the map.

"Let me show you where you'll be living when we get to America." She nodded, staring at the map, swallowing the rising fear. It was going to be a long, hard trip.

She looked up. Damian stared at her again. Unable to meet his gaze, she looked quickly back to the table.

"It should be a fascinating journey," she said. "Absolutely intriguing." Her head pounded—as long as she didn't get seasick—as long as this unrelenting nausea did not overcome every waking hour. She inhaled deeply and closed her eyes for a moment. She was always tired.

Everyone in the room looked at her now. She could feel their eyes upon her. Christel was worried. Ravyn was growing hostile. The air was thick with tension.

What was Damian thinking? Had he decided that he had been trapped into this sorry state and that she really wasn't worth the effort anymore?

He might have decided she simply wasn't enjoyable enough material, as far as a wife went.

To her astonishment, she felt a prickling of moisture at the corner of her eyes. It was the baby, she decided. She had never ever cried so much.

She could not forgive her husband—not so much for smuggling, but for being so damned certain he did nothing wrong. She hated him at times.

Most men went out of their way to be charming to her, while Damian never gave her the courtesy of believing in the smallest feminine lie. She wanted to best him. She wanted to prove to him English ladies had always been made of sterner stuff. She wanted to prove to him she wasn't afraid, that she could do anything he wanted her to do and do it better than he thought.

And she was intrigued. By his eyes, dark brown one minute, nearly black the next —the sadness that was always there, buried beneath the façade he painted for the rest of the world. She was fascinated by the hard muscled grace of his body. She was determined to deny him and equally determined he never lose his desire to have her.

She had married him, and she was going to have his baby. The baby would be born in America. The babe would not be English. Her hands shook. What if something went wrong?

Two women had been kidnapped and made to do horrific things to stay alive. Things so bad they were too ashamed to return to their own people.

"My love?" Damian murmured, watching her, his brows furrowed together.

She was going to travel across the Atlantic. "I've never really ventured very far from home," she said. "Well, let's see. I have gone to London. And then I found myself spirited to this remote location and denied the company of my family." She looked up, her chin high. "This will be quite different—fascinating. At least I won't be left alone for weeks."

He smiled, another of his taunting, amused smiles. Yet she thought there was a glitter of admiration in his dark brooding eyes. "Not so very much. You still won't see your family."

"Will you write my father? Can I see him before we leave?"

"Of course. I would never want you to be too distressed. I'm not evil or mean spirited. I would not deny you your family."

"I just don't understand what you want from me," she murmured. She spun around suddenly, feeling as if she would faint at a moment's notice.

She wasn't about to let him know she was feeling ill again. He might mistake it for cowardice. She was not afraid, she decided. "Please excuse me..."

She didn't care if they excused her or not. She needed to escape, to run forever. There was nowhere to run. In a few months they would arrive in America.

~ * ~

It was early spring.

Damian didn't return to the newly purchased townhouse in Baltimore, Maryland, until it had grown very late. Amorica had thanked Feroz for seeing to her comfort as well as bringing her pamphlets on the territory where they were going.

He hoped she would weather this journey as well as she had weathered the cross-Atlantic sail. She seemed to adapt well to everything.

The expression on Amorica's face when they'd sailed into the harbor had been worth remembering. Because of the picture he had painted, she must have imagined horrific sights. He regretted what he'd said to her, and yet in the last moments, he'd had second thoughts about her traveling in her condition.

She had been determined to show him she wasn't afraid. When they'd been in the parlor in England and talking about the Indians, he'd seen her spine stiffen and her chin go up a notch.

For a while, he walked along the river, glad of his decision to stay in Baltimore until she adjusted to this phase of their trip. He would find a doctor to bring with them or a midwife. She needed the security of a good midwife and the knowledge she wouldn't be going into labor in the middle of some God-forsaken trail. The rivers ran strong and pure in this new land, surrounded by endless forests and tall mountains.

It was beautiful here. The air was clean and cool. The sun set upon the forests that were dark and rich with plants. It was a rougher place than England and even the wild untamed Highlands.

This was a place of freedom and opportunity. He'd left Aric behind in England to tie up all the loose ends. Eventually, he hoped, Aric would join him here Ryder would arrive tomorrow.

He paused, listening to the run of the river at his side and looking back at the small sprawling town. A farmer waved to him, and he waved in return. The homes surrounding the town were spaced far apart, and yet everyone seemed to be aware of the safety of the others.

Damian had been warned by the governor of the town that one of the Indian tribes was showing hostility to the settlers. Oh, they were miles from town and as long as he stayed within the perimeter of the township, he would be safe.

Amorica would be safe. She'd proven herself time and time again on the way over. He sighed, ready to kick himself. In so many things she was a dutiful wife, not because she gave a damn about being dutiful to him, but because she was determined to prove she could do anything. She was an extraordinary woman. Hell, the Nor'easter they'd sailed into hadn't sent her screaming, it had intrigued her, as well as the whales they'd seen and the dolphins that had followed the ship.

Distractedly, he ran his fingers through his hair. In her mind, she had faced a smuggler. Nothing else compared to that ordeal. Nothing else was quite so horrific.

She slept with him every night because she was his wife. She never protested his touch. Night after night, he felt the passion simmering there; felt she could be magnificent, that he had only to coax her surrender to her passion. Yet she held herself away from him, distancing herself from the love they both could share.

And that was it, of course, in a nutshell. Amorica was not about to surrender.

Yet he had come so close. There had been a languorous look in her crystal-green eyes. She had leaned against him so softly; she had sighed and moved so sweetly. The slightest smile had curved her lips, and even the promise that she might return the least of his desire had sent a near-maddened longing to his senses. He must have been insane. He'd mentioned Ryder and the next ship or shipment to come into port. He'd never told her what his real purpose was. He had never thought he could trust her.

The lights in town were burning lower. The air was beautiful, but growing colder. He stared back at the town. All was well. A horse whinnied from somewhere. The scene was peaceful.

Somewhere out there was a land he wanted to explore, and he wanted Amorica by his side.

Tomorrow Ryder McClaren would arrive. It would be a very long day. He didn't have any idea how Amorica would greet Ryder.

Damian set his jaw, his teeth grating. He had obligations. He'd be expected to entertain Ryder as well as the refugees, finding them lodging and work. Amorica would have to swallow hard and accept it. But what if she didn't? He determined that he'd best be prepared for the worst.

Feroz, he thought, would be doing the cooking for their arrival.

Sholeh had chosen to remain in England. He started back, along the water, through the myriad of houses, and finally to his own.

When Damian slipped inside, he found that Amorica had blown out the candles on the bedside table, making it difficult for him to move about in the darkness. He would manage.

He crawled into their feather bed, wondering for a wild second if she would be there. Yes, of course, she would. Though she didn't know it, Feroz always kept vigil, and if she had thought to go somewhere, Damian would have known it long ago.

As his eyes adjusted to the total darkness, he realized she was bundled from throat to toe in a flannel nightgown. She was as far to her side of the bed as she could manage and her back was to him. She was awake, he was certain. She was lying there too tensely to be asleep.

He leaned close to her. But before he could say a word, she whispered fiercely, "Touch me, and I'll scream until every man in Baltimore is awake."

"My love, I am far too weary to touch you tonight. You should know that I don't give a damn if you scream until you're hoarse. In fact, princess, I have a word of warning for you. Be courteous tomorrow. This meeting is important to me—to us—I hope. Am I understood?"

"I am always courteous."

"Perhaps in your mind," he sighed. "But don't worry about your precious solitude this evening. My pillow offers far more comfort and warmth than you do. But take care tomorrow." He warned her.

He turned on his own side. He didn't touch her. The inch between them lay like a great chasm.

~ * ~

Ryder appeared the next day with a small group of refugees, some who would now be moving on in wagons and some who would stay in Baltimore.

They arrived early and were greeted by Feroz. Damian waited in the parlor for Amorica.

Earlier that morning, Damian had slipped from bed while it was still dark to dress, and he had mounted his horse to ride out to the bay to meet with Ryder when he disembarked from the ship.

He wondered just how much he could tell Amorica. Damian chanced a glance at Ryder and realized Ryder did not trust Amorica with the knowledge of their deeds. Yet he knew Ryder would leave it up to him because he did trust him.

He would have to tell her sometime. She was his wife. He could not keep the secret forever.

The refugees had houses to go to before they all met in the afternoon to formulate plans. He had been pleasantly surprised when Aric Lakeland stepped down the gangplank along with Ryder.

He didn't look forward to this evening. Indeed, he shuddered at the thought and how Amorica might retaliate. He didn't doubt she would be subtle and above reproach, but the underlying feelings would still be there.

She would make sure he understood her adamant disapproval.

He hadn't gone near her himself all through the day, but he had asked Feroz to see to her whereabouts now and then, and he knew she had spent the day with their new housekeeper, Elizabeth. Presumably, she would show up at the dinner table. He thought that he had made his threat strong enough for that.

When he returned home to shave and change for the evening, she was nowhere in sight. She had been there recently, for the hip tub had been brought in for her use and the water in it was still tepid.

Whatever she intended, she intended to do it clean, he thought wryly.

He hadn't meant to bathe, but the water was there, and so he made use of it, shivering when he rose. It wasn't quite as warm as he had thought and the night was growing chill. He dressed and shaved quickly before he went to find Amorica. Feroz stopped him, presenting him the full menu for the evening. They would begin with a wild turkey soup. There would be a mixed vegetable platter composed of yams and fresh greens. He'd arranged for the best deer steaks. And Elizabeth had picked wild mushrooms.

"Very nice, Feroz."

"And we will be eating on china your wife purchased today in town, sir," Feroz said. "I think you will be satisfied."

"I'm sure I will. She helped you today?"

"Oh, yes, sir. This was all her idea. She and Elizabeth worked all day to make this a grand night."

"You don't say," he said wryly, cocking one eyebrow in speculation.

He wasn't sure what to think.

When he walked past Feroz, he nearly tripped over several small boxes that Amorica must have purchased today. He swore beneath his breath, then realized she was spending his money quite nicely.

He strode into the parlor. Ryder was sitting in a chair, lazily tipping a brandy glass. Aric stood by the window looking out at the bay and the ships rising and falling with the incoming waves. Amorica stood by the fireplace. There was no one more striking or beautiful than his wife.

Amorica was silent, perhaps she didn't know what to say to the two men she loathed almost as much as she despised him.

Amorica had outdone herself by changing into the most elegant wear.

He wondered if she had shopped for herself this afternoon too. How much had she spent? He admonished himself. He didn't care what she spent. She was in a gown of rich green taffeta with velvet and black lace trim. The gown had a slightly high collar at her nape, but the handsome edge work was cut low across the bosom. It hugged her upper body, and the skirt fell in elegant folds down to the ground partially concealing her pregnancy.

Against the rich coloring of the gown, her hair had never appeared more midnight black, nor her eyes so endlessly green.

She had dressed for the occasion, he thought uneasily. Everything she had done for tonight was meant to impress.

He strode across the room, acknowledging Ryder and Aric when he turned and nodded. He had expected a few of the refugees. He had wanted to talk with Henri, who was said to be one of the finest philosophers of his time. But there were no others here.

Amorica's eyes rose to his. She studied him for a moment, her expression grave, and he wondered what went on within her head. He tried to convey his own warning to her through his eyes.

Coolly, she looked away.

He came beside her, slipping an arm through hers. "Evening, Ryder, Aric."

"There are things you should know," Ryder said, his gaze transfixed on Amorica, his voice cold.

Beside him, Amorica trembled. She turned to him. "I know what you do."

"I'm a smuggler." He said calmly.

"Henri visited earlier. When you weren't here, I spoke to him. He told me everything. He was the man who had to return to Germany when I interfered."

"Hopefully, you showed him your sweeter side," Damian said, a slight intonation to his voice.

She blushed. "I have not changed my opinions about you or smugglers. But at least I have given my own welfare to a nobler cause than French brandy," she shot back.

Silence fell around the room. She filled her glass with a fine

Bordeaux. Since the baby, the wine made her ill. She needed it tonight, but she could do no more than sip at it.

"Yes," Ryder said harshly."

Chapter Sixteen

Amorica wasn't in their room. Fear knifed into Damian's heart. He tried to assure himself nothing could have happened to her. This was a city. Yet there were sailors and ruffians of all sorts. A waterfront harbored all sorts of criminals.

Walking alone at night was not recommended. He spun around, nearly crashing into Feroz. "She is in the garden. She should be safe enough if she doesn't venture beyond the hedges. I'm afraid for her though. She seems so sad."

"I'll bring her inside, Feroz. Thank you."

Feroz nodded and disappeared into the townhouse. Worry for her safety spurred him. He stomped through the garden and beyond, his eyes focused on her. She had ventured farther than was prudent, walking along the river bank past the boundary of their home. She heard him coming and whirled to meet him. The expression on his face must have been as wild and untamed as his temper because she turned to run, when there was nowhere to run. She had barely taken a step before he was beside her, swinging her around. He did not want the anger, nor did he want her wandering into danger. She did not seem to understand this was not a rose garden in London.

"What are you doing?" she cried out.

His hands on her shoulders, "What the hell do you think you're doing?"

"Nothing that should cause you to terrify me, Damian." To no avail, she pushed at his hands.

"You cannot wander anywhere alone. While the town may seem

civilized, it is not. I repeat. What the hell are you doing?"

"Looking at the gardens. I needed fresh air."

"So, you just walked away from the house and along the river? Do you know how far you have gone?"

"All right, I needed to be away from you and your friends. I needed to distance myself from the information I just now received."

"And you didn't stop to think that I might worry? That some drunken sailor would take advantage?"

"I—" She faltered for a moment only, looking around as if there might indeed be some threatening person in the vicinity, then straightened her shoulders. "I didn't think any harm would come."

"Amorica, Bloody eyes, madam, you will have to learn the difference between safe and dangerous, prudent and wildly ridiculous. You cannot make a habit of wandering alone."

"I just decided I needed to take a walk."

"A walk? In the dead of night? Along a river bank! This is not England."

"I needed to be alone—"

"Like hell. You were hoping I wouldn't find you. That I'd give up and go to sleep before you came tiptoeing back."

"I will never bow down to your whims or fear your threats. Nor will I be on my best behavior because you command it." Her chin high, her words scornful, she met his gaze with her own. Maybe the wine she had drunk was giving her an added boost of bravado.

"You'd best be—tonight. Just because we are in America does not make us safe from the spies who seek to find the men we have transported here. They might have followed us here. Your life as well as mine could be forfeited if you give us away."

She was breathing hard, both defiant and uneasy. He wished that wanting her, aching for her, desiring her so desperately would not plague him so when he longed to shake sense into her. He was so afraid for her.

She could not act this way when they traveled deeper into the countryside.

She would have to heed his warnings.

He couldn't keep his hands off her, despite his most stalwart efforts.

He shot out, holding her hands, pulling her toward him. It was a mistake.

He could feel the trembling in her now. Her eyes were luminous with her anger. Her hair tumbled about her shoulders and fell down her back in wild disarray. Her scent was sweet against the rich earthy smell of the river and the breeze. Dear, God, how he wanted her, ached for her.

"Let go of me, Damian." She jerked free from him and started to walk away. She stumbled and caught her balance. Was it a rock in her path? Or the wine she had drunk?

"Get back here." He pulled her back into his arms. Her eyes went wide. Maybe she wasn't frightened.

"Let go of me," she insisted.

He smiled crookedly. He wasn't quite sure what seized hold of him, but he knew he would never let her go. Maybe it was her defiance, her passion, maybe it was even the depths of the hatred she seemed to bear him. But it felt as if an inferno had suddenly found roots within him, streaks of the blaze ripping throughout him. Tonight? He wouldn't let her out of his sight.

"You're not afraid of me, remember?"

"Damian—"

He lifted her, carrying her in his arms, her own arms wrapping around him, despite her outraged shrieks of protests. He started back to the townhouse, kicking the door open when he reached it. He didn't want to hurt her. Lord, but all he wanted was for her to understand that he wasn't the man who killed her mother. All he wanted to do was make love to her until the sun rose.

She pounded fiercely against his back. "Put me down. Your friends might still be awake. What would they say, what would they think?"

"One, I don't give a damn. Two, any friends of mine would probably applaud my efforts. You are my wife."

She thudded his back again. "Don't," he warned.

"Damn you. Put me down." She whispered fiercely.

"Soon enough, my love."

She fell silent, braced against him as he strode his way to their bedroom. In seconds, he had set her down on the bed. He tried to walk away from her. He found he could not. He spun around. She lay in the green gown, her face flushed, her eyes flashing, her hair cascading magnificently around her. Her breasts were heaving over the velvet bodice of the gown. She sat up then stood quickly, her hands clenched into fists at her sides. "I won't give you whatever it is you want. I can't. I don't want to. You can make love to me, but the act won't change how I feel." She rose from the bed and started to walk past him.

"I have really tried—" he began, reaching for her.

She spun to meet his gaze. "And tonight, I have done everything you asked of me. I have tried—"

He interrupted her with a loud snort. "Tonight you have defied all that is prudent and reasonable, putting yourself and our unborn child in jeopardy."

She stood still, stiffening. Her eyes were green fire. "Since it appears you are determined to sleep here tonight, I shall go to one of the guest rooms."

"Oh, and what if you encounter other smugglers? Ryder, Aric, they both stay here. They are both staying in guest rooms."

"There are more than enough rooms. I will sleep on the sofa if I cannot find one that is unoccupied."

"I see." His anger grew unabated. He had little to no control yet he seized the opportunity to try and calm his escalating emotions.

"Perhaps, I would even prefer a drunken sailor tonight," she said furiously.

He caught hold of her wrist, turning her around until the backs of her knees were against the bed. "You sure as hell aren't going anywhere tonight." Bloody hell, but he didn't want to fight her tonight. He wanted her warm and passionate in his arms.

She fell back her arms spread wide on the bed, watching him, catching her breath. She wasn't about to stay down. Her courage was something he'd always admired, but at times it bordered on being foolhardy. She would fight to the death to protect what or whom she loved. He wanted her to love him.

He could not force her love but he could have her tonight.

She sprang up easily again, determined on walking from the room.

She was no fool. He could see her weighing her options. Since the opportunity to best him was not going to come her way, she was seeking her ever-majestic lady-of-the-manor dignity to use against him. She inhaled, as if with a great deal of patience. "I will not stay here and listen—"

"Sit down, Amorica," he repeated, stripping his shirt over his head before ridding himself of the rest of his clothing.

"I'm far too tired to hunt you down again tonight. I do not want to chase after you just to ensure your safety when we could both be comfortable in bed." She swallowed hard, clenching her fists. He knew she was fighting to think of some way around him. He was far stronger.

She tossed back her hair, smoothing it down. Her words were polite enough, but he heard the grate of her teeth that preceded them. "Perhaps this thing can be discussed some other day."

"It will be discussed right now. I warned you to be courteous, Amorica. I warned you."

"And I did nothing wrong." She stood again, her chin up, her hands folded before her.

He hated that stance. It was so damned superior.

"You've had a fair amount of brandy with your smuggling cronies—"

"Oh, that is rich, Amorica. From the delicate lady who was downing wine like water? No, Amorica. That won't work. I've had some brandy, but I'd need a hell of a lot more to forget your lack of concern for the child you carry as well as your own person." He kicked off his boots and pulled off his buckskin breeches.

She seemed to pale somewhat. She was accustomed to the sight of him naked. Tonight it seemed to disturb her.

She pressed a hand dramatically against her temples. "I have a tremendous headache and you're making it worse. I'm leaving," she said flatly. "You'll just have to pretend you're capable of being a gentleman. I mean it, Damian. It was a wretched night."

"Amorica, we're starting a new life. You have to find a way to forgive or you will never find true happiness."

Maybe she hadn't. For a second, she was silent. "I'm not terribly worried about my happiness, Damian, or yours." And that, he realized, was most likely the absolute truth.

"Amorica—"

He moved toward her, at that moment wanting to comfort her no matter how angry he was. But she scooted away quickly. She was still too upset to accept anything from him. She jerked away from his outstretched hand. "Don't."

Unable to stop himself, he reached out with such lack of control that his hold upon her sleeve tore the gown. She glanced down where the sleeve and bodice gaped from her body. "How dare you..."

He'd never meant to hurt her, or to rip her gown. The damage was done. She wasn't going anywhere, he determined fiercely. Eyes focused on hers, he caught the fabric once again and ripped harder. She gasped as the whole of the garment began to fall from her, exposing her undergarments and her swollen belly.

She inhaled a swift deep breath. Then gasped out, her fists slamming against his chest as she defied every word, every command. He picked her up and set her down upon the bed. "Despicable man," she cried out. "I would not give myself to you and so now you command me to do so."

"I do not command anything, Amorica. Say no and I'll walk from this room. It will be yours for the night. But do it now, Amorica. Tell me now or hold your peace. Buck naked, my love, you might decide to stay in the room. If you say no, I will leave. But I will not have my wife wandering around the gardens or Baltimore alone at night." He turned her onto her stomach, trying to loosen her ties. The chemise resisted him and he ripped it impatiently, only to be greeted with another flurry of fists.

"Hold still, Amorica or I might not hold myself responsible for anything that might happen between us."

She stiffened, going dead still for a second. He used the opportunity to untie the rest of her undergarments. When she choked and began swearing again, fighting to unseat him from his perch atop her, she afforded him the chance to strip off the last of her garments. She lay face down and bare, her breath heaving. Her back was sleek, her hips and rump rose smooth, delectable—and tempting.

"Smuggling bas—" she began.

"One more word, my love, and—"

"And," she cried in desperate challenge.

He tensed, swallowing hard, willing himself to walk away. He didn't want the battles. What could he do when it seemed that something from the past always arose to come between them? Tonight it was the reminder of his past. What would it be tomorrow? Would he ever be able to build a life with her?

Amorica was trembling. Never ready to surrender, never ready to call a truce. He bit into his lower lip and pressed a gentle kiss against the small of her back, intending to walk away from her.

He might just as well have burned her with a branding iron. She shrieked out, bucking against him and turning beneath him. Tears stung her eyes. Her fists landed against his chest. Very suddenly she went still.

He became aware he was straddled over her now with his sex laid low against her swollen stomach and it was aroused and hard against her softness.

Her eyes narrowed on his. She moistened suddenly dry lips. "I hate you, Damian. I hate you for what your kind did to my mother and I hate you for all the French brandy you smuggled into England just for money, for your greed."

"Listen to yourself, Amorica. You hate me for things someone else did. You have no real knowledge of what I have done. Aric and Ryder touched on just a small part of it. Would you have it in your heart to give us a chance?"

Tears stung her eyes. "Can't you understand?"

"Lord, but I have tried. I've tried to meet you half-way, but

Amorica, with you there is no middle ground and the deeds cannot be taken back because you will it."

"Get—"

"Amorica, you don't hate me—"

"Trust me, I do."

He shook his head again vehemently. "I don't really believe that. And I want you, Amorica. I want to touch the spark of magic that is always there, just below the surface. So, let us pretend that you don't hate me tonight. Lie still beside me. You claim you are such an excellent wife. Be one for me." Yet he didn't want her to lie still. He wanted her passion and her wild response to his touch. He wanted all she could give him, all he imagined she possessed.

"Damian," she rallied. "I weathered the trip across the Atlantic. I slept with you in your bed. I carry your child."

"You are here, yes, but your spirit has always been somewhere else.

Amorica, this is your life now—accept it, embrace it—and me. The fire is there, I can feel it. I can nearly touch it. But you deny all of it."

"I don't know what you're talking about."

He pulled her up by the shoulders, searching out her eyes. "Liar, you know. You fight me. You fight yourself. You could taste the sweetness of fulfillment, but you deny yourself the chance. It's within you, I know it.

You know it. You possess a rare passion."

Her eyes were liquid with emotion. "Perhaps I do fight you." She whispered vehemently.

"I know something sweet and rare is locked within you."

"But it will never be yours to possess."

He eased his weight back, holding her still, shaking his head slowly.

"No, Amorica, it's not me. Maybe I'm not what you dreamed of and imagined, but I am your husband. And I swear to you, I've sought to give you all that I am. I know I've touched your passion. You hold back because you have never learned to forgive and heaven help us it seems you cannot forget. But I would not wage war with you any longer, at least not in bed. No more."

"Don't—" she began.

"Amorica, give me a chance, give us both a chance—for our child."

"Damian—" she began anew. But he was done arguing. His lips touched hers. For a moment, he felt her tension, tasted the salt of her tears.

But it did not feel like resistance. She pressed against him as if she wanted all of him. Her nails bit into the flesh of his shoulders, pulling him closer.

"A chance, Amorica," he whispered, lifting his lips just a breath from hers. His voice was low, rich, deep, demanding, even pleading.

She inhaled on a ragged little sound.

He touched her lips once again. Tasted them, pressed past them, felt the desire in him flame wildly as he took in the sweet warmth of her. He wanted her so badly. She was in his arms, and he could have her. They'd waged this battle before. All he had to do was take her. Ease his hunger.

He could not. He must have her surrender, and her compliance, her passion and her courage.

He lifted his lips from hers. Thought himself insane. Her crystal-green eyes were on him. Her lips were damp from his touch, still so tempting.

He smiled ruefully. "Your choice, Amorica."

"Damian?" she whispered, amazed.

"I will not force the issue."

He rolled beside her. She quickly turned her back on him. He ran a finger seductively down the length of her spine—up again, down again.

What was the matter with him? What if this didn't work? It had to work.

The most seductive touch he could manage, down the bareness of her back, caressing the very base of her spine, softly, gently, over the rise of her hip then the fullness of her buttocks. He drew circles with his fingertips, pressed his lips to her back, followed the touch of his fingertip down her back. Up again.

Bloody hell, he thought to himself.

She swung back around.

"You said—" she began to accuse him, her eyes wild.

"I said your choice."

"It's not my choice when you touch me."

"Amorica, tell me to stop. Say the words."

His fingers threaded into her hair. His lips silenced any possible words of protest.

She still tried to keep up the pretense, shaking her head slightly when his mouth rose above hers. "Amorica, do you know what you're doing to me?' he groaned softly.

Despite herself, she smiled. But she was ever determined. "You said—" she began again stubbornly.

"Your choice," he finished on a breath.

He couldn't really leave it that way, not as things stood. She still needed some persuasion.

He swept an arm around her, bringing her fully against him. The length of his body shuddered. He found her lips. Caught them, held them.

Stroked the rim of them with his tongue, parried between them. She would fight him now. She would protest again and tell him, no.

To his amazement, he heard a soft moan rumbling in her throat. Her hands pressed upon his shoulders, pulling him closer, not pushing him away. Her fingertips dug into his flesh, holding him.

He took her tightly into his arms, afraid to let her go. He kissed her lips, stroking her back softly, feeling the sensual curves and planes. He broke from her lips to touch them again, his tongue tracing the shape of them before slipping deeply into her mouth. He caressed the silky skin of her back, sweeping the length, creating sensual swirls once more at the base of her spine with his fingertips, stroking the curve of her hip, the rise of her buttocks.

There was a difference tonight. She hadn't returned his hunger as yet, but the pulse was there, as was the heat. The promise was in his arms.

Determined to discover it, he trailed his kiss to her earlobe, along her throat. He lifted the mass of her hair and kissed the nape of her neck, then shuddered, sighing deeply, burying his face within the ebony cloud of her hair, enjoying the scent and silken feel of it. He moved her about, shifting the fall of her hair once again and pressing a kiss against her upper spine.

He bathed her shoulders with his caress then moved lower against her spine, his fingers stroking fire while his lips delivered their liquid heat, down to the very small of her back, over the rise of her hip. He paused, sensations sweeping through him in a staggering manner from the taste and feel of her, as she suddenly sighed and shuddered.

He held her in his arms once again. Her eyes met his, very wide, soft, dazed.

Perhaps she hadn't really expected this—to feel the burning inside, the need like raw hunger. "Damian, please," she mouthed.

"Please what?" he asked, both tender and determined. "Tonight, my love, we are bridging the gap between us."

"It's the wine," she whispered. "You're taking advantage of my confusion."

"Damn right." He laughed huskily. "I take every advantage I can get.

And it isn't the wine so much, because I've noted that you barely touch the stuff since you've been carrying our child."

"I tell you—"

He pressed his case, capturing her mouth, and feeling the duel of her tongue with his. Hunger seared through him. His hand moved fervently over her breast, discovering the peak pebble hard. He delivered his kiss there, teasing the nub, savoring the sweetness of it, suckling upon the fullness of it. She shifted beneath him, gloriously giving back the passion she received. Even as she did so, longing gripped his loins tightly, a savage heat swept through him and he moved against her, his hands never still. There was a greater demand to his touch now, an urgency that filled his body.

She could always arouse him. But tonight, she was a breath of magic.

Perhaps hatred was close to love, perhaps the passion of anger danced narrowly close to that of desire. Maybe they had just been building to this.

She was liquid and supple in his arms. He stroked her breast. She rose against him, and he whispered soft words to her. "Feel the touch, my love.

Here, and here...feel it become a heat that begins a swirl inside of you, deeper and deeper, here." He stroked her upper thigh, set his palm over the rise of her ebony triangle. Here," he whispered, then slipped a finger deep inside of her. "And here..."

She gasped and trembled against his touch, and shifted as if she would deny it. If the fires were not sizzling through her then, they were running rampant within his body. Still, he took his time. She was stretched out on her back. Her flesh was damp with an exotic sheen, touched by the gold lamplight. Her hair was a tangle. Her limbs were long and beautiful and her breasts were rising and falling in a rush. Her eyes were soft—glazed, as if he had taken her quite by surprise. Perhaps he had. Perhaps it had been building as he had said, and tonight he had finally begun to tear down the walls between them.

An anguish tore through him. He wanted her. He wanted more tonight than he had been willing to settle for before. He wanted those haunting green eyes to fill with the passion he knew lurked behind the shadow of her lashes. He wanted to feel the bowstring quivering of her slender form, the ardent rhythm of her hips.

He rose above her and gently touched her lips with the breath of his own. He drew a pattern between the valley of her breasts with his finger.

He followed it with his tongue. He lowered himself slowly against her.

Wherever he caressed her, he kissed her. Lower and lower until he lay between her legs—touching her, parting her, caressing her, kissing her.

A soft fervent cry escaped from her. Her fingers tugged upon his hair.

He caught her hands and held them firmly within his own. She moaned softly. Her head began to toss, her body to writhe.

If it was the wine, then bless that wondrous fruit of the vine. Magic surrounded them. Beyond their bedroom, the night breeze stirred, making their flesh seem even more searing. In the endless sky, the stars rode the heavens. They seemed to dance within the room. They rained down upon him in bursts of radiant light. She was beautiful, vibrant with her passion.

He smiled wickedly. All the torments of hell could take hold of him now and he would endure them gladly. He found the bud of her greatest sensuality and played mercilessly upon it, laving, teasing, and demanding with caress of his lips and tongue. She began to shudder, and the golden gleam of light upon her began to shimmer with the growing undulation of her hips.

"Damian, please," she cried out again. "I can take no more." And she could not. What had happened tonight, she wondered. Why couldn't she fight this fire?

She couldn't think, the sensations were so strong. And it was wonderful, erotic and sending her into such sweet spirals of sensation that she couldn't fight. He was whispering things to her and in her mind, she was seeing things of startling beauty. A rosebud, so dark and rich and ivory, flowering beneath a radiant heat, stretching, growing, parting to burst into an open beauty. Even as she saw the image of the rose, she was aware of the very graphic reality around her, the large bed, herself, the glow of light that touched them, the bed beneath them. Damian.

The power of his hands, his fingers locked around hers, the taut muscled feel of his body, the weight of him between her legs, and the way he touched her. The things he did. The tension grew inside her, hot, wonderful, painful, and sweet. It grew until it was anguish, until she was arching wildly against him, and until sounds filled the night, soft, anxious, breathless. Sounds she was making herself.

Then something seemed to burst. Sweet, so achingly sweet. It fractured with wonder over her, with light then with dark—with stars across a velvet sky. Like a million shots firing into the night. It was the sweetest rapture within her. It was so, so good. She floated with it. Saw the light, saw the darkness.

Then he was atop her. His eyes dark and wicked in the gleam of light, his naked body slick, hard, and muscled and fascinating her still. She cried out softly, closing her eyes, trying to turn away from him. He wouldn't have it. His body slid into hers. "Oh, no," she whispered.

"Oh, yes," he corrected.

Her fingers fell upon his shoulders. She shifted; amazed he could feel so wonderful within her so swiftly.

Tonight the spiral began again, the heat deep inside. Curling, deepening. It could not come again. The velvet black, the exploding of light, the molten stars bursting warmly throughout her body, so sweet, so delicious, so wonderful.

The spiraling and the hunger that led to it were so easily coming alive again. She was achingly aware of him, as if all sensation of her flesh had become heightened. She felt his hair-roughened legs and chest, the hardness of his arm muscles, the rock of his hips, and him inside of her—the fullness of the movement, the thrust...

She gasped. The spiraling was rising again. She arched to meet him.

She dared open her eyes. His blazed into hers, and she bit her lip, her lashes falling. His face remained so taut, his length so vital yet rigidly hard. He moved, demandingly. His arms held his body above hers. He thrust into her and his eyes locked with hers. He moved faster and faster, his face fraught with tension. She cried out, unable to deny the quickening within her. Her hands fell upon his shoulders. Her fingers raked across them. She was pulling up to him, meeting his thrust with a rhythmic arch of her own. Her lips fell upon his shoulders. She covered them with ardent kisses. Her fingers played upon his back, massaging, digging, clinging.

She felt him thrust incredibly hard against her just as the sensations seemed to split and explode within her in a wild frenzy of fire and hunger.

She gasped, clinging to him, as she felt the force of the climax burst upon her. Darkness fell. Light burst. Liquid stars seemed to rain down upon her once more. For a moment, she was so encapsulated in shimmering ecstasy she did not realize he remained above her, the heat spilling from his body was filling her own.

He fell to her side, slick with sweat, breathing hard.

She shuddered, turning to her side as sudden tears warmed her eyes.

Dear God, she'd never imagined such a piece of heaven.

But yes, she had. She had known Damian could bring her to it, and she had been fighting it fiercely. She felt the desperate need to deny Damian and the emotions she'd just surrendered to him. She was so very afraid she might be falling in love him.

She had married Damian.

She could lie to herself and to Damian. She could tell herself that he was not desirable, that she did not care for him. Yet she could not deny what had just happened between them.

He had seized hold of her, turning her from all she held dear, taken her from the life she knew and the one she'd planned for herself.

He had given her something more.

Admitting she cared for him went against all she'd fought. They were enemies who had clashed head-on, but they were enemies too because they were both strong, determined, willful.

He had never really given her a choice but she'd accepted marriage.

He was beautiful, whipcord strong and lean in his physique, rugged and handsome in his face. Indeed, he held the key. He had touched her heart and found all that he had demanded of her.

He stroked her arm gently. "Madam, I take it back," he murmured. "You are an excellent wife."

Was he gloating? She had certainly given him all he wanted, whether willingly or not. She had always wanted to surrender everything she was to him. But she had not known how to give up her own demons. Every word he had spoken had been true. She had teetered on the precipice night after night, tasting the wonder, refusing to let it come to her.

Yet tonight it had been undeniable. It had taken her in a torrent.

"Excellent..."

"It was the wine," she whispered.

"I see," he murmured.

She started to stiffen, unsure if he mocked her or not. But then something miraculous happened. She felt something, not wild and exciting...

Different. She inhaled sharply.

Deep, deep inside of her the baby was moving. It was just a flutter. So curious. So light. Then it came again.

She gasped.

"What is it?" He was over her instantly.

She smiled up at him. "The baby. It moved."

"Is it all right? Did I hurt—"

"It's fine. It's so strange."

His palm moved over abdomen. "I can't feel it," he said.

She smiled at him again. The darkness cast shadows over them both.

"No, you can't feel him, not yet. It's just inside. I think it takes time to feel the movement on the outside. But—oh, there again. He's kicking."

"He's what?" Damian asked with an eagerness that surprised her. His palm still lay gently against her flesh.

"He's alive and real—so very real."

His hand went rigid. He pulled her back against him. "Go to sleep. You need your rest."

His body encompassed hers. The comfort was there. But suddenly something was lacking. She felt an emptiness inside her. And she wondered if he thought of another child.

A child lost.

She knew he blamed himself.

Chapter Seventeen

Sunlight jerked her awake. She pulled a cover over her head. "Rise and shine, my love. It's a beautiful day and should not be wasted in bed." Amorica's dream, all the peace-filled images crashed to a halt. She had been sheltered the night before in a cocoon of warmth and safety.

She'd surrendered more of herself than she should have, and now in the aftermath she was afraid of what he might think.

She had thought excuses would explain away her actions, the wine, and the anger —None of those things played an important part in what she'd done, all she'd felt. Now, all she wanted was to hide beneath the mountain of covers and never look at Damian Andrews again. She wanted to forget her heart.

"Please—leave me alone. I'm tired."

"Amorica." At first, he'd sounded gentle as if what happened the night before meant something to him. Now he sounded impatient, commanding.

"I'm still tired," she said, and pulled a pillow over her face. "Go away." For a moment, she thought she might have heard his deep chuckle.

If that weren't irritating enough, she felt him tugging the covers as well as the pillow from her.

"Amorica, we have things to do. I want to show you something. There are people I'd like you to meet. You can't do that unless you get up and get dressed."

Indignantly, she opened her eyes, staring at him. She turned her back on him, struggling with the covers, knowing her actions would be for naught. When Damian wanted something... "Damian, please, just —"

"Just what?" he interrupted, his fingers still tugging the covers away.

"Let me stay a moment longer. I need the sleep, the baby—" she hedged.

"I know the child makes you tired. But you can't sleep the day away." He said, catching her arm and rolling her over to face him. He had apparently risen some time ago. He was fully clad in his tight-fitting buckskin pants and a white linen shirt. She heartily resented the fact that he could appear so devastatingly handsome after so little sleep.

He was a striking figure, imposing as well. Yes, he'd done things to her she had never imagined. Now, when he touched her, she remembered.

Her face heated, her body warmed. She didn't like admitting it, but she wanted him.

"You have to get up. The day will be gone, and you will still be abed."

"I don't want to," she said impetuously, wishing he would go away.

A smile curved his lip. He bent down so he could whisper close to her ear. She immediately regretted her hasty words. "I do like you in bed, Amorica—very much so. And I would like to join you, especially after last night. Last night you were—amazing."

He stroked her shoulder.

"It was the wine," she whispered, pushing his hand away. "I cannot be held accountable—"

He laughed softly in apparent good humor. "I see—the wine. And I thought it was my irresistible charm. Amorica, Amorica, are you so sure it wasn't? Perhaps I should try again. If you weren't sure, that is."

"I am sure. It was the wine." She pushed back against the headboard, distancing herself from him, from temptation. She didn't want to remember anything about last night, yet she couldn't seem to put it from her head.

So much still lay between them. So much that she had to put to rest.

She knew it had to come from her, yet she had lived a lifetime of hating men such as Damian. She didn't know if she could put her hatred behind her. To find peace, she had to find a way to do just that.

"I need sleep. If you would please just leave me be—" she began.

She swallowed hard, shrinking back as he suddenly pinned his arms on either side of her, bracing himself as he studied her eyes as if he could see inside her soul. "Amorica, I won't change last night, and I won't pretend it didn't happen. Neither will you. I won't let you." He spoke softly. "Everything I've longed for from you, I found in your arms last night. I never meant to press my point, but you responded, wildly, passionately and perhaps with passion yourself. Yet the night was everything I'd ever imagined because it did not end in anger." She felt trembling deep within her. She didn't want to feel the surge of warmth that flowed through her. She didn't want to fight with him.

There were times when it seemed he longed for peace between them and there were times she would not give over to the sweet peace offerings.

This morning she needed distance. She needed to step backwards and figure out what happened last night, to try to understand what motivated Damian. And why she'd given in to the sweet passion he generated within her. "Don't," she said. She saw the quick darkening of his eyes, saw them narrow and harden as if her one word built the wall again. "You're a smuggler because you didn't have the ability to earn a decent honest living."

His brow arched. His lip curled. She wondered fleetingly whether he was amused, furious, or just simply tired of everything. She hadn't meant to deny him or to taunt him.

"I'm a smuggler because I'm a second son. I'm a smuggler because there were people who needed help. It was simply a way to disguise ulterior motives behind a lesser crime."

"Now you are making excuses for your actions. You cannot change who you are or what you have done. You must make amends." She wanted to avoid further discussion of motives and crimes. Now she was just as involved as he was. "And last night can be attributed to the wine.

Only the wine."

"Then perhaps I will try to seduce you with the wine every night," he said, tracing a gentle line down her arm that sent shards of heat racing through her.

Panic rose within her. He could hurt her all too easily. To guard her heart, it seemed prudent to strike out first.

Yet she could not find the words. Tears welled in the back of her throat. Yet neither could she rid herself of the image of her mother lying in a pool of blood.

She had not been watching him. She had closed her eyes for a moment. She cried out as his fingers traced a lone tear down her cheek.

With the back of her hand, she wiped it away. "I will never—" Suddenly he wound his fingers around her upper arms, and she found he was lifting her from the bed and pulling her against him. "You will." The tension within him frightened her. She wanted to tell him but she couldn't find the words. Last night had begun with anger, yes. But they had come so close to something being right between them. How could daylight change it all?

"I'll get up," she cried out, afraid of the emotions and the feelings he brought so clearly to the forefront.

He laughed then. "Of course you will. Are you afraid of last night happening again? It will, my love. But cheer up—perhaps I won't make love to you again this morning. Perhaps I am tired of sleeping with someone who wants nothing more than to deny all the wild passion and love she possesses. Perhaps I am tired of a woman who seemingly preferred a simpering popinjay to a real man." He was balanced upon their bed on one knee, holding her so close she could feel the ripple and play of his muscles against her. She should just give in, she thought. She should get it over with, give him what he so diligently and painstakingly sought.

But she refused to lie and give promises she could not in good faith keep. She could not promise him love, nor could she guarantee him the same passion night after night. Not until she could clear the images of her slain mother from her mind, not until she knew he loved her.

She narrowed her eyes at Damian, unsure of what to say to him, shaking her head and knowing in a few moments tears would flow.

He released her so suddenly she fell back, unprepared. Her hair spilled over her shoulders and breasts, and the covers fell away from her.

He stepped back, his hands clenching into fists at his sides then unclenching again. "This is your new home. If God is willing, we're starting over," he told her.

He stared at her and the depths of the passion in his eyes startled her.

She wondered if the burning emotions within him then were hatred or desire, or perhaps a combination of the two. Despite his anger, despite his harshness, she wanted to cry out, to reach out to him. To mend the wounds, they had somehow created together. She wanted to hold him close to her heart and find some measure of forgiveness. For in truth, he had not murdered her mother. He was not guilty of the sins of another.

The moment vanished. He had turned and was walking away from her, leaving the room. Before opening the door, he paused. His back to her, he spoke again. "I would make all this easier for you if I could. If somehow I could create the right words, do the correct things to make you happy I would. Nothing I do or say, it seems, will change your opinion of me." He turned back to her, brows narrowed over dark brooding eyes.

"I'm not asking you to change what you feel. I'm just asking you to put it behind you so we can paint a new life together. Would you try?"

She nodded, attempting some dignity about herself, smoothing her wayward hair, tugging at the sheets to cover her breasts. "I cannot promise you anything."

"Save to try."

"To try," she repeated, meaning the words yet still unable to figure out how to do what he asked. What was so deep within her heart was so very hard to vanquish. It was a battle within her. A war she did not know how to win.

He smiled and she wondered just what he was thinking. "My love, I will do my best to meet you half way."

When he turned to leave this time, he did so without another word.

Amorica threw herself back on the bed, fighting a new rise of tears. He didn't understand. She tried every day, and every day it seemed she wanted him as much as he wanted her. Yet it was not enough.

She rolled over with a groan, her face against the sheets. As she lay there, she became aware that there was a faint smell of her husband about the bedding. It was rich, pleasant, masculine.

Damian.

What is it we have brought upon each other? Why are the demons so hard to vanquish? The sheets reminded her of the night that had passed between them—of the passion she had felt for her husband, and the heat.

She'd never imagined such a night. Maybe a few previous occasions had hinted at such glory, but she'd been too naïve to imagine what incredible physical sensations could be reached. Damian had known, of course. He had been married and had known long before he had met her—before she had become his wife.

Yet she had to give him credit where it was due. No matter what her protestations he had always been determined to sweep her into his fire. He had been a giving and a determined—lover. He had done so because he had wanted her surrender. No, he'd wanted her passion. Passion was different.

He had wanted her to know the richness of sensation and emotion he sought for her. Any time he had touched her with lovemaking in mind, he had been determined to teach her the sweetness and the beauty of the act.

She clenched her teeth. She did not want to appreciate or admire Damian Andrews—or love him.

A sigh escaped her and she trembled suddenly. The bed had grown cold without him. Her head ached. She was tired and once again she only wanted to close her eyes and go back to sleep. For the sake of their marriage, she needed to forget her past and look to their uncertain future.

Her lashes fluttered closed. Then they flew back open. If she didn't show up downstairs soon, he would return.

She rushed from the bed, dragging the covers with her. There was water. Damian had seen to that. He was, she thought, always courteous in such things. He pampered her when he could find the time. It seemed he was always busy, always going somewhere. People needed him.

She hurriedly washed and more hurriedly dressed. She shifted through the clothing still on the floor, his and hers, an aftermath of last night's lovemaking.

An opened letter fell to the floor. She picked it up, thinking it was the letter Damian had read the night before. She started to refold the parchment then wondered what it really said. For a moment, she stared blankly at it, deciding whether to invade his privacy or not.

The letter was from Richy. How curious, she thought. Indeed, she sat on the edge of the bed, knowing it was none of her business but unable to stop herself. Perhaps it would mention her cousins or just give some news of London.

She suddenly realized she did not miss the parties or anything about the city—only her cousins. And she wondered if they had succeeded in dissuading the men. Against her better judgment, she opened the letter.

The words jumped out at her.

"So, you have won the wager but you are also difficult to keep track of. Who would have thought you would run off to the States after you wedded and bedded the object of our bet. You are indeed a lucky fellow..."

The object of the bet—The letter fluttered to the floor, the rest of it unread. Amorica felt herself sway. She would not faint. But she could not shake away the words—the awful horrific words. The men had wagered on their ability to get them into bed.

Of course, Damian had won the bet. He had been the first to wed her and nearly the first to bed her without benefit of marriage vows. And then she'd secured the deal by eavesdropping. He had jumped on that and used it to bind her to him.

For the sake of the bet—Once, she had been willing and she had thought herself falling hopelessly in love with him. She moaned softly to herself. She had almost seduced him that night in the cottage, before Aric showed up.

Before she discovered he was a smuggler.

Before she shot him.

You and your cousins wagered too, she reminded herself but to no avail. It did not seem to be quite the same thing. A wager to lose the men was not the same as one to get them into their bed.

To wed them.

She could not forgive him the lies, the dishonesty—the bet. He could have told her. If she had not discovered his identity that night when she shot him, he would have won the wager then and there.

She buried her face in her hands. He would never have married her.

She would not have traveled across the Atlantic to go to an untamed, uncharted, uncivilized land. She would not have once thought him an honorable man.

~ * ~

Damian whistled as he walked along the waterfront. He'd just visited the home of Louise, the little girl, and the baby he'd rescued that storm swept night almost one year ago. The moaning cave had proven to be their savior. He had hoped to see them, and he meant to take advantage of the meeting. Their welfare was important to him, and he hoped they would visit this afternoon.

He wanted Amorica to meet Louise and her family. Perhaps when she saw one selfless result of his work, her heart would soften at least a little.

He wasn't all about French brandy.

The trio was doing well despite the fact that the father died in his attempt to flee. Damian had set up a trust for the woman and her children.

She'd refused the help but agreed to keep the money for the children—just in case.

When he walked inside his home, Amorica was dressed and beautiful.

Her eyes rose to meet his—beautiful and as green as a moss covered glade. She hadn't wound up the bountiful wealth of her ebony hair but rather let it hang loose upon her shoulders.

"You've been busy?" she asked.

He nodded. "I have." She was probably the most amazing, intriguing woman he had ever seen and the most beautiful. He felt a surge of desire sear through his body, and he knew the one benefit to the marriage had been Amorica herself. No matter what words passed between them, no matter what gulf separated them, he ached for the nights. He had felt sometimes that he lived through the day just to touch her by night.

He turned away, determined not to let her see the pleasure he found at just watching her. It wasn't amusing. It was painful to want his wife the way he did. To want her every waking moment.

There was something special within her. She possessed a passion sweetly strong, feverish, and dynamic. He had sensed it, felt it, and he had longed for it. Now he had touched the passion. For one night, he had known Amorica. As he had suspected, there was nothing in the world like making love with Amorica when she made love in return when she held no part of herself back. It was dangerous to remember last night, because it made him forget everything else he was doing.

Night would return. And he prayed the moments would be just as sweet.

He had to keep a smile from curving his lip once again. He sobered, determined to make his gaze a warning one as he watched her finish with the table. Even as he did, his eyes fell upon a letter on the sideboard. It had not been there earlier, he was sure. He walked to pick it up. Instead, he was stopped by Feroz who summoned him.

A horrific feeling pooled in the pit of his stomach. He had the sensation he should not ignore the letter yet for the life of him he could not recall what it was or where it had come from.

Louise and her family would be here in a few minutes, he told Feroz.

The knock on the door shook the memory of the letter out of his head.

He inhaled swiftly, ashamed of what he had done. Wishing fervently now that he had been able to figure out a different path.

"Louise," he said, holding his hand out in greeting. "This is my wife, Amorica." Good, God but the letter told the story of the wager. Richy had written of his amusement. He had also spoken of his desperation for a wealthy wife. Damian knew why the bet went to the back of his head, because he had felt an immediate fear for Ravyn. Richy's father disowned him and Richy had lost all his fortune. Richy might try anything to have Ravyn.

Amorica turned her bright, beautiful smile upon the woman and her child. Louise had chosen to leave the baby behind with the nanny Damian had provided for her.

Damian wondered at the rush of resentment that filled him. Why was she so quick to smile for everyone save him? Bloody hell, perhaps she'd read the letter and knew about the wager. Bloody hell, but she could not; once he'd vowed to himself she'd never find out because he would never be able to explain how he had been coerced into the wager. How he'd had no choice and that he'd had to play the game.

Because of the smuggling. Because he'd had so many identities to protect and so many innocents to shelter. Because he had played a deadly game. It seemed Louise and her child formed an instant attachment to Amorica. He was sure Amorica would never be able to find fault with her.

Amorica was laughing at something the child was saying.

Damian watched and when Amorica turned her attention to him, her gaze was frigid. Yet he read so very much in it. He could not remember every word Richy had written but he remembered enough to know it was damning. Where Amorica was concerned, it damned him to an eternity of hell. For a moment, silence fell in the room then Amorica began a lively chatter with the little girl, ignoring him. He breathed in a deep sigh of relief. At least for the moment Amorica had chosen not to confront him.

She would save her condemnation for a private moment.

"You will never know how grateful I am to your husband," Louise spoke softly to Amorica who handed the child a doll.

Damian could have said something then, but he was too curious to see what his wife intended to do next. He leaned back against the sideboard, watching her.

Her body was relaxed and her smile spoke of her pure enjoyment of the moment. She folded her hands in front of her. Her chin rose as she watched the little girl, Amorica's grin contagious. "I hope you have a good life here and that you are never afraid again. I'm sure my husband appreciates your well wishes as I hope he no longer continues with his escapades."

Escapades, he thought wryly. Well, perhaps it was better than smuggler, and she hadn't uttered it with the usual disdain in her voice.

She turned her attention to him. The flash in her crystal green eyes and the set of her mouth made him absolutely sure she'd read the letter.

He supposed he should explain. If only an explanation would whisk away the problem.

"I will let you speak with Damian. You may need more funds. I am quite aware he has come into a substantial windfall." Amorica had never appeared more the lady, Damian thought, his gaze keenly upon her as she swirled around. For a moment, her eyes touched his. There was an instant of wariness within hers. There was the slightest trembling to her lower lip then her jaw tightened. Her lashes lowered, and she walked by him.

He felt something pull at his heartstrings. He didn't know if he'd ever meant to tell her about the wager. But had he told her before she discovered it on her own, she would have laughed. He could have recounted that first meeting of theirs, and the way he'd stumbled upon her, losing the list of names then crawling around on his hands and knees to find it. He'd been intrigued and fascinated by her the moment he first set his eyes upon her. Now the fascination was greater.

She was an amazing woman. He didn't deserve a wife such as Amorica. He'd known that from the beginning. Now he was planning to drag her into a wild untamed land—territory that belonged to the Indians.

Many of the tribes took white women as slaves. Sometimes they tortured their captives. He knew a number of frontiersmen kept ammunition set aside to kill their own wives and children before letting them fall captive.

A shudder ripped through him. He could never put a bullet through her heart. Amorica was young, strong and beautiful. If the Indians took her, they might well make a slave of her, but the hope for freedom would always be there. She was a fighter. He would not take the chance for life away from her.

Besides, Amorica's sentiments were strong and now that she knew about the wager, her misconceptions about him would be stronger. To Amorica's way of seeing things, she'd already bedded a smuggler. What worse could happen to her?

He paused for a moment, straightening his shoulders, stiffening his spine. God Almighty, what had he done to them both? Why in hell had he ever taken her away from England and her precious family?

How the bloody hell had he ever made the stupid move of falling so deeply in love with her?

Chapter Eighteen

"You know about the wager." Damian strode into the room, watching Amorica, waiting for the expected outburst. Instead, she greeted him with silence.

Amorica sat in a high-backed chair. Her fingers moved rapidly over a piece of needlework. Her jaw clenched tightly. Her wealth of ebony hair flowed around her. He wanted to see the crystal green fire of her eyes but she she didn't look up.

He cleared his throat then poured them both two fingers of brandy.

"It," he began, "the wager, it's not what it seems," he said, handing her one of the drinks and sipping from his own. If it was fortitude he wanted, the brandy wasn't going to give it to him. It seemed peace would never exist between them. Something would always create an unbridgeable chasm. Every link he'd built over the past months had just burned to the ground.

It occurred to him he could have told her about the wager. But he'd forgotten about it until Richy's letter arrived. At the time, he'd not thought it important. His gut churned. He clenched and unclenched his fists. He didn't want to deal with this right now.

She looked up, needle poised over fabric, her eyes shuttered by dark lashes. "It's not what it seems?" she queried softly. "Pray tell, explain then."

He smiled, sensing her forgiveness even though he knew she would fight him, perhaps make him plead for it. Yet something did not bode well.

When he looked more closely, her lips trembled, her eyes filled with liquid moisture. Sadness settled around her like a cloud of doom between them.

"I had no choice," he said.

"I don't believe you." A lone tear slid down her cheek. She wiped it away with the back of her hand. "You have always been in control." She watched him then as if he would have an answer she could believe.

"I—" he began once more.

"A wager?" she nearly cried out, her anger and desperation pulling on his heartstrings. He had not wanted this. He would have told her if he'd thought of it. The wager had seemed inconsequential after all that had transpired between them.

"I was caught between good and evil. I had to pretend to be what I wasn't. The wager was a part of the game they played." Her jaw clenched tight, yet tears streamed from her eyes. It didn't seem to make a difference that she tried valiantly to push them away.

"And yet you chose not to tell me."

Her accusation rang too true and yet it was wrong. "I would have peace between us. I beg your forgiveness." He would get down on his knees and truly beg if he thought it would help.

"I can never forget what you did," she said, her voice trembling, her shoulders shaking with restrained emotion.

This was for the best, he thought. If she could forgive perhaps in time, she would also forget. He had time. They both had time.

But something felt hollow and empty inside him. He worried they would never find the happiness he sought so desperately. His heart beat too strongly. He worried now about their trip west—about the Indians— the unforeseen dangers. He clenched his fists. He couldn't bear to lose her.

How had he become so entangled? He could not love her!

He raked his hands through his hair, unsure of what to do next. His pulse throbbed. His mind reeled. "Richy and Dicky suspected me from the start. I had to convince them, I was nothing more than—"

"A simpering popinjay?" she queried. He kneeled beside her, touching the back of his hand with a fingertip then picking it up. Her hand was cold, her palms damp from the tears. He almost wished he could hide behind the scarlet coats and a flamboyant neckcloth.

"Aye," he said. "Forgive me," he tried to take the command from his voice. He loathed the feeling that she might indeed prefer the simpering English dandy to the man he was.

She nodded. She didn't speak, just removed her hand from his and turned away, wiping more moisture from her face. She looked upward as if she might find answers on the ceiling. Then she looked back, her gaze boring into his. "I cannot forget. Will that be enough? I don't know how I feel right now. Used, battered, ignored, taken for granted, I suppose the list goes on forever. I would have you on your knees before me, begging me to forgive. And I think I can—forgive, for the baby, perhaps, for me, perhaps. I don't' know."

"For now," he said, "it is enough."

He stood, unsure of what to do next. He walked around the room, wishing for answers, praying for peace between them. This would not be their home, and he didn't relish telling her they would be leaving as soon as the provisions were purchased and arrangements finished. Spring would be here soon and he wanted to make the trip before she was too far into her pregnancy. She had seemed to settle in here well enough. Would she adapt to their next home? A house that would not be nearly so grand as this one. Together, if they could reconcile all the lies and all the misunderstanding, it would be a home for the baby. Ah, but for the baby they might never bridge the chasm between them. And the night before might never be recreated. Ah, he thought once more but for the wine, and the downfall of his own heart.

What would her feelings be tonight when they lay together? She was furious with him. Forgiving but never forgetting his past misdeeds.

Perhaps it was how it should be. He had deceived her, and he'd never meant it to go this far. What would the night be like? Would her emotions turn into a tempest again? Perhaps the night had not been as special for her as it had been for him.

With Amorica watching, he paced the room. The tears in her eyes did not vanish nor did the pain in his gut. He wanted to leave but knew walking from the room was the coward's way out. He wanted to take her into his arms and vanquish all the demons in her heart, but knew he would only create more. It was not enough to tell her how sorry he was but it had to be. Words would never undo the wrongs. Yet he could ill afford to show his weakness toward her, could not let her know he'd fallen in love with her.

The room darkened, evening was approaching. Feroz entered with deer stew and a bottle of wine. He poured her a glass. She looked at the wine with a wary eye then at him. She shook her head but he left it on the table. A few seconds later, she sipped a small amount. Ah, but for the wine. He never wanted her to come to him because of the wine. He wanted her to come to him with love in her heart and the wild unrestrained passion he'd known last night. He watched the play of the flames in the fireplace.

The night drew on and the silence seemed comforting. He watched her eyes close and knew she fought sleep. She slid more deeply into the chair then rested her head on the desk. For a moment, she opened her eyes.

"You should go to bed," he told her.

She shook her head. "No, I cannot. I won't."

"Because of me?"

He watched her sleep. When he was sure she wouldn't fight him or tell him to leave her be, he picked her up in his arms and carried her to their room and to their bed.

He pulled back the covers and settled her on the sheets then he covered her and lay down beside her, the quilt creating a barrier between them. He wanted to take her into his arms and comfort her. Yet he knew he did not have that right. He understood she had to find a way to reconcile the lie he created with the life she had to live.

~ * ~

She remembered closing her eyes. And she remembered Damian pacing around the room. She had wanted so very desperately to give what he asked for. Yet she could not say the words.

When she woke, the room was dark. She found herself stretched out and comfortable. There was remarkable warmth at her backside.

Disoriented in the darkness, she slowly became aware that she was no longer in the chair. Damian had brought her to the bedroom.

She stiffened. He had picked her up and carried her here, to lie beside him. But he wasn't touching her. He was drawn to his own side of the bed, the quilt a great barrier between them.

"What's wrong?" she heard his voice, deep and low. He wasn't sleeping. He had sensed her slightest movement.

She didn't answer him. Her heart was suddenly thudding and she was afraid. She wanted to feign sleep. She wanted to forget the wager. His as well as hers. And she knew she should tell him the rest of the story. But she could not find the courage.

He wasn't going to allow her to pretend. "What's wrong?" he repeated.

"I—"

"Bloody hell, when did you become afraid to speak your mind?" he asked raking his hands through his hair.

He still wasn't touching her. He knew her exhaustion went soul deep.

She caught her lip between her teeth. It was difficult to talk to him about anything. Nothing seemed normal.

"I still don't know how I feel." She reminded herself she had a secret too. And she really had no room to condemn him for the wager. She had been a not so willing participant with her cousins in a wager concerning him. "I'm not asking you for anything right now."

"I think you should know—" she began.

He looked impatient. "What?"

"That my cousins and I made a wager too."

His brows drew together, his eyes darkening. She felt as if she could read his mind. Yet he smiled as if the thought amused him.

"And what was the wager?"

"We sought to dissuade you and your friends. Just long enough so we could return home."

"Well that's royal. I'm guessing you lost."

She was facing him, yet she was so very tempted to turn from him and bury her head in the covers. She was glad for the darkness. He certainly did not intend to make anything easy for her.

She inhaled quickly and spoke in a rush. "I understand if you are angry too—that you have every right—"

"To what Amorica? I'm heartily glad you lost your bet."

"I—"

"I know, Amorica. My God, what kind of a wretch do you think me? I regret nothing that has happened between us. I mean to look to our future only. I will not dwell on the past or our differences which were birthed in the past."

"But I am not able to forget what you did. I can't put it from my mind. It is loathsome."

Hell, yes, Damian thought. Richy and Dicky are spoiled English aristocrats. Both were looking to marry fortunes since they had lost their own. Many English men did the same.

"I have quit smuggling," he said quietly staring at the ceiling above them, "but I will not apologize nor will I tell you everything I did was above reproach. I will tell you this once again. I never murdered innocent women or children."

"Damian—" She broke off.

Damian rose up on an elbow. She was trying to apologize and to thank him. It was a unique experience. And if he reached for her, she might even respond.

But what would be her reason? He wanted more from his wife. He wanted it all. He didn't want her apologies. He didn't believe she'd done anything wrong. He had never wanted her anger and he didn't intend to be angry with her.

He wanted magic again. The kind he had touched last night.

"Go to sleep, Amorica," he said.

He sensed the stiffening within her once again. He turned his back to her, closing his eyes tightly.

She smelled like roses, sweet and delicious. Her hair fell in a cascade of ebony silk, enough to entangle him straight to hell and back. When he had returned to the room, she had been so incredibly beautiful, innocent in her sleep, all her defenses down. She had appeared vulnerable. He had wanted to take her into his arms—cradle her—love her.

The scent of roses still teased his nose. He clenched his eyes more tightly shut. Not tonight. Tonight there would be no battles fought, no peace discovered. He did not have to have her. He had warned her she was not irresistible. But he lied.

Why did her scent haunt him so? Why did he long to turn to her?

Bury his faced against her neck and the sweet-smelling silk of her hair and forget the frontier and the death that stalked it.

He grit down hard on his teeth. Who am I taunting? Her? Myself? The answer was obvious. His was the tortured soul. But then, he was the one who had so foolishly fallen in love, lost his heart.

Still he lay there, frustrated by his torment, his back to her. Pride. What a foolish emotion and such a waste of time. She lay beside him. She had waited for his touch.

And just last night, it seemed, they had evoked the angels when they had made love. Bloody hell to his pride, he would hold her again.

At last he turned yet when he did, it seemed she slept again. He felt her breathing, slow deep, and easy. It was very dark. He smoothed some of the hair from her face and felt her cheeks. They were damp.

Amorica crying? Moisture in her eyes, yes, a lone tear sometimes, but she'd never shed copious tears. She was proud and possessed immeasurable strength.

"What is this hell we have made for one another?" he whispered softly aloud. He slipped his arms around her and pulled her close against him, holding her as she slept. His hand fell beneath her breast. Her back lay against his chest, his hips curved around her derrière. The ache of his desire was not eased.

But something within his heart was. She slept beside him so easily, curved against him naturally.

It was right just to hold her. Last night she had felt their child moving.

There would be a new life created. He shuddered, remembering Meara.

Meara had died. With all his strength, he had to protect Amorica. He had planned to take her west. He should send her home. But he could not send her away. He had found he could not live without her.

~ * ~

"So, this is it." Amorica stood on the wide veranda of her new home.

"It's not a castle."

Damian laughed softly. "True, but it will be our home and perhaps a castle of sorts."

"It is not that far from the city." They traveled well over two weeks.

She didn't know how far from Baltimore they were. Amorica felt reassured, that if need be, she could reach town in a day. A small village lay about three miles from them. A stream ran behind the home. The forest surrounded them.

"The land as far as you can see—even farther—is ours." Damian wrapped his arms around her waist, holding her close. His strength as well as the sheer power of form he possessed reassured her.

She breathed in deeply. The air was clean and fresh.

"You will farm the land?" she asked. Behind her, she felt him nod his head. She walked inside. Dust covered the floors and the simple furniture.

"People lived here before?" she asked Damian. Once again, he nodded yet it seemed he hid something from her.

"What happened to them?"

"They left. The lady passed away and her husband wanted to go farther west."

"I see," but she didn't—not really. She didn't think she wanted to know more. She was looking around the house when she paused. It was dark but a lantern on the porch gave off enough light to see three men

236

approaching.

They were the first people she'd seen since leaving the village, and it made her think of the previous lady of the home. She walked slowly to the door, staring at the men.

The night was cool yet they wore flannel shirts. They were dressed in boots and buckskin breeches not too different from the ones Damian often wore. They carried hunting rifles and wore knifes sheathed at their belts.

She shivered. There was nothing civilized about them. The very way they walked seemed to speak of their freedom and of their fierce determination to cling to that freedom as well as the land.

"Damian—" She moved closer to her husband even while it seemed, he walked toward the men.

"Mason. Slater," he said slowly. He had been watching the newcomers too.

Her heart slammed against her chest. "Why are they here?"

Damian shrugged. "They've come to check on me, I suppose." The men nodded toward the back of the house. Damian disappeared with them.

Amorica tried to settle into the house but she could not do so. There was too much to do and too many things to think about. She was so completely utterly alone. Damian had taken care of the meal before the men came. The bedding was arranged and the bedroom was comfortable.

She rummaged through their belongings that were still in the cart outside the house. She found the hip tub and brought it inside. She did relish her bath; she had felt almost as caked with mud as the earth itself.

She almost wished Damian would come in while she was still in the water, since finding her in a bath tended to give him an urge to action rather than conversation. She was sure she wanted to be held—to give in one more time—to touch that beautiful height of paradise that came even here in the wilderness.

Her nerves stretched thin, she could think of nothing save the night to come. Damian had barely spoken with her since they began the trip. He hadn't touched her since they had left and with the hectic days they'd spent preparing for this journey, they had both retired exhausted.

She left the bath, dressed, paced the room then sat at the top of the steps watching the foyer below and the front door. Damian still hadn't returned. She leapt up suddenly. It seemed, he was usually angry with her anyway. It didn't matter if he wanted her with him or not now that the men had come. She was longing to see people again.

She threw a shawl around her shoulders and left her room and the house, heading in the direction Damian and the travelers had disappeared.

There was no one there to stop her. Feroz didn't seem to be around. He surely would have stepped in front of her if he'd seen her.

She continued on her way, a speech already in mind if Feroz did step from the shadows. She told herself Damian would not mind, but she knew he would. She paused just short of the stables, wondering if they were inside or if they'd gone off into the woods. Inside, she heard Damian's voice but she couldn't understand what he said. She stepped inside, stopping at the door. Two of the men stood off to one side, near the horses.

One of the men was speaking with her husband.

"It was just a few months ago when you smuggled French brandy across the channel. Now there is nothing to keep us in England. The patrols get closer every day. The refugees want passage. Austrian spies are all around, seeking the men who escaped as well as the men who helped them."

Amorica's eyes widened as she realized these men had been promised certain things and now it seemed Damian meant to keep those promises.

Damian stood straight and tall, nodded sagely to the man before him.

"In good faith, I will do what I can for you. I've moved on though."

"I hope you are right. My men are used to the money your business generated. They will not be pleased to find out you have no more work for them."

Damian leaned forward. "I have begun a new life. However, I

would give safe keeping to any who need it. But I have given up smuggling. Let others do what is necessary. Someone will take my place."

"I do not control the forces directing this, but I will pass your word on to them."

"And you can exert your influence," Damian said.

The man before him—a tall man and with a solid, muscular build—inclined his head. "So we reach an agreement and hope that in good faith all will be right."

"I am agreed," Damian said simply. He stood. The meeting had evidently been completed.

The man turned. He had been about to walk away, but he stopped, standing dead still as he saw Amorica. Damian, who had been involved with the other man, saw her too. His brows furrowed, his fists tightened.

Amorica flushed as the other man studied her from head to toe.

"My wife, Slater," Damian said. The man didn't really acknowledge Amorica, he nodded to Damian.

"She is a beautiful woman." He studied Amorica again in silence, turned back to Damian and bowed, then proceeded out of the stables, nearly brushing by Amorica as he left. The other two men followed him in silence, their eyes studying her with the same blunt appraisal.

When they were gone, Damian exploded. "Bloody hell, of all the foolish things—what do you think you are doing here? I would have thought you had learned your lesson about too much curiosity," he said, his tone low but shaking with the effort to keep it so.

"I don't—"

Feroz appeared from a corner. Amorica had not known he was there and for a moment, she wondered if the men had known. Feroz rarely spoke let alone in her defense, but it seemed he meant to stand up for her this time. "Damian," Feroz said, "Surely it can't be your wife's fault to have stumbled upon us in the midst of—"

"Feroz, I will handle this," Damian snapped. He started toward Amorica. "And Amorica. You need to learn to stay in the house."

"What good would it have done me to stay in the house? What difference would it make" Amorica retorted, wishing she had never come, and miserable for both herself and Feroz. "Those men are smugglers, aren't they?"

"Those men are dangerous and should not be taken for granted. They are very fond of taking women and selling them for slaves."

Feroz cleared his throat. "I will take my leave."

"Go back to the house and make sure everything is in order."

Feroz nodded. He didn't look pleased. He strode from the stables.

"You have no right to speak to me in that manner," Amorica whispered fiercely.

"And you don't need to put your life in jeopardy because of an avid curiosity or boredom. There are plenty of things for you to find to manipulate your time. These lands as well as the times are dangerous." She stiffened, whirled around and strode toward the house almost blindly. She nearly tripped over the rough ground.

"Amorica!"

She heard him, but she looked straight at the house and pretended she did not. Furious and heartsick, she strode on across the rocky pathway until she reached the back door.

He was behind her, catching her by the arm, spinning her around.

"Amorica, don't walk out on me like that again."

"Then don't yell at me like that again."

"I'm just afraid—"

"Then you shouldn't have yelled." Tears welled in her eyes. She didn't want to cry. She never cried.

He threw up his hands. "Right. I wouldn't want to show concern or fear for your safety. You've no idea what life will be like here. What precautions you will have to take to stay alive and healthy. This is not England."

"And you do?" she queried, wondering what practical experience he had in these matters.

"I have lived here. I have worked with men like those you just encountered. In some ways, I've grown to respect them."

"You never told me."

"There is much I have done in my life I've never told you,

Amorica."

"Oh!" she cried, and threw up her hands in frustration. "What right do I have to know about my husband? Why should I be reassured that I will not become a slave to one of those men." Angrily, she pulled a dishtowel from the counter and threw it at him. He caught it and tossed it to the table, advancing on her. She backed away quickly, but found there was nowhere to go. He was nearly upon her when she began talking. "I didn't mean to cause you difficulty or interfere," she whispered. "I just wanted to know what was happening. Do you have any idea how hard is to wait, not knowing?"

"You intruded on something dangerous, potentially explosive. I cannot protect you if you continue to act foolishly." She turned away, trying to keep her fingers from shaking as she poured him a brandy, handing it to him. To her surprise, he accepted it from her. His eyes were still hard, dark brown fathomless. She quickly tried to play her advantage.

"I will try to do better."

"You will have to."

"There is so much that I want to understand. It seems those men trust you. Why?"

Damian shrugged. "He tolerates me—more than he is willing to tolerate most men." He leaned forward suddenly, wagging a finger at her.

"His men should have never seen you. They are dangerous and capable of anything, even kidnapping. They have a small camp with quick access to the ocean."

"But—"

"Slater may trust me, but I would never wager on the rest of them."

"But—"

These men can move like the wind. They like to travel through the forests as well as on the ocean. There are paths that seem to open only for them. They take women and sell them to the highest bidder." A chill slipped over her. "But Damian, this house is not so very far from the village. Surely we are safe."

"We are not in the city," he reminded her tautly.

She felt the ice in the marrow of her bones. "I will be careful."

He was up suddenly, hands folded at his back, pacing the space between them. "See that you do stay close," he commanded. He stopped in front of her, his voice sharper than she had ever heard it to one of his men.

"Be very careful. The next few days will tell a tale all of their own. Feroz will be here, and you must always be somewhere where he can see you."

"What?"

"I am going to be working in the fields. And I will be looking for people to help. I will be here part of the time, in the village as well, and I might have to leave for a few days."

Amorica nodded. "You will be close though?"

"I will be home late and I will leave early."

Amorica shook her head. "I did not know you would be gone. I thought—"

"This is not England. There is danger everywhere. I would have my wife safe in my bed when I return each night. I trust Feroz more than I do most men, no matter what his color."

"If you trust him so much, why are you so angry with me?"

"Bloody hell!" he seemed to roar. "I've been trying and trying to make you understand."

"Stop swearing at me like that," she countered, her fingers tightening into fists. "I can understand what you are saying even though I don't like the confinement. I will be careful."

To her amazement, he paused. He swooped her up into his arms and walked up the steps to their bedroom. He sat down at the foot of the bed, keeping her in his arms and staring at her then smiling.

"I have work to do, Amorica."

"But—"

"Will you miss me?"

Heat rushed to her cheeks. "Damian, really—"

"Come now. Admit it. You will miss me just a little."

"You're crazy, you know. We didn't have to leave England. And now we live in a place where you tell me I cannot leave my house."

"You're right of course."

"I—"

"I've got tonight. Then I can almost guarantee you that we will see very little of each other. I will not spend the night with this distance between us."

"But you are still angry with me. You'll yell and then expect me to do your bidding."

"You are most likely right." He stood, lifted her high, and set her down upon the bed. "I don't want to yell."

"But you do."

"I'm doing this for our future, Amorica."

"Fine," she said, repeating his words.

"You," he said, pointing a finger at her. "Unless I have a promise from you to stay in the house, I will never feel safe about you."

"Damian—"

"Will you miss me?"

She moistened her lips. "Maybe."

His laughter was deep and rough. "It will pain me every second I cannot look upon you."

"You are a liar," she accused him.

"I am furious with myself. There will be no distance tonight, Amorica. When the night has passed, you will surely miss me. Whether you do with pleasure, I cannot be certain, but you will surely be aware of my presence tonight and that it is gone tomorrow."

A heat rose within her. She lowered her eyes quickly, avoiding his.

"What, no protest? No excuses?"

The candlelight was very low and very soft. She stared down at her hands, studying them. No matter how she fought it, she felt a wave of crimson coloring rush to her cheeks and her words were soft and breathless. "Don't tease me so? I would truly like to please you. I have given all of myself to you. What more do you want?"

"Everything you have to give me," he said and he came down

upon one knee, taking her hand from her lap to slide between his own.

"Everything."

She inhaled, feeling the fire of the darkness in his eyes as they sought to impale her own. She refused to meet his gaze, shaking her head. "I did give you everything," she murmured. "I swear. I have ceased the fight.

I've no argument with you."

"You insisted it was the wine."

She lowered her head, wishing he were not so close, so very demanding. "Perhaps it was. Perhaps it was not. I still don't understand what it is that—that you still want of me."

"Everything, Amorica. I told you I want everything. But more than anything else, I want you to come to me. Not because I might defend you or protect you. But because you want me. Would that be too difficult?" She shook her head, swallowing the lump in her throat. Her eyes met his at last. She tried to speak, moistening her lips with the tip of her tongue, seeking words, unable to find them. Perhaps he understood her dilemma, perhaps he knew exactly when to push her and when to retreat.

Damian never retreated. He released her hands, his arms slipping around her. He rose, bringing her to her feet along with him. His mouth descended ardently down upon her, seizing her lips in a fierce, hungry kiss. But one that gave so much more. One that teased, one that coerced and even cherished. One that was hot and fervent, one that elicited fires to burn in deep secret places she had so recently discovered within herself.

Those fires seemed so quickly fanned. In the fierce sweetness of his kiss, she swiftly understood more of what he sought from her, and with that honeyed excitement sweeping though her she dared to respond to him with newly leashed passion. Her arms slipped around his neck. Her lips parted willingly to the pressure of his kiss. With each passing second, she teased and taunted in return, her tongue playing a sensual dance with his.

Her fingers stroked the hair at his nape, caressed his cheek, curled into the muscles of his shoulders and arms. She felt the rampant beating of his heart, a hardness, a quickening within him. He lifted his head from hers at last, dark glistening in his eyes as they touched hers. "My God, Amorica," he whispered, and she smiled. He spun her around his fingers impatient on the hooks of her gown. When the material slipped from her shoulders, he spun her again, his lips touching down on her flesh, searing and wet, causing her breath to catch, and the flame within her to sizzle and soar. He eased her dress downward and it fell, pooling on the floor.

He sat, pulling off a boot. She knelt before him, taking off the other boot. She paused for a moment, aware that he was quickly shedding his shirt. Her eyes met his again and the searing spark of desire within them sent a flutter cascading from her heart to the center of her womb. She rose slightly, curling her arms around him. Her lips just feathered softly across his then pressed to his neck, to his collarbone. She teased his flesh with the tip of her tongue, tasting the salt there. Her fingers moved over the bronzed length of his arm, testing the ripple and play of muscle. She sat back, watching with fascination as she brought her hands easily over his chest, her fingertips dancing lightly over the crisp whorls of dark hair upon it. She came close again, kissing his chest testing with the tip of her tongue, finding a rising excitement in the fascination of his body.

"Amorica," he whispered her name huskily, rising suddenly, bringing her with him. She stood on tiptoe. Her lips caught his, left them. She stroked his back then lower. A husky groan escaped him, startling her. She found herself swept up and laid back upon the bed, dizzy with the sweet feel of her own passion, so alive and vital, anticipating the wonder of his lovemaking. Yet when she saw that his buckskin pants were off him, she did not wait. He had said he wanted her to want him. And she did. A raging inferno swept through her. She ached for his touch everywhere. He had said he wanted everything. Dear God, she gave him all that she had.

The inferno seared inside of her, and the longing was deep and rich.

Even as he walked toward her, she rose again. With a little cry, she raced toward him. She found herself swept up again. Her legs locked around his back as he spun with her, kissing her. He held still. She slid down the length of him. Fingers and lips covered his chest. Stroke him. Her eyes found his. She questioned silently.

"This?"

A deep, guttural groan gave her sweet reply. "This," he said.

Against the softness of her flesh, she felt the hard arousal of his sex.

Her heart hammered. She didn't dare—she couldn't. She closed her eyes, leaning her forehead against this chest. She teased him first, inadvertently, with the brush of her knuckles. She felt his breath catch, his heart thud.

She closed her fingers around him. An exclamation exploded from him.

She grew bolder, stroking the hardness, exploring beyond her hands touching him, testing. Whispers fell from his lips that she scarce understood, yet she did not need to hear the words, for the desire and the approval were so rich in his tone. She was lifted suddenly again and found herself breathless as she lay flat. She cried out softly, for he was touching her and the feeling was amazing.

Her legs locked around him, holding him close. He brought her soaring to the very crest of a pinnacle then withdrew. She felt his lips upon her, upon her shoulders, upon her breasts. They were so sweetly upon her breast, teasing, bathing, suckling, first one and then the other. She was whispering frantically herself, demanding that he cease the torture and come to her. But he did not. He stroked, caressed, and bathed the length of her with his kiss. He demanded everything from her with a hungry passion of his own. When he was done, he lifted her over him, drawing her slowly down, his eyes impaling hers even as his body did the same. He taught her to move, his eyes fully upon her. His hands curved strongly around her buttocks. He guided her until the natural force of her desire brought her hungrily against him, sweeping them both into a maelstrom that exploded into an ecstasy beyond all that she had ever imagined, sweet, volatile. He brought her crashing against him at last, entangling him in the wild fall of her hair. Even as it seemed that the world burst into brilliant shards, it fell to darkness, and then burst into bountiful rays of light that surrounded them.

She heard his whisper, deep, throaty. Teasing perhaps, but yearning, too. "Everything?"

"Damian—"

"Is that everything?"

God yes, she might have cried out. I have nothing more to give. She might have cried out how much she loved him.

"Bloody hell, if it takes that long, I might be provoked to try again." A gasp escaped her. She was suddenly, fiercely, in his arms again.

He made love to her, slowly, fervently, thoroughly. He erased all thoughts from her mind, other than the hunger that ragged within her for him. "Everything? If not—"

And the sound of his laughter was warm, as were his arms around her.

"My love, I have given you all that I have because you gave me everything. Thank you."

Chapter Nineteen

The following days moved slowly for Amorica. If she woke with the sun, she saw Damian for a few minutes and at times, she would wake to a goodnight kiss before he slipped into bed beside her.

She had promised Damian she would give him everything and she did. But he wasn't there during the day to see it nor was he there at night to claim what she so desperately wanted to give him. She was amazed to discover that while she waited for him to come home each night she lay awake, aching for him physically as well as with her heart and her soul.

She wondered if there would ever be a time when she could tell him how she felt. She lay awake in agony, wondering at all the secrets he kept locked within his own soul, wondering about Meara, wondering about the child he had lost.

Several weeks after they arrived at their new home a man from a nearby village brought mail. She received a letter from her cousin, Ravyn.

While I seem to have adapted well to London, the parties as well as the stream of aristocrats that come courting, Christel is homesick. She is pale and listless most of the time, and I worry over her. I wish you were here. So many times, you knew just the right thing to say to her. I'm afraid for her.

Aric Lakeland speaks of Australia, and Richy is ever farther into debt.

He planned on catching the infamous smugglers, but it seems the man and the woman disappeared. He doesn't know what to do about his money problems. I saw him the other day at one of the coffee houses near the racetracks. I'm sure he was betting on a horse or two. I heard later he'd lost quite a bit of money. His father is threatening to send him away. But it doesn't help. Richy just needs to be given some responsibility, and he'll do fine. Speaking of Aric Lakeland, it seems Ryder, Damian's other dark friend has been staring openly at Christel. I do hope he is not someone looking to take advantage of her. I believe whole-heartedly that I need to get Christel away from London. But putting her in the countryside might be worse. Is there any chance of sending her to America? The two of you could look after her, and I wouldn't worry as much about her there. Or do I need fear that she'll wander off and the Indians would capture her? No, I'm just being silly. Damian would never put you, and the unborn child in such danger. Oh, I do need to go. The Duchess says I have a caller. I grow tired of the string of men coming my way. I wish I could find a true love, one such as yours.

Love,

Ravyn.

Amorica let the letter dangle from her fingers, imagining what home would look like now. The spring flowers would be starting to bloom. The landscape would be alive in colors.

"Homesick?" Feroz asked her.

"I guess."

"But you have a new home now. You'll come to love this one."

"You understand, don't you? How many places have you called home?" she asked then smiled slowly. "I admit this has all been fascinating. I think I've always had an adventurous heart."

"This America," Feroz murmured. "There was a time I'd never heard of this place. I knew nothing of anything save the great vast sands of the desert."

"At home there are balls and parties; endless hours of wasted gaiety while children starve in the slums."

She didn't want to finish.

"What will you do?" Feroz asked. "Damian may not always be content to stay here. The west calls to him."

"He is my husband. I will do what he wants."

Feroz smiled. "I suppose one could say that home is where the heart is."

"I will make it so," she said with more force and determination than she thought possible.

Amorica wiped her hands on a dishcloth and walked outside to stand on the back porch. She put her hands at the small of her back and stretched. She had felt the baby kick. She knew the baby would be born here, and she wondered if the village had a doctor or a midwife.

Feroz was inside working. She could hear the pounding of nails as he worked on the stairway. The house was big and spacious. It was warm and the fireplaces added a kind of warmth. The floor was not dirt as she had been led to believe. Everything seemed huge to her. When she looked outside, she saw mountains and forests. The sunset over lush green trees and she too at times wondered what was on the other side of the mountains.

A spring sun beat upon the earth. She lifted her face to the sky, inhaling the fresh cleanness, enjoying the warmth. She walked off the porch, wandering a bit, knowing she was not supposed to leave the house yet resenting the confinement. A cat darted into the stables. She followed, watching it and wondering if perhaps there were kittens.

She was rewarded with the sight of five tiny orange and white kittens.

She knelt down beside the small nursery the mother cat had arranged and picked up one of the kittens. They would be good mousers.

A hand wrapped around her mouth an arm around her waist dragging her backwards. She tried to scream. Her arms and legs were free. She used them flinging her arms and kicking out with her legs.

She found the air cut off from her lungs. Her head spun. Slowly her legs gave out, the world turning a strange hazy grey. She fell limp against the man holding her. Somewhere in the back of her mind, she knew the man slung her over a horse. He tied her hands around him so she could not slip from the mount. She heard the words, "Let's ride." then she knew nothing more.

~ * ~

It was almost dawn when he walked into the house. He'd spent the night riding in hopes of getting home and seeing Amorica for a short time before he would have to ride out again. Even for the early morning, the house felt empty.

How strange, he thought, to have had such strong feelings of anticipation. He punched the wall. Then he raced through the house, upstairs, then down to the kitchen and the parlor. He ran to the stables.

He saw Feroz.

"Good, God!" he gasped out.

He found Feroz in the middle of the floor. He was bleeding, but had managed to come to him. He had crawled on his belly to reach him.

Damian cried out again, shouting for help that wasn't going to arrive.

He lifted the man who had been his friend and companion for so long, trying to find the wound. It was a head wound. Blood poured from it. He ripped up his shirt, packing the wound to stop the flow.

"Damian—" Feroz was trying to speak.

"What the hell happened?" My God! I've got to get you a doctor."

'No."

Feroz found the strength to rise. Shaking his head vehemently, he fell back.

"Don't worry about me. I've survived worse."

Feroz beckoned to Damian to come close to his lips and he spoke quickly. "The smugglers, only I don't think it was Slater but the men he was with, they took her. They jumped me. I never saw them until it was too late to help."

There was blood everywhere. But Damian knew head wounds bled profusely. He prayed Feroz would recover quickly.

"Amorica—" he whispered.

Feroz reached for him. "When I saw them, I managed to drag myself around to the stables, but I was too late to save her. One of them knocked me out cold."

The men would sell her to anyone who could name the right price.

They had no other reason to take her. There were discontents out there.

Men who did not want to give even one concession—men who hated the English. Amorica might well pay the price. He realized staying inside the house that day would not have saved her.

A cold shiver ripped through Damian. More horrible than anything he had ever known. Amorica, she had been boldly stolen away from her home. A home protected by him. His reputation, he had thought, would be enough to keep Amorica safe.

"Don't worry about me," Feroz said. "I'm going to be fine." He tried to stand. For a moment, he seemed he might, inhaling long deep breaths.

"I'm going with you."

"You can't stand let alone ride," Damian said. "I want you stay here—recover so you can give assistance when I need you."

Feroz nodded. Damian helped him into the house, found bandages and doctored the man who had been loyal to him for so long. Then Damian strode quickly to the stables, anxious to reach his horse.

Dear God, Amorica was out there somewhere. All that he'd feared might well face his wife. She had courage, and Damian prayed she did not have too much courage because she loathed smugglers.

~ * ~

They rode, walking the horses then trotting, knowing the horses would have to be traded soon for fresh mounts. By then, Amorica was fully aware of her fate. She knew as well that Damian would not be home until the evening.

Nothing was said. She didn't know if this man spoke English or French. She recognized him as one of the men who had stared at her the first day they arrived.

"My husband will come after you," she finally said.

His hand fell to the knife at his belt. He paused for a moment, "I am supposed to be afraid?" he asked with a sneer.

They rode once again, keeping a steady pace. In front of them, paths seemed to open and close—the forest thick.

She knew she should fight but she was so very afraid if she did, the man would hurt her. She wanted to live to find time to escape. She needed to get back to Damian. Then there was the child. She would never risk the babe. Damian would come for her. Damian would come.

If he still wanted her. If he had not already died. For she had no idea if he'd been attacked. If he did not lay dead in a pool of his own blood, would he want her back enough to risk his life?

No, she could not believe it. He could not be dead. He could not. She would not be able to bear it if he was.

Tears spilled again from her eyes to her cheeks, but they went unnoticed, for the wind dried them even as they fell. She never would be able to lay down her pride and tell Damian she loved him. She had been given everything in the world, and she had not told him how she felt. Now she had lost the opportunity to reach with all her heart for the things that once had been given to her so very freely.

She closed her eyes against the wind, and in misery, she endured the long and wretched ride.

They traveled for several days, stopping at trading posts to change the horses. Then the rugged journey ended at last, Amorica was close to unconsciousness. She could not stand when the man dismounted from his horse, and despite herself, she fell into his arms. A man lifted her and carried her until they came to the largest of the shanties. There were many, many men here. They followed along behind her, laughing and making derisive noises. Their gestures were lewd, but they did not touch her. The man pushed them away, and she was brought into the house. There was a sudden and curious silence. Someone spoke, and she was set down. She heard a rustle of movement then saw a man was staring down at her. She tried very hard to focus upon him. He was dressed like the other in tight fitting black pants and wearing a cloth around his head. Dark hair fell to his shoulders and was parted neatly in the center of his head. His eyes were incredibly dark, and the very strength of his features was arresting.

Startled, Amorica dampened her lips and tried to speak. "Please," she whispered. "Slater?"

"So, Damian's woman is here," he said in acknowledgment. His face blurred in front of her then vanished. He returned to her, putting a cup of water on the floor beside her. She tried to drink, having little strength left.

He lifted her head for her. The water was sweet and wet. He let go of her then, and let her fall back onto the floor.

He rose then, strode to the entrance to his house, and spoke sternly to the people outside. Amorica was dimly aware that he argued fiercely with the man who had kidnapped her.

While they argued, Amorica heard a rustling, and then someone came close to her. She opened her eyes again. It was a young woman. She called herself Chastity.

"Mason says you are his slave. He captured you. It is his duty to decide if you should be sold or kept here for his comforts." Amorica trembled. She was exhausted and heartsick. Her head throbbed, her thighs hurt, and her body seemed alive with agony, and still she didn't want to die. She remembered the stories about women who were sold into captivity and how it was better to kill yourself than to suffer that fate. But these men were not Indians. Pirates had kidnapped her.

She would never kill herself. She wanted to live, to survive this and see Damian one more time so she could tell him she loved him.

"Oh, God," she whispered. She tried to pull herself up to a sitting position. Chastity helped her. She inched backward looking for something to lean against.

"Mason comes back," Chastity whispered. "They will decide nothing until morning. They will let you rest."

Amorica moved back to the pallet. She stretched out and closed her eyes. She sensed the presence of Mason as he walked over to her, staring down at her. He spoke to Chastity, and Chastity answered him softly in return. He made a snorting sound and turned away from her. He sat before the open fire with the smoke hole above it in the center of his shanty. He snapped out some order—a command for Chastity to come forward, for that was what she did. Something was cooking, and Amorica thought he ordered Chastity to prepare a dish of food for her, for she did that too.

It seemed hours passed and Amorica lay awake, staring at the smoke hole, watching the gray haze dance through the opening. She thought hard about escaping, but she knew she must wait until she was stronger. Right now, her only hope of survival was with Mason.

Finally, he stretched out near her.

It wasn't too long and she heard him breathing. He slept.

She watched him, thinking about escape as well as revenge. She longed to rise, find his knife, and slit his throat. She shook, aching to do so. But she was smart enough to know she wouldn't succeed. How many times had she promised Damian she would temper her actions with common sense? She had never been a rash-thinking person. Not until she met Damian and had been driven to a life she was ill prepared for.

She wasn't going to die—at least not without fighting. She would go down fighting. She had never wanted Damian so very much. She needed to pray but she couldn't find the words. Finally, tears damp upon her cheeks, she slept.

The next day arrived with the sun shining into the house. The day began with renewed terror. She heard the sound of raucous screaming.

Looking upward, she saw a dozen women staring down at her. They laughed, pulled at her hair and spit at her dress. She tried to scurry back away from them.

Her temper flared and exploded. Amorica leapt to her feet and threw herself at the young woman who attempted to remove her hair from her head. She brought the woman down to the ground but Mason returned to the shanty. The women all fell silent.

He laughed and stood with his hands on his hips, watching all of them with a smug grin. "All of you behave yourselves," he spoke to the women.

"They tried to kill me," Amorica cried out. Then she remembered this man held her life in his hands, and she gritted her teeth. She still met his eyes. He smiled and shoved her back to the women.

"You are dirty and you smell. They only wish to bathe you."

"That is all?" she whispered hopefully.

"For now," he told her. It seemed he didn't mean to enlighten her further. He left the house, and the women latched on to her arms.

The women dragged her past the village center. She didn't want to look at the shanties. But it seemed almost normal, almost as if she were being led through a village of normal people. She almost fell, buckling over with such strength the women had to jerk her back to her feet.

They had not been the only prisoners. It seemed Mason had raided other farms in the area.

Move, don't look, Amorica told herself, urging her feet forward. She squinted her eyes until they entered into a trail of trees, and from there they came to a river. The women set upon her, tearing her clothes until she was left shivering, naked, and panting from the fight she waged against her captors. The cold shocked. Amorica rose from the chilling depths, gasping for air. She was quickly joined by the women who did not seem to feel the cold of the water. Set upon again, they scrubbed her thoroughly with handfuls of sand and stones. Amorica hated every touch. No matter how she screamed and fought, she was viciously scrubbed.

Finally, exhausted and panting, she was left upon rocks to dry beneath the sun. Then she was given a dress to wear, like the other women. She was not given shoes. Amorica thought she was kept barefoot to hinder any thoughts she might have of escaping.

The women brought her back to Mason's house then gave her a bowl of meat in gravy. Amorica looked at the food suspiciously, but she was ravenous, and when she tasted the stew, it was delicious. Chastity came back soon and told her the meal had been rabbit, and that she need not fear eating it.

What is going to happen to me?" Amorica asked Chastity.

"The men meet. They will discuss your future there. Mason says he wants you, and that he will have you. Slater says no, that he is in charge, and he will wait and see if your husband comes for you."

"He will come. He will bring all of his men with him. Is that what you want?"

"You have great courage and perhaps too much confidence. All of his men? They are spread across the oceans," she told her.

"How do you know all this?"

"I listen and I watch..."

"Why do you even care?" Amorica asked.

"I am sure if Damian is alive, and if he can come, he will. Mason thinks Damian should die, but Slater says Damian has been honest with him. If Mason wants to fight Damian for you, that will be all right.

Whichever man lives will have you. If both die, you will belong to Slater." Amorica wrapped her arms around herself. The chills would not stop.

In the afternoon, one of the women returned with a bag of grain and mortar and pestle, telling her she must work. Amorica shook her head refusing to give over to what they wanted from her. She would not become one of them, she vowed. She would not stay here long enough to belong to either of these men.

The young woman looked at her angrily then returned with one of the matrons with a long reed. The older woman lashed at her with hard, stinging blows. Amorica screamed and covered her face.

Suddenly the blows stopped.

"Stop it! Stop it!" Chastity shrieked. "She will be no good to anyone dead." Chastity was on top of the woman wrenching the reed from her hands and wresting her in a fury. Amorica staggered to her feet, surprised yet hurrying to her aid. Just then, Slater walked into the house.

In a rage, he tugged up both her and Chastity by the hair. The older woman—with a bleeding nose, thanks to Chastity's tender touch—began to rant and rail and lash out at Amorica again. Slater thundered out in anger and pushed her to the far rear of the house. He sent the women away.

Amorica held still, watching the tall, muscled man pick up the reed.

He came to her and waved it in front of her. "Everyone works. You will work. Next time I will let them beat you until the blood flows from your flesh."

He dropped the reed, turned and left them. Chastity picked up the grain she was supposed to grind. Looking at Chastity's smudged face, Amorica smiled. "Why did you defend me?"

Chastity flushed. "She was beating you. You will learn what you must do to survive here. If you are dead, you will be no good to anyone." Amorica shrugged. She would do what was necessary. She set to the task. If it could remain so, if she could grind wheat by day and have Slater's protection by night, then she could survive until Damian came.

Chapter Twenty

"Damian, I love you. I love you with all my heart," Amorica whispered to the empty room. She spoke the words even though she knew no one would hear them. Yet the words eased her heart. Damian will come for me. Those words became her mantra.

That night, when Slater returned to the shanty, he dragged her to her feet, the gleam in his eyes unreadable. He smiled, slowly and curiously.

She gasped, stunned, when he ripped open her garment, baring her to the waist. She tried to cover herself, and he grabbed her hands, wrenching them around behind her back and holding her tautly to his chest with one hand to imprison her.

"You tempt me. Indeed you do." She clenched her jaw against the humiliation and pain as he moved his fingers over her breasts, pausing to flick the nipples. She wanted to lash out at him; she was afraid she would fall, and she didn't have the strength to free herself from his powerful hold. "You tempt me, yes—but Damian Andrews is a man of character. I will give him a chance."

She opened her eyes wide, aware that Slater taunted her but she knew she would be spared rape because of the man her husband was.

He tied Amorica securely. His dark gaze found hers. "Don't make me forget who you belong to," he warned her.

"Damian will cut out your heart," she said.

"He can try."

The night proved to be long and cold. She could not sleep. Yet she knew she must. She didn't know if Slater would change his mind and take what he could so very easily or if he would remain a man of his word and leave her be.

In the morning, Slater slit the ties that bound Amorica to the pole before he left the house. Amorica stared at him with hatred in her soul, but he impassively ignored her. She refastened what she could, trying to hold her dress together.

"You are nothing but trouble." Slater spat on the ground. "For Andrews, I have kept you from the hands of your true captor."

"But I—" she began but he cut her off.

"Stay here. I will come for you soon enough. You are a dangerous prize—someone will pay the price for you."

He turned and left the house. Terrified, she tried to race after him.

Chastity waited outside, shaking her head slowly. "You must go inside."

Amorica stepped inside and sat down. Chastity followed. "Chastity, please—what will happen?"

"I don't know. Everyone is talking, so something must happen. But now, in the midst of this there is more. I don't know quite what happened myself, but Slater and Mason have gathered with someone I've never seen before."

A sharp command came from outside. One of the other women was warning Chastity to leave Amorica alone.

"I don't dare stay longer. Their tempers are so high. I think someone must die—"

Another roaring command came from the outside. Chastity jumped up, stared at Amorica, then hurried from the house.

Amorica sat on a pile of furs, trying not to shake. She wanted this agony to end.

But then, just as the thought came to her, she felt movement.

The baby was moving again. After all that had happened, the baby was alive inside her. She had to live. No matter what happened to her, no matter what Slater did to her, she had to live. If nothing else, she meant to see to it that she delivered her baby. If Slater had any sense of honor, he would see to it that Damian received their child.

She lowered her face to her knees and fought the tears that threatened her. What would come now? How would she survive?

Would Slater return? He had said she should have been punished.

It was then she heard the drums, a slow, steady beat, continuous, chilling. They seemed to go on for hours and hours. Hours in which she thought she would lose her mind. They warned of something soon to come.

What?

Damian would know.

Tears, unbidden, slid from her eyes. With the back of her hand, she wiped them away. It was then she looked up and terror struck her heart once again. Someone was there—tall, indomitable—filling the entrance of the house.

~ * ~

It was up to him, Damian thought. He would have to trust Slater, and he would have to go to the man in peace even when his heart cried out in anguish.

He looked up at the spring sky and swore with a sudden vehemence.

He had known. He had known not to trust the smugglers, but he had not known Slater was a pirate.

He rode fast and hard yet he never stopped looking for signs of Amorica's passage. He'd been traveling, riding hard, weary beyond anything he'd ever imagined. He wondered if he wasn't imagining this. He reached Baltimore and knowing Slater would be camping on of the many inlets of the Chesapeake Bay area, he boarded one of his ships. So many coves and inlets existed in these waters he despaired of ever finding her.

When he finally saw the small camp and Slater's ship, he felt chills slip down his spine. They were to go back to Baltimore and send for Feroz, Ryder and Aric.

A strange sensation prickled his skin. He was in Slater's territory.

There was something so unnerving about the sensation he was tempted to turn his ship about and sail as hard and as fast as he could in the opposite direction. He could never do that. Even if the desperate, all-consuming need to find Amorica vanished, he could not turn and run.

When he'd arrived here with his grandiose plans of building a home for himself and Amorica, he'd never imagined he would be walking into Slater's encampment seeking his wife. He prayed she still lived. And he prayed he could think of something to bargain with when he demanded the return of his wife. He had nothing save honor, truth, and dignity.

Damian moored his ship in a small cove before he set off on foot toward Slater's camp.

Another chill crept up his spine, as he watched one of Slater's men disappear into the dense foliage. Suddenly three men blocked the trail he followed. Within minutes, men had slowly encircled him. No one moved to their weapons. They kept their distance as an escort into the camp.

He hadn't reached the first pathway through the shanties when he saw an old man step out, barring his way. For a moment, he felt his muscles tensing then he relaxed.

It was Blue Boy, once an English dandy—a Lord of the realm. The man lifted a hand in greeting to him.

"Andrews," he said.

Damian dismounted, walking the few feet that remained between them. "I've come in good faith. I've come for my wife."

"You have something to trade?" Blue Boy asked.

He nodded. "Yet if my friend Slater seized my wife, I wish to think he would bring her home to me—no matter what."

Blue Boy lifted his arm, indicating Slater's shanty. "There is trouble over your wife," he commented.

Damian's heart slammed against his ribs. He tried to still the panic rising in his breast and followed Blue Boy into his home. He entered then sat with his legs crossed.

Blue Boy produced a pipe. It was an exceptionally fine pipe. The stem was carved. The tobacco was exceptional. Damian could only believe it was a good sign.

The man respected him and wanted to remain his friend.

Damian tried to conceal his impatience, inhaling deeply on the pipe before speaking.

"What is this trouble with my wife?" he asked, his heart pounding.

All manner of horrors raced through his mind. "As Slater is my friend—"

"Slater does not refuse you your wife. He has been waiting for your arrival."

"Then—"

Blue Boy shook his head and inhaled deeply before speaking to Damian. "Slater said that this has passed from his hands. That by their laws he has the right to claim your wife as his slave. Mason captured her.

She is his. A man should have control of his own home." Damian's insides shuddered. He recalled the meeting between his wife and the other men, and he had known only harm would come of it.

"I understand though I don't agree," he said.

A shadow fell across the door opening. Slater and Mason entered and accepted a mug of ale so they could be involved in the discussion. Slater stared accusingly at Damian. Mason seemed to be challenging him.

Damian realized the man who had come to him before as Slater's emissary was gaining an equal footing with Slater as leader of this crew of cutthroats and thieves. If that happened, all the merchant ships as well as their passengers sailing within the area would be in terrible jeopardy.

"She is well," Slater assured him, and Damian wondered just what had given him away.

"Then I may take my wife and leave—" Damian began.

"No," Mason said.

"There is the matter of which man here has the right to the captive," Blue Boy told Damian. "Mason was the man to capture your wife. Before we knew of your coming today, they had disagreed about her. Mason challenged Slater, and they agreed to meet with knives to settle the dispute."

"I will not give her up," Mason said. His eyes met Damian's at last.

"You are not my friend. I owe you nothing."

"I will not leave without my wife." Damian insisted.

"Then Slater must be taken from this dispute," Blue Boy spoke. "And you, Andrews, must be ready to meet Mason in his stead. Is your wife worth this?"

She is worth my life, he might have said. But he kept quiet for a moment and searched for the words. "She is mine. I will let no other man have her."

"Or die in the trying," Mason said with quiet menace.

It was more than just keeping Amorica from this man, Damian realized. It was a power struggle within the pirate ranks.

"Or die in the trying," Damian agreed.

"It is settled," Blue Boy said. "When the sun rises, you will meet with knives. The fight will be a fair one between two men in our fashion with our laws. The crew will witness."

"If I win," Damian spoke slowly, defiance and determination within his heart. "It is agreed, on your honor, that I leave here in peace with my wife."

"It is agreed."

Blue Boy started to knock the burned tobacco from his pipe—a clear sign the meeting had ended. It was time for them all to rise and leave the house. Damian, though he knew the etiquette, sat still.

"I will fight in the morning. I want to be with her tonight," he said.

"That I will not agree to—" Mason began.

But Slater held up a hand to silence the other man. "The woman is Andrews' wife and has been. She carries his child. He may well die tomorrow. There are matters to solve between them. I say he should have the night." He looked to Blue Boy.

Blue Boy nodded. "We have kept our two captains from meeting one another and perhaps killing each other when leadership means survival.

The fight will be good and fair, the outcome just. Slater, you will see that your friend reaches the woman, and you will tend to his needs for the fight to come.

They all rose. Damian could feel the heat and fury from Mason. He knew the pirate longed to slit his throat then and there, but his captain had spoken against him, and to retain face he must wait for the fight.

Damian had the night though.

They walked through the camp. Most of the pirates paused and stared at him. Many of them knew him. They all understood Amorica was a hostage.

They knew about the trouble over her and now knew that he meant to claim her.

Slater came to a halt in front of a shanty. "You must leave her at dawn," he said. "You will come see me. I'll see you are dressed properly so your opponent will not have an advantage.

Damian nodded. "Thank you."

"You are a rare man, Andrews. You have always kept your word with me. I hope you live to do so again."

Damian smiled. "So do I." he said.

The guard in front of the house moved aside for him. He stood in the doorway for a moment, letting his eyes adjust to the darkness. His pulse quickened, an inferno raced through him. Amorica. Slater had told her she was fine.

A fire burned in the center of the shanty. Beyond it, a shadow moved, sat up then backed away. He strode forward, anxious, anticipating this first meeting. Anger and fear swamped him, yet he wanted nothing more than to hold her. She wasn't moving, he realized. She was frozen as still as ice.

He heard her shifting her position, inhaling swiftly. She was afraid of him.

"Damian!" she cried out.

Her startled gasp reverberated in the tiny room, and he realized she hadn't know until that instant it was he who had come upon her.

Pressed against the wall, curled as if she meant to move through the wall, her entire body shook with fear. The fire played over her, and he saw that she was dressed in a soft flowing skirt and a shirt that barely covered her, slipping off her shoulders. He saw that her hair was free and

Amorica's Wager

long, flowing down her back. In the meager firelight, he could not see her eyes but he sensed her fear and perhaps her relief at seeing him. He was suddenly terrified himself. He wasn't afraid of fighting Mason. He had fought too many times and survived.

He was only afraid that he'd come so far, that he'd found her and now he would lose her again this time to death—his own. If he died, if he was not the victor, he was afraid of what would happen to Amorica.

Amorica, damn you, he thought. But then he remembered everything and all he'd put her through. He remembered that even if she had followed his instructions and stayed within the house, nothing would have changed.

His hands shook. He was so glad to see her safe and unharmed.

Suddenly, if his fate was to die in the morning, he wanted nothing more to stand between them. He wanted her in his arms, and he wanted to taste her sweetness once more.

He reached for her, catching her wrists when she continued to stare incredulously at him. He pulled her to her feet and brought her crashing hard against him.

"I have been so afraid," he told her. He didn't mean to sound harsh or condemning, but the depth of his feelings and hunger combined with the fear for her if he should die on the morrow gave his voice a rough-edged quality. His hold was tight, and he didn't want to let her go, ever. He brought her closer against him. He wanted to touch her, explore all of her from the soft planes of her face to her fingers and toes.

He ran his fingers through her hair, stroked through its long silky length, tilting her face, forcing her gaze to his. Hands on both sides of her face, she held still as his lips lowered until they hovered just above hers, and he felt her soft breath against his lips. He thought the moment had never been sweeter or more bitter. Yet he wanted to hold onto each second as if it were his last.

"I might die tomorrow—" he hesitated for a moment, trying desperately to search his mind for something more reassuring to tell her.

Yet he knew if he died, she might stay here for the rest of her life. He realized now in this hour nothing that had gone on between them in

266

the past made any difference. Tonight, she would love him because the drums and the wild music would not stop beating, because he would live or die for the glory of her touch.

Tension seemed to burn in his body, hotter than the bluest streaks of flame within the fire. "Tonight we will not think of our future or our past." His lips melded with hers, hard, questioning, and yet she gave back to him everything he asked and more. She demanded of him just as he did the same of her. It seemed he burned with fire, passion, and a force he could not name.

"Damian," she said as his lips softened and he pulled away from her for a moment. Her eyes were as green as the finest cut emeralds. The primitive and erotic sound of the drums had entered his blood. It seemed to enter hers too.

She pressed against him, threw her arms around him and clung to him. Her fingers moved over him, through his hair, across his shoulders, exploring him as if she did not believe he was here and in her arms. He drew her away from him, the anger, the tempest, the fear still alive within him. "Amorica, make these moments worthwhile—memorable. Revel in what we can be, what we might have been, and perhaps what we will achieve if tomorrow proves victorious for me." She stared at him. He swept her into his arms and set her upon the furs. "Love me," he said.

She watched him as he stripped, her eyes on his, waiting. Then he came down beside her, his hands upon her, removing her clothes.

She didn't refuse nor did she answer his plea. Yet her flesh seemed to burn beneath his touch, her skin supple, smooth and so very soft. He began to tremble with the need to have her, the need for her to love him in return.

There was so very much he yearned for. He might have only one night with her.

He was sure in his heart that she was fine. They had not maimed her or harmed her in anyway. She would keep nothing from him, he decided.

She wouldn't fight the sensations he evoked within her, and she would concede all to him. He whispered to her. "Give in to me, Amorica.

Give me all that you possess. Surrender your passion to me." He straddled her. Her skin was beautiful, ivory and gold in the firelight. Her breasts were so large now, full, evocative, the nipples nearly crimson, hardened. He could just feel the rise of their child in her belly, and he prayed suddenly, fiercely, that they all might live. Beneath him, she trembled, and he didn't know if it was desire for him or if the endless incantation of the drums had entered them both.

She reached for him, her fingers just touching his shoulders, tracing his collarbone, her eyes wide, luminous. She moistened her lips to speak, and her words were soft, quivering, yet filled with a passion that touched his soul.

"Everything," she repeated his words. "Damian, I will give you all I have to give. I would give you more if that were possible." She brushed a wayward lock of hair from his eyes, her fingers so soft so gentle. Guilt swamped him. She should not be here. He should have never taken her from Baltimore, never made her leave her beloved England.

Tonight was different from all others. He separated himself from the accusations, the anguish, and the whispers. He loved her and tonight that love was all that mattered. He didn't know how long he had loved her so intensely, maybe it had been forever. For all else paled beside this. No love he had known could be so deep, no hunger could be so intense.

He found her lips. They trembled beneath his and parted. Heat rippled and burst between them, spreading rampantly. His hands moved swiftly, circling the heavy fullness of her breasts, rounding over the rise of her belly, touching her.

The softness of her body seemed to meld to his. She twisted and turned, accepting his caress, wanting his touch. Soft sounds escaped her, sounds that sent desire rocketing more deeply into his mind and body.

"For myself, I am not afraid to die. But for you—you must make some promises to me. You must not anger anyone. Someone else, Ryder or Aric, will come for you. Feroz knows where I am. You will be saved. You must hold on." He promised her. His voice was harsh and fierce and yet what he tried to say to her overrode all else.

The urgency of her touch, pressing against him, set his flesh ablaze once again. Holding his breath, he let her have her way. Upon her knees, she leaned forward and kissed his shoulders, her fingers bit into his flesh and muscle. She kissed his lips, his chest. Swept into a newer, even sweeter fire, he caught her hand and guided it to the fullness of his sex.

A ragged cry escaped him. He pulled her into his arms then laid her flat against the hides and fur of the bedding. He caught her ankles, spreading her legs. He hovered over her, lips ravaging hers again, eyes seeking her own. His body screamed that he must have her then.

But something within him knew that he could not for he had to touch her more, had to feel her, see her, kiss her, touch her, taste her. He wanted to protect her shelter keep her from all harm. All he had was tonight.

Once again, his lips covered hers. They covered her breast. They bathed her belly, and even as she cried out, his kiss, his lips, his tongue stroked and teased her inner thighs, the cleft between them. A cry escaped her, then whispers and gasps. She urged him to her, near sobbing as she brought him into her arms.

"Amorica," he cried out.

He felt alive, vital and so damned, desperately hungry with desire. He scooped her into his arms. Sensations sheathed and sheltered him as he thrust into her. Her limbs wrapped around him, the liquid fire of her body accepted and encompassed him. He moved and let the thunder of the drumbeats call his rhythm, for he was far beyond reason, feeling the incredible rise of his climax. He fought the explosion, savoring the feel of his wife beneath him, the sleekness of her flesh, the undulation of her body, rising against his and meeting him. He felt the ragged rise and fall of her breath, the pure thunder of her heart.

But the wonder of the moments seemed as primitive as the throbbing drums. Passion within him took flight and soared, then burst in a violent climax. He felt the trembling beneath him, felt the explosion within her.

"My love..."

The words escaped him. He didn't know if she heard him or not.

He didn't care. He clenched his teeth, feeling the final thrust of his body, the last of the little explosions that shook him.

He held still. Felt the satiation fill his body. He lay down beside her, sweeping her damp, cooling body into his arms.

She began to speak.

He touched a finger to her lips, silencing her. "We have the night." She curled against him. She touched his face but her eyes would not rise to meet his gaze. "It will be gone before we know. And then—" It didn't seem as if she wanted to finish the sentence.

He smiled. "You have so little confidence in my abilities?" he queried softly.

"They trade in people. They are savage cutthroats. What do you know of their ways?"

"I am a smuggler." He reminded her.

She rose up, trying to see him in the flickering firelight. "Damian, I know I did not do as you asked. I have no right to expect you to understand the whole of it. Feroz—" There was a glaze of tears in her eyes.

Damian hesitated. "Feroz is alive and as I told you, he knows where I am. He is recovering and will make sure if something happens to me—he will move heaven and earth to bring you home."

"Oh, God," she whispered. "I pray he will not have to do so." Her fervent words touched his heart and he knew she spoke with such great sincerity. He prayed himself that the man who had been his good and loyal friend for so many years would be able to do his bidding if something happened to him.

Feroz wasn't here now. The real world was all he had, this shanty, the drums beating all around them, the flickering fire bathing them in its gold light, and the promise of the violence that would come with the morning.

"Damian—"

He reached up to her, threading his fingers through her hair, amazed himself that he could want her again, so desperately, so quickly. It might be all that he would have.

"Come here," he whispered, pulling her head down to his. His lips just a breath from hers, he told her, "We haven't that long." He rose, pressing her back down to the furs. But she moaned deep in her throat, protesting, tossing her head. She looked at him, her eyes wide and incredibly green, her hair wild and entangling them both.

"Damian, you said you might die. I don't understand."

"I am to meet Mason in the morning. We will fight for you with knives."

She inhaled sharply, and a shaking seemed to overtake her. "You—you can't meet him. He could kill you—"

Until now, he had thought she understood what was at stake. She had not. "Again I ask. Do you have such little faith in me?" She shook her head. "Oh, my God, Damian, it's just that—"

"I know. Hush now. Do not think on it. Tomorrow will come soon enough."

She swallowed hard, her lashes falling over her eyes. "I didn't think, Damian—"

"Not tonight," he said roughly.

He tried to capture her lips again, but she was speaking quickly. "Don't you see, this is your life. I can't think of a future without you. Damn you Damian, I don't want you to die for me. I don't want you to die for honor, not for my sake."

"Amorica, you are carrying my child," he reminded her.

She fell silent, breathing, her lashes once again covering her eyes. The longing in her eyes nearly broke his heart. "Before you came, I asked Chastity to bring you the baby if anything happened to me. You can change your mind. You don't have to fight."

"Amorica, even if I chose to, I couldn't leave you. My honor is at stake."

"Damian, you've never been one to let others dictate to you. And as to honor—" she broke off.

"Amorica, the night is waning. The morning is nearly here. I must prepare."

"Dawn?" she whispered.

"I have to go."

"No, you must sleep," she said desperately.

"I will sleep," he said. He threaded his fingers through her hair. "I will sleep soon enough."

"I—"

"No more protest."

She had no chance to do so for his lips claimed hers, and the kiss was deep and sweet, stealing the breath from her.

When he finally slept, she stared down at his face, memorizing the strong angles and planes, feeling tears form and fall. She jerked back, lest her tears wake him. If anything happened to him tomorrow, she had no one to blame save herself. If he died, she did not want to live. She loved him, desperately, deeply, with all of her soul.

"Live. Live to see your child. Live so that I may hold you once more," she whispered. Finally, she lay down beside him certain she would never sleep.

Yet she did, and when she woke, he was gone. The fur beside her was cold and empty. She heard cheers and chanting. She lay, staring at the ceiling of the longhouse. And then she remembered.

She jerked up. Damian. Oh, God, it had already started. He fought for his life as well as hers and she slept. She leapt up and found her clothes, slipping quickly into them. She burst from the house, afraid someone would stop her. But it seemed the entire village had vanished to a distant spot. She heard the cheering and followed the sounds.

When she saw him, she almost didn't recognize him. He was dressed in pants that were cut off at the knees and his skin had been rubbed with grease.

A knife had been given to both men. They circled each other, waiting and watching to see how the first exchange would be made.

Slater dropped his arm and the fight started.

Mason did not wait any longer. Snarling, he burst for Damian, casting him off-balance. Both men came down to the ground, writhing and rolling and viciously attempting to stab each other. Mason's knife skimmed Damian's back.

Amorica almost cried out, stopping herself in time. She did not want to draw Damian's attention away from the battle. She closed her eyes, feeling a mind-numbing terror freeze her. She heard the pirates give out a roar of approval, and she opened her eyes. Blood streamed down Damian's back.

They backed away from each other, circling then both balancing on the balls of their feet, awaiting the next move. Mason leapt high and came down upon Damian, smashing both of his feet against his chest. The air went from him, and he fell, stunned and dazed, unable to move.

She screamed.

He looked up and saw that Mason rushed him now with the sure fire of triumph in his eyes, his knife raised and aimed for Damian's heart.

Damian rolled. The man smashed into the earth. Damian leapt up then fell upon him. Both had been smeared with grease, and it was impossible to get a hold upon him.

The two men appeared evenly matched. Both men were superbly muscled, agile and alert to the slightest movement from the other. Mason made another flying lunge at Damian. The two men went down.

The men gathered tightly around the circle. Amorica could not see anything. She tried to push her way through the crowd jumping and stretching this way and that in an effort to see what was happening. She weaved her way through bodies, but was blocked again. She tried to twist through, and fell to the ground, crawling through on hands and knees.

A gasp escaped her. Tears welled into her eyes. Damian was upon the ground. Blood streamed from a gash across his chest; another sliced his thigh. His eyes were closed; he lay on his side in front of her.

No!" she cried in anguish, sure he was dead, sure she had lost the man she had grown to love. "Damian—"

He lay so still, so silent almost as if he slept. She could not let him stay there. "Damian!" she cried out once more. "Don't leave me." To Amorica it seemed he heard her. He groaned and moved, sitting up slowly yet coming alert. She would stop the fight. She would go with whoever wanted her. She could not let him die.

His lips curled suddenly. "I'm not going to die, at least not today.

He pulled to his knees. Amorica suddenly felt herself wrenched to her feet, held back by one of the men. She wasn't going to be allowed to come close anymore.

"No," she cried but to no avail. The man's hold upon her tightened and she found herself drug back into the crowd. She could just barely see the men moving. Circling, coming closer and closer.

Damian had wounded Mason. He had not gone unscathed, and yet she could not stop the shaking that swept through her, nor the horrific agony.

A war whoop shook the air. One of them had lunged. She could see their bodies entangled upon the earth. Arms and legs flailing, kicking, one man on top then the other.

She had never felt so helpless as she did now. The grease seemed to keep either man from getting a hold upon the other. She saw the man's dark eyes upon Damian, sizing him up, as they both seemed to hesitate.

Damian's jaw tightened, his muscles flexed. They were both losing blood. The blood dripped into his eyes from the wound on his forehead.

He had to win. She had seen many things in Mason's eyes. He hated her and he hated Damian. Yet it didn't matter. Nothing mattered save Damian's life. He had to win.

"I love you, Damian," she said over and over again. She prayed he heard. She prayed that in some small way the words would help keep him alive. She prayed. Love could be the strongest weapon of all. He would not die. They lunged again. The sound jarred and knives dug into flesh and bone.

Chapter Twenty-one

The men closed the circle tighter.

"Damian!" she cried out his name. Tears ran from her eyes. She wiped them away with the back of her hand, stretching, trying desperately to see inside the circle.

"No," she tried to rip away from the man who held her. He didn't release her, but the woman in front of her moved. She saw the bronzed chest of a man. He lay with his face pointed up to the sky covered with blood, grease, and dirt. The hilt of a knife protruded from the side of his rib cage.

"Damian..." she whispered. She started to fall. It was Damian, and he was dead. She really didn't care what happened to her anymore. Her knees were too weak to allow her to stand, and she would have fallen if the man had not held her upon her feet.

"Mason." She heard the name, and she inhaled swift and sharp, her heart nearly stopped. It was not Damian who had fallen. He was alive, and he was speaking and the men who held her so rigidly was at last moving forward.

Damian was alive. He was covered in as much blood as he was covered in grease and dirt. Standing seemed to be nearly impossible for him. He wavered and staggered yet he stood, and the other man was down.

He was talking to Slater.

"I am sorry for all that has come between us. Everything is in order and I would have leave to go home and live my life in peace. I promise I will not seek revenge. We have our honor. Let me take my wife and go home."

Amorica felt the man's hand upon her loosen yet she could still not wrench free to run to her husband. She watched as Damian exchanged more words with Slater. Then Slater nodded. He lifted a hand. The man released Amorica.

With a soft cry, she raced the distance to her husband. The weight of her against him almost caused him to keel over. She straightened quickly, made painfully aware of how he had been cut and injured. She tried to support his weight upon her shoulders, yet he would not lean upon her.

"Andrews, you are a brave and honorable soldier. Take your woman and return to your home."

Amorica inhaled a ragged breath, gazing at Damian. He smiled and stepped forward.

But he wasn't walking. He collapsed onto the ground.

"We must stop the blood," Slater said.

~ * ~

Damian woke with a jerk. "Amorica." He had dreamed he had died, that he'd been enveloped in an inferno of blood and flames.

"Hush," her voice floated across him like a sweet spring breeze. "You will live," she said.

When he opened his eyes, he saw her smile, smelled white roses and saw the crystal clarity of her fascinating green eyes.

"Don't laugh," he admonished.

"I am so happy you are alive. I will laugh and I will smile whenever I please." She leaned over him, a cool cloth pressed now to his forehead.

He blinked, trying to see her. Her face was very white and drawn. He tried to smile, but the effort seemed too much. He tried to rise.

"It's all right. You're going to be fine," she said.

He nodded. He wanted to talk to her. The effort seemed too much. He closed his eyes.

When he woke again, he felt stronger. He heard a soft whisper, and saw that Chastity had come to him. She brought a bowl of a thin-looking gruel. She smiled, offering it to him. He sipped the substance. It was something made from deer meat, he was certain. He downed it all, determined he would get his strength back.

"You should leave with your wife in the morning, Andrews. It is not safe here—for you or Amorica."

"We aren't welcome here?" he cocked an eyebrow.

"It's not that. It's just—well, you need to take her home and have a healthy baby."

"I understand."

Chastity smiled. "She has worried over you. She loves you very much."

Chastity disappeared. Damian lay down again, wishing he were still unconscious. They had survived. He closed his eyes. She was so warm beside him. He reached out, putting his arm around her, pulling her closer.

He slept again. When he woke, it was morning. Amorica was awake and watching him, setting cool cloths on his head.

He sat up to abruptly. His head throbbed, and his body burned with pain. Yet he had no choice. "We have to leave today." Panic touched her eyes. "You are not ready. You can't ride. You—"

"We must go. There is no choice." He touched his forehead, stifling a moan of pain. He was well bandaged with Amorica's old dress.

"We can't stay here," he insisted. He staggered to his feet. She followed along with him, supporting him. He stepped outside. Slater stood just outside with Blue Boy.

"Your hospitality will not be forgotten," Damian told him. "We are ready to leave if we can take a horse."

Slater nodded gravely. Chastity brought two horses. "There is food in the saddlebags and a skin of water. It will take you some time to ride home."

Damian nodded. "But I don't intend to stop except to eat and rest if necessary."

Slater nodded once more. "God be with you. I will leave you in peace and I promise no one will go near your property again." Yet the expression on his face did not speak of optimism. He reached out a hand to Damian.

Damian grasped it.

Blue Boy set Amorica on a horse. He assisted Damian onto another horse. "It is yours," Slater said.

Then Slater grinned and waved to Damian. Damian waved in return.

Following Damian, Amorica slowly rode from the camp. They traveled for several hours. Amorica rode up alongside Damian.

"You need to rest."

"We need distance between the camp and ourselves. While I trust Slater, there are those among his companions who were not pleased at the outcome of the fight."

"But they let us go."

"I want to be as far away as possible," he told her.

A while later she tried to talk to him again. "Thank you, Damian." He clenched his teeth, wondering just what he dare say to her. "For what?"

"For risking your life. You didn't have to come for me. You could have left me there and forgotten about me."

"Bloody hell, Amorica. You're my wife. You carry my child."

"Never the less, I am grateful. I didn't want to stay there."

"I don't want your gratitude."

She fell silent and allowed her horse to drop back.

He was stubborn and determined. More than anything he didn't want to say something to Amorica he would regret and even more than that he wanted to take her back to Baltimore and put her on a ship to England where she would be safe.

They rode until twilight. He dismounted, groaning inwardly at the strain. But before she could leap down from her mount, he stood beside her, reaching up to her.

She let him ease her to the ground then she quickly broke away from his touch. Moisture welled in her eyes. He wanted to brush the tears away and tell her all would be fine. But nothing would be the same again.

They had stopped at a beautiful, bubbling stream that was shaded by tall trees. Amorica unrolled a saddle blanket and spoke to Damien behind her. "Sit please, rest. I'll get the food from the saddlebags and the water." He stood for a moment then he obeyed her. She brought him water in the cup from his bags then returned for more, drinking what felt like half the brook herself before coming back to him. She produced the food and he ate it hungrily, wincing when his back moved against the bark of the tree.

She stood and walked away from him.

Damian watched her. He realized the pain from his wound wasn't half as great as that which now seared his heart. She was standing so proudly, trying to talk. But what was there for her to say?

She was returning to England. He meant to see her on the ship himself. He would never risk her life or his child's like this again. He wanted her with him. But not at her expense.

"Damian, I don't know what you are thinking, but I'm sorry. I will make it up to you. I will never disobey you again."

"It doesn't matter."

"It does matter." She cried suddenly, passionately. She fell silent, then. "Fine, if it doesn't matter, I'm going home just as quickly as I can, and I will not let you stop me!"

His heart was ripping apart. Agony seemed to sear into him. His head pounded; his wounds ached.

"You will return to England then."

"I'm going home because of all that has happened—" she began, but then stopped abruptly. "What did you say?"

"You're going home—to England." The cuts on his back were driving him crazy. He wanted to sleep, to ease the pain, to forget he only had a few days left with Amorica. He did not intend to return to England with her. This was his home now, his land. The last thing he wanted was another fight.

"What did you say?" She gasped out, spinning around. She had been standing by the stream, her back to him, a very noble pride to her stance, her hair free and falling down the length of her back.

She stared at him as if he'd gone insane. He wondered if he saw right because he was having some difficulty with his vision. He was almost certain tears streamed down her cheeks.

"You stupid, stupid, smuggler!"

"Amorica, I am in no mood for smuggler abuse."

"Don't talk to me of abuse. You told me you were sending me home."

"After you said you wanted to go," he reminded her.

"I don't want to go because I hate you. I want to go because I love you. And I don't want your life put in danger because of me. But I had hoped that you might want me to stay."

"What!" he exclaimed. Painstakingly, he rose to his feet. He must have yelled because her face paled and her shoulders began to tremble.

She looked as if she wanted to turn from him and run as far as she could.

"Chastity told me you loved me. That you were terrified I would come for you and terrified I would not. Tell me because I didn't dare believe she spoke true."

'I—" she began but words seemed to be frozen in her throat.

He stepped toward her, fighting for strength. His fingers suddenly curled around her arms. "Tell me."

"You shouldn't have had to risk your life for me. You shouldn't have been near death and bleeding from wounds that were inflicted because of me."

"Not that!" he yelled, shaking her, pulling her closer into his arms. "The other."

Her eyes widened. She caught her bottom lip beneath her teeth. She pushed her hair from her eyes, fingers shaking. "I—"

"Amorica—"

"Was it my imagination or did you just tell me you loved me." She nodded and lowered her lashes, her hair falling across her face.

Beneath his hands, he felt her trembling begin anew and more fiercely.

"Is it that hard to say the words?"

She looked up then, a fire blazing in her eyes. "I have yet to hear you say you loved me," she whispered the words even though he guessed she would have rather shouted them. He was stunned, shocked that after all this time he had not guessed that she could possibly love him.

"I—" She paused. "I said it!"

"Do you mean it?"

She lowered her gaze and then her head. "I mean it." Then her gaze rose to his again, simmering green. 'It's not that I don't want to be with you. I just don't want to hurt you, Damian. I know you would never really wish me dead rather than someone else, but I've been here with nothing more to think about than if perhaps you wished that I was your Meara."

"Bloody hell, Amorica." He closed his eyes tightly, wrapping her tenderly in his arms. "Amorica, she was fine and sweet and gentle, and yes, I loved her, and dear God, yes, I'm sorry she died, just as I am sorry your mother was killed. I have never wished you were anyone but you, and I have prayed only that our child might survive. If you haven't read my heart, Amorica, then you have not looked very closely."

She jerked away from him, her gaze crystal and doubting.

He smiled. "You stubborn wayward little fool," he charged her, glad to see the sizzle of anger touching her eyes. It was the Amorica he knew—and loved. "From the instant I was legally able to get my hands on you, I was obsessed. I wanted you so badly, Amorica, that nothing else mattered.

But then I'd made that damn vow to you. I never wanted to keep that promise, and every waking moment I looked for a reason to break it."

"I—" she simply couldn't speak.

"I could never have let you go. More than anything I wanted you to respond to me."

"I was afraid to. I was afraid I would lose my heart to you. But I already had. I fell in love with you when you wore those horrible clothes. And when I discovered you weren't what you pretended to be and that you were a smuggler, I felt betrayed. I never wanted to love a smuggler." She smiled ruefully. She looked down at the ground again. "Damian, I'm so sorry. I didn't even think when I was so determined to have my freedom. I thought you were simply putting undo restrictions on me. You didn't want me to enjoy the fresh air and the freedom of riding. You'd told me it was safe, and your smuggling days were over. I never thought slave traders would kidnap me."

He lifted her chin. "Amorica, nothing you did that day would have changed the outcome. Only a regiment of American soldiers could have defended our home from Mason's intentions. I never wanted you to know I was afraid, but I was worried about the move. I was too stubborn, and I told myself repeatedly the dangers were minimal and posed no threat. Sometimes I was furious with myself for tearing you away from your home, forcing you across the ocean. But then I knew I could never let you go. That I couldn't live without you. Amorica, we've been such fools, going in such ridiculous circles."

"I felt that I was competing with a ghost." She murmured suddenly, searching out his eyes.

"I am not your enemy. I have never killed anyone. The smuggling I did was only to help people not hurt them."

"But, oh, God, Damian, I have been afraid of smugglers for years. Every time I saw a ship on the horizon, I was afraid. I prayed fiercely they would not land near my home."

"I can undo none of that, but I would if I could." He said softly. His strength was suddenly failing him. He'd been so swept up by her confession, so torn, so anguished.

And then so awed. Watching her speak now, watching her eyes, still so wet with tears, he knew everything she said was true. She loved him.

He didn't know if it was the blood that he had lost or the simple miracle of her words, but he could stand no longer. He started to fall.

"Damian!"

She caught him before he fell to the ground. He leaned against the tree, his eyes closed, sweat beading on his forehead. He opened them.

Tears were damp against her cheeks. He touched them tenderly.

"Don't cry."

"Oh, my God, Damian," she whispered. "Don't die. Please don't die now that we finally understand each other."

He grinned very slowly. "I wouldn't die now. I've held heaven in my arms and intend to do so again."

She caught his hand and kissed each knuckle. "You must sleep." He nodded. "Of all the irony. We are alone, in one of the most beautiful spots I've ever set eyes upon, and I cannot even stand let alone make love to my wife who, after months together, has finally confessed her love for me."

She inhaled deeply then shook her head a smile forming on her lips.

"We will return here and make love. I promise, but now you must rest." She sat beside him, leaning her head against his. He was silent for a moment.

"Amorica, it may not be truly safe here. I have given up smuggling for farming. I still have enemies that might seek me out. We will always have to take care. But your mother—can you live with who I am?" he asked very softly.

She smiled, lowering her lashes, resting her head against his shoulders. "Yes."

"You're' positive?"

"I can live with anything, as long as I am with you. Don't send me away. If you do, I won't go. And if for some reason you get me on some ship sailing for England as soon as I reach land, I will turn right around and sail back to you."

"You would defy me?"

"In that, yes." Her smile deepened. "Just imagine how very, very deeply I love you."

He leaned back. His fingers moved in her hair. Branches stirred and rustled over them. The brook bubbled. "Amorica," he murmured.

"Damian?"

"I adore you." He planted a very tender kiss upon her lips.

Then, his strength spent, he leaned back against the tree and studied her.

~ * ~

Amorica dove beneath the water, the sensual pull of the cool water swept across her naked flesh. She stayed beneath until she had to breathe and when she surfaced, she dove again. After the night before and the confessions, she knew her life would never be the same. The water reminded her of the best part of her childhood, the pond near the castle where her mother taught her to swim, the island where her sisters and her cousins used to play and plan and imagine their futures as well as their husbands.

She surfaced again and swam slowly to the bank. She rose and squeezed the water from her hair. A sudden noise alerted her, and she looked up quickly.

Damian stood on the bank. He'd shed his buckskins. He was beautiful. The long red gashes that ran the length of his legs had been gained in his quest for her. Some of them would scar. Maybe that was good. She would remember for all time just what he had sacrificed for her.

The thought was very sobering because he could have sacrificed his life.

"What are you doing up?" she whispered to him.

"I could not resist watching you," he told her. He stopped before her in the water. The sunlight played upon it, mirroring both of their images.

"I believe I have found paradise."

He walked toward her. He paused for a moment. Maybe not paradise.

There were still problems to deal with. Despite his rippling bronze muscles, he was torn and wounded. And she was beginning to round more daily now with the baby.

He came before her and took her into his arms, kissing her with a slow burning fever and passion. "You should be resting," she reminded him. "I've slept half the day away and I'm feeling fine. I don't care if every gash in my body breaks open, I can't wait to make love to you in a new more delightful way."

"I don't understand," she said huskily.

"With you whispering in my ear that you love me, and with me crying out those same words every step of the way?" he told her.

"Oh, my," she said innocently. He kissed her then he kissed her throat, her lips, her collarbone.

"Damian?"

"What is it?"

"I love you."

Epilogue

May 17, 1818
Landsend, Dover, England

"You're back," Christel and Ravyn rushed up the rocky path to the lookout.

Amorica rose from the boulder where she sat, her heart open as well as her arms as her cousins rushed into them.

"I'm back, but I don't intend to stay. We will take the babe to London so The Duchess can see him and see that we are all fine."

"Where is he?" Christel and Ravyn asked. "We want to meet our newest nephew.

"Feroz has promised not to let him from his sight. He is with the nanny for now."

"Feroz? That giant of a man?" Ravyn asked.

"Gentle giant," she amended.

"And the proud, papa? Where is he?" Christel stepped up to the ridge looking out at the swirling ocean.

"I am supposed to meet him here soon, but for now he is attending some men who would like to buy land in the states. Start new lives."

"How is yours?" Christel asked.

Christel's curiosity surprised Amorica. "I am fine." She didn't know how much to tell her cousins. Yes, she had found two new loves, her husband as well as the new country they lived in, but now she was well aware of the dangers. They would not vanish although it was not as harsh as she had once thought. "The land is truly beautiful, amazing and fascinating. I would that both of you could see it."

"My love," Damian approached, tall and strong. His skin bronzed almost as much as the Indians one saw if traveling farther west. "I hoped I would find you here. I see your cousins have come to welcome us home." He dropped a casual but possessive arm around Amorica. "Perhaps we should talk later."

Amorica smiled. "We have nothing to hide. I know in my heart we will return to the states. I only wish I could persuade my cousins to come with us."

Amorica watched as Christel shuddered and Ravyn frowned. It was too much to hit them with all at once.

"Go on now, go see the baby. Go see the newest of the Andrews and Hepburn clans. I think my husband wants to speak in private." The pair stood on the ledge and watched the cousins ride down the path. Ravyn and Christel both excellent riders, sitting their mares with tall straight backs, hair flowing in the sea breeze. She had come full circle but the circle had not ended. She didn't care what Damian said, what arguments he presented her with, Amorica knew her heart and she was sure she knew Damian's.

"I want to go home," she told him, "back to America." And she smiled, watching his face and the ever-changing expressions, feeling a warmth sweep around her. She loved him so much, yet it seemed she loved him more each day. She touched his dark hair, marveling at the color and the thick rich feel of it. "The point of this story is that England is a nice place to visit, but it isn't home."

"It was my understanding you wanted to stay here for a while." She shook her head and waved a hand in the air. "I might have thought so. But I think I only wanted to see if I could convince either of my dear cousins to travel back with us. I fear they both turned up their noses at the idea. Although I believe they had different reasons." He took both her hands in his. "So, when do we return to that primitive, savage land across the ocean?"

She realized he would do whatever she wanted, despite his own desires. She started to tremble and she reached up and threaded her fingers through his hair. "Oh, my God Damian," she whispered. "How I love you." He caught her hand and kissed her palm tenderly. "Amorica—"

"We can stay here, we can go. Home is where the heart is and my heart is with you."

He lifted her into his arms. She stared at his dark eyes. They were no longer sad and empty.

"What will we do?" she asked.

"Ah—" he said. He whirled around with her and walked with her to a secluded mossy glen. It was down the path but off it far enough no one would dare disturb them. When he reached it, he lowered her to the ground and came upon his knees pulling her against him, entwining their fingers together.

He kissed her. Kissed her long and leisurely, savoring the taste and touch and feel of her lips, the brush of their bodies just barely touching one another.

"What will we do?" she repeated one more time.

He grinned, his lips barely a breath away from her. "I think you know.

As wonderful as Jessie's aunts are, he will want his supper, and soon.

Although there is nothing I would deprive my son of, I want his mother too. And so I must find my pleasure with her now."

"What will we do?" she persisted.

"The future will write itself. It always does." She smiled. And then her smile was captured in the inferno of his next kiss. The flames raged and burned around them. The ocean sounds enveloped them in a tumultuous onslaught of sweetness and secrecy, magic and miracles.

"I love you, Damian Andrews," she whispered to him.

"I love you as well," he told her just before he captured her lips again.

She loved Damian with a strength of emotion she could have never predicted. She, Damian, and their children were destined to build a dynasty in a new land far from England.

Also by Christine Young
Available at Rogue Phoenix Press

Ravyn's Marriage of Inconvenience
Twelve Dancing Princesses Book Three

A REGAL BEAUTY

When The Duchess decides to wed her to a wastrel and a fop, Ravyn Grahm takes matters into her own hands and declares her engagement to another man. Instead of fessing up and telling her great aunt what she has done, she goes through with the pretense. Aric Lakeland is the bastard son of an earl and has a dangerous reputation. But Ravyn is willing to do most anything to keep The Duchess from discovering the lie.

A DEVIL-MAY-CARE SMUGGLER

He'd bought land in America, looking to put down roots and end his life of adventure, but Aric Lakeland got more than he bargained for when he encountered a beautiful heiress who made a promise she didn't want to keep. But the promise could not be undone and standing between them were more obstacles than either ever dreamed. Aric had made plans to spend the rest of his life in America and that was at odds with Ravyn's plan of living in England and running her father's estate. Now, he'll have to choose between his dreams and the woman he loves more than life.

Chapter One

London 1817

Aric Lakeland dodged foot-traffic along the boulevard in a crazy attempt to keep up with the bouncing erratic carriage he followed. The day was intolerably hot and his mood was no better. He resented this mission. He'd left a cool pub and a cold brew to sweat beneath the hot sun.

His idea of fun was not traipsing after a notorious gambler and womanizer. Nor did he want to babysit a spoiled debutante.

Yet, he'd promised. A wave of guilt washed through him.

Sweat beaded on his forehead, dripping down his face. He swiped it with the back of his hand and sidestepped, nearly knocking packages from a lady just exiting a dressmaker's shop.

"You owe me, my friend. When this is done, I will collect," he swore beneath his breath and began thinking of all the favors he might ask of his half-brother, Damian Andrews.

The carriage he followed turned a corner and disappeared from sight. He plowed into a lamppost, swore again and raced through the crowds. Richy Richmond did not deserve this absurd protection. He could deal with his own affairs. The other part of Damian's request bothered Aric. He did not want anything to happen to the lady he followed. His half-brother had reason to believe Richy might do something to compromise her. His gut instincts had never been wrong. Ravyn Grahm, cousin to Damian's wife, was in serious trouble.

Richy's carriage came to an abrupt halt. He jumped from the vehicle. His cane in hand, he strode toward a dress shop Aric had reason to visit on occasion.

Aric watched, fascinated as the scene unfolded. He started forward but noticed Richy race to protect the women Aric followed.

"You ruffians! Get your hands off me!" The white-haired duchess shrieked, her age-lined face mottled with rage, pushing at two little guttersnipes who seemed more intent on shoving the elderly woman around than stealing the packages she carried.

Ravyn swiped her parasol across a boy's head and turned to the other, her eyes blazing, shooting violet-blue sparks.

"Stop it!" she cried out, raising her parasol again and again. "Take that! And that!"

Amused, Aric leaned against a lamppost similar to the one he had run into earlier in his race to keep Richy's carriage in view.

He crossed his arms over his chest, grinning as he watched Ravyn batter the boys who'd had the audacity to try and harm The Duchess.

He chuckled, prepared to step in if needed, but it appeared the two women had the situation under control. Ravyn, he mused, the regal, classy lady who seldom had a hair on her gorgeous head out of place was decidedly disheveled. Her cheeks were flushed, her hair flowed beautifully from its once perfectly coiffed hairdo. Her jacket sleeve was torn and to his amazement, she grinned as if she were having the time of her life.

"Go on, get," Richy stepped in, shooing the two boys away. He grabbed hold of one of the boy's arms and shook him. "Patrol," he yelled, looking around for help. The boy stomped on Richy's foot. Surprised, Richy let go. "Bloody hell! Come back here. Little brat," he yelled as the boy ran off.

Aric cocked an eyebrow, watching and wondering what would happen next, knowing Richy had a card up his sleeve. He had not forgotten he was supposed to be watching Richy, nor had he forgotten the man had suffered innumerable losses at the gaming tables and the racetrack the last few days and he might do something to Ravyn.

Aric pushed away from the lamppost and strode toward the women and Richy. He watched Richy change demeanor. Suddenly, instead of rescuer, he was attacker. Aric's heart stopped for a moment then raced.

Richy, wrenched Ravyn against him, pulling her close, her arm behind her back, his mouth close to her ear as if he whispered something to Ravyn.

"Let go," Ravyn cried out, twisting and thrashing her arms. It seemed to be the opposite scenario as moments before. The crowds that had previously closed around the women had now dissipated.

"Bastard!" Ravyn cried again.

"You're mine, Ravyn," Richy said in a low well-modulated voice. "You should have realized it months ago, and I'd have won the wager. But instead, you ignored me. You taunted me and sometimes you pretended to care while other times you turned up your pert little nose when I walked by."

"What do you think you are doing? Let go of me!" Ravyn cried out, hatred now blazing in her stormy violet eyes.

To Aric, she sounded incredulous, perhaps confused. But strangely, not afraid.

"We..." he paused a moment, "are going to Gretna Green. We are getting married and I will inherit your estate. You will be mine."

"Never." She kicked out at him. And The Duchess who had regained her balance straightened her clothes.

"Now, now, children," she began.

Richy's powdered wig went slightly askew and he let go of Ravyn with one hand to adjust it.

"I cannot! I don't want—" she began. But Richy waved a ringed hand in the air.

"Of course you can. There is nothing stopping you. See?" he looked around, his gaze seeming to move up and down the street.

"Never," she caught sight of Aric. "I am already—"

"Already what?"

"I have someplace to go." Now she appeared panic struck. Terror filling her eyes.

Aric watched her moisten her lips, confusion clear in her expression. He stepped up, "Let her go." He commanded.

The Duchess straightened her skirts. "Young man," she turned on Aric, doing what seemed to him as a complete about-face. "You have no business here. Ravyn is getting married. It is about time."

Aric cocked his head to one side, one eyebrow rising and his smile strangely mocking. "It seems the lady is distressed. I was simply offering her my help."

"She doesn't need help. Richmond is quite acceptable marriage material," The Duchess spoke clearly. She had drawn herself up to her full five feet in height; her hands on her ample hips and it seemed to Aric she meant to drive him away.

"You heard The Duchess," Richy sneered, a leering grin on his face. "We don't need help from a bastard."

Aric's good humor vanished. He had done this to help a friend, but now Richy had made this personal. "Bastard, you say? Well it's better than a wastrel."

"Leave us be, the lady and I are engaged," Richy snarled.

He looked at Ravyn for confirmation. Her face had grown pale. Her eyes were huge pools of fearful astonishment, and she shook her head at Aric while she tried to dislodge her arm from Richy.

Aric looked to The Duchess who seemed content but not completely pleased. He guessed The Duchess was simply using this as an opportunity presenting itself. It was well known how hard The Duchess was working to see Ravyn married. In most quarters, Richy's perfidy was unknown. Perhaps The Duchess had no idea how desperate Richmond was to find a rich wife.

He heard Ravyn once more whisper, "Nooo." But if The Duchess was in favor of a marriage to Richy Richmond, then the situation was no longer his business.

"I will not marry him." Ravyn's gaze darted to Aric then searched the crowd as if she hoped more help would come her way and fearful Aric would back down.

"You will," The Duchess told her. "I will send word to your father. And I will tell him all I know of this fine young man. Then I will notify the paper. I will have done my duty where you are concerned. I will see you wed." Her voice gentled.

"No," Ravyn's shoulders trembled, she pressed her hand to her head and for a moment, Aric was sure she might faint. "You cannot. My father would never agree to this marriage."

"Don't be ridiculous," The Duchess said, waving off Ravyn's complaint as meaningless.

"I cannot," she protested once more.

"Why?" Both The Duchess and Richy chorused.

"Because..."

Once again, she moistened her lips then she bit down on her lower lip all the while looking from The Duchess to him. He had never seen her quite so intriguing and fascinating. He did wonder what reason she would come up with for her refusal of marriage. *I do not want to*, seemed good enough for him, but in his experience, most women needed to come up with something a bit more fanciful.

"Why?" The Duchess asked again, tapping her foot impatiently on the walkway. "Come now child, you must give me a valid reason. I see nothing wrong with this young man. Why, he has been courting you for over a year now and he has always behaved as a gentleman."

"I don't want to."

"Come now, you think you can do better? If your father were here, he would make sure you gave no protest. He charged me with the task of seeing you married."

"I..." She stammered once again, her eyes meeting his. She looked at him as if she wished he would come up with some good reason.

"Children, now, you don't have to go to Gretna Green. If you thought I would stand in your way, Richy, you were wrong. I heartily approve of this marriage."

"Noooo," she said again and a bit louder. Ravyn reminded Aric of a wounded deer, wide-eyed and searching desperately for a place to hide.

"Now, Ravyn," Richy said pleadingly. "I think you do protest too much."

"You are a scoundrel of the worst sort," she said. "I detest you and all you and your kind stand for."

He plucked an imaginary piece of dirt from his scarlet coat.

"You will not speak that way of me when we wed."

No, Aric thought. Richy would most likely hide her away at the old castle and seek his pleasures in London. He would impregnate her first. An heir was necessary.

"We will not wed," she protested one last time, stuttering for a moment. "I will never say the words and no one can force me."

"You are being unreasonable, dear," The Duchess said before directing a pointed glance his way.

He saw Ravyn swallow hard, saw her chin move one notch higher while her shoulders squared. "Because," she caught her lower lip beneath her perfect top white teeth. Then she inhaled deeply. "Because I am already wed."

"What?" Once again, Richy and The Duchess echoed the same

question.

"I am wed already. I went to Gretna Green with—"

"No," Richy cried out. "She lies." He pointed a shaking finger at Ravyn, his face a blotched and mottled red.

Ravyn gasped dramatically, her hand at her throat. "Apologize," she said.

Richy seemed to gain control of his emotions. "No, you are a little liar," Richy's purr changed to a sneer. His true personality rising to the situation.

"I think you best do just that," The Duchess told her. "Apologize to Richy. You know you shouldn't lie."

Richy drew himself up, a smug smile on his face, and gave an approving nod to The Duchess.

"I don't understand what you are doing?" Ravyn spoke to The Duchess. "I thought you wanted us to be happy. I thought you wanted what was best for us. I don't love him."

"Love is not necessary for a marriage. You will learn to love him with time. Your father charged me with seeing you wed. I intend to do just that."

"Duchess—"

She waved a hand in the air. "He is well appointed. His pedigree is implacable. And he has money."

Aric thought he should step in here. "Richy has been disowned by his father and he has lost two fortunes at the gaming table just this week. He no longer has an inheritance or a pedigree. He needs Ravyn's money."

"Bah, 'tis sour grapes," The Duchess said, pointing an accusing finger and staring pointedly at Aric.

"I will never marry him and that should be enough said, but..." Ravyn turned her back on Richy.

Aric shrugged. "Think what you will."

Ravyn shook off Richy's tight hold on her arm and stepped forward, pushing her disheveled hair back and picking up her skirts so she wouldn't trip. She placed her hand on Aric's arm and looked into his eyes before she spoke.

"I cannot marry Richy because I am already wed to Aric."

"We eloped," Ravyn said sweetly, sugar lacing each word.

Beneath her fingertips, she felt Aric stiffen.

Dear God, what will I do? Aric must go along with this ruse. How can I convince him without words of explanation?

Not daring to look in his eyes, Ravyn pressed into him, closing whatever gap there might have been, and trying desperately to convince The Duchess she spoke true. She batted her lashes flirtatiously even though she never wanted to look at Aric again. Yet she was heartened he did not deny her crazy proclamation.

"You're trembling." The concern in Aric's expression and voice gave Ravyn hope. He did care. If only just a little.

Only a real gentleman would go along with such a fanciful ruse. The Duchess would give in, Richy would leave, and she could apologize to Aric as well as thank him for rescuing her.

The Duchess, her Aunt Charlotte cleared her throat, her expression stern. "This is reprehensible. You denied me the privilege and fun of planning your wedding? How could you?"

It was, Ravyn had to agree, worse than reprehensible. She never wanted to hurt her aunt, but she never wanted to marry a man such as Richy. If The Duchess had not accepted him so readily—as a suitor—as a husband...

"She lies," Richy snarled, stepping forward, waving his hands in anger, his face blotchy. "She has been in the city for weeks. She could not have done such a thing."

For a moment, Aric's grin vanished. He pulled Ravyn closer. "Would you want to meet me at dawn?" he queried of Richy. "No one talks about my wife in that manner. She does not lie."

Ravyn swallowed down her panic. Thank God, he played along with her. "Chivalry is not dead," she looked up at Aric and flashed a wide smile, touching his chin softly with one fingertip—a lover's caress.

He leaned down close to her and whispered. "Be careful what you do, little minx. You may not be able to mend the netting."

The warning gave her chills. Be careful? She had no choice. She could never marry Richy, and she thought Aric an honorable man. When they retired to the townhouse, she would be able to tell the story in its entirety to her aunt.

Lord, she hoped she would understand.

"You have a lot of explaining to do, young man." The Duchess parroted Ravyn's thoughts. When she spoke to Aric, her bony finger tapped his chest. "While I approve of impulsiveness where love is concerned, you have gone too far. You should have consulted me. I am her guardian."

"I intend to explain myself and our actions," Aric said, looking at Ravyn. He collected The Duchess's hand in his and placed a gentlemanly kiss on the back of it.

The Duchess blushed. "Of course you will. I don't want to hear you spin any tall tales. You hear me? I want the truth and I want to know why you felt you had to steal away to Gretna Green in the middle of the night without telling a soul. You could have stepped forward and asked for her hand in the normal way."

"Remember who I am, duchess. I'm a bastard—"

"Pishaw. You should know me by now. I want a good, honest, hard working young man for my niece. I want a man who will take charge. Ravyn has a mind of her own, you know. She is in need of someone who can protect her and take care of her."

Ravyn felt dumbstruck by her aunt's words. And The Duchess thought Richy would make a fine husband? When Ravyn looked at Aric, he grinned like a little boy who just tasted his first piece of taffy. But that could never be. No man wanted to be tricked this way. Ah, well, he must think he can explain his way out of this to The Duchess.

She certainly prayed he could.

"You were about to give me to Richy. He has never worked a day in his life." Ravyn felt betrayed; the genius of her declaration of marriage starting to come full circle.

"I thought he would do nicely. But Aric Lakeland, bastard or not, is charming, fascinating, I think, and he can handle you."

"Handle me." She left Aric's side. "I will not be handled by any man."

Aric cleared his throat. "I think we would all benefit by retiring to The Duchess's townhouse and let her know how all of this transpired."

"Yes. I would like to know when this happened," The Duchess said, happily picking up her skirts and heading for her carriage.

"I would too," Richy said furiously.

"You are not coming with us," The Duchess told him. "This is not your concern. The matter will be handled privately."

"It most certainly is," Richy puffed up his chest. "If he cannot give a proper explanation, I will be forced to call him out."

"Really," Aric said. "That might solve any number of your problems."

Heat rose to Richy's cheeks. "Perhaps I will stop by another time," he said quickly, turned on a bespangled slipper and got back inside his carriage, muttering angrily as he went.

Ravyn had never felt quite so relieved in her life. Now all she had to do was tell the truth. The Duchess would forgive her, as would Aric, and he would be on his way. There would be no marriage.

"Why me?" Aric leaned close and whispered to her as The Duchess was helped into the waiting carriage. "You know we do not suit at all."

Ravyn smiled at the grinning man but could not think of the right words.

"Ravyn," he said, the roguish smile vanished, a tone of demand in his voice. It was a side of Aric she had never seen. "I want the truth. All of it."

Fear made Ravyn stumble. Aric caught her and set her right with the same casual grace he did everything. "You were there. And..." She began then quit, not quite knowing what it was she should say. There was no excuse for what she had done to him.

"Are you coming?" The Duchess asked, her head poking unduchess-like from the window of her carriage.

Aric waved her away. "We will be along, shortly. Ravyn and I have a few things to talk over. Don't we, my love." He smiled at The Duchess, nodding to the driver and backing away from the vehicle, his hand closing over Ravyn's elbow in the process.

Ravyn swallowed, having horrific misgivings. She had this strange image of her life in sudden upheaval. His hold on her was powerful, his voice demanding, and she had just put him in a position where he would have to defend himself and the lie he did not deny.

He'd had every opportunity to deny it too. And she was forever grateful he had not.

What now?

She looked at him. "I'm sorry. You must be horribly angry with me. I—"

"That cannot begin to describe what I feel," he spoke slowly, watching her, his gaze implacable. "You put me in a position of lying to a woman I admire and respect. I am an honest and honorable man."

"I—"

"Ravyn, you have much to atone for." He grinned again. Ravyn knew she should not let down her guard. Propagating the lie had been a horrendous mistake.

"I could think of nothing else to say." She shook her head, hoping that one little piece of truth would appease him.

"Well, you best think of something by the time we reach the townhouse, or you might indeed find yourself wed to me."

His jaw was clenched tight and a muscle ticked. He felt his grip tighten around her elbow.

"We will just tell my auntie the truth." She smiled, knowing the truth was the only way.

"And you will find yourself wed to Richy," he reminded her pointedly.

"You cannot mean to go on with this ruse." She cried out in dismay. He could not. She did not want to wed Richy, nor did she wish to spend her life with Aric. While he was nice enough, he was wild and rugged. He fascinated her. Yet she trembled at the sight of him. A strange trembling. One that was not fear but something else, something deeper. His handsome form and a beguiling smile did not a match make, she knew very well.

He'd said so himself. They did not suit.

Aric was a smuggler. While she did not feel the same as her cousin Armorica about smugglers, she did not intend to live a life of deceit. A little white lie, one that could easily be corrected was all right, but an entire life pretending she was someone she was not was far from acceptable.

"I presume you would go to any length not to wed Richy. And yet I have suddenly found I am caught in your lies," he told her. It seemed anger overshadowed his previous jaunty mood. He no longer smiled. "I expect you will have a plausible answer for The Duchess when we arrive at the townhouse."

"Is that why you held me back?" she queried. "I thought it was to tell me how angry you are."

"Furious," he said. "I do not appreciate aristocratic debutantes who play games at my expense."

She inhaled deeply, closing her eyes for a moment then opening them to look at gold-flecked eyes, gazing down at her. Angry eyes, she acknowledged.

"Well, don't worry. I will fix this."

"I will hold you to that," he told her and hailed a cab. He helped her inside and she watched as he leaned back and the cab started up. He seemed to relax but she was sure it was simply a ruse.

They rode in silence. Ravyn stared out the window, her heart in her throat. Nervously, she bit down on her lip. The Duchess had to believe her story, had to accept the lie and her reason for it. If she didn't accept it, Ravyn Grahm would find herself married to Richy Richmond and that she thought was indeed a fate worse than death.

And yet—

If she pursued the lie, she would find herself wed to Aric Lakeland. At least a bastard would not need an heir. She would not have to bed him.

It was the longest ride of her life. Finally, the carriage pulled to a stop in front of the townhouse. When she turned to look at Aric, he was staring at her as if to say, have you thought of anything yet?

He escorted her up the brick-lined walk to the front door. It was opened by the butler. "Mr. Lakeland," he said, "Miss Grahm."

She nodded yet she did not feel any better.

"The Duchess waits for you in the parlor. She has ordered celebratory drinks."

Aric cleared his throat and nodded. The roguish smile she'd admired earlier once again had vanished. It seemed he was still furious. When she looked at him now, his features were dangerous, hard and so very cold she felt chilled to the bone. Yet the first time she'd seen him, almost a year ago, she'd been charmed by his smile. Her heart had fluttered and golden butterflies had danced in her stomach.

"Welcome," The Duchess held out her hands, raking Aric with a happy smile and turning to Ravyn to take her hands. "I have never been so displeased. I have waited too long for your wedding, and now I have only your cousin to see married."

"Duchess—"

She let go of Ravyn and waved her hands. "You do not have to explain. The two of you were so eager you couldn't wait for the proper time to pass. Oh," she sighed, "it is so romantic. I was young once." She looked so wistful Ravyn did not want to break her heart.

"Duchess—"

"Now you, on the other hand, have to apologize. You have deprived me of planning your wedding as your cousin did. So, we will have a huge party in your's and Aric's honor. I have already sent a notice of your nuptials to the paper and I have invitations being printed as we speak."

"Nooo—" She began, blood draining from her face then cut herself off.

"What don't you like?" The Duchess turned, her skirts swirling about her, a strange smile on her creased face.

Ravyn moistened her lips then looked to Aric for advice. He was leaning against the mantle, arms crossed nonchalantly in front of him, watching her. Yet beneath the casual demeanor he seemed angry, furiously so. She prayed his seeming fury was her imagination. He nodded at her as if he was challenging her. She had to find a way to make this right.

"Now," The Duchess said. "I have had a room prepared upstairs for the two of you. I'm sure Aric has missed seeing his bride of—how many weeks? Two perhaps? And, I'm sure the two of you have a lot to talk about—and things to do." She waltzed from the room humming.

Ravyn whirled on Aric, a heated flush to her cheeks. "You haven't said a word. You're enjoying this aren't you?"

He shrugged. "Not particularly. What makes you believe I enjoy lying or watching you squirm? Besides, I have every confidence that you will figure a way out of this predicament."

"Oh," she wanted to stomp her foot. "What are we going to do?"

His brows furrowed together, he pushed away from the mantle and approached her. "I think I might enjoy the wedding night. What about you?" he asked, his voice a hard rasp.

Her face paled and she suddenly felt the floor undulate. "Wedding night?" she repeated. Startled, she looked at him. "You are despicable. We are not married. You cannot think that I would—"

He nodded. "We will be sharing a room tonight. I don't intend to sleep on the floor."

"You cannot."

"Then tell me what it is I should do. Tell The Duchess? She will be humiliated in front of all London. The notice will be in the paper in the morning. Then she will have all her friends to explain this to."

"But you do not want to marry me anymore than I want you."

"I seem to be taking a liking to the idea. At least the bedding part. You are quite beautiful."

"No," she was backing away, wishing the floor would rise up and swallow her.

"Yes," he said, eyebrows rising.

"But..." She was speechless.

"Be forewarned. In one week, we sail for America."

Christel's Sunrise
Twelve Dancing Princesses Book Four

He Made Her An Offer...

Life has thrown Christel McClellan some experiences that could have devastated a less determined woman. Beautiful, self-assured and fiercely independent, she is trying to forget the loss of her stillborn child. But is the child alive?

She Couldn't Deny...

Life is carefree for Ryder MacLaren who loves to see what is on the other side of the sunrise. Laird of Clan MacLaren, he is wealthy, handsome and happily unencumbered... until stunning Christel McClellan enters his life. When he hears her story, he believes the child she thought dead has been sold to a wealthy buyer.

Storm's Passion
Twelve Dancing Princesses Book Five

SHE MADE A PROPOSAL...

Life strikes Storm Graham a shattering blow when she learns her father has bartered her to a man she detests. Storm is beautiful, self–assured and fiercely independent, and refuses to be a pawn in her father's schemes, yet she can find no way out of this bargain made in hell. Going on the offensive she asks the wealthiest man on the eastern coast of England to marry her, never believing she might fall in love.

HE TRIED TO REFUSE...

For Hadden Johnston life has provided everything he ever wanted, including a sanctuary for homeless children. He is wealthy, handsome and happily unencumbered... until stunning Storm Graham marches into his life and proposes a marriage of convenience. Yet this type of marriage to a woman who inflames his senses is far from acceptable. If he's going to be tied down, he will move heaven and earth to have this woman warming his bed.

Gotta Have Fayth
Twelve Dancing Princesses Book Six

A regal beauty with raven hair and piercing blue eyes, Fayth Graham is unwilling to parade herself in front of the wealthy Lords of England during the season. Seeking a means to dissuade any man wishing to wed her, she seeks a way to ruin herself for marriage. When she unexpectedly meets a man with sparkling gray eyes and an infectious grin, she decides this is the man who will keep her from agreeing to obey.

He returned from six months at sea, looking for a few nights of pleasure with a willing lass, but Jarret Kinsley got more than he bargained for when he met a beautiful debutant who responded to his kisses with a wild innocence that touched his heart. Yet the obstacles looming between them might rip them apart. Both had vowed never to marry, so when consequences of their dalliances got in the way, Jarret would have to choose between the life he's always desired and the woman he loves more than life.

Ella's Pleasure
Twelve Dancing Princesses Book Seven

A WHISPER OF PLEASURE

Ella Hepburn was an auburn haired debutant from the harsh Scottish coastline—a wild innocent to be seduced and tamed. A spirited beauty, she captivated Drake Montgomerie's jaded heart—while succumbing to the smoldering desire she felt for her unyielding suitor.

A WHISPER OF DANGER

In Drake Montgomerie's glittering world of money and privilege, young Ella discovered passion and desire could overcome everything she'd been taught to resist—entangling Drake, the heir apparent, in a lethal coil of aristocratic family intrigue. But grave peril would only nurse the sparks of a love that knew no limits and a magnificent ecstasy that would not be denied.

Eveleen's Seduction
Twelve Dancing Princesses Book Eight

A WHISPER OF SEDUCTION

A brutal attack on Eveleen Hepburn's cherished island off the Scottish coastline leaves her shattered and bewildered. Learning a man she once trusted can kill as easily as he can breathe even though the deed saves her life, creates questions that need answers. An innocent beauty, she enchants Logan Maxwell's cynical heart—giving in to the raging passion she feels for her mysterious suitor.

A WHISPER OF INTRIGUE

In Logan's Maxwell's world of espionage and privilege, young Eveleen discovers truths about herself she never expected, and a need for passion and love can overcome all her fears if she learns to accept certain truths. She finds herself entangled in a lethal battle for land that was once owned by French nobility, taken from them during the revolution and sold to Maxwell. But grave peril would unleash the flames of love that simmers, creating a magical union that cannot be refuted.

Tavia's Deception
Twelve Dancing Princesses Book Nine

WHISPERS OF DECEPTION

When her father decides to send her to London for her season, Tavia Hepburn resolves to see the world instead. The raven haired beauty decides to disguise herself as a lad and find employment on a ship bound for Barcelona as a cabin boy. But she never bargains on finding passion and love to a red haired sea captain who rescues her from certain death.

WHISPERS OF MURDER

For James Macmurra, the world is black and white until he meets a young debutante, who turns his world upside down. He's unable to deny Tavia's intoxicating effect on him. In a match tense with obstacles, unwillingness to divulge secrets, and unforeseen peril, irresistible desire and passion grows into undeniable love. James would risk his life to shelter and protect the innocent debutante who seduces him with her sweet love.

Larena's Fascination
Twelve Dancing Princesses Book Ten

WHISPERS OF FASCINATION
Fiery, free spirited Larena Graham never wanted to marry a duke. She is thrilled to be in love with the fourth son of an aristocrat, Gavin Broon. But when it seems Gavin ignores her, she set her sights on politics and bettering human life. Unsuspecting intrigue and a plot against her, she continues her dangerous plans despite Gavin's wishes.

WHISPERS OF TRUST
Gavin has every intention of properly courting the beautiful Larena until he must leave the city in order to put his affairs in order. Returning to London, he finds the woman he means to make his own is embroiled in political protests that could lead to a prison ship. Larena must learn to trust the handsome Scotsman whose most pressing mission is to protect her and keep her from harm.

Tira's Education
Twelve Dancing Princesses Book Eleven

WHISPERS OF EDUCATION
Learning how to build ships is Tira Hepburn's only dream until she meets Jamie Lundin and her world is turned upside down. With her raven black hair and vivid green eyes, she tempts Jamie and pushes him to defy his vows. She never bargains on finding an irrevocable love and a

passion to a man who cannot fulfill her dreams despite his burning desire for her.

WHISPERS OF A BARGAIN

Arrogant and self-assured Jamie is brought up short when Tira captures his heart. All his carefully made plans are put to the test when he decides to teach her the art of ship building if she will spend a week with him alone on his ship. He is unable to deny Tira's intoxicating effect on him. When Tira leaves him behind unwilling to live with him without the benefit of marriage, he races after her. Jamie will risk everything to shelter and protect the innocent debutante who seduces him with her sweet love.

Aidan's Love
Twelve Dancing Princesses Book Twelve

Whispers of Love

Aidan McLellan has loved since she first set eyes on him as a young girl. Spontaneous, wild and eager to grow up, Aidan haunts his waking thoughts day and night, insinuating herself into his life. With her fiery red hair and sparkling sapphire eyes, she seizes Blade's heart even while he tries to resist the innocent child until she becomes a woman.

Whispers of Courage

Blade has waited what seems a lifetime to claim the woman who captures his heart as a little girl. Claiming his inheritance before his younger brother takes what is rightfully his, Blade must convince Aidan of his sincerity after years of avoidance and wed her before his father dies so he can return home, securing his rightful place. Everything is put to the test when his life as well as Aidan's is threatened by the man who once called him brother.

Twelve Days to Love

When Archer Steele shows up at Calanthe Durand's failing

plantation with an alligator over his shoulder, Cali thinks she's never seen a more handsome man. During the war she had to defend herself and her servants from both union and confederate soldiers. Independent and self-sufficient, she vows to never marry.

But Archer Steele has different ideas. The first time Archer sees Cali in town, he feels an instant attraction. He decides he will do everything and anything to convince the beautiful Miss Durand he is worthy of her love. During the weeks leading up to Christmas, he gives her twelve gifts in hopes she will fall in love with him. Yet they are faced with challenges they must overcome before Cali can commit to a marriage.

Door to Heaven

Jessica Lawrence is the stepdaughter of a woman born in the twentieth century transported back in time to the year 1868. An acclaimed suffragette, she raises Jessica to believe in the equality of women. Jess Law believes everything she was taught, and when the time is right she becomes a private investigator. Courageous and impetuous, Jess finds danger in her quest to save all women from white slavery. Her passionate mission results in a wedding to Roc Newman, a man she knows can steal her heart...

Roc can't trust the sapphire-eyed spitfire who invades his home in search of secret papers and knocks him flat with her karate moves. Jessica's refusal to obey his wishes serves to inflame the war between them. Still, he cannot control the intense desire his reluctant bride inspires, or make her surrender her independence, until he has conquered the headstrong beauty on the battlefield of love...

Rebel Heart

HER REBEL SPIRIT DEFIED HIS OUTSIDERS SOUL... She was velvet and silk, eyes the color of a summer storm and amber hair. Victoria DeMontville, because of a promise and a codicil to her father's will, was forced to marry one man to protect her from another. She hated Cameron Savage with a fierce passion. But to hold on to her genetic research and find a cure for the deadly Signe virus, she must pretend to love the enemy at her door, come with weapons of fire to melt her icy heart...

HIS OUTSIDERS TOUCH IGNITED RAGING PASSIONS... He wore a mask, disguised as the Phantom, a true legend come to life. Even as war and debate over new genetic research engulfed them all, he would find his greatest adversary in the beauty who'd branded him an outsider and barbarian, the woman he was born to possess, his soul mate.

Safari Moon

Solo St. John, a wildlife photographer, is preparing for a trip to Alaska. Suddenly, Solo finds women of all sorts invading his privacy, his home and his office, all cooing nonsense words and blatantly throwing themselves at him. Solo doesn't know why, and he has no idea how to rid himself of the persistent women. He finally decides to beg a favor of his best buddy Nyssa Harrington.

In love with Solo for the past ten years and knowing he doesn't return her feelings Nyssa doesn't want to talk to Solo. She knows if she accepts his phone call, she will not be able to resist the temptation to hope again.

Straight to Heaven

Running from demons, Alexandra McMurdie stumbles into Forbidden Ground where up is down and elements of nature are contested. Though a strong independent woman in the twenty-first century' she is unprepared for life in the 1800s. Her first site of the formidable James Lawrence makes her heart skip a beat, giving her cause to reconsider her desperate need to find a way home.

Born with a silver spoon, James' life was torn apart during the

War Between the States. Moving west he vows to put the life he once knew in the past. When he discovers a half-frozen woman near Gold Hill, his heart begins to thaw. His love for Alexandra and his need to keep her from a man who has pursued her through time might cost him his life as well as hers.

A Valentine's Anthology

The Lending Library-a fantasy by Christie L. Kraemer
Faeries try to fit into the human world when the forest where they make their home is destroyed by a mysterious enemy.

Chasing Rainbows-a contemporary romance by Genene Valleau
An eccentric aunt, an inventive uncle, a mother who wears poodle skirts, and a brother who wears pearls provide a hilarious backdrop for the courtship of a young woman who yearns for a "normal" family.

The Gift-an historical romance by Christine Young
A man and a woman on opposite sides of the Civil War get a second chance at love after one final battle returns soldiers to their war-torn homes to rebuild their lives.

A St. Patrick's Day Tale
Christine Young, C. L. Kraemer, Genene Valleau

Tumble through time...
...to Ireland in 1817, when tensions are high between Protestants and Catholics and fae people guide the fate of villagers. A lovely Catholic lass stumbles upon the weakly ritual fisticuffing between Irish lads. She falls into the lap of a handsome young Protestant. Family ties, grudges, and two conniving faeries threaten their budding love. But the faeries outsmart themselves when they hijack a time machine that has mysteriously appeared in their forest and are whisked to...
...Eugene, Oregon in the 20th century, amid a property feud

between the local faeries and night elves. The conniving faeries from Olde Ireland try to stir up more mischief. However, a warrior gnome convinces the magic folk to control their own destiny, and forces the intruding faeries to take refuge in the time machine again, spinning their way toward...

...A modern day castle in western Oregon. An eccentric inventor is determined to reclaim his wayward time machine and save his beloved wife from her latest misadventure. If only they can travel safely past the black hole...

a May Day Anthology
Christine Young, C. L. Kraemer, Rosemary Indra, Genene Valleau

Highland Miracle — Christine Young
HURTLED THROUGH TIME, Sean Michael Sterling, landed in the midst of a May Day celebration he didn't understand, assuming the role of Laird Sterling.

ILLIGITAMATE CHILD OF NOBILITY, Reagan Douglas searches for a way out of her half brother's house.

Defying the Odds — C.L. Kraemer
The night elves on the hill aren't happy without their magic. They concoct a plan to punish those who were involved in the act that rendered them almost human. Meanwhile, Uther, the rogue night elf, has returned to woo the Librarian to be his eternal mate.

Love in Bloom — Rosemary Indra
When childhood friends reunite it takes two fairies and a matchmaking daughter to help them admit their true love for each other.

No More Poodle Skirts — Genie Gabriel
After drifting for years in the innocent age of the 1950s, a woman struggles to join today's world by finding a career and a new love, with some help from her zany family.

Once Upon a Christmas Moon
Christine Young, C. L. Kraemer, Genene Valleau

TWELVE DAYS TO LOVE

When Archer Steele shows up at Calanthe Durand's failing plantation with an alligator over his shoulder, Cali thinks she's never seen a more handsome man. During the war she had to defend herself and her servants from both union and confederate soldiers. Independent and self-sufficient, she vows to never marry. But Archer Steele has different ideas. The first time Archer sees Cali in town, he feels an instant attraction. He decides he will do everything and anything to convince the beautiful Miss Durand he is worthy of her love. During the weeks leading up to Christmas, he gives her twelve gifts in hopes she will fall in love with him.

BOOTS AND BLADES

An ancient evil from the old country has arrived in the high desert of Oregon. Gnome children are vanishing then re-appearing, showing various stages of traumatization. Tiamoon, warrior gnome, will put her skills to use alongside Killian, a handsome warrior, also in need of a cause.

CHRISTMAS PAWSIBILITIES

With their world destroyed and their space ship malfunctioning, the dogizens of Planet Canid have little choice but to crash land on Earth. They face tortuous experiments at the hands of the Geeks in Green... or they can trust an eccentric inventor and his zany family to deliver the Canine Queen's puppies and help them celebrate new lives.

www.ingramcontent.com/pod-product-compliance
Lightning Source LLC
Chambersburg PA
CBHW070737180626
46818CB00007B/2880